WRONG
BEACH
ISLAND

WRONG BEACH ISLAND

Jane Kelly

Plexus Publishing, Inc.
Medford, New Jersey

Third printing, 2003

Published by: Plexus Publishing, Inc.
                 143 Old Marlton Pike
                 Medford, NJ 08055

Printed in the United States of America.

Library of Congress Cataloging-in-Publication Data

Kelly, Jane, 1949-
  Wrong Beach Island / Jane Kelly.
    p. cm.
  ISBN 0-937548-47-2
  1. Women detectives--New Jersey--Long Beach Island--Fiction. 2. Long Beach Island (N.J.)--Fiction. I. Title.
  PS3561.E39424 W76 2002
    813'.54--dc21

                                                    2002001458

Publisher: Thomas H. Hogan, Sr.
Editor-in-Chief: John B. Bryans
Managing Editor: Deborah R. Poulson
Production Manager: M. Heide Dengler
Copy Editor: Pat Hadley-Miller
Book Designer: Kara Mia Jalkowski
Sales Manager: Pat Palatucci

Jacket design by Jacqueline Walter Crawford
Cover Model: David T. Panara

To Friends and Colleagues

Chris, Phyllis, Pam, Susan, Mary, Barbara,
Carolyn, Carole, Mary, Dona, Suzy, and Kathy

Chapter 1

"That's her story?"

Andy nodded.

"And she's sticking to it?"

Again, he nodded.

"Let me get this straight. Page Spenser told the cops that she and her husband had a small argument so he decided to go kayaking. In New Jersey. In February. In the Atlantic Ocean. At night."

"Yes." If Andy's mind housed any skepticism, his face betrayed no doubt.

"Dallas Spenser, a fifty-five-year-old man, says he is going kayaking in the middle of the night...."

"Well, not actually the middle. He went out a little before midnight."

"Close enough." I took a deep breath to punctuate my statement. "Her fifty-five-year-old husband...."

"Fifty-three."

"Okay. Her fifty-three-year-old husband says he is going out in an ocean kayak...a tiny little boat...in February...in the Atlantic Ocean...and she believes him?" I paused. "And the police believe her?"

1

Andy shrugged. "The cops see surfers and windsurfers all winter. You've seen them. I know I have."

"Fifty-three-year-old surfers?"

"I never check their I.D. Besides, Dallas planned for the cold; he had a wet suit. They found it on the beach."

"Near the body?"

Andy shook his head. "No, right in front of the house."

"Let me just go over this again...."

"Meg...." Andy sounded exasperated.

"I just want to make sure I understand." I cleared my throat. For sarcastic effect. "Dallas Spenser has a fight with his wife. To work off his anger, he takes an ocean kayak and a wet suit down to the beach."

"They live at the beach. He had to move a thirty-pound boat maybe seventy-five, one hundred yards." Andy's voice was rife with impatience.

"Okay. He takes the two items to the water's edge...while wearing Gucci loafers I might add...."

Andy interrupted. "It's not as if he had to worry about his shoes. Money was not a problem...."

"Okay. His dress was completely appropriate." My tone added *not*. "So he never puts on the wet suit."

"The cops found it on the sand right outside the house so that would be the assumption." Andy was being annoyingly fair minded.

"Okay, instead of putting on the wet suit, he gets shot in the back. A shot no one hears, I'll just mention. Then the shooter steals the kayak but not the wallet in his pocket. The wallet that contains close to $500 in cash. Which is nothing compared to what the watch on his arm cost."

"That's one scenario."

"Dallas encountered a crook who wanted a kayak and was willing to kill for it. Some crook who didn't need cash? Some crook who couldn't recognize a solid gold Rolex? Some crook armed, coincidentally, with a low caliber pistol?"

Andy offered no reaction.

2

"What? Are bands of roving kayjackers lurking up and down Long Beach Island waiting for a midnight paddler to stumble down to the water alone?" Andy didn't respond. "I can just see the perpetrator leaving the house. 'Okay, honey, it's about eleven-thirty. Think I'll wander down to the beach and see if I can pick up that kayak Junior wants for his birthday. It's about time all those night-owl-partying, polar-bear-club-joining kayakers should be headed for the water. Yep. I have my gun. I know I could pick a kayak up on half a dozen porches around town, but I enjoy the challenge of stealing from the victim directly. We don't need any cash, right? Or a watch? I'll leave the wallet, all valuable jewelry, and any negotiable securities the victim might be carrying.'"

"Okay. Okay." Andy waved a hand that begged me to stop. "Maybe the shooter didn't steal the kayak. Maybe somebody decided it was lost, seized an opportunity, and took it." Again, Andy shrugged. His tone was even. "I only told you the facts. I didn't speculate. You're speculating."

I shook my head and continued. "Sure. Okay. Maybe Dallas Spenser was simply on the wrong beach at the wrong time, but let me understand the facts: The tide comes in, grabs Dallas, and goes out again only to bring the body back and deposit it a few blocks away by sunrise?"

"Apparently."

"You can't believe this." I met Andy's eyes with a steady gaze. He turned his head away. "I know, but...it's her...Page...."

I tried to appear sympathetic. I guess no man wants to think that his old girlfriend is capable of murder. Apparently, Andy had fond memories of Page Spenser. From what I heard, Page was quite beautiful. And, let's face it, men did not always think with their heads. But this story? No one was that beautiful.

Andy stumbled through an explanation. "I never said the kayak was stolen. Maybe the tide carried it out to sea."

But the incoming tide hadn't brought the boat back. Thursday morning's high tide had, however, carried the fully clothed body of Dallas Spenser to the Loveladies beach. The corpse had been surprisingly undamaged except for the single bullet hole in the back. Dallas hadn't been dead long when a morning jogger stumbled upon him. Since Dallas wore khaki pants, a yellow cashmere sweater, and one Gucci loafer, the young man astutely assumed that something was amiss. Despite the January thaw that lingered into February, the forty degree temperatures didn't encourage swimming even by the fully clothed—and accessorized.

Just my luck. Dallas took his wallet kayaking. If only he had forgotten to put his billfold in his pocket—or remembered to take it out—or simply failed to change his address with the DMV in a timely fashion. If only the tide had come in later. If only the I.D. had been made later. Even one hour later. An hour later, Andy and I would have been sitting with our seatbelts fastened and our tray tables in a closed and upright position. An hour later and the flight attendant would have already instructed all passengers on the flight to Antigua to turn off all electronic devices. An hour later, the 767 would have been rolling down the runway for a flight to the Caribbean. Unfortunately an hour earlier, we were still in a cab mired in traffic on the Van Wyck when Andy dug the ringing phone out of his satchel.

"No. Yes. I understand. Of course. I am so sorry. I can be there in three hours."

I'd heard only one side of the conversation, but I knew his next sentence would ask the driver to turn the cab around. It did. The following sentence was directed at me.

"Meg, a friend, an old friend, needs me. She needs a friend, and she needs a P.I., so it looks like I'm it. We'll have to delay our trip a few days. You don't mind, do you?"

At that point, I didn't mind. I was disappointed, but I didn't mind. What did a few days matter? Andy and I would be sailing the Caribbean for the next four months. Andy's apologetic tone told me that he realized I'd sublet my apartment, deferred graduate school, and stored all my winter clothes, and now he was asking me to linger in the northeastern United States in February. But hey, a friend needed him. What did a few days matter? And, Andy assured me that we would only be on Long Beach Island for a few days. I didn't mind. I said so. And at the time I wasn't lying.

I declared *no problem* before I met the widow who placed the call to my current boyfriend, her old boyfriend. Before I met Page Spenser. The same Page Spenser who told Andy that the cops had no suspects in her husband's murder. The same Page Spenser whose story Andy had relayed to me with a straight face.

Eventually, I met Page Spenser. Eventually, I minded.

Chapter 2

After the cab reversed direction, Andy and I spent the next five hours in taxis, on trains, and in Andy's classic Mustang convertible that we retrieved from the garage he'd rented in Point Pleasant. I used the time to wheedle some information out of an increasingly taciturn Andy. He provided the facts—and only the facts.

Andy Beck and Page Bennett had dated for about a year when they were both in college in Washington DC. Within a few months of their breakup—Page dumped Andy—Page Bennett left school and married Dallas Spenser, a man twenty years her senior. The couple had moved to California and managed separate careers there until the previous year. Last January they had purchased a co-op on the Upper East Side of Manhattan. Last July they opened their new summerhouse in Loveladies, an affluent community on Long Beach Island in central New Jersey. Dallas had been found dead near that home early that morning. And yes—I had to push for this answer—Page was quite beautiful.

Five hours. Five hours alone with Andy and that's what I found out. We rode the last twenty miles in silence as Andy grew more and more pensive and I grew more and more apprehensive. I'd never heard Page Bennett's name before. What had she meant to Andy? What did she mean to Andy now? It seemed that he hadn't seen her in quite a while. Silently, I prayed that his college sweetheart had gone to seed.

When we turned into the sandy driveway toward the pile of cubes on the beach that the Spensers called home, I wasn't surprised by the size of the house. Loveladies was full of houses that could post the sign: This is NOT a hotel. Because the town on the northern end had been developed later than most of the other towns on Long Beach Island, many of the houses were modern. Masterpieces if you liked contemporary design. Monstrosities if you didn't. The Spenser home was typical of the new breed of Loveladies architecture. Andy told me the house slept twenty-seven. I could think of no reason to doubt him— and no reason why a childless couple needed a house that slept twenty-seven.

Andy brought the car to a halt with a jerk and hopped out. He was moving at running speed as he headed for the front door—two red slabs suspended in a wall of glass. I caught up with him only because he slowed to avoid a loose board on the wide wooden staircase. He advised me to do the same. Then, he marked the dangerous spot with a tiny pine tree in a clay flowerpot.

Only a few seconds after Andy rang the bell, the door was opened by a woman who did not recognize Andy. I felt a sense of relief that this long, lanky blonde with round brown eyes was not Page. The woman introduced herself as a friend of Page's from New York—although I detected a distinct southern accent. When the woman heard Andy's name, she virtually gushed. "Oh, Page will be so happy you are here. Thrilled. She's been anxious for you to arrive." Then the woman paused. "I should have known it was you. Page said you were tall and very handsome." She was flirting. Yes, I am the jealous type, but I was right. The woman was flirting. I checked the woman's ring finger. She was married. Happily, I hoped.

In strides twice as long as mine, the blonde led us through some oddly shaped spaces that I guessed qualified as hallways into a large room with two walls of windows. Posed at the intersection of the two was a statuesque woman in a black wrap dress that didn't wrap far enough for my taste. As she greeted us, her face lit up, although I don't think it was the sight of Andy and me arriving together that excited her. She took a few steps toward Andy and extended her hand to the man who had only two weeks before declared if not undying, at least current, love for me. "Andrew." The single word constituted an invitation. Andy accepted and moved forward. The two hugged for ten seconds before Page noticed me. "Oh, I'm sorry...." She didn't actually say for what. She didn't have a chance. Andy interrupted.

"Page, this is my friend from New York, Meg Daniels."

Friend? I thought Andy and I had crossed the friend threshold when he invited me to move in with him on his boat in Antigua.

"Meg, how nice to meet you." Page clutched my hand with a soft, squishy handshake—surprising from such a slender hand and repellent from any type. "I'm sorry our meeting comes under such unpleasant circumstances."

Despite my experience in hosting funerals, I never know what to say. I mumbled something incoherent. Page didn't care. She had already refocused her attention on Andy—giving me the opportunity to study her. I had to admit that Page Spenser was an attractive woman. Broad shoulders. Long legs. And Katherine Stewart's coloring. Don't strain your memory. It's unlikely you'll remember Katherine; she was in my third grade class. I don't know if Katherine was pretty, but I found her beautiful. She was the first person I ever saw who had black hair and blue eyes so pale they appeared supernatural. Page had the same dark hair, cut short and close to the head. Her haircut might have been boyish, but there was nothing masculine about Page. Not her face. Not her body. Not the way she used those pale blue eyes—the ones she had trained on Andy.

8

"Oh Andrew, I can't thank you enough for being here for me." Page wrapped a long slim arm around the man I'd come to think of as my boyfriend only weeks before. She kissed something. Possibly the air. I suspected his ear. He demurred that it was no problem. She thanked. He demurred. She thanked. He demurred. I stepped aside and took a seat overlooking the Atlantic Ocean. Neither Page nor Andy noticed that I had moved away. Page grasped Andy's hand and told him about her morning with the police. I noticed that her eyes remained focused—and dry.

At the entrance to the room, the tall blonde nodded approvingly as Andy and Page chatted. I watched too, but not at all approvingly. I hated what I saw as I observed Andy chatting with Page. Chatting. They weren't chatting. They were communicating. Deeply. Intensely. Meaningfully. Andy watched Page with his cool green eyes. I couldn't resist those eyes; I wondered if she could. I wondered if she wanted to. The woman violated every rule of personal space. Did she lean close to share secrets with Andy? Did she consider her old beau such an *old* beau that he'd become hard of hearing? Or did the woman simply want to cuddle my boyfriend? A lot of women would.

Andy Beck looks good enough when he hasn't just spent two relaxing months sailing the Caribbean—and he *had* just spent two relaxing months sailing the Caribbean. Andy is tall, well built, with hair like strands of golden silk that he flips in the cutest way when he's happy, angry, or flirting. I eyed him executing the move now. He was making a condolence call so he wasn't happy. He hadn't been involved with this woman in years so he wasn't angry. Oh God. He was flirting. And if I weren't mistaken, Page Spenser, the widow, was flirting back. Why not? Dallas Spenser had been gone for more than twelve hours. No use living in the past.

I tore my eyes away from the two and searched for clues about Page in the décor of the Spenser's vacation home. Not a single memento or photo marred the austerity of the decorating scheme. Wide expanse of hardwood floors. Bare windows overlooking the beach. White walls. Black furniture, what there was of it. All Corbusier and Barcelona chairs. Abstract art with a hard edge. The Spensers went for abstract oils, probably over-priced and definitely oversized. The walls were huge, but the space was not quite large enough to show the paintings to their best advantage. Few rooms outside of Versailles were. I liked the look, but for what I wasn't sure. Not for living. Where did one curl up in the room? I gathered one didn't.

When Page's friend reappeared with a tray, Andy and Page moved to a couch across from me. "Lauren, I was just telling Andy about the police this morning."

Lauren groaned. "They were so rude. You would have thought that Page shot Dallas." She batted heavily mascaraed eyes at Andy. "I certainly hope private eyes are more polite." Andy smiled at her, and explained that the police just needed to explore all options, but Lauren was having none of it. "I was appalled at their lack of sensitivity toward Page, who has been through such a terribly tragic experience. But Andy, now you are here. Our Page needs someone to depend on. She needs someone to see her through this horrible ordeal." Lauren reached over and patted Andy's knee with beautifully mani-cured fingers jammed with heavy diamond jewelry.

Did anyone notice me sitting on the couch? The only proof that I had not, in fact, become invisible was that Lauren served me tea and sneered when I took four sugar cubes. That was probably four more sugar cubes than the size-2 woman had consumed in her entire life. After serving tea, Lauren said a brief good-bye to Page and promised to return for the funeral. She told Andy it was nice meeting him. She told me nothing.

After Lauren had left, Andy turned in my direction. "Meg, I think Page and I need to speak in private. Would you mind...."

At that point, Page broke in. "Andy, we can use Dallas's den. Marge can sit here and enjoy the view."

Andy didn't even correct her about my name. He agreed that hers was a good idea. The two slipped through double doors into a room to the north. They closed the doors behind them. I don't want to tell you what I pictured going on in that room. Perhaps my olive eye color makes me prone to the green-eyed monster. I know that jealousy is an unattractive trait. Knowing makes no difference. I am relentlessly jealous. It's not that I'm hopelessly insecure. I'm just realistic. Let's face it, a woman cannot be all things to all men—or even to all the moods of one man. I'm a five-foot-six buxom blonde, not a five-foot-nine sleek brunette. If Andy Beck happened to be in the mood for tall, flat, and brown-haired—and my eyes told me he was—I was out of luck. And out of sight.

I wandered to the window and gazed out at the ocean. It was a beautiful, clear day. The kind of day I'd hoped it would be. In Antigua. Knowing the temperature lingered somewhere in the forties, I didn't even consider stepping out on the deck on the south side of the house. I watched the waves through the window while fighting the urge to speculate about what might be going on in Dallas's study. Instead, I pondered how the Spensers' neighbors were taking the news of the murder in their town. With the possible exception of jellyfish, crabs, and an occasional sandshark, corpses didn't generally wash ashore on Loveladies' beaches. The Loveladies beaches did not play host to uninvited bodies—living or dead. The beaches are ostensibly, by law, public, but as far I could ever figure only to those who skydived in. You try finding a parking space in Loveladies.

Anyway, Long Beach Island, an eighteen-mile-long barrier island whose population swells by more than one thousand percent in the summer, is typically the site of happy memories, not the brunt of a lot of body-part jokes like, say, the East River. People retreated to Long Beach Island to get away from the type of violence that Dallas Spenser's death represented.

My thoughts were interrupted by the sound of the door opening. Andy stepped into the room first. His face was flushed and he appeared agitated. "Maggie, we should go." The fact that he used his pet name for me worried me. What had happened in that room? When I asked him—after we were back in the car—he answered gruffly. "Page told me her account of what happened that night. And gave me some ideas she had about who might have killed her husband."

We drove south through the many towns that line Long Beach Island. We were headed to Beach Haven on the southern part of the island where Andy had a friend willing to host our visit. According to Andy, Oliver Wilder was downright thrilled to be our host. He didn't care if we stayed for months. I urged Andy to make it clear that would not be necessary.

As Andy shared with me what he felt he could about his meeting with Page, I looked for new sights and missing land-marks. It had been five years since I had visited LBI and I was a vigilant opponent of change during my absence. "You know, Meg, that there are things I can't share."

"Does that mean Page is your client?"

"Well...." He dragged the word out. I knew he didn't want to tell me what would follow. "It would be hard to turn her away. She is an old friend. And I'm the only private investigator she knows."

The word "referral" crossed my mind but didn't arrive on my lips. I continued to play the good sport. I agreed with Andy—at least I nodded that I did. I never referred to the delay the inves-tigation would cause in our interrupted trip to Antigua. I addressed the case. "Was Dallas a friend?"

"Not really. I only met him at the wedding. I mean I saw him a few times, but that was the occasion I actually socialized with him. At the wedding." Andy's voice assumed a defensive tone. Why, I couldn't figure out. I didn't believe I'd been on the attack.

"You were invited to the wedding?"

"Of course. It was all very civilized. Dallas was an extraordi-narily civilized guy. Very British you know."

"If he's English, how come he's named Dallas? Was he named after the television show or something? They ate up that JR thing over there." I shook my head, answered my own question, and asked another. "Nah, he's way too old. What did he look like anyway? I spotted not one photo on display in their house. Don't you find that odd?"

Andy didn't. "Maybe they're camera-shy. Maybe all their mementos are in New York. Not everyone crowds up their shore house with pictures, you know." I wondered if Andy's comment was a negative judgment of the photo-crammed bookcases in my New York apartment. I didn't think so. He sounded more factual than judgmental.

"Was Dallas handsome?"

Andy protested that as a guy, he wouldn't know.

"Well," I persisted, "was he ugly?"

"No."

"So he was ordinary?"

Andy shook his head. "Not really."

"Better than average?"

"Maybe a little when he was younger."

"Have you seen him recently?"

Andy kept his eyes on Long Beach Boulevard. "They've been living in California for years. Page talked Dallas into moving back east. They built a house in Loveladies. Just opened the place in July."

I nodded. Days would pass before I realized that Andy had not given me a straight answer.

Chapter 3

Six days after we arrived on Long Beach Island, Andy and I joined the guests crammed inside a small chapel that might have been airlifted from the Vegas strip and dropped in the woods of South Jersey. A good crowd—both qualitatively and quantitatively—had assembled to send Dallas Spenser to his final rest. A lot of very attractive people wearing appropriately sober expressions arrived in very expensive cars—most with New York plates. Considering the Spensers' recent relocation to the East Coast, I was amazed that so many mourners had made the two-hour trip.

The crowd was dominated by tanned, silver-haired men in gray suits and power ties. Their companions were just as handsome. Most of the men were accompanied by women who might be their nieces. I guessed, however, that I was looking at a lot of wives—seconds, thirds, maybe even fourths. Trophies for the men in the $2,000 suits they clung to—just as Page had been for Dallas.

When I first saw Dallas in the casket I couldn't suppress my shock. "She dumped you for him?" I eyed the body. "He must have had some personality."

Andy shrugged. "He looked better when he wasn't dead."

I hoped so. Dallas Spenser certainly wasn't looking so good in his coffin—although under the circumstances I shouldn't have been surprised. There appeared to be well over six feet between his thinning red hair and his surprisingly petite feet. From what I could tell his height/weight ratio appeared to be in line with medical standards. His body seemed okay but his face...heavy makeup did nothing to soften the sharp features. I suspected the mortician's efforts only emphasized the deceased's resemblance to a crow. A contented expression might have helped, but the undertaker had not succeeded in eliminating a frown. Dallas's mouth was drawn down at both corners. He was, however, impeccably dressed in the latest styles. I eyed the gold Rolex on his right arm. Looked real to me. "He isn't taking that with him, is he?"

"Page said he loved that watch. She gave it to him as a wedding gift. I don't imagine it's still running after a long soak in the Atlantic." Andy nudged me away from the casket and toward the receiving line. I resisted—not from a reluctance to say good-bye to Dallas Spenser (after all I'd never said hello) but to avoid greeting the merry widow. I spotted her when we walked in. Her, and the way she gazed at Andy.

Andy had spent most of the last six days helping Page—with what I wasn't sure. I'd spent most of those days bonding with Oliver Wilder, Andy's old friend from Beach Haven who was our host. Okay, I actually spent my time with Oliver wondering what Andy was up to, and pretending to be a good sport. Yes, I admired Andy's loyalty to an old friend. I just wished the old friend didn't have a face that rivaled Liz Taylor's in her prime.

I greeted Page politely and briefly. Then, while Andy checked on the funeral arrangements, I found a seat, observed the mourners, and conjured up depressing scenarios—all of which ended with Andy riding into the sunset with Page.

I had to admit that Page was beautiful. And, an appropriately dressed woman. My attire, on the other hand, was not exactly what you would pick from a fully stocked closet before leaving for a funeral. My black spandex mini-dress and thin-strapped sandals were more suitable for cocktails than mourning. But I had an excuse for my outfit. I was supposed to be in Antigua. If I hadn't tossed the small black sheath and high-heels into my bag at the last minute, I could have been wearing a bikini and flip-flops. If I had, I could not have felt any colder.

My ruminations were interrupted by the ring of a cell phone. I didn't turn around, but I knew that the call was taken by a mourner in the row behind me. It wasn't my fault I could hear every word the man said. I think he believed he was whispering. "It's him. Yes. I'm sure. I know him when I see him. Older yes. But definitely him. And dead." I assumed that by "him" he meant Dallas, since his appeared to be the only corpse in the immediate area. The guy spoke in a light accent that had its roots somewhere in the British Commonwealth's working class. My guess was England. "Hey, don't blame me. I didn't kill him." He paused for a moment. "Look, I don't know who did it. I know it's a bad deal for you."

Despite his claim that he didn't know who killed Dallas, I suspected this was a man Andy would want to interview. I checked around the chapel, but Andy was not in view.

Behind me the man was silent for over a minute. "Oh, come on. This was just about played out anyway." He listened for several more minutes without speaking. "That's overkill, Eddie." Again, he listened. "Eddie, I did not see Frankie. I'll sit through the whole bloody service if that's what you want, but I never saw Frankie anywhere near him. Not in years." The man tried to interrupt but the voice on the other end of the phone won. "What makes you think that Frankie wanted him dead? For all we know, that little sneak was hitting him up, too."

Now there was something to report to Andy—unless I was reading too much into the word "hitting up." I hit Andy up for cash. Andy hit Oliver up for a place to stay. Charities hit people up for donations all the time. Hitting someone up didn't have to be bad. Maybe the caller represented the United Way. Frankly I wasn't buying my own story. I glanced over my shoulder to catch a glimpse of the man. He was leaning forward in the false belief that his position would muffle his words. I glimpsed only a bald head on top of a dark pinstripe suit with ridiculously wide stripes—the kind that rarely make their way into U.S. stores.

The man continued to talk into his phone in a stadium whisper. "I have not seen Frankie Wexford in years." He paused. "Yes. I know what Frankie looks like. Hey, people change their hairstyles. I doubt that square bangs in front and a tail in the back are still cutting it for Frankie. Look I got to go. Hear the organ music?"

What we all heard was a tape of organ music—signaling the start of the event. But apparently the man wasn't going to stay for the service. As I peeked over my shoulder I saw his shiny suit headed for the back of the chapel. I checked for Andy but he was still missing in action. I grabbed my bag and followed the man into the vestibule just in time to see a bald head disappear down a narrow stairway.

I found my way down the steep stairs to a moldy hallway no wider than the staircase. Three doors opened off the corridor: Ladies, Men, and No Admittance. While I waited to run into the man as he exited the men's room, where reason told me he had gone, I decided to see what lay behind the No Admittance sign.

The door opened easily. No way I could make a surprise entrance. The light from the hallway, as dim as it was, would give me away. So I called out, "Anyone in here?" No one answered. I reached around the frame of the door and found a light switch. When I flipped the switch, the room wasn't exactly flooded with light. Seemed the large basement relied on one sixty-watt bulb for light. Pews, robes, stacks of hymnals. The only thing out of the ordinary for a church storeroom was the smell of cigarette smoke. Someone had been downstairs recently sneaking a butt.

Out of the corner of my eye, I sensed movement across the room. A church mouse. Probably mechanical—a faux rodent for a faux quaint chapel. I backed out and slammed the door behind me. As I did, I crashed into a large form. "I am so sorry." I turned around and gazed into the eyes of a man in a shiny pin-striped suit. He had to be the caller with the cell phone. At least I hoped that was what he had in his breast pocket. He seemed amused. "Don't they teach American children that curiosity killed the cat?" He smiled, revealing one gold tooth.

"I just had the urge to peek in there." I was actually telling the truth. "Don't know why."

The guy reached around me and pushed the door open. "Not much to see, is there?" I shook my head to agree. He flipped the light out, smiled insincerely, and moved closer.

I took a step backward, which meant into the wall. "Guess I'd better take care of what I came for." I pointed to the ladies room door. "Nice to meet you, Mr...." I left space for the man to fill in the blanks but instead he answered, "Nice to meet you too, Miss." He did not allow space for me to fill in my name.

Leaving the task of checking out the storage area to the stranger, I spun into the ladies room and into Page. Literally. I slammed into her at the mirror in the cramped facility. I couldn't imagine that if I were burying my boyfriend of five months I would bother to put on makeup at all, let alone refresh it. Yet here Page was—about to bury her husband of almost fifteen years—and her focus on eyeliner was unmistakable.

She caught my eye in the mirror and her brow furrowed.

"I'm Andy's...friend."

"Of course, Marge. I know you."

I know I'm the one who sounds like a crank. You'll say that she had just greeted hundreds of people—many of them strangers—in very little time. She felt distressed, stressed, and tired. And she had no one to walk her to the ladies room. That's what you can say, but I swear she knew my name. She just didn't use it.

Anyway, I corrected her gently, expressed my sympathy again and slipped into a stall. I was in the compartment only a few seconds when I heard Page's voice again. "You shouldn't be here." She didn't so much whisper as hiss. "Are you nuts?"

Of all the bathroom stalls that offered minimal privacy, the chapel's were built to CIA requirements. I felt sure that no one could see in because I certainly couldn't see out. Nor could I hear anything. Yet I sensed communication. Someone was on the other side of the door arguing with Page. I tried to peek under the door but all I saw were nondescript oxfords on the feet of a small man—or a woman with questionable fashion sense.

I tried to hurry. Before I could get out of the stall, I heard the click of a purse snap followed by the creak of a door spring. I detected hushed but not friendly voices until the slam of the door cut them off. I did my best to rush, but when I stepped into the hallway, Page and her anonymous visitor were gone.

Chapter 4

The funeral service for Dallas Spenser was short, impersonal, and conducted to the accompaniment of sniffles—which Andy attributed to an excess of emotion and I attributed to an excess of floral arrangements. Either way, the mood was lighter—but only slightly less fragrant—at the post-funeral bash. Okay, I called it a bash. Page called it a small gathering. She also called the house where the small gathering was held a summer cottage.

I'm not sure why Andy brought me along since he explained that he would be working the crowd. I was sure why I came along. The funeral was the closest I'd gotten to a date with Andy all week. On my own in a sea of mourners who appeared no more saddened by Dallas Spenser's death than I was, I wandered from cube to cube feeling like a not-particularly-popular guest at a gallery opening. While I checked for ugly pinstriped suits and even uglier brown oxfords, I accepted hors d'oeuvres and wine from servers in short red jackets and surveyed the art. I feigned appreciation for a large canvas bordered with black and red dots. I don't mean to criticize the painting. Well, I do, but I feel guilty about it. I'm certain the piece spoke to someone. I, however, was not that someone.

Neither was the guy who positioned himself beside me at a bleached pine bar in the room where I'd first met Page—the far southeast cube that served as the main public space for the house. His gray suit told me the stranger was less affluent than most of the guests. His rubber-soled shoes—size twelve minimum—told me he possessed less fashion sense. His questionable taste did not hide the fact that he was better looking than most of the men in the room. At least I thought he was. Of course, I'd drunk two glasses of wine in ten minutes, a personal best—or worst, depending on how you viewed it.

"So, you think I could sell them my kid's refrigerator art?" The man stared at the painting but he spoke to me.

"Only if you have a 30,000 cubic foot refrigerator." I eyed the lone canvas on the wall behind the bar.

He studied the painting for another fifteen seconds before reaching his conclusion. "Nah. I think my kid's stuff is too good." The man checked me out with a not very surreptitious glance. I checked to see that my coat remained closed. It didn't. I pulled it around me. "You one of Dallas's girls?" The man—tall, dark, but not traditionally handsome—asked the question.

"I didn't know he had children."

"Who said anything about children?" The man smirked.

I stared at him until his meaning hit me. "You would approach a woman who was one of 'Dallas's girls' and ask them that question? Why would anyone say yes?"

The man chuckled and planted both elbows on the bar. "Appears to be some sort of sorority." He nodded at a group clustered before a window and a wide expanse of Atlantic Ocean. Silhouetted in the hard midday light were three lanky, lean women laughing, giggling, and working on winter tans that were already deep enough to make the average dermatologist squirm. "Those gals met through their relationships with Dallas. There were more of them at the chapel. Apparently not everyone who attended was on this guest list."

I'd only seen Dallas at his own wake, but I didn't get his appeal. I wasn't impressed by the tall—or should I say long, since I only saw him reclining—redhead. Possibly the pale blue of the silk casket liner was not a flattering shade. Maybe his British accent was the secret weapon. American women loved those British accents.

The stranger leaned close enough to encourage conspiratorial gossip, but I had none to tell. That didn't mean I would mind trying. The guy had an appealing smile with surprisingly white teeth for a man over forty. Despite his stature, maybe six-two, six-three, his square build suggested stocky. His unlined skin stretched across the most formidable bones I'd seen outside the Kennedy family. His hair was almost as black as his eyes. Not my type but appealing. And interested in talking to me. What did I have to lose? I was at a funeral.

"You know the widow?"

I checked my watch. "Yep. For about six days, three hours."

"Know the guy with her?" He nodded over my shoulder. I turned to see Andy huddled with Page in front of an abstract painting that suggested either a tropical paradise or Dante's fifth circle of hell.

"I thought I did." I polished off the second glass of wine and pushed the empty towards the bartender for a refill.

"He yours?"

I turned to face the stranger. "Well, I'm certainly not his."

The guy laughed. His arm brushed mine as he held my glass out to the bartender. The stranger made a point of studying my ring finger. "You two living together?"

I shrugged. "Sort of. Traveling together. Or trying to. We were on our way to Kennedy when we got the news. About Dallas."

"Been together long?"

I glanced at Andy. "Possibly long enough." I wanted the stranger to understand the irony of my situation. How Andy had gone to such effort taking jet planes, prop planes, trains, boats, taxis, and water taxis to invite me to join him in Antigua. How I'd been minutes away from taking off for four months sailing the Caribbean with Andy when the call came. How the best romantic fantasy of my life was going up in smoke—which I recalled was actually what Dallas was doing at that exact moment. I stopped whining. Even I had to admit that my problems paled when compared to those of Dallas Spenser.

I nodded at Andy. "I met him late last summer. In Ocean City. We hung out for a couple of months and then he went away. We've only been back together for about two weeks. So...." I eyed Andy. "If it doesn't work out it's pretty much easy-come, easy-go."

"You knew the victim?"

Victim? I felt like the victim. "Oh, you mean Dallas. Never met him. I'm here on a date."

"Did Beck know Dallas?"

The warm glow faded. Suddenly, the shoes made sense. "Now officer, letting on that you know Andy's name was a rather unprofessional slip. I suspect you're better at your job than that. Why would a policeman with all these possible suspects running around want to talk to me about my boyfriend?"

"We're interested in anyone who had contact with the happy couple since they arrived here."

I shook my head. "Andy hadn't had any contact with them...." The look in the officer's eyes stopped me cold. His was one of those expressions any woman hates to see—the kind that mixes pity and sympathy with a *soupçon* of amusement. "I mean...I know Andy has seen Page since Dallas died." The man's expression intensified but didn't change. "Why don't you do the talking." My ignorance of Andy's activities had already told the cop what he wanted to know. "And while you're at it why don't you give me your card."

Studying the homicide detective's business card gave me the opportunity to think. Why should I care that Andy had seen Dallas and Page recently? I had to give the guy credit for all the trouble he went to in luring me to sail with him on the *Page One*.

Okay, you noticed. Andy assured me the boat's name had nothing to do with Page Bennett Spenser. He'd christened the boat in honor of a case. Andy had negotiated a fee that provided the cash for purchasing the sailboat with enough money left over to enjoy some time off. The murder case had landed him, actually us, on page one of several regional newspapers. So when he explained how the *Page One* came by her name, I'd bought the story—hook, line, and sinker. I know. You have land to sell me. Of course the truth seemed obvious—now. Now that I'd seen Page Spenser. But I'd never heard of the woman when I learned the sailboat's name.

I didn't share these thoughts with the cop—Detective Jerry Petino according to his card. I did share a third glass of wine. And I listened. Not that the cop told me much. He wanted me to hear what he wasn't saying. That my boyfriend appeared pretty cozy with his old flame even right in front of me. That my boyfriend enjoyed the attentions of his recently widowed ex. That my boyfriend had been meeting with his old girlfriend behind my back—and the back of her husband—the same back that ended up with a bullet in it. Most importantly, Detective Petino wanted me to know that my boyfriend might have a motive to put a bullet in that same back. I shrugged off the cop's last suggestion with a laugh. It was his earlier comments that plagued me. There was no denying what my eyes saw: Andy gazing at Page with expressions recently reserved for me. He'd been doing that for a quarter of an hour. Didn't the widow have other guests to entertain?

I redirected the conversation away from Andy. "Got any suspects?"

"You must watch TV. You figure it out. And, if you feel like talking, you have my card, Ms...." Petino waited for me to fill him in.

"Daniels. Meg Daniels. I thought you would have known that."

"Why not just ask? I like to try the easiest approach first. I'm not that much of a zealot."

"Did you mention that to the victim's family?"

"Don't worry, Ms. Daniels. You can trust me to get the job done." He flashed a smile. The glare of the sun off those teeth was bright but not blinding. I saw the threat the cop presented. I'd heard Page Spenser's account of the night the crime took place. I hated to have any thought in common with the cop. But I did. Neither of us believed Page Spenser's story held water.

Chapter 5

When Andy found me a ride from the funeral, I didn't complain. As he rushed me out the door, I did try to fill him in on my conversation with Detective Petino. Andy, however, was preoccupied. He put me off, dismissing me with a light kiss on the lips. "I've got work to do. It's got to be boring for you hanging around here. We'll talk tonight. When we're alone."

That made sense. No use being overheard. I didn't want to start any rumors. Plus, if Andy was committed to finding the killer, he might as well work hard and solve the crime fast so that we could catch the next plane south. I didn't resist as he guided me to a decrepit hunk of steel that I suspected was a car.

The pile of metal had a driver's seat. In it sat a kid I'd spotted on one of my tours of the house. His age, 25 tops, and his clothes, sport coat and khakis, set him apart from the tycoon guests. The moment I first laid eyes on him, I knew I was looking at a kid called Opie throughout childhood. Actually, this kid's impish face made the real Opie look sinister. The kid was still clearing McDonald's bags and soda cans from the passenger seat as I climbed in. Climbed? Landed would be the better term. Andy shoved me through the car door with a brief introduction. "Jake Chandler. He'll drive you home." The door slammed. Andy waved over his shoulder as he headed back to the house. Without any greeting, the kid put the car in gear and we jerked down the driveway. Jake kept an eye on the rear-view mirror at the expense of the sand-covered lane lined with vehicles boasting prices I still associated with real estate.

"Watch out." I screamed as he veered toward a Lexus SUV.

"Sorry." He jerked the wheel but glued his eyes to the mirror again. I was relieved when we made the left onto Long Beach Boulevard and he turned his attention to the road.

"Thanks for the ride. I'm Meg Daniels."

"Nice to meet you. Jake Chandler." Although Jake Chandler's transmission languished somewhere between second and third gear, he took his hand off the shift to shake my hand. In the interest of auto safety, I kept my grip light and my grasp brief.

"Lucky for me you were leaving, eh?" I pretended I was happy to get the bum's rush from Andy.

"Not so lucky for me." Jake spoke with a hard, clipped accent that suggested he was not from New Jersey.

"Oh, I'm sorry if this is a problem...."

"Oh...no." The kid realized how I interpreted his statement. "It's not bad that you're here. It's bad that I'm here. I didn't exactly plan on leaving yet. However," he cleared his throat meaningfully, "I was never actually invited—except to leave."

That explained the two thugs—excuse me, gentlemen—in black suits I'd seen guiding Jake through a sea of Jaguars and BMWs to the old Japanese compact car that might have been blue. Once. On the outside. I couldn't begin to guess what color the interior started out. Every inch of glass and vinyl inside the car was currently encrusted in tan residue. Residue of what? I didn't want to know. I didn't ask. We rode in silence.

Jake bent forward and reached around the floor until he found a piece of cloth. He rubbed the inside windshield with what had, in a former life, served as white jockey shorts—

presumably Jake's. From my perspective the rag could only add grime to the already opaque glass. Jake, however, seemed pleased with the results. "I wasn't exactly a fan of Dallas Spenser. You?"

I recoiled as he tossed the scrap at my feet. "No."

"I hated the bastard."

I'm not sure I admired the kid's candor. I certainly didn't admire his clothes sense. It's not that there was anything intrinsically unattractive about his khaki pants, blue shirt, and navy jacket. I just didn't understand the fit. Had his grandmother who had not seen him for fifteen critical years of the growth cycle sent his outfit from a far-off state? Had he been given the wrong order by his dry cleaner? Had he been cursed by a tribe of pygmies? His small head appeared shrunken peeking out of the wide abyss that was his shirt collar.

"Obviously you weren't alone in your dislike of Dallas."

"Meaning?" He seemed abnormally interested in my observation not to mention what he could see of my black cocktail dress. This guy could keep his eyes anywhere but on the road. Luckily at this time of year traffic wasn't heavy. Who cared if we used two lanes?

Surprised that an explanation was required, I provided one. "Meaning someone killed Spenser...I doubt they did so based on a sincere sense of admiration and appreciation." Jake was still checking out my sheath. He was puzzled, not excited. I answered the question on his face. "I know this is an odd dress to wear to a funeral—especially in the winter. It's all I had with me. Right now I am supposed to be on a sailboat...."

The guy wasn't interested in my woes. "Why do you think Spenser came back to the East Coast? To Long Beach Island? To Loveladies?"

I looked out the window for signs identifying restaurants that were open all year. "I've been too busy wondering why I'm in Loveladies, Long Beach Island, East Coast to give Dallas

Spenser's motives much thought. As I mentioned, I'm supposed to be in the Caribbean right now. Andy and...."

Jake still wasn't interested. He interrupted. "I've heard some interesting tales about Spenser. You must have heard things." His tone gave the word *things* a menacing meaning.

"I didn't even know the guy. I was only a date at the funeral. Andy's." I clarified. "Andy's date, not Andy's funeral."

"Don't know him."

"The fellow who put me in your car." I eyed the kid quizzically.

"Never met the guy. He just saw those fellows tossing me out. He said you were bored and asked if I could give you a lift. I said it was okay since I was leaving anyway."

Andy sent me home with a stranger? A gate-crasher? A guy who was being ejected? From the funeral of a murder victim? Shouldn't all invited guests, let alone uninvited guests, be considered suspects? I studied Jake Chandler for traces of evil. With his small stature, wide eyes, and bright red hair, I found it hard to imagine his conceiving, let alone perpetrating, a crime. Jake appeared to be the Mickey Rooney of his generation, a generation with absolutely no desire for a Mickey Rooney—even the youthful cinematic version that sang to a pubescent Judy Garland. Jake's voice contained Mickey's optimism as if at any moment he might yell, "I know. Let's put on a show." That optimism was apparent as he asked his next question. "As I said, you must have heard *things* about Dallas Spenser? Seems everyone has a story."

"Really? I don't. What kind of *things* have you heard?"

"Well, a lot of women attending today's events were his lovers."

"Really?" I wasn't about to share what the cop told me. "What about his wife? Isn't she suspicious?"

"From what I hear she wouldn't care."

"She have some action on the side?" I couldn't hide the anxiety in my voice.

"Do you know Barney Wainwright?" Jake's eyes were drawn to a beat-up van. His eyes went left; his car went right. "Left. Left!" I screamed.

"You know those guys?" After a final backward glance, Jake returned his eyes and the car to the traffic lane.

"What people?" Over my shoulder, I barely caught a glimpse of a couple disappearing into Joe Pop's.

"I thought you were yelling for a reason."

"The reason was that you were headed for a pedestrian."

"Oh." While he considered the information I brought the conversation back to Barney Wainwright. Page already had a lover—this was great news. "Who is Barney Wainwright?"

"If you read the San Francisco society pages, you would know." Jake's interest in Barney Wainwright appeared to wane.

"He lives in San Francisco?" I didn't conceal my disappointment. "Not here?"

Suddenly, Jake was interested again. "Have you seen him here? Have you heard that he's visited here?" Jake's eager tone grew even more eager—which until that moment I wouldn't have thought possible.

"No. As I said, I never heard of him."

"How about Spenser's business cronies? Know any of them?"

I shook my head. "I told you. I was just Andy's date. Page is an old friend of his."

"He met Dallas through Page?"

"Yes."

Jake was clearly disappointed. "Did he know Page before he knew Dallas?"

"Yes." I kept the answer short. No reason to elaborate.

"He didn't know Dallas before he knew Page."

"He barely knew Dallas at all. You ask a lot of questions. How come?"

"I'm a reporter. Why'd you think they threw me out?" He chuckled. "Were you worried that I was a suspect?"

"No," I lied. Adding "not now" would have made the answer true but I didn't bother.

"Look, I've got something I want to look into today. Maybe later in the week I could drop by. I'd like to talk to you. We could go out for a drink...."

"Oh, no. I mean that's very nice of you but...." Then I took a deep breath and said the sentence for the first time. "I'm only going to be in town for a few days."

Chapter 6

Here is my recipe for a good dinner: Locate a six-ounce bag of potato chips, original flavor. Find one quart bottle of skim milk with a freshness date of today or later. Pour eight ounces of milk into a paper cup. Rip open the potato chip bag. Eat potato chips. Drink milk. The recipe can serve two, but I find it works especially well when you're dining alone, as I was that night.

When Jake Chandler dropped me off in front of the orange and blue house that Andy and I were calling home, I found I had the place to myself. The renovated Cape Cod cottage was in Beach Haven or Beach Haven Terrace or Beach Haven Crest or Beach Haven Gardens or Beach Haven Inlet or Beach Haven Park—I never knew where I was. Even as I referred to the entire region between Brant Beach and Holgate as Beach Haven, I knew I was wrong. I always thought of LBI as the kind of barrier island where if you stood at the bay you could see all the way across the strip of land to the ocean. I'd rarely ventured too far off of Long Beach Boulevard, from which you could often see both the bay and the ocean. And in a lot of places, that was true. But I'd found out recently, in a lot of places that was not true. Long Beach Island included several land masses that stuck out from the long stretch of land that I thought of as LBI. The place where we were staying was located on one of those intrusions into the Manahawkin Bay.

The house belonged to Oliver Wilder, an old friend of Andy's and a rabid fan of the Miami Dolphins. An astute observer would detect Oliver's partisanship pulling into the driveway. At night even if you missed the fountain—the dolphin that in warmer weather spewed water into a spheroid pond—you could still tell that the siding was turquoise and the shutters were orange. The combination wasn't as bad as one would imagine. Close, but not quite as bad.

The exterior of Oliver's home was merely a preview of what lay behind the orange door with the brass ball-and-bat knocker. The Wilder house represented an odd combination of big money and little taste. Make that unusual taste. From a decorator's point of view his affection for the Dolphins could be seen as good news. Turquoise and orange blended nicely with items representing Oliver's second favorite sport: baseball. I couldn't imagine where Oliver had found chairs that resembled catcher's mitts that caught rear ends instead of fast balls. But he had. Four of them. As well as baseball bat lamps, hockey stick tables, and basketball ottomans.

Oliver had taken great care in tracking and acquiring the items throughout the house. Each of the three guest bedrooms was carefully decorated and easily identified. Andy and I were assigned the Bruins bedroom. "They may not be what they once were but you can't overlook their glorious past." It was just as hard to overlook their yellow and black color scheme. Personally, I would have preferred the simple red and white of the Phillies bedroom—or even the blue and orange of the Mets room. (Oliver supported all New York and Philadelphia teams in addition to his other picks.) But who was I to complain? We had a warm room, a soft bed, and a window with an expansive view of Manahawkin Bay. Plus, Oliver had welcomed us into his home on five hours' notice.

While Andy worked, I'd spent the last six days hanging with Oliver. But when I returned from Dallas Spenser's funeral, Andy's old, my new, buddy was nowhere to be found. I wasn't sure what to do with the whole house to myself. A retired Wall Street exec who now spent his days trading online, Oliver was a seemingly normal fellow who under closer inspection proved to be a wild and crazy guy. Couldn't I find something wild and crazy to do in his house?

After I cleaned up the dishes (open trash can, toss in paper cup and bag), I went for a run. I picked up the remote and ran through all 101 channels. Nothing on. I lost interest in drumming my fingers after about ten seconds. Foot-tapping proved no more fulfilling. The intricacies of the sound system were beyond my abilities.

Then I remembered the computer in the corner. Oliver had given me log-on instructions; they worked on the initial attempt. I checked my e-mail first. No friends had written. Why would they? I was supposed to be sailing around the Caribbean too involved in romance to correspond. God bless American Airlines and Eddie Bauer. At least they wanted to keep in touch.

I sent off a plethora of e-mails hoping to generate incoming mail. In each message, I tried to sound chipper. Not bothered by the delay or the idea that my boyfriend was spending time with his old girlfriend. Okay, I didn't actually mention that second part. I wanted to minimize the "I told you so's." I'd had enough of "You're thirty-four years old. You should know better." Problem is that what I know has little impact on what I do.

I'd decided to run off to Antigua with Andy instead of starting graduate school after knowing him only four months. Okay, four months total. For two of those months we had been separated while he tasted Antigua and I stayed in New York. I'd accepted his invitation to join him in the Caribbean for reasons that—despite my friends' reservations—I considered obvious. Let's see...sailing over beautiful aquamarine waters through balmy breezes with a handsome man. Riding the M5 bus alone through slush and snow to boring classes in drafty classrooms.

Right. I was gonna opt for the Amsterdam Avenue bus instead of the *Page One*. Most of my friends didn't agree with my decision—but most of my friends hadn't met Andy.

Anyway, to minimize the notes of recrimination, I downplayed the delay as I wrote e-mails. When I finished an hour later, I still had the house to myself. In the hopes of a change in my situation, I stared out the front window for a few minutes. Not only did no car come up the driveway, no vehicle of any sort came down the street. Oliver's house was tucked away on one of the spits of land up and down Long Beach Island that I never knew existed. Off the beaten track of the north-south highways, their streets saw little traffic. There was little to watch out Oliver's window. I gave up.

I checked the 101 channels one more time. Still nothing on. I returned to the computer. Between Andy's investigation and Oliver's curiosity, we had already seen the stories on Dallas's murder from the New Jersey and New York papers. It was unlikely that I would locate any news about the crime that had not already been found. I went to Yahoo!, typed in Page Spenser's name, and hit the enter key to search the entire Web.

It took me less than a minute to figure out that "Page" isn't a particularly good search term in a world made up of Web pages. That night I wasn't interested in sites focusing on the poetry of Edmund Spenser and/or the investigative skills of *Spenser for Hire*. I tried Dallas Spenser's name. That search plunged me into the world of television. Who knew there were so many Web pages that dealt with two TV shows: *Dallas* and *Spenser for Hire?* In addition, I'd retrieved a fair number of Spenser family home pages—none of them related to Dallas from what I could tell. I found more than 400 Web sites to browse through. I cursed Dallas and Page for their uncommon names that were such common words.

I dismissed most of the sites quickly. I was sure that Helen Pageen Spenser in Dallas was a lovely person; I was also sure that she couldn't give me the information I was seeking. I moved on. While the next page loaded, I tried running through the television channels again. No luck. When I returned my eyes to the monitor, I was shocked. I found the back of a naked woman filling the computer screen.

I was sitting in Oliver's sunroom surrounded by windows through which the entire population of Beach Haven could have seen me—viewing porn on the Web. Assuming, of course, the entire population of Beach Haven had assembled in Oliver's backyard or on the water beyond to monitor my activities in the hopes of catching me viewing porn on the Web. Seemed unlikely but I took no chances. I hit the back button as quickly as my limited eye-hand coordination allowed. Just as the next page began to load, I saw it. The caption. Bad Girl Page waits for Daddy Dallas...you know where the story was going. Could the naked bad girl Page have been the same bad girl Page I'd seen at Dallas Spenser's funeral? I hit Forward to load the Page page once again, but only after turning on the outdoor flood lights to make sure no one would sneak up on me undetected.

As the page loaded, I leaned close to see if the picture was of Page Spenser. The hair was the right color. Since Page had elected to appear fully clothed at her husband's funeral, I'd never seen her nude—although I did know someone I could ask. I hoped it wouldn't come to that. At that point, her hair color was the only feature I had to go on. The woman's face was carefully obscured. I clicked on the image to enlarge the photo. The display was painfully slow. When it finished, however, the larger image told me little. How would I know if Page Spenser had a rose tattoo on her right cheek—the right cheek pictured on my screen. I clicked to the site's home page. Whoever this Page and Dallas were, they were certainly willing to share their fantasies with me. With anyone. With everyone. The couple provided one picture as a heading for each of their interests, and they had many. They were active proponents of BDSM. (I looked it up. By most accounts it meant Bondage, Discipline, Sado-Masochism, although some assign the D/S to domination and submission. Either way you get the picture.) But they did not limit themselves. They were also interested in group sex, voyeurism, and a number of fetishes that I'd never heard of. Or let me put it this way, a number of activities I never dreamed could be fetishes. Apparently I lacked the creativity to think of sneezing as a sexual activity.

When you selected a topic, the site offered choices. You could read the text of a story or you could look at a series of thumbnail photos that conveyed the plot—supposedly. The series I picked had four participants—two of each gender. Given the size of the photos it was hard to figure out what was really going on. I picked a group shot and clicked to see a larger display. The dark-haired woman's face was not visible. The photographer had not gone to the same lengths to hide the blonde's face. I could only see her from the side, but I suspected that I was looking at Lauren.

Each of the photos resembled the first one I'd found; the face of the woman with dark hair was obscured through some device—generally a body part—generally not her own. The only clear identifying feature was the rose tattoo. At least that was the woman's only identifying feature. I'd rather not discuss the identifying features of the male participants. I will tell you, however, that none of the men were redheads.

Now I have no problem with anything that goes on between two consenting adults. Or three. Or four. Actually, I think I counted six in one photo. But I was a little shocked by the couple's need to share—not to mention the poor quality of the photography. I followed the links Dallas and Page had created on their home page to stories about their fantasies and activities. My mouth fell open as I read the stories. As I said, I have no problem with whatever consenting adults want to do. But....

How could they broadcast their activities to the world? Why did they think others would want to read their memoirs? Who would read this stuff? Okay, I read fifteen stories in all—but I had an unusual motivation.

My mind was spinning when I finished. I scanned the stories for any reference to drug use. I found nothing. No mention of cocaine. No mention of Ecstasy. The drug, that is. I glanced at the photos. There wasn't enough cocaine in Colombia to loosen me up that much. Whoever this Page and Dallas were, they were certainly less inhibited than I was. I was amazed and repulsed at the same time. I was also wishing Andy would come home.

Andy. Andy who had possibly visited this couple weeks before. I went back and checked the date on the stories—especially the one accompanied by a photo of a young blond man. Last spring. I sighed. Last spring the Spensers were still in California. Plus, Andy didn't have brown eyes or...well, never mind.

As I logged off, my mind was racing. Could this couple really be the Spensers? How many couplings of a Dallas and a Page could there be? And with a friend bearing a close resemblance to Lauren? Although the name was mentioned occasionally, Dallas was not in any of the photos. Was he the photographer? That would be consistent with the voyeurism tale. Did Detective Petino know about this site? Did he know if the couple was the Spensers? If so, he wouldn't tell me. How could I find out? Could I ask Oliver? No. I didn't want to explain why I was surfing porn sites. Andy? No. I didn't want to explain why I was investigating his girlfriend. He might mistakenly think I was checking up on him. I wouldn't do that. Would I?

I went back to the photos and studied the male participants one more time. Just to be sure. Andy was not among them. Not that I was checking up on him. I wouldn't do that. Would I?

Chapter 7

You might think that trip down the information super-highway would make me lose my appetite. It didn't. Apparently cruising porn sites makes me hungry because I was starving. My hearty dinner of milk and potato chips was beginning to feel more like an appetizer. I went back on the Web and called one of the taxicab numbers listed in the online directory. I was pretty sure that Oliver wouldn't have minded if I took his keys off the rack in the kitchen and drove his Porsche, but while I didn't know the current price tag on the 911, I knew it was more than I had in my bank account. Don't do the wreck if you can't write the check. I'd just made that up and, although it was true, doubted the term would ever become a popular catch phrase.

The cab arrived within ten minutes. When the headlights came down the street, I was waiting at the door in my one outside outfit, the clothes I had chosen for the plane ride from winter to the tropics. I met the taxi at the foot of the driveway. Luckily the driver, Tad, was a cheerful type who knew where I could find an open restaurant. He took me to Kubel's Too in Pehala Park—at least that's where the driver said the restaurant was located. If I'm not standing under a water tower on LBI, I have trouble figuring out what town I am visiting. I accepted the driver's word. "They stay open all winter and you can still find something to eat this time of night." He dropped me off at the door and promised to come back for me in fifty minutes.

I entered the restaurant through the bar area. I had fond memories of Kubel's in Barnegat Light and was willing to extend that good will to the Pehala Park branch. The bar was hopping—or at least crowded, noisy, and smoky. I took a table in the first dining room and regretted immediately that I hadn't brought a book. There wasn't even anything to read on the placemats. So I stared into the fire. To do so, I had to stare past some other late-night diners who apparently thought I was watching them. So I switched to studying the décor.

"I think I can help you."

I turned my eyes from a photo of old LBI to a childlike face on a tall body. I couldn't decide if the person who slid onto the chair across from me was a man or not. I knew he was male but I didn't know if he was a boy or a man. His brown hair was cut short with a crown of tight curls on top. His skin was so smooth that I couldn't imagine that it hosted a razor on a regular basis. His face was wide and attractive, almost pretty. Not fat but soft. He resembled an overgrown baby with the innocent visage to match. If I had to guess, and I did, I would put him in his early twenties.

"I don't believe I need help." My words did not welcome the stranger to the table.

"That's not what I hear." His intonation was flat. Not friendly. Not threatening. Not normal.

"You've heard about me?"

He nodded. His face, like his tone, was devoid of emotion. The blue-gray eyes were flat and lifeless. I searched them for the telltale signs of overmedication—legal or otherwise—but didn't find any.

"Who told you about me?" I couldn't imagine any of my friends associating with this odd creature.

"You know someone from Texas who recently died." He did not exactly ask a question, but I could tell he was waiting for confirmation. He stared past me as if the answer was perched on a flashcard on my shoulder.

I shook my head. "No." I thought back to when I started working after my first stint in graduate school, after I earned what I now called my mercenary degree—the one that catapulted me into a career in business. Back then, I'd spent more time in Texas than in my home base, New York City. But that was a long time ago. All the friends I'd had in the Lone Star state had moved on—either to other locales or out of my life. "Sorry."

"You're wrong. Think it over." His tone was more emphatic than surly.

I didn't need to think it over. I needed to get rid of this guy. "You must have the wrong person." I tried to disguise my grimace as a smile. I really wished I had brought reading material. I'd pretty much exhausted the entertainment potential of the wall treatments.

"No. It's you. I was having a drink at the bar...."

Well, that explained it. The guy had obviously had more than one drink at the bar.

"And I was pulled in this direction." He looked around. "You're the only one here."

I glanced at the other table where two couples had sat between me and the fire. The man was right. They had left. "Well, I'm eating a little late tonight...."

The man-child cut me off. "I'm seeing Dallas. I'm sure of it." He shook his head slowly. "You know they have that funny tower there. I haven't been, but I've seen pictures. You must have a friend from Dallas. Think." He moved his eyes to meet mine.

I returned the man's stare. His gaze was relentless. I should have asked for take-out; instead I heard myself making the admission. "I knew someone named Dallas who died."

The guy smiled with the corners of his mouth. The rest of his face remained impassive. "I told you so. It must be him."

"Him?"

"He's here."

Rather than taking my expression as a sign to leave, my scowl prompted the stranger to continue.

"He says you need help."

"Help getting rid of you?" Okay, I didn't say that out loud. It was, however, what I was thinking as the man went on to explain in a long string of short sentences that he had a gift. As he described his talent, he communicated with people who had changed. Changed was his euphemism for died. "He wants you to know that it wasn't a woman. He knows that you think it was a woman. It wasn't. Do you understand what he means?" The man didn't look to me for an answer. He sat silently staring past me. "Was this man changed by the act of another?"

I stared at him blankly.

"Was he murdered?"

"Petino put you up to this, right?" I adopted the man's habit of answering a question with a question.

"Who's Petino?" His eyes reflected no surprise. No guilt. No knowledge of Petino.

"Oh, that's right. You only speak to the dead. You wouldn't know him. Yet. He's still alive and working as an investigator for Ocean County."

The guy shrugged. "Never met him." He brushed off my remark and stared over my shoulder again. "He just wants to be very clear that a woman didn't kill him."

Page. It hit me like a rock. Who else would have hired someone to speak for Dallas? Especially to communicate that his killer was not a woman. But to me? Why me? Why not go to Petino? "Why does Dallas want to talk to me?" I didn't hide the sarcasm in my voice.

The guy shrugged. "Just because a ship goes over the horizon doesn't mean it doesn't exist. You can't see Dallas, but he is still with us. He is just as much a part of your life now as he was when he was living."

"That I believe."

All the muscles in the man's face contorted, proving that they could actually move. "You didn't know him during his life here, did you?"

"Almost forgot that, eh?"

"No. He's telling me that. But, he likes you." After the brief flurry of activity, his facial muscles again retired.

"He feels you care."

"About Dallas?" Amazement permeated the two words.

"About the truth." The stranger stared at me with no discernable expression.

The time to unload my visitor had come—make that visitors, since I assumed the man-child would take Dallas with him. Even as I spoke I tried to memorize the fellow's nondescript clothing to describe to the cops—if the occasion arose. I had the uncomfortable feeling it would. "Listen, I don't care about Dallas Spenser, although I'll admit I am interested in identifying the person who killed him. I don't know who put you up to this. I hate to insult you but...."

The man-child interrupted. "Hey, it's no skin off my teeth. I'm just the messenger, and you know what they say. Don't shoot the messenger." His slammed his hands on the tabletop as if he were going to lift himself out of his seat. Instead, his stare returned. Ten seconds passed before he directed a forced smile in my direction, "I apologize. I guess that really wasn't funny given the circumstances."

Chapter 8

I had to face the facts. There was a chance that I was a loser. After we found the driveway at Oliver's house empty, I had Tad—my new friend and cabby—drop me at the beach so I could count the ways. The concerned taxi driver warned me to keep warm. He offered to come back to pick me up, but I explained that I could walk the few blocks to Oliver's.

As the cab pulled away I questioned my decision. I was already shivering. Long Beach Island is a great spot for a vacation. A summer vacation. The contrast between LBI and Antigua is probably never more marked than in February. Even in my one outdoor outfit—the jeans, shirt, and cotton sweater under the lightly lined trenchcoat I'd planned to wear on the plane—I was freezing. I thought of turning back, but why? What was waiting for me at Oliver's house? Nothing. No one.

I read the list of rules and regulations posted at the path to the beach. Generally I believe those prohibitions were meant for summer. And even then for teenagers. Not for mature adults with a need to slip away and feel sorry for themselves. I didn't intend to obey any curfew, but according to the signs I wasn't breaking any laws.

As I plodded along the path through the dunes, I had to admit that the facts were irrefutable. I had sacrificed any semblance of a life to follow a man who was following his old girlfriend. And not just any old girlfriend. An old girlfriend who not only indulged to excess in every sexual aberration known to woman but advertised the fact on the Web. And wait...I'm not finished...an old girlfriend who might well have killed her husband. And...I'm not done yet...it appeared that my boyfriend preferred spending time with this exhibitionist murderess than with me. Okay, I'd seen Page. I'd seen the pictures. I understood. Kind of.

Without a full moon, or light thrown from beach houses that sat dark for the winter, the only visible sight was the trace of the whitecaps that broke in thin lines close to shore. Those same whitecaps were responsible for the only sound. Considering that the moon was just growing into a sliver, I could believe that Dallas had been taken by surprise a week before. There was not enough light to see intruders but just enough sound to drown out their noises. But a gunshot? I gave Page the benefit of the doubt. Maybe she wouldn't have heard gunfire in front of her house.

I assumed I was alone on the beach but I didn't really know. Occasionally, I sensed a moving figure closer to the water or to the dunes, but I couldn't be sure. The night was too dark. Like my mood.

Objectively, Andy had done nothing wrong. He was helping a friend. It wasn't his fault that his friend was a woman. A beautiful woman. A beautiful woman who appeared to have the hots for him.

I plowed through the sand toward the water's edge and a harder surface to walk on. I tried to admire Andy's loyalty to an old friend. Admirable, yes. But inconvenient. Why did Dallas have to die now? Why couldn't he have waited until summer. If Andy left me for Page in six months at least I would have had memories. But no. Dallas had to die the very week we were scheduled to fly away. I was relatively certain that Dallas spent his entire life pissing people off. What had he done differently this time to bring this fate on his head? Detective Petino clearly felt Andy was involved, but I knew that idea was ridiculous. Wasn't it?

I pulled my coat around me and headed south with the wind at my back. I didn't consider what that would mean on the return trip. I was too preoccupied. How well did I know Andy, anyway? Well enough to know he was hiding something but not well enough to figure out what that something was. But murder? No way. I couldn't love anyone who could be involved in such a deed.

And I did love Andy, didn't I? Whenever Andy said he loved me—and the words seemed to come easily to him—I always said "me too." I'd actually upgraded to "I love you too." Okay, I hadn't gone first yet. But I would. I might. Soon. Someday.

Why not? There was a lot to love about the man. He was kind, considerate, and sweet. I hate sweet. Yet on this guy sweet looked good—never like a sign of weakness or insecurity. He could talk to anyone—and they would talk back. He could find common ground with larvae. Andy didn't feel any obligation to follow a specified path through life—as a matter of fact, he appeared obligated not to. And that was fine with me. I had no idea where we were headed; I felt no need to know. I just wanted to enjoy the present. And, no matter how often Andy reassured me, I feared that Page Spenser threatened a very nice present.

I had reached no conclusion when the cold drove me from the water's edge. Well, the cold combined with the exhaustion from walking into the wind on my return trip. Clumps of the soft sand slipped under my feet as I headed up the beach towards the path to the street. Focusing on my feet and my labored breathing, I wouldn't have noticed the University of Southern California marching band parading down the path through the dunes. Who did come down that trail? It wasn't USC's band. It was someone carrying something soft but heavy—something that slammed into my right cheek. The force knocked me to the ground. I was in shock. I hadn't seen the blow coming. I screamed as I pulled myself up onto my knees. I wasn't sure whether my sobs came from rage or pain. All the disappointments of the last week—perhaps my entire life—were channeled into my roar. A lot of sound came from my lips, but no words. I sounded like a wounded animal. Not a kitty—a big animal. A large, enraged, wild animal.

My right eye was out of commission. My left eye squinted to catch a glimpse of my attacker in the darkness. I saw nothing. I heard rustling that might have been the sound of my attacker fleeing. Wrong again. I felt the same heavy instrument on my back.

"Who are you? What do you want?" My words were mixed with sobs.

I got no response—verbally. I felt one last wallop on my shoulders and then nothing. I curled into a fetal position, head in the sand, and wailed for an hour. Okay, three minutes that felt like an hour. When I opened my eyes, they weren't much help—and wouldn't have been even under a full moon. Tears blinded my vision before streaming down my cheeks. The tears stung; my eyes snapped shut. I struggled to a sitting position and continued to cry. The tears could have been from the blow, but they weren't. As I said, I had to face it. There was a distinct possibility that I was a loser. I was thinking colossal loser.

Chapter 9

On Thursday morning, in search of sugar and caffeine, I staggered down the hallway and into Oliver's sun-soaked kitchen wearing my traditional indoor attire—white shorts, T-shirt, and flip-flops.

"I put some soda in the fridge for you." Oliver Wilder appeared in the doorway in Yankee blue, an homage to Joe DiMaggio. "What the...?"

"What?"

Oliver looked aghast. I wasn't shocked. Mornings weren't the highlight of my day, but people weren't usually as repulsed as Oliver clearly was.

"Your eye."

"Oh yeah." I'd forgotten the previous night's run-in, although I noticed my head felt worse than it did most mornings. My right eye was watery and the skin around it felt tight. "How does it look?" I poked the spot where I'd been hit. I jumped. The area was sore to the touch.

"Not good." Oliver's expression told me he wasn't lying. "I'll make you an ice pack. What happened?"

"I don't really know." I tried to catch a glimpse of my eye in the oven glass. I could see discoloration, but the dark glass did not make a good mirror.

"Did you fall?" Oliver asked the question from inside the deluxe refrigerator that housed more beer than food. He was slamming the palm of his hand against something. I think it was the icemaker because I heard a loud crackle followed by the hum of a machine.

"No. I don't think so. Not at first anyway." I lifted my face in the hopes of seeing the damage in the chrome oven handle. What I saw was a mass of purple and black. I feared the dark mass was the skin around my eye and on my cheek. What else could it be?

"So?" Oliver pulled his head out of the fridge and turned around with a fistful of ice. He ran a few steps to the sink, dropping ice cubes and scattering them with his feet on the way. He dumped the few remaining cubes into the sink. I wasn't really surprised at his clumsiness. Andy had warned me that Oliver was at two with the universe.

"I think someone hit me." Oliver made no move to retrieve the ice cubes strewn across the floor, so I did. I noticed the task wasn't as easy as it would have been the day before—the day before I'd been knocked to the sand in the Beach Haven dunes. I reached around Oliver to drop the ice in the sink.

He was still rubbing his hands together to chase the cold. "Think? You think someone hit you?" Oliver knelt to dig into a low drawer. He emerged with an old-fashioned icebag. I smelled something unpleasant when he unscrewed the top, but Oliver seemed oblivious.

"It happened so fast." I went to the fridge and pulled a cola out of the rack on the door.

"Who hit you?" One by one he dropped ice cubes, including the ones from the floor, into a glass and also the soft bag.

"I have no idea." The events of the night before seemed unreal in the light of the day. I popped the tab on the soda can, accepted a subway series tumbler full of ice from Oliver, and shuffled past the two armchairs shaped like baseball mitts to my regular spot. After spending a week in Oliver's house, the soft turquoise leather sofa had saved the imprint of my body. Sunlight fell through the skylight directly onto my spot so the leather felt warm and welcoming. I pulled a World Series throw over my bare legs and gazed out over the water at another gorgeous-looking day. Blue skies. Bright sun. Small swells on the bay. I was willing to bet the day didn't feel as gorgeous as it looked.

After a stop at the coffeemaker, Oliver tossed me the icebag and allowed the catcher's mitt to catch him. "Come on. Let me hear the story." His bright brown eyes betrayed that although he was concerned, he was also expecting some good gossip. He drank from a baseball-shaped mug as I explained.

"Last night I walked on the beach late—maybe around eleven or so...." I grimaced as I rested the icebag on my eye. Now the injury really hurt.

"Alone?"

"Andy was working, so I thought...." I laid my head back and balanced the pack of ice on my eye. The pain began to fade. Slowly.

Oliver interrupted. "With what happened to Dallas, you walked on the beach late at night?"

"Get real, Oliver. I don't think LBI is playing host to a homicidal maniac. After all...."

"You don't? You don't think that somehow your attack and Dallas's murder are connected?" I peeked from under the icepack to see Oliver push his eyebrows high to emphasize his incredulity.

"It never occurred to me. Besides, I wasn't shot. Someone came out of the dunes and hit me. I think. I didn't see...."

Again, he interrupted. "What else could have happened?"

I laid my head back and hid under the icebag. I couldn't really come up with another scenario.

"Did you call the cops?"

"No." I moved the ice onto my cheek.

"Why not?" Oliver worked his eyebrows again. The effect was comical, but I knew this wasn't a good time to laugh.

"Whoever knocked me down didn't rob me or touch me... except...you know...except for knocking me down. I'm fine."

Oliver allowed for a long, meaningful pause before he asked his next question. "Do people routinely knock you down?"

"Of course not."

"So...don't you find what happened a little unusual?"

I stared at Oliver over the icepack. "I guess so."

"You guess so?" Somehow he made sipping his coffee underline his point.

"I've had some unusual experiences since meeting Andy. It isn't...."

"What does your getting attacked have to do with Andy?" Oliver's face betrayed serious concern. Instead of pushing his eyebrows towards his forehead, he let them merge in a genuine expression of concern.

"Well, nothing...."

"Do you want what happened to you to happen to someone else? This could be the start of a major crime spree on LBI. I don't mean to scare you, Meg, but you may have encountered Dallas's killer last night. You'd better report the attack. The police need to know that Dallas's murder was not an isolated event."

"Dallas is dead. I have a bruise. I think his murder *was* an isolated event."

"You're being naïve, Meg. Notify the police."

I mumbled that I would.

"I'm sorry." Oliver's voice grew suddenly soft. He stared into his coffee cup.

It never occurred to me to blame Oliver for my injury, but it had occurred to him. He felt that if he'd been home to entertain me I wouldn't have gone out. As he spoke, he seemed embarrassed to meet my eyes. He kept his attention riveted on his coffee. I tried to persuade him that he was not to blame.

"Things like this happen."

Oliver regarded me with amazement. "Not really."

Andy's friend displayed the slow, broad smile that he exhibited frequently. Oliver stood about the same height as Andy's six feet, but Andy had at least forty pounds on him—and Andy was easily described as slim. Oliver reminded me of Mick Jagger without the lips, the hair—or the energy. Nice looking in a rugged kind of way that suggested that his past had been more exciting than his present. It wasn't the forces of mother nature that had weathered his face. Late nights and the artificial stimulants Oliver had used to sustain his lifestyle—both at work as a hard-driving Wall Street type and at home as a hard-core partier—had left their mark, including some crevices so deep they cried out for guard rails.

"You know, Meg, I don't mind keeping the heat up to eighty. Believe me, it's no problem to have you hanging around in your summer clothes—I've actually thought of turning the heat up to ninety in the hopes you'd change into a bathing suit. You must be getting sick of hiding under covers. Borrow my car and go shopping. Pick up some winter clothes."

"Thanks, Oliver. Both for the bathing suit remark and for the offer of your car. But we won't be here that long. Not that here isn't nice." The room where I'd spent most of the last few days opened onto a wide wooden deck that overlooked a dock and two slips that in winter had been emptied of a wide array of grown-up toys. Beyond them, the Manahawkin Bay stretched west, providing a much better view than an elderly couple watching C-SPAN, the one from my New York apartment.

"Hmmmh." Oliver averted his eyes.

"What does 'hmmmh' mean?"

"Just that if Andy wants to solve this crime...it might take more than a few days. You only have one outfit suitable for the outdoors." He referred to the jeans, shirt, and cotton sweater combo I'd worn the night before. "I just think you might need more."

I thanked him and rejected both—the offer and the idea that I would need a wardrobe.

Oliver was surprised that Andy was already gone and that I'd only glimpsed my boyfriend when he got up that morning. Oliver didn't understand why Page needed so much help from Andy. "After all, it isn't like she's a viable suspect or anything." He studied my face for a reaction. Learning nothing in my expression, he moved to the window with long, purposeful strides. He observed the only activities on the bay, tiny white-caps. "Page never would…hurt Dallas. Not that way. Never. It's ridiculous."

I grunted to hide my disappointment. I liked painting Page as a villain.

Oliver appeared wistful. "Funny, Page was not real popular with us—Andy's friends. The guys, that is. Actually, the girls liked her even less."

One of Oliver's best traits was his constant dissing of Page. I'd known Oliver for less than a week but during that time, he took every opportunity to denigrate her. If I turned a page in a magazine, he'd start. "Page, I didn't like her at all when Andy brought her home." If his pager went off, he'd talk about Page. "Page, in the old days I never knew what Andy saw in her." Considering she was Andy's old girlfriend, she spent a lot of time in Oliver's consciousness. But then again her husband had just been murdered.

Oliver reached for a football—one was never out of arm's reach of a sports-related toy in the Wilder household. He twirled it in the air as he spoke. "We couldn't see her charms back then. But Andy had it bad for her. Took him a while to get over her. He'd hate me for saying this, but I don't think he truly got over her until you came on the scene. We were all pretty shocked to hear that you were on your way to Antigua with Andy."

"Really?" My heart leapt. Pathetic, eh? The man had barely acknowledged my existence for the last seven days and I was hanging onto the slightest reference to our relationship. He likes me. He really likes me.

I loved listening to stories about the efforts Andy's college gang made to avoid Page. "Andy didn't mind having her all to himself. If you think she looks good now…." Something in my expression prompted Oliver to change tacks. He feigned a cough. "Andy met her in DC in college. He'd bring her home in the summer—just one summer really. She was hot. He was right about that, but…." Oliver shrugged and gazed across the bay.

"What?" I asked anxiously. What was Oliver holding back?

"That guy never came back to take his boat out of the water." I pulled myself up and followed his gaze.

I spotted a sailboat still sitting at a dock. "But?" I prompted.

"May I be blunt? She had Andy whipped. We hardly recognized him when she was around. Whatever she wanted, he did. Page needed someone who could stand up to her…Andy was just…not the one."

"I can't imagine Andy in a domestic situation."

"I didn't say she wanted domesticity. Page was a wild little thing. You should have seen…wait…I was cleaning out some files the other night and found some pictures…." Oliver passed the football to the other catcher's mitt and admired his throw before he crossed the room in three steps and dug into a drawer under the wide TV screen. He found the photos easily and plopped them on the edge of the couch at my head. "See, here's Page with Andy…and that's me." Oliver went on to describe the others in the photo, but I didn't hear a word he said. My eyes were riveted on the young couple in the center of the frame.

I'd never seen the young Andy before. Oliver told me it was a twenty-year-old who stared into the camera with an intensity that I recognized. But in the photo, the intense eyes were set in a baby face. The physical changes weren't what made Andy's face look so different—although he had shed some puffiness around the jawline. What had changed Andy was the intangible force of aging. I had to admit that he looked happy in the photo. The cat that swallowed the canary came to mind. I wondered if Page was responsible for his contentment. I could see how she might be.

Young Page had a lot more hair—as the era dictated. She smiled into the camera, but I wouldn't say she looked happy. She looked seductive. She looked alluring. She looked smug. Would I have had the same reaction if she weren't resting her chin on the head of my boyfriend? Would I have felt the same if she hadn't posed with both arms wrapped around my boyfriend? Would I have felt the same if she had cuddled with Oliver for the photo? No. I probably would have said she was a beautiful young woman who looked great in a bathing suit.

I glanced at Oliver. He was studying the picture with nostalgia. Checking how he looked in the photo, I suspected he was recalling a really great high—if one could, in actuality, remember a really great high. "Yeah, Page liked to party. No wonder Page went for Dallas. He was quite the partier in those days." It didn't take much prodding to start Oliver describing those days. "Page could hardly turn down a man with an unlimited supply of coke." My heart leapt. Drug debts. Unsavory characters. People with criminal records—and motives. I wanted to explore the topic, but Oliver wanted to hear about the funeral and the murder.

I told him what I knew. No crime scene located. No obvious motive uncovered. The cops had a bullet but no murder weapon to match it. No suspects identified. From Andy, Oliver had already heard Page's timeline for the night of the murder. Dinner. Video. Argument. Kayaking. Page had no candidates for the role of murderer of her husband. At least that's what she told Andy.

"How was Page at the funeral?"

"You should have come." Even as I said the words, I wondered if Oliver possessed any clothes that would have been suitable. As far as I knew he didn't own a single item without the insignia of a major sports team emblazoned across the front—or back—or front and back. And that included his socks and shorts. (For the record, I saw his underwear in the laundry room.)

"Was Page okay?" Oliver persisted.

55

"As I said, I don't know her but she acted okay. No tears." I shrugged and tried being kind. "But people go through those things in a state of shock."

"Was everyone being nice to her?"

I scowled at Oliver. "Why wouldn't they be?"

Oliver shrugged. "You know with murder...the spouse is always the first suspect."

Now there was a thought I could buy into. Page could vie with me for Andy's affections—but not very aggressively in horizontal stripes. Did convicts still wear those outfits? I envisioned Page in one of those awful orange scrub suits. With dismay, I realized she wore the color fairly well. But certainly with all the resources of the free world at my disposal, I could look better— or at least competitive.

A frown overtook Oliver's features. "Who's that?"

I followed Oliver's gaze down the hallway. Through the glass panes that surrounded the door, I saw a tall, dark, not quite handsome man coming up the front walkway. "Detective Petino. I met him at the funeral."

Oliver radiated hostility. His eyes narrowed into slits that followed the cop to the front door. "Why is he here?"

"He's a homicide cop. There's been a homicide."

Oliver turned to me and repeated his question. "But why is he *here?*"

"With any luck he was completely charmed by me at the funeral and has come to see me because he finds me fascinating." I whispered as the cop moved closer as if he could hear through walls. "Of course, there is one problem with that theory."

"What's that?"

"I'm not that charming."

Chapter 10

The doorbell played the theme from Monday night football. "I'll get it." I pulled myself off the couch and padded down the faux marble hallway to the door. Detective Petino saw me coming through the glass side pane, averted his eyes, and disappeared behind the door. That couldn't be a good sign.

Cops scare me even when it's obvious we're on the same side, and this situation wasn't quite that obvious. I plastered on a happy face to greet the detective. "Detective Petino. I must say I'm a bit surprised to see you here."

"And I must say that I'm a bit surprised to see you've been beaten up since we first met."

It took me a moment to interpret his question. "Oh, this. I was actually going to call...."

"What happened?"

"Someone kind of attacked me last night on the beach." I touched the puffy skin lightly. Yep, it still hurt. I poked it one more time just to be sure.

"Someone." He shrugged. "I admire you for not using the old 'I fell' excuse."

"What is that supposed to mean?" I tried to frown emphatically, but the effort hurt.

"I've heard Beck has a bad temper."

"What?" I was genuinely shocked. I'd seen Andy remain calm under circumstances that would have pushed me over the edge. Like the time I mistook him for an intruder and hit him over the head with a crystal vase. He'd remained completely calm. Of course intitially he was unconscious. But when he came to, he displayed no tendency toward violence. And if there was ever a time a man might lose his temper, that was it. The detective forced a short smile—well, about 25 percent of a smile. He curled the corners of his mouth, briefly, revealing no sign of his formidable dental work. "I'm looking for Beck." The detective changed directions.

"Not here."

"Where?"

"Don't know."

"Oh."

"He's working. I just don't know where."

"Oh."

"Would you like to leave a message?" A hint of impatience crept into my voice. The day looked warm and sunny. It *was* sunny, anyway. The detective wore a heavy tweed overcoat. He was prepared to stand on the doorstep all day. I was not. The skin on my legs had already gone to goosebumps. I had a keen interest in closing the door. When I did, I wanted the cop to be on the other side.

"No. No message." Petino studied the house over my shoulder. He seemed particularly taken by the Super Bowl XXXV poster in the hallway.

"Bad game. Good poster." I smiled.

He didn't. "How long were you folks planning to stay here?" His black eyes were narrow, almost hidden under thick black lashes that I'd barely noticed the other day.

"At Oliver's?" I shrugged. "Only a few days. I told you. We were on our way...." Suddenly I didn't want to tell the detective about our plans. "We were going…out of town, but now…we …it's open ended…our stay…the duration." I took a deep breath and aimed for a complete sentence. "We haven't made any plans. After all, we just got here."

"Hmmm." The detective surveyed the view. "Oliver Wilder must be a good friend of Beck's to let you two stay here."

"They go way back."

"And you?"

"I told you, I met Andy late last summer." I moved the door toward a closed position. But only by inches. I wanted to appear cooperative.

"I mean Wilder."

"I just met him." I moved the door a bit more so that I could use it to shield the right side of my body from the cold.

"Did Wilder know the victim?"

"A long time ago." I shook my head vigorously. "I think he's run into Page around town, you know, since she's been back here. But mostly he knew Page a long time ago—like Andy did." Remembering the detective's revelations, I shrugged. "Mostly."

The cop nodded as if I were only confirming information he already knew. His bright white teeth remained hidden. Detective Petino wasn't wasting any smiles on me today. In fact, I figured he had intimidation in mind.

"You don't know where Beck is?"

I shrugged, shook my head and slipped a bit more of my body behind the door.

"Well, I have a hunch I can find him." He chuckled. "If you see him, tell him I said I'd catch him later."

Great. Cop humor.

As the detective turned to leave he stopped, then turned back to me. "If you want to get dressed I'll drop you at the station to report your attack."

"I am dressed."

"Oh."

"I'm supposed to be in the Caribbean."

"Oh. Right."

This time when I peered into the cop's eyes I saw sympathy. I preferred the hostility.

Petino turned to go again, but stopped abruptly before I managed to close the door. Did all cops of a certain age suffer from Colombo syndrome? "By the way." His slicked-back hair combined with a glance-over-the-shoulder pose made the cop resemble a model—in the Sears catalog circa 1982. "What was the first thing you thought when you heard Dallas Spenser had been murdered?"

Easy answer. "Who is Dallas Spenser?"

"You had no idea who killed him?"

"How could I have an idea when I didn't even know he existed?"

The detective shrugged. I watched him through the window until his car pulled away. As soon as the dark sedan disappeared onto Long Beach Boulevard I dialed Andy's cell phone. I reached his voice mail.

"Andy, I know you're busy but we have to talk. We didn't really have a chance earlier...and now...well...Petino is looking for you. Please call me at Oliver's as soon as possible."

Chapter 11

Would you like to know how I found out that Beach Haven has its own police department?

When Andy hadn't called back in an hour I borrowed an oversized Giants jacket and a dilapidated bicycle from Oliver. I wanted to bike to the police station to report the previous night's attack. Oliver offered me his Porsche but didn't seem at all concerned when I said I wanted to bike. He asked me if I knew where the police station was. I said I had passed it many times and he didn't question me. The stock market was open; his attention was focused on the screen of his laptop.

I had the whole day ahead of me with nothing to do. I had time to tour the entire island by bike. I had, however, planned a more modest itinerary. I hadn't ridden in a long time. *They* said riding came back to you like, well, like riding a bicycle. I hoped *they* were right.

The day wasn't frigid, but it was too cold to invite a leisurely course. I rode up to the ocean and headed north, staying as close to the water as possible. Motivated by the cold, I cycled toward the police station with increasing speed—and comfort. Turns out riding a bicycle did come right back. I even did a little no-hands riding. The bright sun provided unexpected warmth. Luckily, I rode in the sun most of the time. I zigged and zagged to make sure of it.

My legs were shaking by the time I followed the sign to the police department and rolled the bike up the ramp at the Long Beach Island township building. I was in no mood for the information the officer on duty provided—even though he delivered the news in a gentle and kind manner. Since my assault, as he called the incident, had happened in Beach Haven, I would have to go to the Beach Haven police station—a building I had apparently passed within minutes of leaving Oliver's house. The officer went on to explain that there were four police departments on Long Beach Island. Beach Haven, along with Surf City and Harvey Cedars, had their own police forces. I tried to smile as I thanked him, but I didn't feel very happy knowing I was about to cycle more than one hundred blocks back toward where I started.

As I climbed back onto the bike for the return ride to Oliver's, I felt better about the cops and my legs. I had one of those inexplicable bursts of physical energy. I don't know why I felt so good—but I did. I even sang a little. Okay, a lot. It was still winter. No one was around. I did *West Side Story.* Recently I'd figured out I had a perfect voice for the lead—unfortunately, the lead was Tony.

By the time the dark sedan pulled alongside me I'd finished three numbers. I was riding in the bike lane on Ocean Boulevard, before the road becomes Beach Avenue. The car's bumper stayed even with me as I pumped the pedals on the old thick-wheeled bike harder. You'd think that would make the bike move faster wouldn't you? Yeah, I did too. It didn't. So I slowed to let the car move ahead. The motorized vehicle slowed as well. I waved for the driver to pass me. How cautious could a driver be? The car had more than a full lane to itself but, apparently, no plans for passing.

I glanced at the car. The fading paint was navy. A Ford, I guessed. I recorded the information for the cops. At best, this guy was stalking me. At worst? I thought about the night before.

Maybe the attack hadn't been random. In the next block, a furniture delivery truck blocked the bike lane. If the situation did not change in five hundred feet, I'd be squashed between the car and the truck.

To my left, the passenger window of the dark sedan slid down. "Ms. Daniels. Nice to see you."

I glanced into the car. I didn't recognize the torso or the thighs, but I did recognize the voice—okay, and the badge on his belt.

"Is that you, Detective Petino?"

He bent his head down so I could see the flash of his wide white smile. "Yeah, I was wondering if I could offer you a ride somewhere."

One hand let go of the handlebars and pointed to the bike beneath me. "I've got wheels, thank you."

"Well, I didn't know how far you had to go. You appeared kind of uncomfortable riding. Agitated even."

Maybe my rendition of *America* made me appear a little frazzled. No need to share that. I sneered to ask him if he was nuts. "I'm fine. I ride all the time."

"Oh." He made the word sound meaningful.

"What?"

"I felt concerned that you were worried or agitated."

"No reason to be." At least before he pulled up beside me. "I'm fine, although riding and talking is getting a bit scary. Maybe we should say good-bye."

"Sure. I just wanted to ask you about the trip Beck made from New York City to Long Beach Island last week."

Looking back, it was my shaking that made the bike veer out of control. At the time, I would have sworn my bike careened across the macadam for no reason at all. I saw the front wheel headed for the police car's passenger door and jerked the handlebars to the right. The next motion was inexplicable and unstoppable. The rear wheel of the bike seemed to rise into the air. The seat tilted to the right, and I went with it.

I was never quite sure how I cleared the bicycle. When the action was all over, the bike was sprawled on the pavement and I was sitting cross-legged on the scratchy winter-brown surface of a well-manicured lawn of an equally well maintained Cape Cod cottage. Detective Petino was out of his car and kneeling before me with a concerned expression on his face. The shiny black circles that were his eyes seemed less threatening than they had only hours before at Oliver's. "Are you okay? I feel I contributed to your fall."

"Contributed? You caused it. I should sue the city."

"Actually the county...."

"Fine, I'll sue the county."

"Let me help you up." He grabbed my hand and yanked. I accepted the assistance—I needed it. "I don't see any bumps or bruises—that is, any new ones." He inspected me from head to toe, front and back. "No rips or tears—no cuts or scrapes. Luckily your outfit...." Petino stumbled over the word as he checked out my jeans and Oliver's jacket. "Your clothing was...protective. You're fine."

"No thanks to you. You swerved."

"I didn't swerve."

"You swerved."

"I didn't swerve."

"If you didn't swerve, then why is that bike laying on the ground and why am I sprawled on this lawn? I should be crossing the state streets by now."

"You swerved."

"I swerved?"

"Yes, you swerved."

"*I* swerved?"

The cop nodded. "When I mentioned that Beck had been here last week, you swerved."

I sighed. Maybe the detective was right. Maybe I did swerve and in doing so told him what he wanted to know—that Andy Beck had failed to share this information with me.

"Well, it doesn't matter how it happened. It happened. And I'm fine." I lifted the bike and rolled it back and forth a few times. "And the bike appears fine." At least as fine as it was when I'd taken it out of Oliver's garage. "So if you'll excuse me." I threw one leg over the bike. "Don't worry; I won't sue."

"I'm not worried."

I put one foot on a pedal but stopped. "You know, Detective Petino, you can drop the subterfuge. Andy had nothing to do with the murder of Dallas Spenser, so if you want to ask me anything I am more than willing to cooperate."

"I never said I thought Beck had anything to do with his murder."

"Right." Well, technically the cop was right. He hadn't. But why all the interest if he didn't think that.

"Okay. I'll ask. Was Beck with you on the night of the murder?"

"You believe that was last Wednesday night, right?"

The cop nodded condescendingly, as if questioning my uncertainty about such an important date.

"He was with me in New York from Wednesday morning until we got the call on the way to the airport the next day, except...."

"Yes?"

"Except when he took his car back to the garage he rents."

"And that would be?" The smirk on Petino's face told me he already knew the answer.

"In Point Pleasant." I didn't have to tell the detective where the town was. I was relaying the news to my own consciousness. "New Jersey."

Chapter 12

I pedaled to the Acme supermarket at 96th Street. I wanted something good to come out of my ride to the police station at 68th Street. After Petino's revelation, I felt that need for some Pepperidge Farm Mint Milanos. Some do drugs. Some do alcohol. I do Milanos.

To survive our delay on Long Beach Island, I'd need to restock Oliver's refrigerator. Actually, I needed to stock it. To restock Oliver's fridge all I needed was a thirty-pack of Budweiser. Even if I'd wanted to I couldn't manage that box in the bicycle's basket, so I settled on some staples. Cookies. Chips. And whatever else struck my fancy.

I got a shopping cart and started wandering the aisles. I'd secluded myself in Beach Haven for the month of October many years before to focus on my thesis. Along with my activities at the Spray Beach laundromat/car wash, trips to the Acme had been the mainstay of my social life. I grew sentimental as I wheeled the squeaking cart across the linoleum.

I'd been up and down three aisles and the only thing in my basket was a jar of capers and some Q-Tips. I decided to check the fruit and vegetables I'd passed on my way in. Maybe if I stared at healthful foods long enough I would learn to like them.

I recognized her from behind—even with her clothes on. When she turned and reached for the basil, I knew. Page Spenser was in the Acme pushing a cart full of fresh produce—the kind that I couldn't identify on a food chart. Great. She cooked. Andy had an old girlfriend who looked great and cooked. Of course, on the downside, she killed her husbands. Okay, one husband. Allegedly.

What was she doing in the food store anyway? Didn't she have leftovers from the funeral repast? And even if she needed food, what was she doing on my half of the island? There was only one bridge to LBI from the mainland. To get to Oliver's, I turned right and drove south. To get to the Spenser house, Page would turn left, drive north, and, hopefully, stay there. But she hadn't remained in Loveladies. She'd driven half the length of the island to get groceries. She must have passed a store on her way south. Okay, offhand I couldn't think of one. But that did not mean it wasn't there. She could have gone across the bridge to Manahawkin, which was loaded with shopping options.

I considered saying hello. Considered. Why should I? I had nothing to say to her. And I couldn't imagine she had anything to say to me. I didn't say hello. Yet, I couldn't tear myself away. I'm not proud of my behavior but neither am I surprised by it. I followed her.

Page looked depressed and slightly less than beautiful. Slightly. Dark circles outlined her big blue eyes. Even at a distance, however, her eyes were striking. Her pace was slow and her expression dejected as she surveyed the produce. That I could understand. The selection was more limited than usual. I bet the produce in Antigua wasn't suffering from seasonal limitations.

I watched as Page selected several varieties of lettuce and additional items I couldn't actually recognize without moving closer—close enough to read the labels. I was keeping a discreet distance, feigning interest in fruit. If I were a professional P.I. like Andy, I probably would have known better than to observe a suspect while selecting oranges. If I shopped more I would have known not to pick oranges off the bottom of the pile. But I wasn't and I didn't. I selected an orange absentmindedly. Not just any orange. Apparently the orange I wanted served as the lynchpin of the entire stack. Suddenly, the oranges started to move. All the oranges. I tried to be inconspicuous as I worked at a frantic pace to stop the avalanche. I glanced up and down the aisle. No one, including Page, appeared to notice my problem—a problem that seemed to have no end in sight. I was still fighting the oranges when Page disappeared around the corner.

Eventually, a kid in a white apron came to my rescue. I left him juggling oranges and pushed my cart off in search of Page. I caught up with her at the meat counter where she picked up some fresh items. I followed her as she added some exotic oils and premium coffee to her cart. But Page didn't stop at the cookie aisle. I did. That's when I lost her.

I wasn't worried. I saw no way Page could move through checkout ahead of me. I qualified for the Express Lane. I figured I would go outside first and wait for her. Then I would observe her. Why? I wasn't quite sure. I knew from hanging out with Andy, however, that a lot of surveillance is watching nothing happen.

I maneuvered my cart into the express lane. Only one person was ahead of me—a man in motorcycle gear. A man with a really big order. I glanced at the sign above the register. Eight items. There was no doubt; it clearly said eight items. I checked out the items on the belt. Certainly looked like more than eight to me. I counted. The guy caught my eyes moving methodically through his order. He made a great show of counting and grouping his items. I counted thirty-two. I felt pretty sure he counted eight. That's because he counted three six-packs of toilet paper as one; six cans of soup as one; and six cans of tuna fish as one. Okay, maybe they were open to debate. But piling six packets of assorted meat cuts did not make the six packages a single item. Putting all your vegetables together didn't help. The sign said eight items—not eight food groups. I checked out the heavy chain hanging from his belt and decided not to call for a recount.

I kept one eye on Page. Just my luck. She got the most efficient cashier on the planet. The only cashier who spent more time ringing up groceries than flirting with the bagboy in the next aisle.

My cashier finally scanned the last of the biker's groceries. "$72.73." The man's brow furrowed. Apparently, he labored under the impression that groceries were free. When informed that, in fact, payment was expected, he dug into a seemingly bottomless pocket for his wallet. For a moment I believed he had forgotten it. After about thirty seconds, his large hand pulled a battered leather billfold from the deep opening. He fumbled as he opened it. He glanced at the total on the cash register. He counted the bills in his wallet. He studied the total again as if he could will the amount lower. Then he began a systematic search of his pockets. Many, many pockets.

Two lanes away, a checker with the hand–eye coordination of a Wimbledon champion was totaling Page's order.

I looked back to the man in front of me. How many pockets could one outfit contain? He was still digging for coins. "I thought I had more." He mumbled an apology to no one in particular.

While the guy counted change—lots of change—Page's groceries were flying into the bag at the hands of a kid who appeared to have won the "Bagger of the Year" nationals.

When his effort ended, the man in front of me did not smile. I had a feeling I would not smile either.

I knew what was coming. "I guess I'm gonna hafta put somethun back."

The cashier appeared more annoyed than I did—which was going some. Her sigh could have blown some of the larger items off the belt. It might have been a coincidence but the guy's roll of paper towels tumbled.

"What?" She snapped.

"What?" He mimicked.

"What item do you want to put back?"

Page was closing her wallet while the man in front of me was doing more meticulous counting. "I'm only $2 short."

"Not any more you're not." I moved his cart, which he had long since forgotten about. I leaned across the basket and shoved two singles in his direction.

"Oh, I can't."

"You can." I said with authority and a crisp smile.

"No. I can write a check." He pulled a ratty check book from his pocket. "I know I have a check-cashing card here somewhere."

He was right. He did. He'd filed it behind his other cards. Lots of cards—health insurance, library, AAA. Behind a photo of the lucky woman whom I assumed was his girlfriend. Behind driver's licenses. Not one license—I swore I saw multiple licenses.

He presented the check card to the cashier without apology. What? No coupons?

Page had stopped near the front door to dig in her handbag. She checked her watch as she pulled a cell phone from the depths of the soft imported leather pouch.

For my part, I'd been a little too quick to dismiss the coupon issue. "Oh, look." Apparently, the motorcyclist had found one in his checkbook. "Almost forgot."

The cashier with the patience of Job opted for adjusting his total as opposed to resorting to physical violence. The man still didn't have enough cash. He started filling out the check.

"Hey." The guy stopped only after he had completed writing the check. "Can I have some cash back?"

He wrote VOID seven times on the check and started over.

I checked the Cash Only sign surreptitiously as the man wrote his second check. The multiple I.D.s outweighed even the chain at his waist as a motivation to remain silent. I couldn't think of one good reason why a person needed multiple I.D.s. Reasons. Yes. Good reasons. No.

Gotta give it to the guy. He was thorough. He even filled in his check ledger and did the subtraction to come up with a new balance.

Near the door, Page appeared impatient as she spoke into her cell phone.

In my lane, the cashier counted change. When she put it in the man's hand, he recounted it—carefully. Then he placed every bill in the bill compartment, making sure each president faced in the same direction.

Finally, he rolled his cart away—about three feet away. He was still blocking my carriage when he stopped to rearrange his items. Why couldn't he roll into the exit aisle and block Page? But no. He wasn't finished annoying me.

Page finished her call and checked her watch. She didn't appear in any hurry to leave the store. Fifteen feet away, the cashier could at last address my six items. Five items—plus the one that needed a price check. While the bagger ran to check, Page rolled her cart out the automatic door.

I consoled myself. What did it matter if I missed my opportunity to watch Page get into her car? Following her was ridiculous. Did I really think she'd be revealing the secret of her husband's murder in the Acme parking lot? When I finally got my change, I didn't even rush. I figured Page would be long gone. I figured wrong. Page was finishing loading groceries into the back of a Mercedes sedan—one of the big ones.

She politely pushed her cart out of the way and climbed into the front seat. I feigned interest in the notices posted on the glass wall as I watched her ride away.

When she stopped at the stop sign with her left blinker flashing, a head—clearly a male head—popped up beside her. A small scream, more of a yelp, escaped my lips. Was someone going to kill Page, too?

While I observed from behind the glass wall, the head appeared to plant a quick kiss on the woman's cheek. Then it disappeared from view. Page made a left and headed north up Long Beach Boulevard. I watched with puzzlement. Lately, I'd witnessed some pretty odd happenings, but this one was really weird.

Chapter 13

By the time I pedaled up Oliver's driveway, I was putting a lot of effort into making biking appear effortless. My legs shook as I applied the brakes and buckled as they took my full weight. The bike almost knocked me off my feet. With difficulty, I retained my balance and my dignity. At least a modicum of dignity. I concentrated on staying upright as I opened the orange garage door. The accomplishment required a lot more concentration than you might imagine. It wasn't until I pulled the bike inside and turned to close the door that I noticed the car. There couldn't be two cars like that in existence—let alone within a forty-mile radius.

I dropped the door handle and strode across the lawn with long strides that grew more purposeful as my legs adjusted to the land. As I passed the concrete dolphin leaping above the cement fountain my view became unobstructed. I was right. It was definitely the same car. The driver hid behind a newspaper, but I knew he wasn't reading. He was watching Oliver's house and those of us in it.

I went directly to the passenger door and climbed into the front seat. I glimpsed a half-eaten Big Mac just before it flattened underneath me. "Jake Chandler. What a coincidence!"

Jake let the newspaper drop and turned his undersized head in my direction. His face was as red as his hair.

You *should* be embarrassed. I didn't say that out loud. I maintained a friendly, naïve pose. "What are you doing here?" he sputtered.

"Jake, you are awfully easy to spot. If you drove a low profile vehicle—say, an innocuous four door sedan—you might get away with such blatant surveillance."

He sputtered with more intensity.

"So why are you watching us?"

Jake did what he considered folding his newspaper. I would describe the action as crumpling. He pushed the paper into the backseat. When it resisted, he finished the job with a punch that didn't subdue the newsprint. If Jake couldn't win a fight with a daily newspaper, maybe he should think twice about the way he plied his profession.

"I guess it looks like I'm watching you, doesn't it?"

I let a raised eyebrow be my answer.

"I...I...."

"Just say it. 'I am watching you.' Then tell me why."

Jake exhaled and stared past me. "I was waiting for your boyfriend to come home. If he's in there, he won't answer the door. At the funeral, I had no idea...look, I don't like to be the bearer of bad news."

"Bear it," I commanded.

That's how I found out that if Detective Petino never said Andy was a suspect in the murder of Dallas Spenser, he certainly knew how to intimate the idea. Not only to me but to Jake Chandler. He intimated that Page and Andy were lovers. He intimated that Page stood to inherit a lot of money. He intimated that Page needed a conspirator to carry off the murder. "I don't think the cops are right," Jake reassured me.

Yeah, right. What was Jake going to say to me?

"I'm sure you don't believe their accusations, right?" Jake inserted just enough optimism into the end of his sentence to warn me that he felt we were on the record. Not that he meant to alert me. Jake simply wasn't good at subterfuge.

I ignored his question. "Jake, Andy isn't here. I don't know when he will be back. If you want to sit here all night that's fine with me. I won't call the cops, but I can't speak for the neighbors. I don't believe they get a lot of loiterers on this street."

I pushed the door open with my right shoulder and climbed out. After I scraped the Big Mac from the seat of my pants, I handed the mess back to Jake. "Sorry I can't invite you in." I sucked a spot of special sauce from my finger.

"Hey, I understand." Just as I slammed the door he called out, "How about my story?" Through the glass I thought I heard him add, "You didn't say anything, but you must have liked it."

Chapter 14

I could have asked Jake to show me his story, but I didn't want him to see my reaction. Whatever that might be. With legs that didn't have much left in them, I pedaled to pick up the last *Press of Atlantic City*. I stopped at Buckalew's not so much to eat as to rest. I wondered if a cab would take my bike back.

The lunch crowd had thinned. I got a table for four and spread the newspaper across the top.

Jake was right. I did like the story. I was finishing the last paragraph when I heard the increasingly familiar voice. "We have to stop meeting like this." Detective Petino dropped a newspaper on my table, called for a cup of coffee, and slid into the chair across from me.

"*I* think we should." Detective Petino was joking; I meant it. "I don't know why you're following me."

"Hey. Don't flatter yourself. I'm off-duty. I'm here for a late lunch—or an early dinner. I'm here because I'm hungry. I just thought I'd be polite and say howdy." He smirked. "Howdy." He flashed his wide expanse of white teeth. There was not an ounce of sincerity in his smile.

"Howdy back."

The cop grabbed one of the rolls from my basket and ripped a piece off. "After just a few hours, your eye looks better. Did Beck bring you flowers to make up for it?"

I released a deep sigh before I spoke. "I told you before and I will tell you again. Andy Beck had nothing to do with my black eye. Besides I haven't seen him since we last talked. Gee that must have been…what…fifteen minutes ago?" I feigned a glance at my watch.

Detective Petino smirked. It seemed he barely used his facial muscles except when he cajoled with a fake smile or smirked—which he did often.

"I think you're spending a little too much time worrying about my boyfriend. I would think that this information would lessen your interest in Andy." I pointed to what I considered pretty big news. Jake Chandler had a byline in the *Press of Atlantic City*. "Now this should provide some leads." I slapped the newspaper with the back of my hand. The noise startled a baby at the next table who regarded me with wonderment, then disappointment, then fear. "Did the bad lady scare you?" his mother asked as the baby's face crumbled. Within moments his cheeks were covered in tears—and it took a lot of tears to cover that chubby face.

"Sorry." I shrugged as an apology to the young mother. A weak apology. I thought the bad-lady tag was a bit harsh.

Jake's story revealed that Dallas had been Dallas Spenser only for the last fifteen years. Before that it appeared that he had been Denver Spears, a Pennsylvania businessman presumed drowned fifteen years ago. Denver Spears had left a wife, the former Emily Burton, and two children—a son, James, now nineteen, and a daughter, Bonnie, now seventeen. Denver Spears had emigrated from England, and purchased a small direct marketing company near Pottstown, Pennsylvania. Over the next six years, he had grown the business, expanding into electronic media where he made his fortune.

I studied the two photos that appeared with the story. There was little doubt that Denver Spears and Dallas Spenser were the same person—although the Dallas Spenser iteration was clearly the more recent. As Denver Spears, the man stared into the camera with a blank expression. I detected no charm. No charisma. No hint of the sexual appetite he revealed on the World Wide Web. The same was true of the man in the photo labeled "Dallas Spenser," except that in the more current picture he had acquired a confidence that was better described as arrogance. I leaned close and studied the studio portrait. I still did not get the deceased's appeal.

I tried to reconcile Dallas Spenser's image with the man Andy had described. Spenser had boasted of an English, public-school, upper-class background and described himself as a man whose greatest failure in his own estimation was never finishing at Oxford. According to Andy, Dallas claimed that he was too anxious to plunge into the rigors of the business world. He gloated that his success far exceeded that of his classmates who trod the well-beaten path. Dallas (or Denver, or whatever his name was...I decided to call him "DS") apparently boasted of following the unbeaten path—a path where he might have met a lot of people interested in seeing him dead.

In my opinion, the revelations about Dallas Spenser's former life provided a fair number of motives for murder. I don't know about other women, but if my husband faked his own death, leaving me with two young children to raise, I would have killed him. I hoped the police were investigating the possibility that Emily Spears, the woman in Philadelphia who'd believed that she was his widow, did just that.

Detective Petino could hardly sound less interested. "Yeah, we're checking into that angle." The cop's tone suggested not hard enough.

Checking into it? Jake Chandler had identified abandoned relatives, colleagues, and customers. All left in the lurch by Dallas, then known as Denver Spears.

"I hate to admit it, but little Jimmy Olson did a good job on this one." Petino scowled at the newspaper.

Jake Chandler had done a good job. He, not the cops, had uncovered Dallas Spenser's real identity and the memorial head-stone in a suburban Philadelphia cemetery.

"That happened fifteen years ago. As far as we know no con-nection exists between Spenser's past life and his death." Petino dismissed the article with a wave that let him grab his coffee mug from the waitress in the same move.

"But you're investigating, right?"

"We know how to do our job."

I was painfully aware of his evasive reply.

"You know, I've heard rumors—just rumors of course—that Dallas Spenser was involved in drug trafficking."

"Trafficking?" The cop snickered. "Hardly. From what we can tell he kept a little stuff around the house for business purposes. Since he dealt with some show-biz types on occasion. It does not appear he used drugs himself."

"But you're investigating that angle?" I ignored the sandwich the waitress slipped in front of me.

"No need to. Spenser was at the bottom of the drug-world food chain." The cop took a long drink of coffee to punctuate the sentence.

"Or so you think."

"So we know." The cop grabbed a french fry from my plate but apparently didn't view eating my food as a bribe. He was not swayed by my opinion. "He was at best an occasional user. A dealer? Hardly. Spenser was too smart for that. Maybe he did a little informal distribution—not that I'm saying he did—but guys at his level don't get rubbed out because they owe their friendly local dealer two hundred bucks. Spenser could easily cover whatever he may have put up his nose." He grabbed another french fry.

"That's it. He had a lot of money. Who knows what his involvement was?"

Petino shook his head. "We think we know where we're headed with the murder of Dallas Spenser."

"But that whole drug angle...."

The cop interrupted me. "I think our investigation is on the right path." He sneered. "Even if you don't happen to like the route we're taking." A cop who used metaphors. I was impressed, but not happy.

"If you for one minute think Andy killed Dallas, you're wrong."

The detective's eyes narrowed as he studied me. "You keep making that accusation. I didn't say Beck killed Spenser." He bit into yet another fry.

The cop was right. He hadn't said it. Very pointedly.

Chapter 15

I left Andy a voice mail message warning him about Jake Chandler's surveillance, but by the time the P.I. came up the driveway, Jake had left or at least relocated his car to a more subtle position. When Andy got into the house unaccosted, I assumed Jake had left. I hoped it was because he'd gotten a better lead. I suspected, however, that his absence had more to do with the thermos I'd seen on the floor of his old compact. But right now Jake Chandler was only one of the things worrying me.

Detective Petino's comment about Andy's visit to Page had gotten to me—like Waterloo had gotten to Napoleon. I hadn't even questioned Andy about stopping to see Page on his way to Cape May three weeks ago. And, now, it turned out he had stopped to see Page again last week—before Dallas died.

"Did Petino find you today?" I spoke from my standard spot on Oliver's sofa.

"No." Andy didn't bother taking off his coat. He plopped and let the mitt catch him. "What happened to your eye?"

So I told the story of the twenty-seven-hour period since I'd last spoken to him. I started with my conversation with Petino at the funeral and carefully omitted my amateur spying. I didn't mention my journey into cyberspace or the aborted attempt to follow Page from the grocery store. Still, there was a lot to tell.

His first concern was the attack at the beach. "What did the cops think about that?"

I shrugged. "I don't know what they think." I told him about my trip to the wrong police station.

"You'll go tomorrow, right? To the correct police department. You should have Oliver take you. I'm sure he won't mind. By the way, where is our host?"

I shrugged. "I think he's on a date. This morning he told me he wouldn't be home tonight. I think he meant all night. If you get my drift. If I got his drift correctly."

"About time. No reason for you to sit here alone. How about going on a road trip? I interviewed eleven of Dallas Spenser's cronies over the past two days and the only clue I got was in the newspaper. I set up a meeting for tonight. Come along for the ride."

"Don't you want to hear about Petino? He stopped here today looking for you. I tried to call you."

Andy nodded. "I picked up the message. I tried you but Oliver's voice mail picked up. Want to go with me tonight? We can talk."

"Petino's visit is only the tip of the iceberg. He came here and ran into me twice today. Accidentally? I think not. I mean 'ran into.'" I told Andy about my fall from the bicycle. "He couldn't wait to tell me that you stopped to see Page last week. If you had given me an opportunity to talk to you last night, I could have let you know that he also asked about your visit to Dallas and Page on your way to Cape May last month."

"I didn't see Page last week. Get your coat. Ride with me." Andy appeared totally unconcerned about Petino.

"He thinks you did. Why would he think that?"

"Why would you think that?" Andy grabbed my coat from the pile in the hallway. He called over his shoulder. "Why did you believe him?"

"I thought...well, it was just that...I thought you came to New Jersey for the car. I didn't know...." Why did I believe Petino? I knew the cop was manipulative. In deference to the man, his ability to manipulate people probably made him good at his job. But what had made me believe him, a stranger, over Andy? The answer was simple: fear. Petino was a stranger, but a stranger in uniform. Not physically, but metaphorically.

I stared into Andy's eyes as he pulled me to my feet. "Andy, Petino believes you are involved in Spenser's death, you know."

Andy shrugged. "You'd better bundle up. The temperature is really dropping."

"Andy, Petino has led Jake Chandler to believe the same thing. That's why he was trying to ambush you."

Andy shrugged. "I have no comment." He pushed my arms into my raincoat.

"Petino wanted me to be your alibi for the night of the murder."

Andy shrugged yet again. "And?"

"And I told him the truth."

"No problem." Andy pushed my left arm down a sleeve.

"Do you have an alibi?"

"I can take care of Petino. Like I said, don't worry about it."

"Don't worry about it! He believes you killed Dallas Spenser."

"Do you believe that?" He adjusted the coat on my shoulders.

"You're kidding, right?"

Andy stared into my eyes but didn't answer.

"Andy, I know you couldn't kill anyone. I could never believe...okay, maybe that one time...but that was quite a while ago and I hardly knew you. I know you now. And, I know that you could not murder anyone." He continued to stare into my eyes. "Really, Andy. I trust you. Really."

Andy ran his hand up under my chin to caress my neck. "I'd like to tell you everything, but there are some things I can't tell you. I wish I could but I can't. It's professional...the reason. I need you to trust me."

"Of course; I trust you." I paused. "But if you're in love with Page tell me now. It'll be easier that way."

He laughed but then thought better of it. "Maggie, I am not in love with Page." He buttoned the top button of my coat. "I swear it." His eyes said he was telling the truth. "I know I'm spending a lot of time with her, but it's because I want to wrap this investigation up so we can leave. The cops do suspect she's involved, and she needs my help." Andy moved down the row of buttons until he'd fastened every one. "Don't worry about my being in love with her. I'm not." He reached into my pockets in search of gloves.

"Good thing. I saw her making out in the Acme parking lot tonight."

For a man who wasn't in love, Andy's reaction was a tad on the extreme side. "She was *what?*" He stopped checking for gloves in my pocket.

I told him the story as he resumed his search in Oliver's pile of winter clothes. He found a pair of gloves, big but pink, indicating they were intended for a woman. "You'd think she'd know better. This is not the time. She knows the cops are watching her." He pushed my right hand into the left glove with a vengeance that revealed his dismay. "Are you sure the woman was Page?"

I nodded as he corrected his glove action.

"And the guy?"

"I have no idea. He was waiting in the car." Andy got lost in his own thoughts. I called him back to his own problems. "You'd better straighten Petino out."

He tied a heavy wool scarf in a bulky knot that propped up my chin. "Page will tell him that I wasn't at the house on the night of the murder." He smoothed my scarf. "I was in the same state—New Jersey. The most densely populated state in the nation. That is about the extent of his 'proof.'" He stepped back and admired his work at bundling me up against the cold.

"I hope so. But shouldn't Page have explained this to him by now?"

He shrugged. "I'll straighten it out. Now let's go."

"Can we pick up my bike? I hid it behind Buckalew's and took a cab home."

"On the way back. Now let's go." His expression grew serious as he studied my face. "What's wrong?"

I looked a bit sheepish. "I have to go to the bathroom."

Chapter 16

Andy pulled his classic Mustang up to the home of the very late Denver Spears at eight o'clock sharp. As Denver Spears, Dallas had lived in an appropriately elite neighborhood in an appropriately elite town in an appropriately elite region. The Main Line, an area named after the train line that ran from 30th Street Station in Philadelphia twenty-five miles west to Paoli, once served as a summer retreat for the city's old money. The area now served as home to a wide variety of people. Nonetheless, the words "Main Line" continue to carry the cachet of its former exclusivity. Denver Spears had settled in one of the pockets that still merited the exclusive label.

After Denver's death, Emily had raised the two Spears children in their English Tudor mansion on Church Road. James Spears had gone off to college six months ago, but Emily and Bonnie still lived there. The house stood at the end of a long, tree-lined driveway. In season the home would be surrounded by a beautiful English garden. In February, it was pretty much surrounded by sticks.

Andy took the lead as we climbed a low flagstone stairway to an entrance that would not have clashed with the décor at Windsor Castle. Andy found the illuminated doorbell to the right of the heavy oak door easily. A few bars of "Rule Britannia" announced our arrival.

"How did you persuade her to see you?"

"No convincing was necessary. I told her I was working for Page."

The answer made no sense to me, but I didn't have time to pursue the topic. I didn't mind. The night wasn't frigid, but in my light clothes I felt happy that the door was answered promptly.

"Mr. Beck?" The woman who greeted us seemed relaxed—almost cheerful. When Andy nodded she extended a warm hand and a matching welcome. Not just to Andy but to me, introduced as a colleague. "Please come in. I've been expecting you."

In the time it took the woman to greet us, I'd already assigned her a stereotype. Emily Spears looked like any Main Line matron in her forties. I could have passed her a million times driving her Volvo station wagon, buying fresh produce at Genuardi's, or selecting tasteful pieces at Wayne Jewelers. Emily was dressed formally, as if she were expecting real company—not some P.I. and his "colleague." Her blonde hair, once natural I guessed, was pulled back into a neat ponytail. She wore a loose silk shirt tucked into black satin trousers. I wished I had taken Oliver up on his offer to go shopping. Or at least that I had washed my one pair of jeans. Emily Spears had not accessorized her outfit with McDonald's special sauce.

"Please be careful." Emily cautioned me as she led me over protective cloths and under scaffolding. "Denver decided the entrance hall wasn't magnificent enough. Not that this house wasn't more than enough when we bought it. We had a wonderful country-style home in Bryn Mawr. Lovely stone place. But no. Denver was English so we had to live in an English Tudor. Now that I know he won't be returning, I'm trying to bring the house back to a little less magnificence."

I peered up three stories to a frescoed ceiling. The wood paneled walls and ornate balustrade seemed magnificent enough to me—even without the heavy oil painting that still covered the left side of the ceiling. I cut my observation short as I slid three feet on an oil cloth. Andy caught my flailing arm and steadied me without a recriminating glance. I appreciated the support—physical and emotional.

"Oh, I'm so sorry!" Denver's widow sounded solicitous and behaved that way as she directed us through the minefield that was her entrance hall. I think she felt relieved when we said we'd keep our coats. I doubt she could have found a closet among the scaffolding and covered furniture. She directed us into another paneled room with a hand that still wore a diamond engagement ring and wedding band. No wonder Emily Spears hadn't remarried. The light from the many-carat stone could warn off ships at sea, let alone prospective suitors.

The decorating in the large living area Emily led us into reflected a masculine hand. Dark wood furniture. Dark oriental rugs. Dark suede and brocade upholstery. Dark lampshades took the room beyond muted to lugubrious. A fire roared in the tall stone fireplace but shed little light through the heavy iron grillwork. Through the darkness, I made out a collection of oils on the walls. Given Dallas Spenser's artwork, I was amused by the paintings Denver Spears had chosen. Formal portraits of Denver's parents' and grandparents' generations, apparently sniffing three-day-old fish, decorated every wall. The gold frame that surrounded each portrait was topped with a cluster of pointy leaves and a shield that appeared to comprise a family crest. "Are they portraits of your family?"

"No. Of Denver's imagination. Or pretentiousness, I should say." Emily offered us seats on the maroon brocade sofa and perched formally on a forest green wing chair opposite Andy. When she sat, Emily's legs appeared endless and elastic. She crossed her legs and wrapped her loose foot around the other leg. She laid her arm on her thigh and hunched over in a position that said rich, Republican, and, in this case, responsive. The ring set was placed front and center on her dangling hand. I couldn't take my eyes off the diamond. We were talking close to ten carats.

A uniformed maid appeared with a silver tray bearing a tea set and cake platter. Emily poured tea into a thin porcelain cup and passed it to me. I didn't want to admit I never drank the stuff. I smiled appreciatively as I took the cup and saucer from Emily's hand. She didn't see me kill the taste with four lumps of sugar. She was busy serving Andy.

"I must say I expected the worst of Denver, but I actually never thought of bigamy. I knew there had to be other women. He was away so much at the end. I never thought his business required quite that much travel. It makes so much sense that he was laying the groundwork for another life." She paused for effect. "Now." She laughed.

"How did you learn that Denver was still alive?" Andy asked in a gentle tone.

She gazed into the fireplace. "That reporter. Jake Chandler."

"Did he say how he found you?"

Emily shook her head. When she met Andy's eyes, I searched for signs of tears and found none. "He said he had to protect his sources."

I figured Jake must have gotten lucky with that source. Dallas had been dead for only a week.

"I assume the police have talked to you?"

She nodded. "They just wanted to verify that we didn't know Denver was still alive all these years. They were concerned that we knew. Especially if we knew where he was living. I've heard from my friends that they interviewed them as well. From what I understand they are satisfied that we are telling the truth. I provided phone and credit card records. My appointment diary for the past seven years—that's all I retain. I gave them everything they asked for. I have nothing to hide. The police were very polite. From what I can see they saw this part of the investigation as a formality, which I can certainly understand. I have the impression that they know who did it."

"They said that?" Andy did a poor job of keeping the apprehension out of his voice. If Emily noticed, she didn't show it. "No. Not in so many words." She paused before asking. "Do you know who killed Denver?" Her voice was almost teasing. "No. I know who didn't kill Denver."

We all knew he meant Page, his employer.

Emily nodded knowingly. She didn't push for an explanation. "There are any number of people who had reason to kill Denver—or Dallas."

I'd arrived viewing Emily Spears as a suspect. I felt disappointed to sense my conviction fading. For one thing, Emily Spears liked to talk too much. Her manner was calm. Her tone was clipped. Her words were well chosen—but there were a lot of them. Information flowed from Emily's lips easily with very little prompting from Andy. No way this woman could hide a crime. Plus, I didn't feel that Emily felt the need to kill Denver Spears. After all, she'd only known that he was alive and then dead again for a few days. She seemed to have adjusted pretty well to the news. She had already started redecorating.

"When did you see Denver for the last time?"

"The day was nothing special. A Saturday. Denver had developed a sudden interest in fishing that spring. Very quickly he became obsessed with the sport. Denver could be that way. Obsessive. He bought a boat. A big thing. Thirty-five feet. Two huge engines. He kept the boat in Cape May. I was foolish enough to feel gratified that he named it after me. Or I thought he did. *Emily's Escape.* He spent all his spare time on that boat." Emily seemed to enjoy reminiscing about her late husband. The traces of a smile curled the corners of her lips. "I went out with him a few times. I love the sea. I just don't love the morning. Denver would be at the dock at sunrise. Sometimes I would drive down and meet him in the evening. That's what I did the day he disappeared. I decided to surprise him and meet him for dinner. But he didn't return. At first I wasn't worried—it was a lovely evening; it had been a gorgeous day. Blue skies. Bright sun. Calm seas. I understood why he would have lingered. But

I was growing more and more worried. At midnight, I alerted the Coast Guard. They found his boat the next day. Denver was not onboard. Nothing was amiss except that one of his fishing rods was flung in the corner of the deck. The police found traces of blood and hair on one of the winches. I think that's what they call them. I'm not a boat person." She took a deep breath. "The other thing they found was some spilled oil with what looked like skid marks in it. The police assumed that Denver slipped on the oil, pitched forward, hit his head on the metal, and fell overboard—probably unconscious. The authorities figured he ran into some freakish bad luck. Maybe a swell hit the boat at the exact moment that he slipped. That's all it would have taken. The Coast Guard searched, but I don't think they ever expected to find him. At least alive."

"And no one ever saw him again?" Andy confirmed.

Emily shook her head. The ponytail bounced cheerfully. "No one who knew him as Denver Spears."

"No signs that he was alive?"

Again the ponytail bobbed up and down with a jaunty attitude incongruent with her topic. "No one ever touched his accounts. His wallet and his glasses were on the boat. And, his gold Rolex. That's how I knew, or why I believed, he was dead. I couldn't believe he'd leave that watch behind." Apparently, the same woman who couldn't believe that Denver would leave his watch would believe that he could leave his family.

"We considered every possibility—but that watch. I still can't believe this is all true—because of the watch. It was my wedding gift to him. I had our initials engraved on the back. And the word 'Forever.' Denver loves that watch. Loved it." As much as the identical timepiece that Page had given him as a wedding gift?

Emily Spears finally addressed the cake. I'd been eyeing the sweet since it arrived. I'd just about given up hoping she would cut it when she picked up an elaborate silver cake cutter and sliced what she considered a piece of cake. I saw it as more of a sliver. She handed me a delicate porcelain plate along with a heavy sterling silver fork. The piece might have been small, but I was happy to see the cake was chocolate chip. My favorite. I ate while Emily answered Andy's questions easily—even the one that I found toughest to answer. Andy wondered why, if she accepted her husband's death, she had delayed redecorating until now. She had used the phrase "now that I know he won't be returning...."

"I know you'll find it pitiable, but I always nurtured a hope that he wasn't dead. I mean...without a body. Who really knew? And I just had a feeling...my friends found it touching at first, then sad, then pathetic. Even though I never really liked this house, I wouldn't move in case he came back. When he came back, I wanted him to find us."

By "us" I assumed she meant the family and the watch.

"And if he did come back I wanted him to find everything as it was." She issued a rueful chuckle. "To be honest, I was afraid for him to find anything changed." She went on to explain that although Denver ruled the roost with a firm touch, he was never violent. "He never touched me or the children." Odd answer considering the question had never been asked.

"Now it all makes so much sense. His behavior. He set up a business with this Page woman. Took out an insurance policy to protect a joint venture. Faked his own death. The company collected the money."

"Page never knew."

Emily and I both reacted to Andy's statement. She believed Andy. She believed Page. I believed Andy. I didn't believe Page. Of course, Emily hadn't met Page yet.

"I understand that he left the money to his new identity buried in one of a hundred contracts in his files. It wasn't life insurance per se. So when he couldn't complete a job, his business paid. I never realized Denver was that clever."

The idea sounded like a good one to me—although an awful lot of effort in a no-fault divorce state. Andy seemed to see the situation the same way.

"Why did he go to so much trouble? Did he ever ask you for a divorce?"

"I wouldn't have let him go easily. I loved him." I saw the trace of a smile touch the corners of her lips. "For Denver, disappearing was probably more profitable than divorce. You see, most of the money was mine."

Chapter 17

We'd been talking with Emily Spears for half an hour when a young woman whom I assumed was Bonnie Spears rushed into the room followed by a sheep dog that I assumed was a good candidate for obedience training. The girl ran to Emily and kissed her cheek. The dog ran to me and kissed my crotch. At least that's how it looked. In truth, she was snacking on the cake crumbs on my lap. I let the group think the dog loved me at first sight. Especially after Emily indicated that she felt animals were the best judges of character.

"Maisy!" Bonnie called the dog, which ignored her. "Stop that."

Maisy did—but only when all the crumbs were gone. Bonnie said, "Good girl." But I knew the truth about Maisy. She turned her attention to the coffee table. I turned my attention to pulling long, white dog hairs off my sweater.

After polite introductions and a brief apology for Maisy's exuberance, Bonnie slipped into the wing chair beside her mother's and assumed an identical position. I attributed the similarity to genetics. Bonnie was the daughter and younger child of Denver Spears and Emily Pemberton Spears. The girl looked vaguely familiar to me but that was because she looked like so many other teenagers. Shaggy hair combed forward on her face, big black glasses and traces of metal everywhere—on her ears, her lips, and her nose. Bonnie's style was clearly radical enough to torment her determinedly suburban mother. Despite the tattoos, piercings, and corresponding attire, which I am sure horrified Emily, Bonnie's appearance betrayed an underlying republicanism. I could picture Bonnie in the same position as Emily, deeply tanned, in golf clothes and a ponytail twenty years from now. That's how her mother and her mother before her had looked. Bonnie was pretty much doomed by genetics to a life of elegance.

While Bonnie listened, Emily continued with her story about Denver. I got the impression that she liked telling it. No wonder she had welcomed us so warmly. We were a new audience. Probably all the neighbors were bored by now. Even the dog didn't want to listen. Maisy wandered away from Emily's absent-minded strokes and settled on the floor beside me. The dog was no fool. Of all the people in that room, I would be most likely to let crumbs hit the carpet.

It seemed Denver Spears had not led an exciting life. He had been a conscientious businessman with a flair for spotting trends. "Denver is smart. He found his own little niche and dominated it."

I had grown bored with marketing discussions when Andy inquired about their social life. This was where the story *really* got dull. Saturday and Sundays on the golf course. Saturday night at the country club—though not at one of the more prestigious cricket clubs, much to Denver's regret. At least according to his former wife. If she ever had any, Emily retained few illusions about the husband whom she believed had left her a widow.

Mrs. Spears looked puzzled but not as puzzled as Andy did when I spoke. "Sounds like your lifestyle was pretty routine. Tame. Was it really what it appeared to be on the surface?" Their expressions called for an explanation. I did the best I could.

"Well, listening to you, I'm just struck by how normal your life sounded. I just wondered if it really was...that...ordinary."

Andy looked at me as if I had two heads but Emily sounded not at all nonplussed. She caught on to what I was saying and denied the allegation quickly—too quickly. "If you're asking if we enjoyed some sort of drug-induced sexual hijinks in our marriage, I can assure you that my answer is no." Again Emily answered a question that wasn't asked.

"When Denver disappeared the police told me all they found to focus on was his business." She emphasized the word *told*.

According to his wife, after Denver's death an extensive investigation had revealed no impropriety in his business dealings. "Although some considered him ruthless. If his ethics were suspect, he never stepped over the line." She took a tiny piece of cake and chewed it thoughtfully. "They investigated his disappearance as a possible homicide. I can't figure out how they missed that insurance policy. I guess it was only one piece of paper among many."

Emily settled back in her chair with her cake. She raised her eyebrows questioningly at Bonnie, who declined the sweet with a quick shake of her mop of brown hair with a reddish tint that she'd inherited from her father. Luckily she'd gotten all of her facial features from her mother.

That Emily spoke so freely in front of Denver's daughter surprised as well as concerned me. Andy must have felt the same way. He was clearly uncomfortable with questioning Bonnie. "Do you recall anything about your father and his disappearance?"

Bonnie's voice sounded light—almost perky. She crossed the room to a table draped in maroon brocade and opened a highly polished mahogany box with brass trim. She pulled out a number 10 envelope and handed it to Andy. "This is all I remember of my father. He left when I was two." Andy glanced through some photos and then held up a piece of stationery. "What's this?"

"You can read it." Emily gave the response. Andy slipped a piece of ecru paper from the envelope and unfolded what I could see through the paper was a typed letter. Bonnie read the letter over Andy's shoulder. A wistful smile filled and then suddenly vanished from her face. The smile was replaced by a bereft look. Bonnie's eyes left the letter. She stared off into space as she spoke. "Denver Spears was my father in name only. I barely remember him. My mother made a good life for me. And my brother." Bonnie presented her case clearly and concisely and without passion. "Someday, I know I'll forgive him." She nodded as if to confirm the thought. Her mop of hair bounced emphatically.

I marveled at Bonnie's maturity and rationality.

"Mother asked me to stay and say hello." Bonnie nodded at Emily. "If there is anything you want to ask me, please do." Finally sounding like a teenager, "I'd like to go out."

Andy ran through a number of routine questions. Bonnie answered each calmly and dispassionately. No, she hadn't seen her father. Yes, she believed he was dead. She only found out that he was alive when Jake Chandler approached the family with a photo of Dallas Spenser. She did not recall exactly when that was.

"Was it after Dallas Spenser's death?"

She seemed more perplexed than angered by Andy's question. But not rattled. "Of course." This was either the most self-possessed kid on earth or the most sociopathic. And polite. She shook hands before vanishing into the hallway.

Emily grew suddenly pensive. "There were a lot of things about Denver we never knew." She glanced up. "Never will, I guess." She smiled with restraint. "I know people don't understand me. I'm not sure I understand myself. I always felt...knew...that he wasn't dead. Even after we had him declared legally dead, I never actually accepted his death. I told myself that he couldn't come home or he would come home. I had a million stories about why he couldn't get back to us."

I would have liked to have heard them but Andy didn't ask. So I didn't. After all, this was his investigation and I was already in trouble for the lifestyle question.

Emily nibbled halfheartedly at her sliver of cake. Embarrassed that my comparatively ample slice had disappeared—apparently into my stomach, I slipped the china plate onto the mahogany tray table. Maisy cleaned the remains from the Royal Crown Derby pattern.

Andy remained silent, and eventually Emily resumed her monologue. "I knew what Denver was like. Early in the marriage. Before James and Bonnie were born. But I didn't leave. He had a hold over me. For a lot of years I was obsessed sexually. I think he really did me a favor when he left. I never would have had the strength. I feel sorry for Page. I really would like to help her. I know how…powerful he can be. Denver was quite something when he was younger. Perhaps he hadn't changed."

Okay, I'd only seen the guy when he was dead, but I just didn't get it.

Chapter 18

"What was the sex, drugs, and rock and roll question?" They were the first words out of Andy's mouth. He waited until we turned out of the long driveway before he asked. He seemed more amused than angry.

"I never mentioned sex or drugs. She did. Immediately. Rather a quick disclaimer, don't you think?"

"You have to drop the drug thing. It's a dead end."

"It's not just the drugs. Drugs are only symptoms of a lifestyle." I didn't want to tell Andy about the sex angle in the dark car. I couldn't wait to see his face when I provided a visual display on Oliver's computer. I changed the subject. "What did the note say?"

Andy gave me a general idea and then repeated the last sentence verbatim. "Emily, my love, if you are reading this, I am gone and it is time for you to turn to the next page in the book of life."

"A pun?"

Andy bit. "Hard to think it isn't."

"What a bastard! Mocking her that way."

"We don't know what their marriage was like. Sure, she seemed nice and she said she loved him. But what do we really know. She smirked when she said the money was hers. For all we know she yanked his chain like crazy." Andy grinned. "I thought she was lucky. He looked for an alternative to divorce. He could have killed her."

"Andy, just because he was capable of getting killed didn't mean that he was capable of killing." I said the words without conviction. The man faked his own death. Who knew what else he was capable of? "You know what I noticed most?"

Andy crooked an eyebrow and turned his head in my direction.

"A couple of times she slipped and referred to Denver in the present tense."

Andy claimed I was reading too much into it. "People do that all the time when people die."

"Fifteen years after people die?"

Andy and I dissected our visit to the Spears home as we drove the backroads from the Main Line through Conshohocken to Chestnut Hill at the northwest tip of Philadelphia. Bonnie was the more perplexing personality, although I couldn't say I had a good handle on Emily Spears. Both women seemed awfully well adjusted to recent events. I pooh-poohed Andy's contention that Denver had been dead to them for fifteen years. The deceit was fresh. To me they were dealing with the pain of the duplicity much better than I could have. Of course, that was my perspective—the perspective of a woman once told that, aside from being the most vindictive person on earth, she appeared to have no emotions at all. I was angry enough for Emily and Bonnie Spears that I could have killed this guy myself. Given the political climate, however, I did not mention that—even to Andy.

We entered the Chestnut Hill neighborhood from the north. I'd talked Andy into a sentimental journey; the sentiment was all mine. To Andy, Chestnut Hill was out of the way. I'd gone to school in the area and with my friend Nanci spent many afternoons window-shopping instead of studying. Or actually instead of attending classes. When we came to maturity, or as close to maturity as we were ever going to get, we would often return to Chestnut Hill. Specifically to McNally's, a neighborhood bar. I directed Andy to take the first parking space on Germantown Avenue. We reached the bottom of the hill without seeing an opening. We reversed direction.

I was searching for an opening big enough for Andy's classic Mustang when I saw her. "That's Bonnie." I swore I saw Bonnie Spears. She was climbing out the passenger door of a dilapidated van. The person who hopped out of the driver's door was male and tall. "Why would she be here?"

"*We're* here."

Andy had never lived in Philadelphia. I hadn't lived in the City of Brotherly Love for over ten years myself. But I knew that people didn't routinely travel from the Main Line to Chestnut Hill for no good reason.

"What makes you think she has no good reason?"

"She lives all the way on the Main Line."

"You have friends in Europe."

"Sure. I do. I'm a grown-up. She's only in high school. Why would she be here?"

"Is this one of your twenty-year-old assumptions? Like those directions you gave me earlier?"

"Hey, they've redone a lot of building in this city since I was last here—and don't try to change the subject. Why would Bonnie Spears be here?"

"She has friends here?" Andy's tone suggested the answer was obvious.

"Then why can't she find them?"

The couple was standing on the sidewalk that fronted the row of the stone storefronts—each more charming than the next. Bonnie—and I was certain it was Bonnie—was looking up and down Germantown Avenue. And when I say up and down, I mean up and down. Unlike some towns with the same name, Chestnut Hill in Pennsylvania was not assigned the name undeservedly. Bonnie was looking up the hill as we drove by to find parking.

"Maybe that's her brother." I slid down in my seat.

"Why are you hiding?"

"Well...well...." I didn't know. "Don't you think it's suspicious? Her being here?"

"No." Andy did not elaborate. "And if it were suspicious, she, not you, would be the one to hide."

"Maybe we should follow them."

"Well, assuming they move," he glanced in his rearview mirror, "which they haven't, I would still oppose trailing them. You know why?" He answered his own question. "Because we have no reason to follow them."

"We'll discover the reason after we follow them."

"See, the way P.I.s do it, we don't just pick people to follow at random. In legal circles we call that stalking."

"I can live with that. Let's stalk them."

"Maybe after we eat." Andy didn't argue.

Situated at the top of the hill in Chestnut Hill and marked only with a small brass plaque, McNally's was my home away from home for a couple of years when my summer job kept me in the city. As we walked towards the bar, I shared memories with Andy of those great times for my crowd between the freedom of being a student and the responsibilities of being a grown-up. I was looking forward to running into loads of old friends. As I was every time I visited McNally's over the past decade, I was disappointed. I spotted no familiar faces along the bar or at the row of tables.

"I can't believe no one I know is in here." I bit into my roast beef sandwich.

"And you were last here...?"

I shrugged. "Four, five years ago."

"Just for the record, do you recall what you ordered the last time you were here?"

I eyed my sandwich sheepishly.

"You expect everything to remain the same while you run all over the world. You did it in Ocean City. You did it in Cape May. And now, you're doing it here. You were upset they changed the menu."

"Not once I found out they still had good roast beef. I just like some continuity in my life."

Andy faked a spit-take. My life had no continuity. I wanted others to remain static and wait for me to return.

"You're being pretty good about Long Beach Island. Why?"

Unlike points south, I'd had limited families to mooch from on Long Beach Island as a child. To the annoyance of the natives, the denizens of the metropolitan areas that bordered New Jersey saw the state as clearly divided. Island Beach State Park and north belong to the New York metropolitan area. Brigantine and south belonged to Philadelphia. Long Beach Island, right in the middle, was claimed by both regions. Since I grew up in Philadelphia, most of my childhood summers were spent farther south.

As a New Yorker, however, I often stopped at LBI—including for a full month to finish my thesis. I loved the rustic feel of the island. Despite an incredible building spurt, the town still had the feel of the barrier islands I remembered from childhood. Maybe the pine trees (and I assumed cedars in Harvey Cedars) helped. Even the most outrageously oversized of the oversized houses appeared nestled in the trees they dwarfed.

Andy knew I'd spent a month on the island when working on my thesis.

"What was the topic of that thesis?"

I didn't feel like a discussion of dull academic topics when I was working on the paper. I certainly wasn't interested now. "Must we?"

We didn't. Instead Andy talked. "I dodged a bullet earlier tonight. You know what Petino said about my stopping to see Dallas and Page last week? That isn't true. But when he said I stopped on the way to see you in Cape May." He cleared his throat. "That was true. Page tracked me down and asked me to do a job for her husband. Dallas was convinced he was being watched when he was in New Jersey. He didn't think anyone was following him in New York. He thought it only happened when he was down the shore."

"Did you tell the police this?"

Of course he had, but they didn't believe him. The police viewed the story as a contrivance created by Andy and Page.

"It should be easy to prove. Didn't Dallas pay you?"

"Would you charge a friend? I stopped and did a couple of nights' work on my way to Cape May. It was no big deal."

I know this was supposed to be about Andy, but I couldn't help thinking of myself alone in the Cape May bridal suite while Andy cavorted—okay, worked—less than seventy-five miles away. I didn't mention that. Instead, I listened attentively as Andy told me about his two nights' work.

The second night he had seen someone in the dunes. From his observation point, the shadow in the dunes appeared to be that of a person—male and under thirty. "But I really wasn't sure. That was just my impression. It could have been a woman, but the hair was short. Light, but I couldn't tell you what color. I thought I was being quiet, but the person heard me and took off." He shook his head. "The only thing I can say for sure is that he or she was fast—and that I'm not as fast as I once was."

I wanted to talk about the stalker in the dunes. "Was the person tall?"

"Not extremely. Beyond that, I can't say. An adult. Not a kid. Not a senior."

"Thin?"

"Not fat, but dressed in loose casual clothes."

"So you reported this to Dallas?"

Andy nodded. "As vague as my description was, it seemed to satisfy him. As if he knew who it must have been."

"That person has to be the killer. Does Page have any idea who it was?"

Andy shook his head. "She said Dallas never brought her into the loop. She didn't even know what I was doing there."

I found it hard to believe that Andy was lurking in the dunes outside Page's home and she didn't know why he was there.

But that was what she told Andy. And he believed her. But then again, Page told Andy a lot of things. And he believed her. I decided it was time to introduce Andy to the secret life of Dallas and Page Spenser.

Chapter 19

"So this explains the sex, drugs, and rock 'n' roll question." Andy didn't take his eyes off the monitor to gauge my reaction. He hadn't taken his eyes off the screen for twenty minutes. Andy found the Dallas and Page Web site even more interesting than I had—and I didn't think it was the technology alone that held his interest.

From the moment we logged on, Andy had no doubt. He was convinced that we were looking at the life of Dallas and Page Spenser. He was also convinced that only one Dallas and Page coupling existed in cyberspace—or the world.

I got the impression he was not totally surprised by what he saw, but his reaction had nothing to do with Page. "If a man would leave his wife and young children, nothing else he does can surprise you. I wonder if Page knows."

I wondered how she could not know—at least that Dallas had taken the pictures. "If she didn't know, I imagine the police would have told her."

"If they know. I never found anything like this when I was searching."

"I found it by accident. I was looking for news, and it just popped up." I didn't mention that the site popped up after four hundred or so other Web sites were retrieved. "I assume that if they go through Dallas's financials they'll find payments to an ISP. Someone is hosting that Web site."

"When did you find the Web site, and why didn't you tell me?"

"When did I have a chance to tell you? Besides, I felt like I had invaded their privacy."

"I don't think you could invade their privacy. They kind of left all the shades up—metaphorically speaking. Unfortunately, nothing in the life of a murder victim is private. Especially this." Andy flipped through the pages with the same rapt attention that I had the night before. He tried an occasional comment but never got beyond "I can't..." or "I never..." or "Why...." I smiled as he twisted his neck for a better perspective. It wasn't always easy to figure out the activities in some of the more complex photos. "None of these people look familiar to me. Do you recognize any of these folks?"

I wasn't about to tell Andy that I'd only checked to make sure the body parts weren't his. I hadn't actually studied the faces of the people in the photo. Their faces weren't the first things to grab your attention. "Aside from this one who I think is Lauren, no. Although if any of them were walking around town naked...."

"I'm going to print a copy for each of us." Andy answered my puzzled expression. "So as we meet new people in the investigation we can check to see if they participated in these...if they participated."

That made sense. "Don't print the thumbnails. Print the blow-up."

"I did." Andy sent the job to the printer. "I guess I should take a look at all the stories." He perused the list thoughtfully. I was interested in what he'd read first. He tried to appear casual. He chose group sex M/F/F. Considering the other choices, I was relieved. I'd been there, done that. The stories, I mean. I had already read the stories. So I picked up *Sports Illustrated*—one

of the few reading selections in Oliver's home—and let Andy
enter the erotic world of Page and Dallas Spenser.

The printer stopped; Andy didn't. He eyes remained glued to
the screen.

"Did you check out the slide show?"

Andy shook his head. "I tried, but I got tired of waiting for
the pages to load."

"Do something else while it runs through and then you can
just use 'Back' to move through it quickly."

Slowly, Andy turned in my direction. His stare was
accusatory.

"Andy, every slide show on the Web is not a porn show."
That was true, but I'd actually learned the technique because,
just like Andy, I'd grown bored waiting for the pages to load.

"I should really read through a few more of these." Andy
mumbled an explanation.

I moved on to the *Sporting News*. I'd exhausted the periodi-
cal and Andy was still reading. I pulled a chair up beside him,
laid my hand on his right shoulder and peeked over his left.
"Which one are you reading now?"

"The one where Dallas...where the husband gives his wife
two of his friends as a birthday gift."

"What part are you up to?"

"She's still blindfolded."

"She is throughout the entire story."

Andy leaned back in his chair and looked at me with disgust.
"Now you've ruined it for me."

I played with his silky hair. "I doubt it." In my opinion, the
blindfold wasn't a key plot twist. We leaned forward and read
on. The characters were taking a long time to get to the point.
Or the points. When they finally got there, they discovered a
lot of 'theres' to get to. I no longer thought of the woman as
Page but as a simple sexual object—which is how she was
portrayed.

Andy waited to express any guilt until he finished reading. And he read all of the stories. "I know these people...at least Page. Prying into their lives makes me uncomfortable." I started to stand up but Andy pulled me back onto the chair. "Let's see who else wrote stories. We can check out some of their favorite links." He backed up to Dallas and Page's home page. "What's a Web ring?"

"It leads you in a big circle to similar sites." I watched as he moved the mouse over the Web rings on which Dallas and Page's site was a stop. "Did you know that sneezing was a sexual fetish? I found out last night and I'm still not interested." I told Andy to keep looking.

He pointed to feet.

I shook my head. "Never did understand foot fetishes."

He moved down the list. I voiced an objection to each suggestion.

"No, that hurts. I think we'd have to find an all-night erotica shop before we could actually participate. I don't even know what that is. Nah, I'd want to lose ten pounds first. Never could understand that one."

Andy sighed. "Well...I don't even know why invisible women would be a fetish, but we know you're not invisible. How about this one?"

Andy and I worked our way around the erotic Web ring. Allegedly erotic. I didn't understand how people could spend hours and hours looking at this stuff. "Hey Andy, look—this one is a classic story. Says so, right here. Must be good."

Andy's eyes asked me to give him a break. He moved on.

"Look, Andy, a free lifetime membership. Now that would look good in your bio." He shook his head. I smoothed his hair as he plunged ahead. Some sites were just plain boring. Some were frightening. None were appealing. Andy and I didn't seem to be succeeding in the world of cyberporn.

I laid my hand on top of Andy's as it grasped the mouse. "Remember the old adage. Those who can, do; those who can't...."

"Surf the Web?" He let go of the mouse and took my hand. "I have always thought of myself as a can-do kind of guy."

"So, Andy, if you can, do."

We logged off.

Chapter 20

I was in the Bayside Diner, eavesdropping unsuccessfully. I could hear okay; I just wasn't hearing what I wanted to hear. Apparently the locals had absolutely no interest in the murder of a New Yorker on their island. At least the locals at the Bayside Diner.

I'd already been to the Beach Haven police department to report my attack. The officer to whom I made my report was kind, concerned, and, unlike Detective Petino, didn't make any snide remarks. Even when I told him about my psychic friend, he simply recorded the facts. Maybe he felt we were on the same side of the law.

The officer wasn't particularly optimistic as he took my number and promised to keep me posted. He gave me his card and said to call if I had any questions or remembered any additional details.

While eavesdropping, I drank a Coke and scanned the *Press of Atlantic City*. I was disappointed to discover no news about Dallas Spenser, although heaven only knew what was left to reveal. Oliver's Porsche was parked outside. I was not in any condition to bicycle anywhere that day. I'd like to blame my infirmity on my attack on the beach, my fall from my bike, or even a surfeit of romance. Truth was my body hadn't been ready for the amount of cycling I'd done the day before. Not only was I unable to ride my bike that day, I was barely able to walk. I considered slipping into the booth a victory. I managed to do so with only a low groan.

I was perusing the local calendar of events when I heard it.

"Good morning."

I didn't actually recognize the voice, yet I knew who I would see when I looked up. Sure enough. I stared into the wide blue eyes set in the baby face. "Funny running into you again."

"Not really. I knew you'd be here." The man-child answered in his usual flat tone.

"Of course." I sipped my morning Coke. Logic would have told me to be afraid of this man. After all he might have attacked me two nights before. But I felt no fear. I felt annoyance, but even that feeling was not very strong.

"What happened to your eye?"

"You don't know?"

"I'm not psychic. I channel the dead." Behind him a young woman dressed all in white looked up from her copy of *Embraced by the Light.*

"Well, then we eliminate any deceased suspects, right?" I took a sip of cola.

"It looks painful."

"It's getting better." I flashed a weak smile. "You should have seen it yesterday." My visitor didn't comment. Neither did he leave. I filled the silence. "Talked to my parents lately?"

He didn't seem offended. "They're not here. That's not why I am here."

He offered no more information. I had to ask why he was standing by my side. I could tell by her expression that the woman at the next table wanted to know, too.

"He likes you."

"Who?" I forced a phony inquisitive expression.

"Don't be coy. You know who. Your friend, Dallas."

"He's here?"

He nodded solemnly. "He's trying to come through. I can feel him." The woman actually turned in her chair to listen. I pretended I didn't notice. In her position, I might have done the same thing.

"Let me ask you something." I wanted to use his name for emphasis but I realized I didn't know it. "First, what is your name?"

"Hap. Hap Hathaway. Hap is short for happy."

I studied the man-child with a furrowed brow. Who could be so miserable that they thought the deadpan creature in front of me should be nicknamed Happy?

He answered the question I didn't ask. "I've always been a happy person." He settled onto the bench across from me.

"And a good poker player, I bet." He didn't understand my little joke, although the eavesdropping woman found some humor in the remark. I didn't think Hap would understand jokes of any size. "Never mind." I pushed my glass aside, folded my hands in front of me and leaned across the table. "Hap, may I call you Hap?"

"Of course."

"Listen, Hap. Are you telling me that Dallas Spenser is here with you today so that he can speak to me?"

"He compelled me to come here. He knew you would be here." Hap's tone was detached.

"Dallas doesn't do house calls?"

The guy's reply was completely earnest. "He cannot speak to you directly. He needs me as his communicator." His tone added, "dummy."

"Listen Hap. I hate to be skeptical, but of all the people in the world that Dallas could communicate with, you are saying that he's chosen me?"

"Apparently." He did his staring thing and then spoke again. "He wants you to know that he trusts you. You are interested in the truth." He paused. His stare intensified. "Do you know someone named Booker?"

I shook my head. This time he was way off course.

"You must. I see a book. It's open to the first page. Page one." His expression changed to indicate puzzlement. "I think he means someone named Booker."

"Could you mean Page?"

"Ah." He sounded reassured. "Of course."

This guy was good. At what, I wasn't quite sure. Nor could I figure out his angle.

I tried to convince Hap that Dallas really meant to speak to Page. "If you give me your number I'll pass it along. I'm sure she would give you a call." Hap, however, was convinced that Dallas preferred to communicate with me. I was getting worried about myself. I interrogated Hap Hathaway as if we were discussing a factual situation instead of a bizarre fantasy or a carefully constructed con.

How did Dallas communicate with him? In symbols. Why couldn't he just give Hap the information? "That's not how it is." Why didn't he just tell us who killed him? "Catching the culprit isn't the point. Protecting the innocent is the point. He tells me a woman did not kill him and he's counting on you. And I get the feeling someone else is, too."

"Got a name?"

Hap did his staring thing but shook his head. "I don't understand what he's telling me. Dallas seems to feel you know. Well, I'd better push off." He meant his statement literally. He put his hands on the table and pushed himself to a standing position.

"So Hap, before you go, anyone else in there want to talk to me?"

Hap might have been annoyed. Given his lack of affect it was hard to tell. "No one is in here. They are over there. On the other side. When they need to, they speak through me. You should be flattered that Dallas has chosen you." With that he turned on a squeaky sneaker heel and left. I studied Hap as he paid his check. Through the window I watched Hap head toward a nondescript sedan parked in front.

Page had to be the one who put Hap up to this ridiculous game. Who else could have? Where did she find this guy? On the Internet? In the yellow pages? What heading did she look under?

Outside the window the young woman from the next table approached Hap. The two spoke animatedly—which in Hap's case meant that he actually moved some of his facial muscles. He bent forward and looked deep into the young woman's eyes. He nodded as he listened to her speak. Finally, they both climbed into the car that I assumed was his. I felt a tinge of apprehension in the pit of my stomach watching the girl climb into the car. I hoped I didn't end up at the police station reporting yet another crime.

I hadn't seen him come in, but as the waitress slipped my breakfast in front of me I could feel the detective's eyes on me. I turned to face him. "What?" I snapped in a tone that might have sounded a tad belligerent considering the man could lock me up on a whim.

"Nothing. I saw Wilder's car outside. I was driving by." The red Porsche was parked in front of the diner. How and why did the detective know Oliver's car? I didn't ask—mainly because the cop didn't take a breath. He was still explaining. "Then I saw you sitting over here." He ordered coffee. "Eye looks great." He was being sarcastic—my eye was still decorated with purple and black stripes. I ignored his comment. "So what have you been up to?"

I continued to pour syrup over my pancakes. "Mostly we've been tracking down Andy's old girlfriends so he can kill their husbands for absolutely no good reason."

"Ms. Daniels, I should warn you. Humor, and I assume your last comment was a feeble attempt at humor, does not play in certain situations. Murder investigations being one of those situations." He drank from the cup as soon as the waitress put the coffee in front of him. Did this guy have an asbestos tongue?

"You see, Detective Petino, by admitting that my comment was humorous you are admitting that Andy's killing Dallas Spenser is a ridiculous thought." I shoved a forkful of pancake into my mouth.

"It's not that simple."

"I think it is." I stared at the detective, who held my stare. When he looked away, I didn't have any sense that I had won. I felt the cop had grown bored with the staring match.

"I was just trying to be nice. I just wanted to see how you were doing—without Beck and all."

What was this guy thinking? "I am not without Beck. As a matter of fact, I'd better go. Andy said he'd try to stop home during the day."

"I think he might have changed his plans."

I couldn't hide my perplexed expression.

"I just came from chatting with your boyfriend." The detective drained his coffee cup, slapped down three dollars, and slipped off the chair. "I'm afraid you won't be able to see him right at this moment."

Chapter 21

*L*aw & Order—not the political position, the TV show—was the first thing I thought of when I heard that the police were questioning Andy. I knew the authorities had to arrest him or let him go. Certainly the cops did not have sufficient evidence to arrest him, I reassured myself. Andy was at the Ocean County prosecutor's offices in Toms River because he was cooperating. That was smart. Andy should cooperate. I would go back to Oliver's and wait for him.

The Porsche that felt so easy to control that morning drove like a bucking Bronco on the way to Oliver's. My trembling hands could barely control the sports car. The way the vehicle swung back and forth across the four lanes of Long Beach Boulevard, there was a better chance I would end up in jail than Andy. Arriving at Oliver's didn't calm me down at all. The street was a sea of white sedans. I understood why my erratic driving hadn't gotten me pulled over. Most of the cops on the island were at Oliver's house. I didn't realize Long Beach Island was home to so many individuals involved in law enforcement.

I pulled Oliver's Porsche behind a blue sedan that I suspected was an unmarked police car. A uniformed officer was posted at the orange door that stood wide open. He blocked my way.

"But I live here...kind of. I'm a guest." Down the hallway I spotted Oliver pacing deliberately from the kitchen to the sunroom—in and out of sight.

"Oliver." I called three times before he noticed me.

"Let her in. She's my guest." Oliver vouched for me with a yell from the back of the house. His eyes were wide as they met mine. "They have a warrant." In his voice I heard shock, dismay, and fear.

I caught up with Oliver in the kitchen. That day his attire honored Dan Marino. He kept picking at the number 13 on his chest as he paced in long deliberate strides that managed to look frenzied despite a lack of speed. Cops were in the sunroom and, Oliver informed me, in the Boston Bruins bedroom I shared with Andy.

"Oliver, I don't care. I have nothing to hide. There's nothing to worry about. Andy didn't have anything to do with this."

My words did nothing to calm Oliver even though he sputtered, "I know. I know. I know."

The cops were moving methodically through Oliver's possessions pretending to be unimpressed by his collection of sports memorabilia. Whatever they were looking for was small enough to hide inside a book. They opened every volume on Oliver's shelf.

"Did you get this signed yourself?" One of the cops held up a baseball.

"Shea, 1986." Oliver said gruffly. "Be careful with it." He covered the small space in a couple strides and grabbed the ball from the cop. "Please," he added at the last moment in a vain attempt to undo the animosity he had created with the policeman.

The other cop stopped the conversation. "Is this Beck's phone book?" He waved a brown leather book at Oliver.

"Hey, that's mine!" Oliver charged at that officer and grabbed the book from his hand.

Oliver's mood was frantic. His body appeared relaxed, but his eyes darted relentlessly. He rambled. I can't say exactly about what. He spoke too fast. At last he took a breath. "This day started out bad enough. My laptop is dead. I have no idea what's wrong." He lowered his voice so only I could hear. "I came down here to use the desktop. Ready to go to work and I find that my inbox is flooded with pornographic e-mails."

"No kidding." I went to the refrigerator, opened the door, and buried my head inside.

"What will the cops think when they see that?" He shook his head.

"Oliver, I think they can only search Andy's stuff." I glanced at the cops moving along Oliver's bookshelves. "And things Andy has access to."

"Not yours?"

I pulled out a cola, met his eyes, and shrugged. "I've got ten pairs of white shorts, ten white T-shirts, one pair of jeans, one shirt, and one navy blue sweater."

Oliver eyed me expectantly.

"Okay, bathing suits and underwear. I'm not worried. The worst that could happen is the cops sponsor a clothes drive for me."

My words did nothing to soothe Oliver.

"I don't think they can touch your stuff. Remember how fast that cop gave you that address book back."

"They have no right to do this." With his hand jammed in the waistband of his pants, Oliver bounced up and down on his toes with such force that I expected him to disappear through the floor.

"Some judge disagreed." I laid a hand on Oliver's arm to stop his fidgeting and hold his attention. "Calm down. I am sure they can only look in our room and public areas for evidence related to Dallas Spenser's murder." I didn't actually hear that from the cops. It was what I believed was true from television. "Plus you have nothing to hide, right?" I assumed Oliver's past was past.

"No. Of course not." He went to the refrigerator, opened the door, and buried his head inside.

Chapter 22

Jake Chandler stuck his head into Oliver's house just as the last of the police walked out. "Knock, knock." He rapped a knuckle on the open orange door.

Oliver and I turned in unison and stared at him with amazement—not just because he was an uninvited guest but because he was incredibly corny. Jake could be held solely responsible for keeping the term bright-eyed and bushy-tailed in the vernacular.

"May I come in?" Jake pronounced the words with such innocence that anyone would feel like a complete jerk saying no. There was no point anyway. He was already inside, inching his way down the hallway toward the sunroom where Oliver and I sat.

"Who are you?" Oliver responded to his question without any trace of hostility. It was virtually impossible to be hostile to Jake.

"Jake Chandler." Hand extended, the reporter came down the hall with long strides that called attention to surprisingly long legs under an abnormally short body. Jake Chandler was short, but he was all leg.

With his usual languid motions, Oliver pulled himself out of the catcher's mitt and extended his hand. "Oliver Wilder. What can I do for you?" He stared down into Jake's upturned smile. With his diminutive size Jake epitomized the concept of cub reporter—another term the dictionary might have been tempted to drop except for the need to describe Jake.

"Jake's a reporter. He writes for the *Press of Atlantic City.*" I tried to sound casual, but my intonation screamed DANGER, DANGER.

"Freelance." Jake tried to downplay the media angle.

"Oh." Oliver let go of Jake's hand but seemed undecided about what to do next. I could tell by the scowl on his face that picking Jake up and tossing him out the door was one of the possibilities.

I took the lead. "Jake, I don't know why you're here but neither Oliver nor I are interested in commenting on the murder of Dallas Spenser. You're wasting your time."

Jake unveiled his "I'm only here to help you" voice. "I know why the cops were here. I know that your buddy was brought in for questioning. I thought you might want to comment."

I eyed the innocent-looking reporter warily. Jake liked to appear innocuous—and he was good at it—but I suspected he was anything but. I wasn't about to become one of the innocent folks who confided in Opie and found themselves betrayed by Kitty Kelley.

"No comment."

Jake took a few more steps into the sunroom. His tone sounded as solicitous as any male soprano voice could be. "You know he is the main suspect in the murder of Dallas Spenser."

"No comment."

Jake focused on me and inched past Oliver. "You know that they don't have enough to arrest him." The reporter tried to sound reassuring.

"Really?" I corrected my comment immediately. "No comment."

With pursed lips that said I *understand,* Jake nodded. Then he abruptly changed his approach. "Cool place." Uninvited, Jake wandered through Oliver's sunroom. He walked from item to item, nodding admiringly as if he were in a museum.

"Jake, as I said, you are wasting...."

Oliver interrupted me. "Cool, eh?" He was referring to the hockey puck table that Jake was caressing lovingly. "I got that table in Boston. You like the Bruins?" Oliver didn't turn to catch Jake's nod. He moved on to a table propped up on baseball bats. "See? I love this thing."

He crouched beside Jake to show him. Jake could see under the table without bending his knees. All he had to do was take a single step backward. "I loved the Super Bowl poster in the hallway. You go to that game?"

"Lousy game but a great time."

Oliver and Jake were bonding. That quickly. I'd thought I was special when I'd bonded with Oliver. Turns out I wasn't the only one with whom Oliver shared his stories. What was he up to? Why was he fraternizing with a reporter? Why was he offering Jake a beer?

I lounged on the couch watching the two talk sports. Oliver could be charming when he wanted to be. I figured out why he wanted to charm when he led Jake, now disarmed by three of the bottled imported beers reserved for guests, into a discussion of his investigation.

"So, bud, tell me why the cops think Andy Beck was involved in Spenser's death."

Jake was a cheap date. Already he slurred his words. "I shouldn't." But he did. In detail.

The cops felt Andy had the strongest motive. He had been in New Jersey on the night of the murder. Chalk up one for opportunity. And, as a P.I. he knew his way around handguns. A vote for means.

"What caliber gun killed Spenser?" Oliver knew what information he wanted.

Jake spoke absent-mindedly as he checked out the sports memorabilia on Oliver's bookshelf. "Like they'd tell me. Low caliber, I assume. They have a bullet. But they don't have a gun." Jake waved his empty beer bottle at Oliver, who replaced it immediately and followed with a barrage of questions. Did the police suspect Page was involved? Yes. Did the police have proof that Andy and Page were involved? They claimed they did. Did the police have any physical evidence?

"Circumstantial. Circumstantial. Circumstantial." Jake sprawled in the center of one of Oliver's turquoise leather sofas. He stretched as far as his diminuitive stature would allow and let a smug expression overtake his fame. "That is what they've got and what they are counting on. They got nuttin'." He affected a gangster drawl. All Jake needed to complete his image was a big cigar. Of course, a big cigar would have dwarfed him. "Myself? What do I think? Andy Beck didn't kill Dallas Spenser. The secret lies in Spenser's past. The cops think that's all history, but they're fools. They are looking into the last few months only. Me, I am digging, digging, digging. You don't see any of the other newspapers covering this story. I am the only one interested in Dallas's past, and I am Beck's best hope. You tell your boyfriend that." Jake wagged a finger in my direction.

Oliver thanked Jake for me and somehow maneuvered the now-jolly reporter toward the door. "Let's get together and watch a game sometime." He slapped Jake on the back—rather gingerly, for fear of knocking the reporter over.

"Sure. And have Andy give me a call." He tossed me a cheerful wave as Oliver ejected him from the house.

"Oliver, you can't let him drive." I started for the door to stop the young reporter.

"Don't worry. I have his keys." We watched Jake stagger toward his car and climb in. The door had barely closed behind him when we heard the blare of a car horn.

"Ouch," Oliver said. "He's fallen asleep on the wheel." The noise stopped. "That's better. Our friend is taking a short nap. In an hour or two I'll hide his keys in the gravel out there. When he's sober enough to find them, he'll be sober enough to drive." Oliver flopped onto the sofa. "By the way, why is his head so small?"

Chapter 23

"Can you come get me?" Andy sounded as if forming the single sentence was an effort.

"If you tell me where you are."

"Toms River. In front of the library on Washington Street. Please come."

"Andy, why...."

He interrupted. "Please just come get me. I'll explain." There was depression, dejection, and despair in his voice.

I borrowed Oliver's Porsche and headed for Toms River. I was worried and frightened. Once I was on the Garden State Parkway, I turned on the radio and beat a drum solo on the steering wheel. The action did nothing to calm my nerves. But it did attract the attention of four teenage boys in an old sedan. The ten-year-old Buick cruised beside me in the left lane as we headed north. When I glanced in their direction the four responded in unison with a nod, a smile, and a thumbs up. I hated to be so superficial when Andy needed me, but I did look good in the car. I smiled back over my Raybans. It was getting dark. I should have taken them off but I had no doubt that the shades enhanced the image. Did these boys love me for myself or for my wheels? It didn't matter. Either way, I bet if I hung around I could have my choice of dates for the prom—which is more than I could say when I was seventeen.

I felt guilty about my good mood as I pulled up in front of the library. Andy was already walking down the path. The P.I. radiated exhaustion as he approached the Porsche. I grew tired watching him. His mouth, however, was not as lifeless as his body. He began talking before he got his right leg inside.

"Look. Don't get all upset. It's no big deal. The cops picked me up for questioning. Admittedly, it wasn't what you'd call a friendly visit, but I was cooperative. I felt like I had to cooperate. If you don't talk, they think you have something to hide." He pulled the door closed against the chilly evening.

"What did you tell them?"

"Whatever I could." He planted a perfunctory kiss on my lips. I appreciated the gesture. His mind was elsewhere.

"Where's your car?"

"I'm hungry."

"We'll eat first, but where's your car."

Andy's Mustang was at the Point Pleasant train station twenty miles north of Toms River where he had parked earlier that day. He planned to catch a train to New York to interview one of Dallas Spenser's business associates. Detective Petino had other plans for Andy. The P.I. spent the last six hours in an interview room at the county prosecutor's office.

I figured there had to be a diner somewhere nearby. We were, after all, in New Jersey. I had three goals in life. One, to visit every state. Two, to ride every subway system in the world. Three, to eat at every diner in New Jersey. Andy assured me that I had a better chance of achieving goals one and two than ever finding all the diners scattered across the state of New Jersey.

I headed back to Route 37, the main drag out of town. As we approached the highway, a road sign pointed both east and west to McDonald's, but I thought I glimpsed a diner ahead. I was right. After a few horn honks and more than a few well-chosen curse words courtesy of drivers turning off Route 37, we made the tough turn into the parking lot of the Crystal Diner.

The Crystal Diner lived up to its name—from the glass chandeliers that dominated the décor to the clear plastic blinds that reflected the lights of passing cars. The cheerful host gave us a table in the nonsmoking area. I thanked him twice as much to compensate for Andy's irascibility.

I took the seat across from Andy at the table for four. We sat silently with our knees touching and our hands clasped. Neither of us looked at the menu. When the waitress approached us with no-nonsense efficiency, I placed both our orders. Andy was in no condition to interact with unsuspecting humans. At least until he got a couple dozen french fries and a burger in his stomach. Then he was ready to talk.

"I didn't have much to tell the cops."

"Did they tell you anything?"

"I think so."

I had to prod him to tell me what he had learned at the police station. Or as he described it, what he thought he'd learned. "I'm not sure the gunshot killed him."

"Andy, the guy washed up on a beach with a bullet in his back. That appears fairly clear cut to me."

"You'd think so, wouldn't you?"

"I think he may have been unconscious but breathing when he fell into the water. The cops were dropping hints in the hopes I'd say something about it."

"They went through Oliver's house, you know. They had a warrant." I explained what I knew of the cops' visit. I could only tell what I had observed. The cops certainly didn't share. I told Andy I'd seen them take a pair of his shoes. "I heard them say they had sand in them."

"Right. That certainly constitutes probable cause on a barrier island. I'm sure you won't find shoes with sand in them in any other house in town." His cavalier demeanor vanished. "Meg." Andy reached for my hand. "I think I might be in some trouble." He whispered so the two couples at the next table wouldn't hear—although based on the decibel level of their conversation I had my doubts that they would have heard if he made the announcement over the PA system. I leaned forward so that our heads were almost touching as he spoke.

As Andy described the day, he spent his time at the police station denying the cops' scenario. The authorities painted a picture of a greedy and unhappy young wife reunited with her handsome—but monetarily challenged—young boyfriend. A boyfriend who knew his way around murder and weapons. A boyfriend who tried to flee the country. He looked at me sheepishly. "They think I'm using you as a cover. I am so sorry." He squeezed my hand. The cops thought I was a cover. Great. That did a lot for my self-esteem. "They think I don't love you. The proof is that I beat you. They think you're lying to protect me."

Boy. I must make a great impression. I wanted to consider that angle but Andy continued. I didn't interrupt. After all, this was really about Andy. "The police believe that Page and I killed Dallas for his money. They think we sent his body out to sea to destroy all the evidence, hide the actual crime scene, and obscure the time of death. They claim that I went to the Spenser house that night. I admitted I was in Jersey and that I took the train from Point Pleasant back to New York. They can't identify anyone who remembers seeing me on the train back to the city. Not that I imagine they tried too hard. I remember the conductor so clearly. A kid. I told them. I don't believe they'll look."

"Certainly Page told them you weren't there." My tone said I was stating the obvious.

"They tried to sell me some story. According to them, Page claims she might have seen me outside. I can't believe they thought they could fool me that way. As if Page would say that. I believe she might have said she saw someone on the beach."

I believed Page would say anything to make her life easier, but I kept the thought to myself and let Andy continue.

"The cops feel that since I'm a P.I., I planned it. They tried to flatter me into confessing. They told me it was a pretty good plan. I spent a lot of time listening to what a creative mind I had. Allegedly."

"Some compliment."

Andy shook his head. "They have no physical evidence. There is nothing. Not on the body. Not on the wet suit. Not on the boat."

"The boat? They found the kayak?"

He nodded. "Not that having the boat will help my case. They won't find any evidence. It's been in the water too long."

Actually, Andy said "too lo...." Then his voice took on an urgent tone. "Wait here." With that he leapt from his chair. I assumed that he was headed to the restroom, but I glanced over my shoulder to see him headed out the front door of the diner.

The people at the next table eyed me suspiciously—and sympathetically. I issued a strained smile for their benefit.

"Your boyfriend know that guy?" One of the men asked in a gravelly voice. Apparently the two couples had been more interested in Andy and me than I initially believed.

"What guy?"

"The boy your friend just ran out after," one of the women informed me.

"Andy?"

"If Andy is your young man." The woman confirmed.

The other man chimed in. "He just saw some kid at the door and he jumped up and chased him. The guy scurried out of here when he saw your friend headed his way."

The fourth member of the party comforted me. "Don't feel bad. I didn't see nothing either. Got my back to the door like you."

"Here he is." The three other members of the party all offered some variation on the statement. I turned in my chair to see Andy coming through the front door—alone. He was a bit confused as to why two tables were welcoming him back—and by name. He was flushed and agitated as he slipped back into his chair. He answered before I could ask. "Jake Chandler, that little creep. He was spying on us."

I was consumed by guilt. I was so busy flirting with teenage boys that I forgot to check if I was being followed.

Andy couldn't believe that I hadn't noticed Jake. "I mean that car of his…it's pretty hard to miss." Andy explained what he had learned in a remarkably short period of time. Jake had followed me from Beach Haven and settled into the smoking section to try to observe us.

"What excuse did he offer?"

"He smokes."

"No, what was his excuse for watching us?"

"He's a reporter. I told him that neither of us would be speaking to him. I did promise that if we had any comment we would call him. Not that I can imagine we'll be making any comment soon."

I reached across the table and took Andy's hand. The tension began to flow out of his body. "Andy…is there anything else I need to know?"

Oops. The tension returned. "Are you turning on me? Siding with your new best friend Petino? I thought I could count on you. You of all people." He plastered disappointment on his features and shook his head as if he'd just been notified that astronauts had landed in a studio in Encino, and not on the moon, in July 1969. But he did not pull his hand away.

"Andy, I'm standing by you here, but there are a lot of things you haven't told me. We both know that. That's all I meant. Let me restate my question. What if any action have you taken in the course of your investigation that may have aroused the suspicion of the police?"

He seemed appeased and relieved. He stroked the back of my hand with his thumb. "The fact of the investigation. They think Page and I are trying to frame someone. They just haven't figured out who."

"They must feel you're not very good at it. Framing people, I mean."

"Apparently." I spotted the tiniest trace of a smile on his lips. "Look, Maggie, they think I am…that I have been…having an affair with Page. It's really important to me that you know…that you believe…that accusation isn't true."

Okay. That was a tough one. I wanted to know...to believe...that accusation wasn't true. I'd gotten past that fear, but I did have relapses. But remember, I am really jealous by nature. Really.

"Nothing has happened between us. Maybe Page...I mean I might have misread...I think she may have given me a few subtle signals. I'll admit it. She did grab me that first day...." Subtle. You gotta love this guy. "But I swear nothing happened."

"Andy, if you tell me nothing happened, I'll believe you." At least I'll try to. I added that part silently.

"I have told you." He squeezed my hand. He sounded sincere. Actually desperate.

"Then I believe you." I leaned forward and stared into his cool green eyes. "What do we do next?"

"Well, I simply change my behavior so I don't arouse any more suspicion."

"Does that mean you're not going to help Page anymore?"

He shook his head. "I haven't told her yet, but the penalty for helping her is too high. For her and for me. My investigation only intensifies the suspicion in her direction."

I didn't even wait a respectable interval before I asked. "So does this mean we can leave for Antigua?" Actually, all I said was "Anti..." before Andy's look stopped me cold.

"Maggie, we can't leave. I mean, you can. You probably should."

I didn't ask where he thought I would go, given that I'd deferred graduate school and sublet my apartment.

"Andy, they can't make you stay here. They haven't arrested you."

"And I don't want to force their hand. I want to appear cooperative." He opened his arms wide to underline his interest in honesty. "I want to *be* cooperative."

"I know," I said, "and I'm staying here with you."

"Meg, we've only known each other for a few months. How can you stand by me?"

"Why wouldn't I?" I laid my hand on his. "You'd do the same for me."

"I love you, Maggie." He wove his fingers through mine and squeezed tight.

Chapter 24

"Sorry about what happened to your house today." Andy greeted Oliver with an apology. "Things back to normal?"

Oliver nodded. "It was nothing, pal. Took it in my stride." Luckily Oliver did not look to me for verification. "So, tell me about your day."

Andy explained how the cops tried to flatter him into confessing with praise for his "plan."

"That must have made you feel good." I watched for a sardonic tone in Oliver's voice but detected none. Andy and I eyed him with amazement as he sauntered to the refrigerator for another beer. "What?" As he turned back with a Bud in hand Oliver seemed amazed to find Andy and me staring at him with wide eyes. "They think you did a good job. Created a good plot." Oliver's reaction to the story of Andy's visit to the police station was at best perplexing.

"Oliver, I didn't plan, plot, or execute anything." Andy just shook his head and went back to his story. "I've been in Page and Dallas's house, so the cops may find physical evidence, but it would be old. And easily explained. When we arrived on Thursday afternoon after the murder, the crime scene unit had already concluded that Page's home was not a crime scene." He dismissed physical evidence as a problem. "Can I have one of those?" He nodded at the beer in Oliver's hand. "And there is no real physical evidence on the body. Or the boat."

"They found the boat?"

"A fisherman found the kayak floating upside down in...."

"I thought those things sank." Oliver interrupted.

"Not that one."

"Any fingerprints on it?" Oliver cleared his throat nervously. "There won't be any evidence, right?"

"Evidence would be good news, Oliver. It could not point to me." Andy snapped the tab on the beer can with a small display of anger. "You sound as if the boat's showing up is cause for alarm."

Oliver mumbled some disclaimer and an apology that Andy waved off. "I know you don't suspect me, Oliver. But they won't find any evidence on that boat. It's been in the water too long."

Oliver apologized again, although I could tell he wasn't quite sure why.

The strain of the day—plus a few beers with Oliver—knocked Andy out cold by eight P.M. After he went to bed, I had time to think. Too much time. I was agitated and desperate to help. I decided I had to take action. I also decided, somewhat reluctantly, that I needed to bring Oliver in on the investigation.

I found our host in the sunroom watching ESPN. You didn't have to be a professional P.I. to track Oliver down. He spent most evenings in the same recliner—remote in the right hand and cold beer in the left.

I checked out the wide screen. Oliver was engrossed in a basketball game being played by men with short-shorts and big hair. ESPN Classics. He knew how this game turned out. He'd known for over a decade. I continued with my interruption.

"How was your date last night?"

He shrugged, but his eyes twinkled. "Okay."

"When will we meet her?"

He blushed. "We're taking it slow."

"So you're free tonight?"

"Sure." He answered quickly. It wasn't long before he concluded he might have responded too quickly. I explained my plan.

"You're a licensed P.I.?"

"Licenses are overrated." My tone was dismissive.

"Especially by the authorities." Oliver made no move to leave the recliner.

"Come on. We don't need no lousy license. I just want to gather a little information. Plus, it's Friday night. We shouldn't be sitting home. Let's go out." When joviality got no response, at least no response I wanted, I changed tacks. I moved a needlepoint Dolphins pillow aside and perched on the soft leather sofa across from Oliver. I leaned forward and plastered an earnest expression on my face.

I didn't think Oliver was eager to hear the details of my plan. Well, I know he wasn't. He said, "Meg, I don't think I want to hear the details of your plan. I suspect it has something to do with Andy, murder, or Andy and murder."

"Indirectly."

"So?"

I explained my contention that Dallas had drug connections that could have led to his murder. Despite Oliver's obvious lack of interest I went on to describe my frustration that the cops were not exploring that option.

"Noooo!" Oliver interrupted.

"At least let me finish...."

"I wasn't talking to you. I was screaming at the Lakers." Oliver pointed at the screen. "Yes!" The "yes" was reserved for a Magic Johnson basket. "Meg, you don't do a lot of drugs, do you?"

I shrugged, temporarily embarrassed to admit that I didn't.

"You don't get killed in drug wars when you're buying a bag every six months."

"You don't know that's all Dallas did. I'm simply asking you to help me contact the local dealer and see what he or she knows. Maybe there's something; maybe there's not. I just need to know. You must have a local contact, don't you?"

"Meg," Oliver interrupted. "I don't get involved in that kind of thing anymore."

I grew concerned. "If this would be a temptation…forget it. I'm sorry I asked. I'll go alone. I need to check this out. You can just tell me where to go."

"Yeah, right. I'd feel real good about that." He pulled his World Series throw under his chin. "Even if Dallas bought drugs, we don't know if he bought them around here. He lived in Loveladies."

"Oliver, I doubt there is an elaborate network of dealers on this island. It's not like we're trying to infiltrate the hierarchy of a major Colombian drug cartel. We're only looking for information about a guy who's already dead. What can it hurt?"

His raised eyebrow claimed it could hurt something or someone. He didn't elaborate. He remained silent.

"All I need is a little push in the right direction. If you gave me enough time, even I could find the local drug dealer."

Again, Oliver raised his eyebrow.

"I could find him a little faster if you gave me a start. Just point me to the right bar and I'll take it from there."

"Right. I am not going to sit here while you go out to commit a crime."

"I'm not committing a crime."

"Not yet. But you're planning to."

"I will not be committing a crime tonight."

"They legalized drugs today?"

"I'm not going to buy drugs. I just want to chat with the guy."

Oliver grew pensive. "You know, Meg, this guy might be harmless but I can guarantee—whoever he turns out to be—he works for some pretty ugly types."

"I'm not going to ask him anything about the organization. Trust me, I know who controls the drug traffic in this county."

Oliver looked at me with a raised eyebrow.

"I read it in a true crime book once."

Oliver groaned as he pulled himself out of his recliner. "I'll go. Go ahead, get dressed." In response to my wide-eyed stare, he apologized. "Sorry. I forgot. You are dressed."

Chapter 25

Although I'd driven by the location dozens of times, I'd never even noticed the bar Oliver parked behind. The nondescript wood building appeared to have been built in four or five stages. The basic shape was oblong—with odd little appendages sticking out at random points. The windows were high and blocked by neon beer signs. The bar offered no opportunity to see inside—or to order any premium beers.

"Are you sure you want to do this?" Oliver asked a question, but his tone voiced the concern that I was, in fact, a complete idiot. "By virtue of your relationship to Andy, you're not the local cops' favorite."

"They don't arrest everyone who talks to a drug dealer." I climbed out of the Porsche—with a little difficulty. I had not yet recovered from my bicycling expedition. "Are you coming?"

The bar was no more attractive inside than out. The walls were cheap paneling that even a bat would realize wasn't wood. The prints that adorned the panels made dogs playing poker look tasteful. The beer signs turned out to be one of the better decorating touches. The garish hues softened the bright, white uncovered lightbulbs hung sporadically in a futile attempt to light the entire room.

Oliver and I found two vinyl covered barstools near the door and ordered beer in a bottle. Oliver because he liked the brew. Me because I wasn't about to let one of the joint's glasses touch my lips.

I surveyed the crowd. Every ethnic, socioeconomic, and age group was represented—united by a desire to drink too much cheap liquor, talk too loud, and dance to bad covers. I looked for faces familiar from the Spenser Web site but recognized no one.

Oliver and I tried conversation over the band that played Creedence Clearwater—or a reasonable facsimile. And over the shouts of others trying to converse above the music. It was hopeless. Too much for my vocal chords. We resorted to non-verbal signals as people came in.

I busied myself playing a game. Alone. My goal was to identify as many faux celebrities as possible. In half an hour I'd spotted a young Debra Winger, an old Britney Spears, and a dead ringer for Brad Pitt. Actually, Brad Pitt walked in quite a few times. Brad Pitt from *Fight Club*.

At last the door opened and a sloppily clad nondescript guy walked through the door. I knew right away that he was my target. The bartender greeted him with a smile and a nod to the right toward a group of preppie types who appeared too young to be buying drinks, let alone drugs.

"There he is." I watched the bland blond exchange ritualistic handshakes with a few pals as he moved down the bar toward the eager schoolboys.

Oliver shook his head. "I don't know that guy."

"He's the one."

"And you know this because...."

"It's always the guy in the 'Just Say No' T-shirt. Don't you watch *Cops*? Dealers are the only guys who wear those T-shirts—which is odd because on *Cops* they're the only guys wearing shirts at all. Plus look at that guy. He has a DARE jacket over his 'Just Say No' T-shirt. What else could he be besides a drug dealer?"

"If you say so. I never saw him before."

I watched the guy for half an hour, during which he visited the bathroom five times. This was definitely my guy. How to approach him? That was the question plaguing me. I couldn't count on Oliver for advice. He'd apparently fallen passionately—if not eternally—in love with a perky blonde in size two jeans and a Led Zeppelin T-shirt.

The man I assumed to be the local drug dealer appeared to be a friendly sort. Of course, salespeople have to be. In his line of work, he had to be charming enough to make sure you forgot that he worked for an organization that sometimes killed its own employees—and its customers.

"Are you ready to give up on this project?" Oliver checked in with me while his new love visited the ladies room. "Face it. You're not even sure he's the right guy—which hardly matters since you're never going to talk to him."

"I'm still reconnoitering."

"You're still procrastinating."

"No...." I tried to protest.

"You know I'm right. You realize this was a dumb idea. Let's go."

"No." I took a deep breath. "I came here to get information and I'm going to."

Oliver looked a bit sheepish. "Do you mind, then, if I slip out with Binky? You can take the car. She'll bring me home in the morning." He laid the keys on the bar in front of me.

I sputtered in response. I hated to keep Oliver away from a woman named Binky, but on the other hand I could use some moral support. I didn't want him to go. Before I could say another word Oliver offered a deal. "If you make your move now I promise not to leave until I see you're okay."

It was now or never. I thought about Antigua. I'd never visited the island, but the Web sites promised a beautiful setting. White beaches. Blue water. Safe harbors. If I waited for the cops to investigate the drug angle, I wouldn't be sunning or sailing until summer came to New Jersey. The only place I'd be visiting

Andy would be at the State Prison in Trenton. Just then, the door opened and cold air streamed in. I shivered. The guy was alone, the band was on break, and the air on Long Beach Island was freezing. It was time to make my move.

The dealer—alleged dealer—was sitting at the bar drinking a draft when I approached. I had no experience buying drugs and Oliver had offered no advice. I was on my own.

I leaned over the stool next to my target. Our clothing made contact, if not our bodies. I propped both elbows on the bar and waved a twenty at the bartender. He didn't seem to notice. Finally, my suspect crooked his little finger. The bartender appeared in front of him. "I think the lady would like to order a drink."

"Can I help you?" The bartender was genial as he took my order.

I ordered a beer. The same brand that the alleged dealer drank.

"Thanks." I cleared my throat. "I...ah...I think you may be able to help me."

"I just did." He smiled.

"Well, I thought there might be another way."

"How so?" The guy seemed interested. He checked out my jeans and sweater, but I had no idea what they told him—with the possible exception that I was not a hooker.

"I'm interested in one of your customers."

"My customers? What makes you think I have customers?" His eyes narrowed. He let heavy white smoke drift out of his mouth and into his nostrils. I hated that. I tried not to grimace. "You know me?"

I ran through a series of coy responses and then settled on, "I hope you're the person I'm looking for."

"Are you sure you have the right guy?"

I didn't go into the significance of his shirt and jacket. I simply said yes. "All I wanted to know is if a man named Dallas Spenser ever bought drugs from you."

The guy's eyes narrowed. "Excuse me?"

The place was noisy but I was fairly sure he heard me over the jukebox, the laughter, and the calls for the bartender. I repeated my request.

"Did you ever sell drugs to a guy named Dallas?"

"Whoa, lady!"

What was this lady thing? I couldn't have had five years on the guy—if that.

"Okay, let me put it this way." I paused. I had no other way to put it. I searched for another way to phrase my question. "Do you know Dallas Spenser?"

"The guy who bought it up the north end of the island a week or two ago?"

"Yeah." I sounded excited. "You knew him?"

The band was playing "Freebird" for the second time. Was there a bar band on Earth that didn't play "Freebird?" Badly. Loudly. Repeatedly. Again, I leaned forward to catch the man's answer. Instead I caught the smoke he exhaled. Again, I tried not to grimace.

"Only what I read in the newspaper."

"That's it? You never met him?"

"We didn't really travel in the same circles." The guy took a long drag on his cigarette. I waited for the smoke to hit my face but he exhaled politely in the opposite direction.

"So you never sold him drugs?"

"Lady, I never sold anyone drugs. Okay? We straight on that?"

I nodded—rather dejectedly, I thought. "You know I'm not a cop or anything."

His smirk was almost kind. "I wasn't worried. I figured out what you're not. What you are? That's what I can't figure."

He checked out his beeper—apparently set to vibrate. Within a few seconds, a guy in a Jets jersey tapped him on the shoulder and he excused himself. My eyes followed him as he disappeared into the men's room. My mission wasn't going well. I searched the crowd for Oliver. Apparently, he and Twiggy or Mitzie or whatever her name was had gone off in search of true love—or a temporary replacement.

The dealer—excuse me, alleged dealer—seemed surprised but not disappointed to find that I was still on the stool next to his. "I watched your beer," I explained proudly.

"Look, lady. If I did sell drugs, I wouldn't have sold them to Dallas Spenser." He smiled a slick smile. "Now, you want anything else from me?" He wiggled his eyebrows.

"I don't mean to insult you. I understand that you really believe in your product. I know you guys think you're king of the world when you're high. I'm even willing to accept that coke helps the creative process. But to tell you the truth, I've never met anyone whose personality was enhanced by cocaine."

The guy seemed more amused than offended. "You don't like my personality?"

"I don't know you. I think you're in a rather risky business. You may be nice and charming, but you work for some very undesirable types. And I don't see a very bright future for you. I'd be careful about using too much of your own product. You'll end up in the hole. You'll have to start marking up to achieve the margins you need to pay off your supplier. You can't be the only game in town. If you have to raise your prices, your customers will go to the competition. It's harder to lure a customer back once you've lost them. You'll end up with a habit, a debt, and no customers. What I am telling you is only good business. I'd have to watch out for the same problem if I worked in a fudge shop."

He stared at me.

"Sorry, I just felt the need to say that."

"Do you have a boyfriend?" The man's question came from left field.

"Why? I know you don't want to take me out."

"On a date? No way. But I might want to go into business with you. I asked about your boyfriend because I thought you might want to take a little gift to him? A free sample."

"I didn't know you guys gave free samples. I mean, you hear the rumors about the kids in the schoolyards but I didn't...."

The guy grew impatient. "Do you want a hit for your boyfriend?" He grabbed my hand. I could feel the plastic packet in my palm. I pushed it back into his grip.

"My boyfriend doesn't need cocaine." He eyed me expectantly. "He has me."

The dealer laughed out loud.

Chapter 26

A ndy was already back from running when I woke up. I found him at the kitchen table sipping coffee and staring at the weekend *Today* show. "Where's Oliver?"

"Haven't seen him. I just got up." I shuffled to the refrigerator for a cola. "Looks like another gorgeous day. Did they give the temperature yet?"

Andy ignored me. "I woke up last night and you and Oliver were gone. Where did you go?"

I shrugged. "Out for a drink." I opened the cabinet and stared at the Pop Tart collection.

Andy turned his back on the TV and stared in my direction. I could feel his eyes boring through my white T-shirt. "You're ducking the question. Why?"

I pulled down a box of blueberry Pop Tarts and opened it carefully. Very carefully. I kept my back to the P.I. "We just felt like going out. We just went out for a drink...that's all...just a drink. I might have picked ice cream, but at this time of year a drink is easier." I threw a grin over my shoulder and went back to preparing my Pop Tart—i.e., trying to rip the package open.

"Where did you go?"

I mumbled my answer.

"Why did you go to that dive?" Andy was on his feet. He took the Pop Tart packet from my hand and ripped the paper easily. He popped the pastry into the toaster, leaving me with nothing to do but face him.

I turned, but my eyes didn't meet his. I stared out over the bay. "Must be windy. Water looks pretty choppy." Andy continued to stare at me. I wasn't going to be able to duck the question. "Oliver knew it. And you know I love dives. So when we wanted a drink...."

Andy interrupted. "What did you do?" I remembered his tone coming from my mother's mouth. And Ricky Ricardo's in *I Love Lucy* reruns.

"Nothing." I was emphatic. Maybe even a little testy. I tried to match his stare. I couldn't. "How about breakfast?" I reopened the cabinet and stared inside as if I hadn't just had plenty of time to memorize its contents. "You like Pop Tarts?"

"Maggie."

I'd always thought of Maggie as a pet name. An affectionate name. Andy didn't sound affectionate. "What?" I tried to sound unconcerned.

"What did you and Oliver do last night?"

I could never stand up to torture. As soon as I turned around and met his eyes, I talked. When I finished my explanation, Andy laughed.

"What's so funny?"

"You. Investigating."

"Hey. I investigate."

"Yeah. Just promise no more investigating." He stared at me and waited for an answer.

"I don't think I did anything wrong." Andy never noticed that I didn't promise. He must have been distracted by my cooking. He likes Pop Tarts. Even as I served him I was thinking that I could find other drug dealers on LBI. Where could I go to meet them?

Andy was a little on the pensive side, but we spent a happy day together—possibly influenced by our Web surfing. It seemed so luxurious to spend the day walking the beach, watching videos, and making love. Almost as good as a trip to Antigua. Almost.

Andy and I lay under the yellow and black quilt, complete with a big "B" for Bruins, and watched the sun head for the horizon over Manahawkin Bay. He held me close and whispered in my ear. "Let me take you out to dinner to make up for this."

"Hey, so it wasn't the greatest. It was fine."

Andy looked confused and then annoyed. "By *this* I meant being stranded here instead of on Antigua."

"I knew that." I shifted gears quickly and asked for the car. If we were going on a real date, I was dressing up. Andy told me where to find the keys to the Mustang. I had less than two hours to transform my image. I headed out alone to find something besides my standard uniform to wear to dinner. That's why I was by myself when I ran into Detective Petino. Or rather, when he ran into me.

I was in Hand's department store in Ship Bottom—the second Hand's I'd visited that afternoon. Closing time was fast approaching and my search for something to wear that night— anything to wear that night—wasn't going well. I had a small amount of money saved for Antigua. I didn't want to blow it all on clothes, but my patience for wearing one outfit was growing short. I was willing to buy just about anything. As long as the outfit was appropriate for February. As soon as I ventured into the clothing area, I realized that Hand's was anticipating summer. I wasn't having any luck. I swept around a rack of sweaters and into Detective Petino. I doubted that his appearance was unrelated to my presence. I had to stop parking in front of the establishments I visited.

"What do you want from me?" I didn't bother with hello.

He smirked. "I'm not on duty. Just happened to run into you."

"In the ladies department?"

His smirk softened into a smile. "You don't know me. Maybe I look good in chiffon." The detective looked pretty good in wool, that was for sure. The red sweater made his dark eyes appear even darker. He had a new, more fashionable haircut, a stylish black leather jacket, and a clone. In his right hand he held the left hand of a miniature Detective Petino. I smiled and said hello in one of those stupid voices that adults use to address children. "What's your name?" The little fellow smirked. Definitely a clone.

"Look, Kyle and I were visiting friends on the island today. I've been keeping an eye out for you all over town." Detective Petino didn't say why, if he was so interested in seeing me, he didn't just come to Oliver's. "I saw the Mustang. I was hoping you were here. I'm off duty but I would really like to talk. Beck with you?"

"No, he doesn't look good in chiffon." I started to rifle through sweatshirts that I had no interest in buying. As I moved down the counter the cop blocked my way. I swear I sensed some concern in his voice when he spoke—although he was going for Mr. Tough Guy.

"Ms. Daniels, I told you that the drug angle was a dead end. Keep your nose clean."

"I don't do drugs." I dismissed his advice.

"That's not what I mean. Don't play Miss Marple. If you stick your nose into the wrong place, it could get hurt." For a moment I had the fear he was going to tweak my nose. I was grateful when he moved away. He headed right for the door, slowing briefly at the exit to adjust his sunglasses on his nose with what I had to admit was considerable élan. Or would have been if the sun hadn't set while he was inside the store.

I found a very sporty navy cardigan. Okay, I tried to convince myself it was very sporty. The sweater did have one great feature—it wasn't the navy blue pullover I'd been wearing all week. With my jeans and one of the many white T-shirts I had at Oliver's, I would have a new outfit. At least I could fool myself into thinking I had a new outfit. Fooling myself is something I have a knack for. It's a gift. Really.

I didn't go right home. It wasn't that I needed time away from Andy; I just wanted some time alone. I stopped by Holgate for a little fresh air. The town at the southern tip of Long Beach Island wasn't on my way. Holgate isn't on the way to anywhere. It's the end of the line—a narrow strip of land where expensive houses grew up around a cluster of trailer homes that had huddled together for as long as I could remember.

Andy's old Mustang was the only vehicle in the parking lot. At this time of year, that was not surprising. I had no idea about the parking situation in the summer. Impossible, I assumed. Maybe that was why I had never actually ventured to the end when the island was crowded with tourists. I walked until signs warned me to stop before I damaged the environment. As I gazed south down the coast, the tops of buildings in Atlantic City peeked over the top of the dunes and the surf that methodically charged the beach. The city lights threw a pink glaze toward the charcoal gray sky that was quickly fading to black. I took deep breaths and let my mind wander. I was thinking more about my future then the past when it hit me. I told Andy as soon as I got home.

"Andy, I figured something out. That guy last night that tried to give me the coke. He was a cop. I'm sure of it. Petino did one of his run-ins today at Hand's. He wasn't even subtle about it. Not that he ever succeeds at being subtle, but usually he tries. He told me to drop the drug angle. When I think about it, why did that guy offer me a free sample 'for my boyfriend.' I think Petino somehow or other knew I was there. I think he paged that guy and told him to give me the drugs. So they could entrap you."

Andy was amazed at the amazement in my voice. "You just figured that out."

I nodded.

"Meg did you think this was fun and games?"

I shrugged. I knew it wasn't fun.

Chapter 27

"This is where I met Hap," I remarked absentmindedly as we pulled into the parking lot at Kubel's Too.

"Hap?" Andy appeared puzzled.

"My psychic friend. But that's not why I like it here." I had a much better reason for liking Andy's choice: We wouldn't run into Page. The restaurant was far too low-key for Page. Plus, she lived a lot closer to the original Kubel's in Barnegat Light. There was no reason for her to drive all the way to Pehala Park to visit Kubel's Too. At least no reason I could think of.

We were already seated at the fireside table testing each other's appetizers when I glanced at the bar and saw her. Page Spenser. I was sure of it. She moved to the doorway quickly, but I was certain I'd seen her. She'd seen us. I was certain it was the power of her stare that made me glance in her direction. However, she made no attempt to say hello. If I'd been alone, her behavior would have aroused my suspicions enough that I would have followed her. But not on my big date night with Andy. All I wanted was for her to go away— unseen by Andy.

I thought I had gotten my wish, but suddenly I spotted her heading for us from the other direction. She'd say she just happened to see us on her way from the ladies room. I knew better. She'd slipped down the hallway from the bar to the rest rooms just so she could pretend to stumble on us in the dining room. She hadn't even taken enough time to fake a stop in the rest room. I know the positive reading of her behavior was that she spotted us, needed to stop in the rest room first, and then dropped by the table to say hello. I, however, could not seem to put a positive spin on anything Page did. Especially when what she did was approach our table.

A jumbo shrimp stopped dead somewhere behind my breastbone—and showed no inclination to move toward my stomach. I started breathing deeply to relax whatever muscle had a grip on the piece of seafood. It was my breathing that drew Andy's attention away from his chowder, to my eyes, and then to Page. She was walking in our direction. I gulped. I didn't want to greet Page with regurgitated shellfish on my sweater. Actually, I did not want to greet Page at all.

To my mind, Page looked gorgeous. Understated. Elegant. And undeniably sexy—in a remote, unattainable way. I could only imagine what the males in the room thought. I looked around. Most of them were thinking something. To my knowledge, none of them were reminiscing. As soon as we arrived, I'd checked all the faces in the room in the hope of locating one of the party participants from the Spenser Web site. No one was there—or if they were I couldn't recognize them.

Although many men admired her, no one seemed to recognize Page either as a friend or a news story. The couple's picture had run in a few regional newspapers, but the Spensers weren't local. I surmised that the locals didn't care much about Dallas's murder. I found their indifference to a body on their beach strange, but more admirable than alarming.

Page's perfume reached our table first. It was rich and floral and reeked of Saturday night. Actually, that's what Page looked like. Saturday night. While I, in my new purchase, looked more like Tuesday afternoon. Or, even worse, Monday. Morning. At a girl's elementary school. In 1955. I vowed to hit a mall for some heavy-duty shopping.

Page was casually and classically dressed—not in a threatening way. So why did I feel threatened? Maybe it was the way the white silk shirt fell across her perky little breasts. Or the way the denim of her jeans pulled at her thighs. Or the way her $1,000 blazer reeked of success. Or was it the million-dollar smile she had trained on Andy. "Andrew." She extended a long slender arm, a long slender hand, and long slender fingers.

Andy stood and shook her hand lightly. "You remember Meg."

"Of course. We met after my husband's death." She scrutinized me with her big, blue eyes, but she didn't offer her hand. I didn't offer mine.

As Andy and Page made small talk about her day's activities, I studied the woman. She didn't notice. Andy, and only Andy, was the focus of her attention. For the first time, I saw her smile. The relaxed expression added beauty to her already awesome face. This woman had gotten all the breaks genetically. Especially if those teeth were real. They were big, white, and perfectly aligned.

Page encouraged Andy to be seated, but he did not reciprocate. I waited for her to say her good-byes, but I had a feeling it was going to be a long wait. As I listened to her speak, I couldn't find much to hate about her. She was a bit boring, but not obviously egotistical. Maybe it wasn't fair to judge her based on her behavior immediately after losing her husband. Had I let my jealousy run amok? I really didn't know Page. Like Andy, she was suspected of evil doings that might well have been out of the realm of possibility. She was independent enough to venture out for dinner alone. And that couldn't be easy so soon after losing a loved one—and finding out that your entire life together was a lie. And having the entire story printed in the newspaper.

"Would you like to join us?" Even I couldn't believe the words came out of my mouth.

Andy certainly couldn't. He sputtered as he confirmed the invitation.

"Well, how nice of you. I hate to interrupt...I know I've been monopolizing Andy lately...but—I'd love to."

With a puzzled expression on his face, Andy rose and held a chair out for Page.

"Thank you. I've been kind of lonely lately. Thank you, Marge." Something in her expression told me I'd been conned. Page had gotten exactly what she wanted—what she had planned.

"So, Page, why are you staying on LBI? I would think you'd want to hurry back to New York." The edge in my voice was unmistakable. If Andy had been confused when I became strangely friendly to Page, this sudden attitude reversal really perplexed him.

It took Page what felt like an hour to answer. Her response included information about where she and Dallas had lived, how much they paid for their apartment, how much they paid for their house, who had decorated each of their domiciles, and which one she preferred. That is not a complete list of topics. I think I blocked out a lot of what she said.

Of course, Page maintained that the main reason she stayed on LBI was to assist in the investigation. As she fell silent, I wondered if her continued presence on LBI was her or the cops' idea. The way I interpreted what she said, decorating the guest-rooms was her only motivation to stay.

Page interrupted her monologue only to order dinner. She mimicked Andy's order—filet mignon with a baked potato. I was surprised—especially with her request for sour cream *and* butter. She struck me as a salad kind of gal.

She snapped the menu closed and was off and running on another monologue. "You know it is so unfair the way they ask all these questions about Dallas's life. They do this, you know. The cops. The victim is victimized twice. Can you imagine?"

Personally, I could. After all, this was a man who had faked his own death, abandoned his family, and lied to his wife about his past. But I didn't say a word. Neither did Andy. We ate. Page talked in thoughtful, well-paced tones. With her left thumb she continuously twirled a large solitaire diamond around the third finger of her left hand—and a wedding band crammed with smaller diamonds.

Page was upset that the police suspected her. "Can you believe that, one, they think I am that kind of person and, two, they think I could do that to someone I love?"

Okay, I could believe it, but I never said so. But Page saw something in my eyes that prompted her to defend her late husband.

"I admit that Dallas wasn't perfect."

I chewed a little faster in anticipation of her revelations.

"But he wasn't all bad. Who is? Sure, he had a tough time in the past. I never even realized how tough until that little nerd reporter delved into his background. And I'm not saying that we didn't have some rough spots in our marriage. Every marriage does. We were no different than any married couple."

Based on what I'd seen on the Internet, I was willing to argue that point—but I didn't.

As she consumed three glasses of Merlot and three bites of steak, she grew wistful. She must have thought to wear water-proof mascara. Not a smudge marred her face as she wept. The tears coating her eyes only served to enhance the bright blue. This woman just couldn't lose in the looks department.

Sometime around her second glass of wine Page's focus changed from Andy to me. Her constant gaze made me uncomfortable. She spoke to me. I glanced at Andy to remind her that he was there. She didn't take the hint. She focused on me—and only me. "I miss Dallas. I do. He could be very mean and very cruel. You could almost believe someone would want to kill him. There were probably moments I wanted to kill him myself. I never would have gone through with it. He could have charmed me out of it. He could be charming. Never needy. Independent. He had a winning personality. Never any feeling of vulnerability. That is what is so ironic. Even when he wondered if he was being stalked, he never showed any fear. To many people he seemed cold, but he was just practical. He knew what he wanted and how to get it."

"What did he want?" The question didn't refer to the Internet sex stuff, but Andy knew where I was headed. He cleared his throat. As if a warning like that would stop me.

She shrugged. "Money. Other people thought the things he did were Machiavellian. He didn't think he was being deceitful or mean or manipulative. He thought that's how to get the job done." Page explained that several ex-employees from California were hostile to Dallas. "But he has no real enemies here." I got the feeling Page was backpedaling as she continued. "I do so appreciate Andy's continuing efforts." I glanced at Andy. There were no continuing efforts. When did he plan on informing Page? "Since we came back east Dallas had been doing investments—and some investment advising. No disasters that I know of. Most of his business relationships were just networking. But who knows in business? The stakes are high. Who knows what you might find out?"

I looked at Andy. He had to tell her that he was discontinuing his investigation. Apparently, he did not feel this was the time.

Page was certainly good at identifying suspects. She had a million of 'em. It appeared this was the list she had given Andy. He dismissed each of them with a short explanation.

At last she took a breath and stared into the fire. "I guess you must wonder how I took the news about Denver Spears." Her explanation was for my benefit. Her eyes bored into mine. "I never knew. It's scary to think that you can be in the grips of a man that you really care for and love, and then find out you don't really know him at all."

I shrugged and gazed into the fire, but I could still feel her eyes boring into me. "Sometimes it's simply chemistry." My tone was gentle. "You know, sexual chemistry can be a powerful thing." I turned back to catch her reaction.

Andy kicked me under the table. Not very discreetly. I shot him a glance that said "back off."

Page neither reacted to my comment nor took the bait. She sipped her wine before answering. "Chemistry will only take you so far and then you have to work. Hard. We worked at our marriage." She tried to go on but I interrupted.

"Oh? How so? I know it's hard to keep the sexual thing alive."

Again, Andy kicked me and Page ignored me. "Dallas was thinking about another career. He felt that would revitalize our lives—and our marriage. He was really into that whole idea that you could reinvent yourself. Well, I guess that's obvious given the Denver Spears revelations. What I mean is, Dallas kept up. He was into technology."

Okay, this had to be my cue. "The Internet?"

Beside me, Andy sighed.

"Dallas was into the Web. Me, I'm an idiot. When it comes to the Internet, I mean."

No argument there. But Page believed she was an idiot because she lacked technical knowledge.

At last Andy spoke. His voice was kind and gentle. "Page, I think Meg is trying to find something out. Something you may already know. If you don't, you should."

Her wide eyes grew even wider.

"We have reason to believe that Dallas had a Web site that featured some personal moments from your life. Were you aware of this?"

It was hard to believe those eyes could grow any bigger but they did.

"I don't understand."

Somehow I thought she did.

Andy was trying to be gentle, but let's be honest—there's no truly gentle way to tell people you've seen their naked pictures on the Internet. Page's big eyes grew yet bigger as he broke the news that not only was she naked in the photos but that she was engaging in a wide array of sexual activities with a wide variety of partners. "Maybe you should go home and check out the site."

"I don't know how to use the computer." She made the statement sound like an accusation.

Andy explained that he and I could be mistaken. "Maybe it isn't you at all." He held her hand and asked if she had a rose tattoo.

Her horrified expression provided one clue. The blood draining from her face provided another. Her holding a napkin over her mouth and running to the bathroom was the clincher. As Page disappeared toward the ladies room, Andy looked at me accusingly. As if my finding the photos caused the problem.

I shrugged. "Must have been the clams."

Of course, we both knew that clams were not on the menu that night.

Chapter 28

I found the story when I spread the front page of the *Press of Atlantic City* across the table. Andy and I were in my favorite booth at the Bayside Diner eating breakfast. We'd had a late night showing Page how to search the Web and then consoling her over what she found there. I, for one, believed she was shocked, appalled, and embarrassed. And angry. If Dallas had not already been dead, he would have been wishing he were.

Anyway, I was too tired to read the newspaper as soon as we sat down. I stared out over the water while Andy checked the sports scores in the Philadelphia paper. When I finally unfolded the paper, I spotted the story immediately.

Whatever his shortcomings, Jake Chandler worked fast. The young reporter had another byline in the *Press*. A story about the late Dallas Spenser. Apparently, the kid wanted to ride Dallas Spenser's murder to a staff position, and I thought he just might do it. His story was on page one. Below the fold—but page one. The headline screamed: DEAD AGAIN AGAIN. Below the headline, in smaller type, was an explanation that explained nothing: Twice Drowned Man Resurfaces.

Jake Chandler's article filled three columns except for the space relegated to three photos—headshots of Dallas Spenser and Denver Spears appeared beside a grainy photo of a man bearing an uncanny resemblance to Dallas. The younger man was obviously of lower social and economic status. A renegade son? A younger Dallas?

I read. Dover Snelling, the man in the photo, had been a petty crook from north London. Snelling worked for a small-time hood who specialized in protection. Dover was a bagman collecting money from shop owners in his neighborhood. Not too far into his career in crime, Dover figured out how to skim from the money he carried. For a couple of years, he did well. Too well, it appeared to his superiors, who began to watch their protégé closely. They decided to test Dover and set him up as the bagman for a big haul one night in March almost thirty years earlier. Dover and his partner for that night's caper, Nigel Sims, disappeared, and so did the money. A badly decomposed body assumed to be Dover's was fished from the River Thames in the late spring. It was hard to determine what had ripped his face and extremities apart, but identification was easy. The clothes, jewelry, and I.D. on the corpse belonged to Dover Snelling.

Apparently, the remains did not. Dover, now known as Dallas Spenser, had been spotted on the beach in Loveladies by someone who had known Dover Snelling in England. The sighting had occurred only weeks before Dallas Spenser had been shot to death. The individual who had spotted him was not named in the article.

I studied the three photos. Dover Snelling's transformation into Denver Spears and eventually Dallas Spenser had not been done with plastic surgery. But the changes were more than superficial. Yes, his hair, clothing, and posture had changed, but there was more. The older man, Denver Spears, stared into the camera with a confidence, make that an arrogance, that came with thirty years of outwitting the authorities and everyone close to him—family member, friend, and business associate alike.

My first reaction was to become indignant. "How can they look at *you* when Dallas had *this* in his past?"

Andy remained unflappable. He scanned the story quickly before he answered. "Because I am here and now. That was a long time ago. Who would care now?" He returned to the sports section of his *Philadelphia Inquirer.*

"The person who recognized Dover Snelling, for one." I grew excited as I remembered the man with the British accent. "Remember the guy at the funeral with the cell phone?" As I recalled, the man on the other end of the phone had cared.

"Yeah. You told me that he was upset about Dallas's death. I'm sure it's in my notes." His voice remained calm. I wondered if Andy was making an effort to remain nonchalant in the face of this news.

"What else did I tell you?" I couldn't remember much about the conversation. I continued without waiting for a response from Andy. "They were hitting him up, weren't they? That's what he said. And they were looking for his associate, Frankie."

Andy thought I was right, but he was lost in basketball scores. Or pretending to be. I had a feeling his mind was spinning as he tried to figure out what this news meant. I hoped it was.

"Maybe Frankie killed Dallas. That makes sense, doesn't it?" I knew he wanted to drop the topic—but I couldn't.

Andy peeked at me over the top of the sports pages. His eyes told me that nothing made sense.

"How on Earth did Chandler get this information? How did he do all this research so fast? How can he find it and the cops not find it?"

Andy put down the paper and stared into my eyes. "The cops didn't find it because the cops didn't look. They think they have their answer here. I just don't want to think about this today. I need a break."

I didn't understand Andy. I couldn't think about anything else. Except how I could make Jake Chandler my new best friend.

Chapter 29

After breakfast Andy and I drove up to Barnegat Light for a walk near the lighthouse that stood sentinel at the northern tip of the island. This had been my daily routine when I was writing my thesis. Breakfast at the Bayside Diner. Lighthouse for a walk. Work. Acme. On special days—days I really didn't want to think about the information usage habits of recent business school graduates—I visited the Spray Beach car wash and laundromat. My car was never so clean; my wardrobe never so presentable. Anything to avoid addressing my topic.

I am sure I have visited Barnegat Light on days when the sky did not provide a perfectly clear blue backdrop, but I can't remember those days. I remember the days like this one. The stark white and red of the lighthouse against a perfectly blue sky made a beautiful and a reassuring sight.

Andy and I strolled to the end of the jetty, and I reminisced about earlier visits to Long Beach Island. Whether we were in Ocean City or Cape May or on LBI, Andy liked to pretend he was bored by my stories of past visits. At least, I think he was pretending. I reacted as if he was. I went on with my tales.

"When I was on LBI my friends who vacationed farther north would park at the end of Island Beach State Park." I pointed across the narrow channel to the tip of the peninsula that extended down from the Manasquan River. "They would drive down from Spring Lake and we would wave at each other."

"And you would do this because...?"

"It was fun?" I sounded doubtful.

"I'm happy that I met you." He wrapped an arm around me and pulled me close. "For your sake."

We started for the car. Walking in the opposite direction down the path was a man with a very familiar face. I just couldn't place it. The guy smiled. His was a slick smile. A flirtatious smile. A sexy smile. A smile I had seen before.

"Andy, that guy smiled at me...."

"Some guy smiled at my girl. I'll kill him. Let me at him." Andy turned and feigned pugilism—not very convincingly.

"No. No." I yanked him over to the metal railing. "Pretend you're admiring the rocks." I slipped to his other side.

"Now look past me. See the guy in the brown leather bomber jacket."

"Sure."

"Is he looking at us?"

'That's unlikely since he's walking away from us."

"I can't decide."

"Decide what?" Andy seemed amused.

"Should we wait here until he walks back or should we run back to the car?"

"I vote for the car...but that's just because it's warmer. I'm a little unclear as to what we'll be doing in the car." He leaned on his right elbow and snuggled up to me as if to suggest some possible activities.

"Andy, you have your briefcase, right?" He nodded. "You have the Internet file in the briefcase, right?" He nodded. "If we go to the car, we will find that man's face on the printouts from the Dallas and Page Web site."

I stayed on the walkway to keep an eye on the guy. Andy went to the car and was back with the file before the man returned from the end of the walkway. He'd been standing at the railing looking out to sea for ten minutes.

Andy handed me the file. "Find him."

I opened the folder and flipped through the pages filled with photos of naked people. "See, here he is." I juggled the folder to pull out the page I needed. I still maintain that a strong wind scattered the papers. Andy claims I dropped them unaided.

In either event, all the pages fluttered to the paved surface. Face up. As I looked at the array of sexual content on the ground surrounding me, the headlines flashed through my mind. Porn King and Queen apprehended at Barnegat Light. "Get them. Quick. An elderly couple is coming down the path."

"There's nothing here that they haven't seen—or done."

I pointed to a group shot with my toe. "How about that one?"

"Okay, let's hope they have bad eyesight." Andy knelt to gather the papers and I positioned myself between him and the approaching walkers.

I looked at Andy on the paved surface. The couple would have to suffer from pretty severe myopia to miss the general impression of what was in those photos. Luckily Andy had good hand–eye coordination and moved quickly. By the time the couple passed, all they could see was the folder cover. Unless they happened to stop and look over the railing.

I cleared my throat and nodded at the lone sheet on a rock below—neatly arranged as if on display. Two boys with angelic faces were hopping from rock to rock. They appeared to be eight years old and headed for the rock that held our lost printout.

Andy sighed. "I'll go."

"Be careful." The state had invested quite a bit of money in signs cautioning visitors against doing exactly what Andy was doing now. While he climbed, I flipped through the photos but couldn't find the man's face. I was sure I had seen it among the partiers. I concluded I'd been wrong about the man when Andy climbed back over the railing and handed me the errant sheet.

"See, it was a sign from God. He pulled this out for us."

"And made it so easy." Andy made a great show of cleaning off the front of his pants.

"Don't be dramatic." I shoved the photo in front of Andy.

The stranger was in a threesome article. The M/F/F threesome article that Andy had read first. Andy remembered the accompanying story in astonishing, and somewhat alarming, detail. "I didn't know you liked that story so much."

"I'm an investigator. I'm paid to remember."

I didn't mention that neither of us had been paid for quite some time now. I addressed the task at hand. "The story gives us a good entrée. We can try to entice him into similar activities." I watched the guy for signs of movement but he remained mesmerized by the Atlantic Ocean.

Andy just stared at me.

"We won't do it. We'll just pretend."

Emphatically, Andy made a great show of counting me, himself and then the man. "We don't have the right gender count."

"Well, maybe he likes variety." I was optimistic.

"Maybe we will take the direct approach." Andy's tone suggested that there was no maybe about it. "It's chilly out here. Why don't we go sit in the picnic area and wait for him to finish enjoying the view? When he turns around, we'll make sure you're right. We can take a walk toward him, simply tell him we recognize him, and why. And I hope we can do it soon because I'm getting cold."

We both got a lot colder. From the covered picnic area we kept a discreet watch on the man. A man with an apparently insatiable thirst for salt air. Finally, we watched as he took a leisurely stroll back along the path to the lighthouse. We started our walk to run into him. Then the man disappeared into the lighthouse.

Andy and I spoke in unison. Only he said "great" and I said "oh no."

"I hope he's only reading the posters at the bottom." I spoke optimistically.

"Why? Catching him in such a narrow space makes conversation inevitable. Unless we hurry, we'll meet him when we're going up and he's coming down. In that situation, conversation is not inevitable." Andy grabbed my hand and pulled me forward. Or tried to. "Come on. We spent all this time waiting for the guy. If we don't approach him, it was wasted."

I disagreed. "He has to come out. We can't miss him if we wait at the door."

"You'll be warmer inside the lighthouse." Andy tried cajoling me.

"Especially after I climb the 217 steps."

Andy's face muscles relaxed to indicate that at last he understood my reluctance. "You know, a little exercise isn't going to kill you."

I wasn't interested in arguing about whether or not climbing 217 steps constituted a little exercise. "Why don't you go. You know what he looks like. Try that male bonding thing."

Andy appeared annoyed, but he went. Alone. I was shivering by the time he returned. He was talking seriously with the man, who was certainly more handsome in person than in his pictures. Of course, he was nicely dressed now. Perhaps clothes do make the man.

He was anxious to see the photos. When he did, the sight knocked his legs out from under him. Literally. He staggered.

"I can't believe…I didn't know…I'm going to kill the bastard who did this."

Andy had to break the news. "Sorry, but you're a little late."

Chapter 30

Andy and I were sitting in Kubel's—the original, in Barnegat Light—with our new friend, Tim Davesi, having drinks. Actually, they were having drinks. I was having a Coke. And steak fries. Andy had beer, while Tim chose scotch. The guy needed the hard stuff. From the moment Andy showed him the picture he'd been a bundle of nerves—all raw. Tim had several reasons to worry. He had a girlfriend. He had a job counseling troubled teens. And, unlike many his age who had computer illiterates for parents, his mother was a librarian. "What if she finds it? Oh God. She didn't raise me to...." Words eluded him. He ordered another scotch.

I could see how Tim warranted an invitation to an event like the one pictured on the Spenser's Web site. He was tall. You could tell he was well built even if you hadn't seen the pictures. Traces of his muscular build were easily detectable under his bulky sweater and leather jacket. His features were nicely chiseled and his skin was creamy and smooth. But I was sure it was his smile that won him the invitations. No matter that his mouth was wide and his teeth white and his bite perfect. What made his smile special was the confidence that oozed out of him when his concerned expression vanished in favor of a wide smile and twinkling eyes. Tim Davesi's unabashed grin was itself an invitation. Here was a guy who was up for almost anything. Or at least he had been until he found himself naked in cyberspace.

Tim could barely look at the picture, yet he couldn't take his eyes off the scene. He'd developed a ritual. Glance at the photo. Look away quickly. Turn the photo over to hide the offensive shot. Fondle the sheet nervously. Gulp his drink. Start the ritual all over again. "How long has this been on the Net?"

We didn't know, but Andy guessed. "I would imagine that Dallas put it up shortly after the photo was taken. When was that?"

"Around Thanksgiving. A lot of my friends were home for the holidays and this friend of mine," he shuffled through the photos, and pointed out a nicely shaped posterior, "introduced me to Clarice. She was really hot. She glommed onto me like old gum to a new shoe. I knew I was gonna get lucky from about the first minute I met her. I just didn't know how lucky." He paused. "Well, at the time I thought I was lucky. When she introduced me to Page, I couldn't believe my luck. This...this group grope...it was their idea. They took me to this incredible bedroom in this even more incredible place on the beach. They kept coming up with new ideas, but you know what...they wanted to stay in that bedroom. I wanted to explore other rooms. I figured that big house had a lot of possibilities. I never dreamt they wanted to stay put so they could take these." He picked up the pictures and slammed them down on the table. "I didn't see anyone taking pictures. Who was the creep?"

"He's dead."

"Good."

Andy and I responded with looks of alarm. He looked at each of us in turn and then issued a disclaimer. "I didn't even know the jerk. I wouldn't know him if I stumbled over his dead body."

"Did you ever see the women again?"

The guy rifled through the photos and came up with another shot. "I was there that night."

I glanced at the picture. Who wasn't? It was a group photo. Really more of a crowd photo. Page was the only female.

Tim pointed to what he said was his naked back. I wouldn't have recognized him. His face was obscured by body parts of other guests at the Spenser home. All paying attention to Page.

"I should have known this was too good to be true." He shook his head.

"How did she find you again for the second...?" Andy never came up with the right word. Finally, he moved on. "Did she call you?"

"I don't even think she knew my name. I had a pretty good time, but I never tried to get in touch with her. She had a husband and all. I thought I'd run into her by accident again. The first time, I guess I told her I hang out at Joe Pop's sometimes. She came in one night. She invited me back to the house. She asked if I had any friends to bring along. Not friends, guys. She wanted all guys. So I invited my guy friends."

I glanced at the photo. Apparently, Tim was a very popular guy.

"Did you ever meet her husband?"

"Are you nuts? She said...what she did...what we did...was how she had fun when he couldn't take care of her needs. I remember how she said the words 'needs.'" Tim smiled—a rueful smile, but a smile.

"She was pretty needy, eh?" I asked that question.

Andy asked the practical one. "Could you give me the names of the friends you brought along?"

The guy shook his head. "I didn't know a lot of the last names. This is just a bunch of guys I talk to around town. At this point, I bet most of these fellows would be happy I don't know their names. But that woman, Clarice." He pulled out the original photo. "I bumped into her around town a few times. The first time, she didn't remember me, which kind of surprised me."

And insulted him, judging from his tone of voice.

"She has a house in Harvey Cedars. She's invited me to her parties when we've run into one another."

"Parties. For the lifestyle. That's what they call it. Swinging. Parties. Orgies. Whatever. I went to a couple of them. Never saw Page there, though. I can give you the address." Suddenly all the blood drained from his face. "Oh God. Does she have a Web site, too?"

Chapter 31

The house in Harvey Cedars didn't look like the kind of place that hosted orgies. No neon lights. No erotic photos. No guy out front screaming "all nude, all the time." The cedar-shake shingled house looked more like the place where you planned the local elementary school's annual bake sale. There was an obvious joke to be made but I suppressed the urge to ask Andy what he thought might be cooking inside.

The beachfront house sat at the end of a short block on a narrow stretch of LBI. Drive one block east from Long Beach Boulevard and hit the ocean. Drive one block west and hit the bay.

As we walked toward the house I pouted. Was I the only person on Earth who didn't have a waterfront home? I thought of the house as modest only because I'd gotten used to the gargantuan homes in Loveladies. The three-story home was certainly nicer than anything I'd be moving into in the near future. How did so many people get so much money—and why didn't I have any? I voiced my sentiments to Andy. He thought my minimal net worth had something to do with quitting jobs whenever someone looked at me crooked and spending every cent I got. Maybe he had a point.

A Volvo station wagon and a minivan were pulled up against double garage doors. Several other late model cars were parked along the street, but there was not a pimp-mobile in sight. I couldn't believe we were headed for the right house. "Hey, Andy, the people next door have a purple Jeep. Maybe that's the place." Andy just shook his head and kept walking.

A Valentine's Day wreath adorned with smiling cherubs hung on the elegant Williamsburg blue door that faced the street. Was the decoration a nice touch for the kids? Or did it stay up all year as a signal to alert people that they were in the right place for love?

Andy reached into the center of the wreath and used the tasteful brass pineapple knocker to announce our arrival. A cheerful woman opened the door a nanosecond later. A *very* cheerful woman. She pulled the door open wide as if expecting someone. She didn't appear so much disappointed as puzzled to see us. I assumed she'd been exercising. She wore form-hugging black tights and a halter-top. I figured she had to stay in shape for all those orgies—or maybe those orgies were keeping her in shape. Whatever she was doing worked. The woman's face suggested late forties, while her body would have made any thirty-year-old happy.

"Clarice?" Andy asked.

"Yes?" She sized each of us up quickly.

"My name is Andy Beck. This is my colleague, Meg. Tim Davesi gave us your name."

"Oh, Timmy! Isn't he a sweetheart?" She threw the door wide open. "Do come in." She extended a welcoming arm.

We stepped into a long hallway that I assumed ran along the double garages and led to the front of the house. Beyond a crowded coat rack to which Clarice added my trenchcoat and Andy's jacket, the narrow space was lined with photos all set in summer. Beach scenes. Boating scenes. Birthday scenes. No orgy scenes.

"I haven't seen you two around town before. Are you new here?"

Andy explained that we were only on LBI for a short time. "We've been bunking with a friend of mine in Beach Haven." When Clarice asked how long we were staying, Andy chose not to answer "until we prove I am not a murderer." Instead, he said our visit was open ended. Good call. Clarice continued to lead us into her home, which she might not have done if Andy had introduced himself as a murder suspect.

The hallway led past a kitchen to a wide room full of overstuffed couches full of people. "You're having a party?"

The excitement I sensed in Andy's voice alarmed me. Had he forgotten we hadn't come here to party? These folks took the term get-together very literally, and I wasn't ready to participate. But the gathering seemed tame. Of course, it was Sunday afternoon. The guests were dressed casually and tastefully. Given the stories Tim Davesi had told us, I felt relieved that the guests were dressed at all—although if a group of people wanted to run around naked, this would be the group. I suspected that any time not spent making out was spent working out. The guests ranged in age from perhaps thirty to sixty; each was more attractive than the next. Andy and I might have stumbled into one of those wine commercials where good friends sat around in expensive clothes drinking cheap wine. It all seemed very innocent. If football season hadn't ended weeks before I would have expected to see a game on the wide-screen TV beside the sliding doors that led to a patio in the dunes.

"We're sorry to intrude while you're busy, but we'd like to talk to you for a moment." Andy tried to be direct with Clarice, but she kept putting him off in favor of introducing us to her guests. We weren't trying to be deceitful. We had no choice. So we stayed and we mingled—with a hidden agenda that we'd made no real effort to hide. Every conversation was designed to discover anyone with a motive to hurt Dallas Spenser. We couldn't even find anyone who admitted to knowing Dallas Spenser— although quite a few of the folks knew Page. They didn't say how well.

The group seemed friendly. Conversation was easy. Clarice's husband, whom she introduced only as Steve, poured margaritas for us, and Clarice breezed by periodically with a new tray of hors d'oeuvres. Andy and I worked the crowd separately. With the exception of one man who let his lechery surface—and at every party at least one man lets his lechery surface—I was feeling comfortable. To the man's credit, I don't think he wanted to stare at my breasts. I think he wanted to stare at my legs. But one look at my legs and the legman had to let his eyes return to the top half of my body. Even through jeans it's obvious that my legs are not my best feature.

"Aren't you warm in that big bulky sweater?"

I shook my head.

"You know, I'd like to see what's under those big, wide cables." He made the big and wide cables seem salacious—and that can't be easy. I moved on.

I was growing convinced that Steve and Clarice had a pretty tame social life when someone turned on the TV. I didn't turn around at first but I watched Andy's eyes. He stood two groups away chatting with a fiftyish couple with classic fifty-something silver hair and tan-skin good looks.

At first Andy tried to look away from the screen and focus on the conversation. Increasingly, however, his attention remained riveted on the television behind me. I watched as his face registered amusement, amazement, and puzzlement. I extricated myself from a conversation with a dentist and a woman whom I doubted was his wife. When I turned I understood Andy's confusion. I couldn't make out what the figures on the screen were doing either. Until the camera pulled back.

Oh, oh. I glanced around the crowd. The guests were gathering inspiration from the characters on the screen. I sauntered to Andy's side and whispered, "The TV isn't the only thing getting turned on in this room."

Andy surveyed the action that began to unfold around us. "I think we've wandered into the seventies." He whispered, "I can feel my lapels widening as we stand here. I better move fast if I'm going to get any more conversations going."

"Don't leave me, Andy." I held onto his arm. "I said I was willing to go undercover—not under covers."

Andy smirked. "You've been waiting to use that line since they turned on the TV, haven't you?" I shrugged and he went on. "I just have a couple more people to talk to. If you don't want to play with folks...and I am kind of assuming you don't...then you can go upstairs. I've already checked it out. You'll pass a few people in the living room but there's a deck overlooking the ocean. I'll find you there."

The action had escalated beyond PG13 as I climbed the open stairway out of the party. As I headed upstairs I saw a voluptuous redhead make her move on Andy. I'm not good at reading signs, but even I knew what the woman was signaling. It was her playful attempt to undo his belt that gave it away.

As Andy tried to extricate himself politely from the woman's grasp, I wished his mother hadn't raised him to be so polite. He smiled and redirected the woman's hands to his waist. She still hadn't gotten the message that there would be no action that afternoon—at least with him. To be fair, I wasn't really sure that Andy had actually sent the message yet. A quick wink in my direction told me that I could go upstairs and not worry. I went upstairs. And worried.

Andy was right about what I would find. A couple of couples were huddled in the living room. I hurried through the room with my eyes averted, but I suspected their activities deserved more than an R rating.

After I stepped onto the deck, I slid the glass door closed behind me. I didn't condemn what the partygoers were doing, I just didn't want to be a part of it. Or watch it. Or hear it. Was I being stodgy? Over the years I had turned down every kinky offer I'd ever received. Why? Because I worried that I would become rich and famous and everything I'd earned would be snatched away when someone came forward with tales or, even worse, pictures of my past indiscretions. My reasoning was fairly fallacious since I'd shown no signs of getting rich or famous. But it could still happen. What if I were drafted to run for president? Although I had no plans for the political life, some odd circumstance could arise. I could become a national hero. Or what if I just happened to fall in love with a man who later became president? I didn't want to risk future blackmail—or embarrass the man I would most likely love. I didn't want a blot like photos at an orgy in my file. They really got to me with that permanent record thing back in grade school.

The air on the balcony felt refreshing—although I knew that in five minutes the chill wasn't going to feel so good. The wind blew off the ocean and the sun had already disappeared behind the house. What little sun was left in the day never reached the porch. I leaned on the railing, took a deep breath, and let the wind burn my face. I pretended the Antigua sun created the glow. I wasn't fooled for a minute.

Behind me the door slid open. Before I could turn to check out the identity of the guest who had joined me a set of strong arms slid around my waist. I hoped those arms belonged to Andy, but I had my doubts that Andy had gone shopping since we arrived. I didn't recognize the dark red silk shirt.

"You must be cold out here." The stranger offered a hug for heat.

"I like the cold. Plus, I have this bulky sweater on."

"I noticed. I saw you downstairs. And I wondered what you were hiding under there. You were with a nice-looking guy. Are you two new to the scene?"

I twisted my neck to catch a glimpse of the man. I saw a nondescript-looking man of about forty. One of those men who makes forty look old. He still had the smooth skin of his youth. Unfortunately he had a lot more of it as his hairline receded and his waistline expanded. He looked like any commuter in loafers and wire rims on his way to his job at the bank...or the law firm...or the local high school. Normal. Nice. Married. And, contemporary. Yet, given his come-on, I was fairly certain he had escaped from 1972.

I was about to turn to wrest myself free when I noticed that the man was growing to like me. A lot. He nuzzled my hair with his nose and whispered in my ear. "I'd like to make love with you."

Funny. I always assumed orgies only happened after dark. And then I realized the sun must have slipped below the horizon. The sky was quickly growing dark. The guy was serious. The thought that someone could expect such a corny approach to succeed made me laugh. Rather, it made me want to laugh. He seemed so earnest. I didn't want to hurt him. Yet I couldn't imagine he would take rejection very hard.

"I'm sorry. I...I'm just...it's my first...I'm not sure about this."

The guy tried to sound comforting. Encouraging. Smarmy. Actually, he didn't try to sound smarmy—he just did. "I can help you. I remember my first time wasn't easy." The man's idea of help consisted of massaging my shoulders, which actually felt pretty good. I waited for an opportunity to slip away, just as soon as he got that knot out of my left shoulder.

"You're really tight here." He dug a knuckle into the offending muscles.

"That's good...right there." Suddenly, I remembered where this guy expected the massage to lead. "I really shouldn't have come," I said—a bit lamely, I thought. "My friend, Page...do you know Page?"

"Hey, any friend of Page is a friend of mine." I felt certain he defined friend differently than I did. "I never saw you at any of Page's parties. I know I would remember you." He groaned as if the massage were giving him pleasure. Uh oh...I think *my* massage was giving *him* pleasure.

"Look, your offer is very kind, but I can't do this. I know it's old-fashioned. I'm old-fashioned. I am sorry."

His hands stopped but his fingers remained dug into my shoulders. "You're not supposed to change your mind after you arrive here."

"Yeah? Well, you're not supposed to change your mind after you leave the altar either, but I read the other day that the divorce rate in this country is still over 50 percent."

The guy spun me around but never relinquished his hold on my shoulders. "Don't get cute with me. You know why you came here."

I got a good look at the man's face for the first time. Well, the first time in person. The last time I saw the face it had been sitting on top of a body wrapped—if you call a big red bow wrapping—as a birthday gift for Page. The man had looked much happier in the birthday photo. As he stared at me, his eyes were narrow slits. Actually, his eyes and his mouth were narrow slits. How seriously was this guy taking my rejection? "There are so many women here. You don't need to be with a ninny like me who's frightened. I saw a lot of beautiful women...."

The man cut me off. "They're all taken." He sounded disappointed. Actually, he sounded disgusted. "When I saw you here I thought I still had a shot."

"Don't get down about it." Actually, I could understand why he was a little less than ecstatic. Getting rejected at an orgy must warrant three years of therapy, minimum. "That's only the first act going on now. There will be a second...maybe a third."

"They'll all be tired after this." The guy's attitude threatened to depress me.

"Is your wife here?"

"She's busy; I saw her."

"Can't you join her group...or any of the groups downstairs?" The guy shrugged. "I guess, but I'm really kind of shy."

I wanted to discuss his claim of shyness, but Andy chose that moment to fight his way through the billowing curtains. I introduced him to the man who responded with a curt, "No last names. That's the rule." He neglected to provide even his first.

"This fellow and I were chatting until you were finished." I smiled encouragingly.

"Well," said the guy, slipping back into his lounge lizard persona, "maybe the three of us could find a secluded spot...."

"Some other time." Andy punched the guy's arm jovially. "We really weren't aware there was a party when we dropped by."

The unnamed man did not seem happy. I eyed his wedding ring. Maybe he could get lucky when he got home. If his wife wasn't too exhausted.

"Andy, he knows Page." I wrapped an arm around Andy's waist and pulled him close. I wasn't sure the partier had given up yet. On either of us.

"Really. It seems a lot of people around here do. Did you ever meet her husband, Dallas?" Andy hugged me tight.

"The guy who bought it up on the beach in Loveladies? Never met him." He did that smarmy thing again. "Page liked to have me around when he was out of town. If you get my drift." Then he let loose a lascivious laugh. Based on his photos on the Web, I guess he earned the right.

"So you posed for the pictures willingly?" Andy asked with forced innocence.

The guy changed from a swinging lothario to an insecure pre-teen in three notes. "Ah...ah...ah. What pictures?" Any blood that had been left in his face drained quickly.

"You haven't seen the Web site?" Andy sounded cheerful, even chipper.

"W...w...Web site?"

"Yeah. I thought I recognized you." Andy spoke as if he were asking if the two took the same train to work in the morning.

"I don't know about any pictures...any Web site." The guy was a collage of emotions—anger, disbelief, nervousness—all badly hidden under a pretense of casual conversation. He looked from Andy to me to Andy in search of clarification. I started to hum "Happy Birthday."

"Me. In the bow?"

I nodded.

"Well, you two enjoy. I gotta run." And with that he did. He didn't even stay around long enough to ask for the Web site address.

I felt a little bad for the guy. A little. "So, what did you find out?"

"I found out they have a spa on the third floor." Now Andy was doing the smarmy thing. Of course, I found the act cute when Andy did it.

"But I didn't bring a bathing suit," I protested with my best impression of wide-eyed innocence.

"I won't look."

"You're not the one I'm worried about." I shook my head. "There isn't enough chlorine in the world...."

Andy gave me a big hug. And a big kiss. And the reassurance that we could lock the door. I didn't think locking the door was in the spirit of the lifestyle. I was beginning to feel like a voyeur. "If we aren't going to participate—I mean really participate—I don't think we should stay. We can be home in twenty minutes."

Andy grabbed my hand and we ran down the stairs. Clarice was still playing the hostess although she explained she was just about to join the fun.

"What about you two?"

"Clarice, we really appreciate your hospitality, but we've got to run. We didn't realize you were having a get-together this afternoon." Andy seemed completely unruffled by the proceedings. "We just wanted to ask you a couple of questions, but we'll stop by again."

We grabbed our coats off the rack by the door and headed out. Then Andy pulled one of those Columbo moments. He stopped and turned back to our hostess.

"Clarice, do you have a Web site?"

"My sons do. Steve and I don't. But I have e-mail." She smiled broadly and sounded ready to exchange addresses.

"The reason I ask, Clarice." Andy seemed pained to break the news—especially after we'd accepted her hospitality. "The reason I ask is that Page does...well, actually, Dallas does...did. But the site is still up."

We didn't have to explain any further. From her expression, she knew what Andy was telling her.

Chapter 32

The next day I dropped Andy at the train station. He was off to ride New Jersey Transit in search of his alibi witness. I headed to the *Press of Atlantic City* in the hopes of finding Jake Chandler, the man I was supposed to make my new best friend. I didn't want to take a chance on getting blown off over the phone. And, I wanted to see his face when he spoke.

It was a dumb idea. I had no reason to believe that Jake had a story to submit that day, or that he would deliver any story in person. Yet as I drove south on the Garden State Parkway, I felt confident that I would be spending the afternoon with Jake Chandler. I attributed this assurance to a false belief that I am, in some way, psychic. I have no remarkable stories to support this belief, but I believe that someday I will have a tale of psychic ability to tell (beyond my prescience that a phone ringing at dinnertime means a call from a telemarketer asking me to change my long-distance carrier).

I couldn't imagine that Chandler would refuse to see me. After all, he didn't know I had no new information about Dallas's murder. I figured I would congratulate him on his recent bylines and pump him for information on the investigation. I knew he'd want something in return. As I drove, I tried to come up with a piece of information that was innocuous, yet would make for a fair trade. I didn't know much more than what I had read in the papers. I did know that the cops were interested in the widow, and her ex-boyfriend, but Chandler already knew that.

The *Press of Atlantic City* is located in a modern building on West Washington Street in Pleasantville. I don't know what I expected, but one look at the glass structure and I lost my nerve. Dealing with a reporter was one thing. Dealing with the organization that filled the office building was another. Plus, I didn't even know if as a freelance writer Chandler had his own workspace there.

I cruised the parking lot twice but did not spot Jake's distinctive vehicle. I considered waiting in the parking lot in the hopes of running into the young reporter accidentally. Briefly. From what I could figure, every parking space in the lot in front of the building could be seen from the windows. All-day stalkers would be easily spotted.

Wouldn't there be a dive nearby where reporters hang out? I think I was living in the 1930s. Or at least a movie from the 1930s. Nonetheless, I drove around hoping to find Chandler's car outside a seedy bar. I found neither. No car. No bar. I checked the newspaper's parking lot again but it appeared that Jake Chandler was not around. I considered going inside and asking for him just to make sure. If my visit served no other purpose, at least I could read the plaque on the impressive chrome sculpture in front of the door. But walking in the door would make my visit official, and that was something I wanted to avoid.

Plan B. If Chandler wasn't at work, maybe he was working at home. I needed to find a phone book first, but after miles of aimless driving, I was beginning to despair of ever finding one. I was asking for directions to the local library when a kind business owner suggested I use their white pages. Luckily, they had a complete set, and I found a Jake Chandler listed in Ocean City. I could only hope it was my Jake Chandler.

The address given for Chandler, Jake, belonged to a modest two-story Victorian. The house was more gray than white, although I'm pretty sure that the paint had once been white. The structure had seen better days but suited the struggling reporter. Or would if he lived there—I still wasn't sure. But as I was studying the building from a parking space across the street, Chandler suddenly charged right by the house, heading to a smaller structure in the back. Even at thirty yards, I could see the scowl firmly in place on his features. He charged across the small porch and went inside slamming the door behind him. I could hear the bang across the street.

I pondered my next move. Did I want to catch the reporter in such a foul humor? I couldn't think of any upside. I could think of the downside. Many downsides. A day wasted. I consoled myself that at least I had learned where he lived. I'd come back again in hopes of finding him in a better frame of mind.

I'd started the car when Chandler ran back down the path in jogging attire. He was still scowling. I reconsidered. Maybe a nice run would cheer him up. Make that a nice ride. He leapt into his car, gunned the engine, and roared off, leaving a cloud of exhaust behind him. I followed as the car zigzagged across town to 23rd Street, where he parked his car in the beach block—just beyond the sign that said "No parking beyond this sign."

The reporter jogged up the ramp and started down the Boardwalk. My calculation was that the run would put him in a good mood. At least I hoped so. It would be easy to bump into him when he returned. I'd used the phones where the Boardwalk ended before. Of course, he didn't know that. He might be surprised to find me when he jogged back to the car, but would he be dismayed? I didn't think so.

It was a beautiful day for hanging out on the Boardwalk. I was surprised to find that I was one of the few enjoying the sunshine. I leaned on the railing and watched the low surf break lazily against the beach. Nature was mellow that day. The few clouds in the sky were white, puffy, and moving at a slow pace across the clear blue sky. The air was not yet warm but the wind packed no uncomfortable chill. The relentless breeze was notable only for its whirring in my ears—the noise that made me wonder if I would hear a jogger's footsteps on the wooden planks. I grabbed a book out of the car and settled on the bench that faced down the Boardwalk so I wouldn't miss Jake Chandler's return.

I was lost in my book when he jogged back. I didn't see him, but he saw me. "What are you doing here?" He didn't sound happy to see me. If the run had improved his mood, my appearance had apparently ruined it again.

"I saw your car." At least I'd learned something from Detective Petino. "I figured you were jogging so I thought I'd wait."

"You know my car?"

I looked down the ramp to the heap parked at the bottom. "It's pretty distinctive, Jake."

The reporter stood with his hands on his hips and studied his car. "Yeah, I guess it is." He sounded pensive. "Ironic, isn't it. I just love classic cars. That's my only real hobby."

I wasn't interested in Jake's hobbies. I wanted to talk about Dallas Spenser, Denver Spears, and Dover Snelling. Andy and I had taken to referring to the murder victim by initials—"DS" referred to Dallas in all of his manifestations. "When I saw your car, I thought I'd take advantage of the coincidence. I've wanted to talk to you but hesitated to call. Can we speak off the record?"

Chandler appeared interested. "If I can ask you a few questions on the record." He wiped sweat from his forehead with the cut-off sleeve of a Boston College sweatshirt.

I didn't want to say anything on the record if I could avoid it. "Look, we got along at the funeral...."

"At that point, I didn't know you were the prime suspect's girlfriend."

"You hinted at that before. Who told you Andy was the prime suspect? Not who hinted—who told you?"

"No one had to tell me, Ms. Daniels. Anyone can see that." He pulled his shirt up over his face to catch the sweat that continued to flow.

"But it's ridiculous. What about the person who recognized Dallas as Dover Snelling?"

"You mean Nigel Sims's sister, Pamela Clark." He laughed. "You should see her. She is the sweetest woman in the world. No way. I bet she wouldn't even know how to get her hands on a gun, let alone shoot one."

"But that whole English crowd is full of some pretty nasty characters." I feigned knowledge I really didn't have.

"In their heyday, maybe. Now? They're just a rather pathetic, overdressed crowd of small time hoods sitting around with fake hair and bad teeth wondering how they lost their hold on the neighborhood."

I pressed for names, but he either didn't know them or wouldn't provide them.

"The money they extorted from Dallas was just their pension plan. Like Social Security. Not a lot, but enough to keep them going. They liked getting their little wire transfer from Dallas every month. They didn't want him dead."

"What about that other family of his? That family that showed up in Philadelphia."

"It seems to me that Emily Spears should have as good a reason as anyone to kill Dover Snelling. But the cops aren't looking at her. You know they think your boyfriend did it, at Page Spenser's request. They figure he'll go down for it. They're less sure they can nail her on the conspiracy story. If I were you, I'd get out while you can. With a little dignity and your reputation."

"Can I say something on the record?"

"Sure."

"Andy did not do it."

"I'll be sure to mention that. When I do write about Beck's role, I'll call you for a statement. In the meantime, keep reading the paper. There's more." The words were accompanied by a teasing smile tinged with pride.

Jake Chandler had no reason to look so smug as he jogged back toward his car. I don't think he even realized that he'd slipped and given me Pamela Clark's name.

Chapter 33

If Jake Chandler wouldn't give me names in England, maybe Pamela Clark would. I called her from the bank of phones at the southern end of Ocean City's Boardwalk. Jake's article had said the person who recognized Dallas Spenser as Dover Snelling lived in Cherry Hill. Luckily, she and her husband were listed as Mark and Pamela. It wasn't easy to persuade Mrs. Clark to see me or even to stay on the phone. Nigel Sims had died at Dover Snelling's hands. She didn't care about justice for Dallas Spenser. I was hoping she would care about Andy, a man falsely accused.

I pleaded Andy's case on a personal level. (If they arrest him they'll never bother looking for the right person.)

I pleaded for justice on an abstract level. (I don't want an innocent man to pay for a crime he didn't commit.)

I pleaded her brother's case. (You should care about justice for your brother; he never got justice.)

Then I tried empathy. (It seems that killing Dallas was not a bad thing, but Andy didn't do it.)

I think that last argument won her over.

The beautiful morning had been only a brief respite from relentless clouds that accumulated threateningly as I drove through the Pine Barrens. I interpreted the weather as a sign—and not a good one. During the drive up Route 40, I practiced opening gambits. I didn't even know what I wanted, or expected, to find out, let alone know how to get to it. By the time I was on Route 38 in Cherry Hill, I still had no idea.

The directions Mrs. Clark had provided were amazingly complete and accurate. I found the neighborhood easily. The sky was dark gray as I turned into the housing development. The rows of brick and clapboard split-levels had served suburban families since the 1960s. The three-bedroom home with attached garage that the Clark family lived in was indistinguishable from the others on Mockingbird Lane. I imagined residents checking the number on the mailbox each night to select the right driveway, just as I did on my first visit.

Oliver's Jeep barely fit into the paved drive behind a two-door Honda. I picked my way up the flagstone path to the front door at precisely two-thirty. A wreath festooned with patriotic icons bore a "welkommen" greeting. Under the intertwined vines, I found a brass knocker and signaled my arrival with three quick knocks.

The door was answered promptly by a pudgy woman of about fifty with the slightest traces of white in remarkably vibrant red hair. I recognized her immediately from Dallas Spenser's funeral. She was one of a half dozen people who had studied the body so carefully that I figured she had come only to make sure Dallas was really dead.

Mrs. Clark could not suppress her natural warmth. Her words said she was reluctant to admit me, but her manner was inviting. She led me the two steps across the flagstone entrance area into a small overfurnished living room decorated in every shade of pink and rose known to man and, I suspected, a few heretofore unknown. I carefully avoided assorted tea cups and figurines as I made my way to the doily covered sofa.

"Your home is lovely," I said sincerely. Mrs. Clark's house reflected care and personality. A lot of personality.

Mrs. Clark settled into a chair as overstuffed as she was. Her feet just skimmed the sculptured rose carpet. "So what might I be doing for you?" I got the feeling she'd rehearsed the hostility—but not long enough. The act wasn't convincing.

"I'm not sure." I flashed an apologetic grin. I provided the details on recent events from my perspective. In the midst of my account, she dropped to her feet. "Oh, the tea! Just you wait here a moment."

With that the plump figure in a pink pleated skirt and sweater set disappeared through the dining area. I had barely a moment to study the dried and pressed flowers on the walls when she reappeared.

"I had it all set. I almost forgot." She laid a silver tray on the table in front of me. "Now, this will make you feel better. Having to go through this horrible ordeal." She quickly filled a cup with tea. "This always does the trick." Mrs. Clark rested the teapot on the tray and offered me a cup and saucer of fine pink and white china with one hand and a matching bowl of sugar cubes with the other. Her eyes widened as I removed four cubes with the silver tongs she provided. I stopped at four lumps based on a sense of propriety. I had no idea that being a P.I. required drinking so much tea.

"What makes you think your boyfriend will be blamed for the murder if he didn't do it?" Mrs. Clark settled back with her tea.

I told her about Andy's visit to the police station. "I don't think he's a very good suspect, but he's the only one tied to the crime by physical evidence. But the evidence is old. Just coincidental."

"How can I help you?" She emphasized the word "I" with a tone of bewilderment.

"You see, Mrs. Clark," I took a polite sip and leaned forward to slide the cup and saucer onto the tray, "I don't know what you can possibly tell me, but I just can't wait for them to cart Andy off to prison."

The woman nodded sympathetically and sipped the brew as I spoke. All traces of her hostile act were long gone. "Now, dear." She smiled sweetly. "That's not going to happen."

"It's going to happen to someone." I sighed in exasperation.
"Like me?" Her voice took on a defensive edge.
I looked shocked. "No. No. Really. That's not why I came. I never thought...." I sputtered. "Never. Not for a minute." My face screwed into a million lines. "You didn't, did you? I wouldn't consider it a shortcoming."
"Nor would I." Mrs. Clark let go a raucous laugh. "No, I didn't. But I wish I had."
She struggled out of her chair and refilled her teacup. She held the teapot over my full cup and frowned.
"Oh, my," I said, grabbing the saucer from the tray. "I've been prattling on." Mrs. Clark didn't flinch at my use of the word "prattle." She smiled approvingly as I gulped the tepid amber liquid. I swallowed with difficulty as she topped off my cup with the last thing I wanted—more tea. I grimaced behind her back and swallowed as she waddled back to her chair.
"No, I didn't kill Dover Snelling." She settled into the deep pink upholstery. "I'm sorry, Dallas Spenser. Same difference. Scum is scum." She took a sip of tea. "I never forgot Dover Snelling. Never. He killed my brother. I believed it then. I believed it all those years. I believe it now." She set her cup firmly in the saucer she balanced in her left hand. "We never got to bury Nigel. There's no grave. Nothing to remember him by. My mum, God rest her soul, believed Nigel was alive until the day she died. She passed on, you know, just a few years after Nigel disappeared. His going killed her. Dover killed her too, really. Nigel was the light of my mum's life."
With effort she climbed off the chair and pulled a picture from a shelf behind me. The photo, a snapshot really, showed three teenagers in dated clothes that probably constituted their Sunday best. The three lined up in what appeared to be a cramped backyard of a small row house. "That's me there in the center. With my two brothers." She handed me the ornate silver frame. I'd already guessed that Nigel was the sullen figure on the right before she told me. "And that is my brother Henry who lives in Toms River."

Mrs. Clark left the frame in my hands and settled back into the chair, her eyes glistening with tears.

"Nigel wasn't a bad boy," she said after a few moments. "My family, we weren't what you would call well off. Nigel just wanted more. He fell in with the wrong crowd to get what he craved. He was quite handsome, you know."

Actually, I didn't know. The photo was a grainy black and white shot snapped by an unsteady hand. Nigel Sims, full of the bravado of his twenties, stared into the camera. Thirty years later I could still feel the disdain. Contempt for the ridiculousness of the middle class convention of family photos poured from his eyes. And it was his eyes that captured my attention. They seemed sharp and clear, unlike the soft face that surrounded them. The face was not disfigured by any ungainly features, yet it appeared muted by adolescent pudginess. I suspected that if he had lived, he would be built like his sister.

Pamela Clark's plump face puffed out further with pride. "Oh, he looked so smart. Made quite a good salary." I smiled at the term salary. "Spent every penny, he did. Should have saved." Mrs. Clark hesitated. "What would it have mattered? Maybe it's good he didn't." A sense of pride crept into her tone. "He'd show up in these fancy silk suits. He was quite fastidious about his appearance, Nigel was. All my girlfriends were quite smitten." She nodded to confirm Nigel Sims's charm. "Twenty-six years. Twenty-six bloody years. He was only twenty-six when Dover killed him. He didn't ever get to marry. Or have children. My poor baby brother." Mrs. Clark laid the teacup on the table next to her and pulled a tissue from the box beside the cup. "I'm sorry." She appeared embarrassed as she wiped her eyes. "It's just that he'd still be young. He'd still be handsome."

She blew her nose hard. I smiled at the surprisingly strong roar.

"I only saw Dover Snelling once. Before last week that is. But I remembered. I never forgot him. I saw him once. The last night he and Nigel worked together. Dover, he came into the pub to meet Nigel. And I'll admit it. I was besotted. I was at a table with my beau. Not a serious beau, mind you. I only met Dover for a few minutes. But he was so handsome."

Dallas? Dallas Spenser? Hard to believe from what I had seen in the coffin, but it must have been true. Mrs. Clark's claim was only one among many.

Her bright blue eyes gazed into space wistfully. "A redhead like me." With her pudgy hand, she patted her short, stiff page-boy. "And there was something about him. Something exciting. Something dangerous. That's why I knew. I knew when they found that body. I always believed that Nigel wouldn't run away with the money. I knew. I did. But in those days we didn't have the tests we have now—and the condition of the body...." Mrs. Clark was unable to continue. I sat silently waiting for her to regain her composure. "And then after all these years, there he was." Her eyes widened at the recollection. "It was so simple. My nephew Parker, my brother Henry's boy, has a house in Harvey Cedars. I was walking on the beach with him and his family. I glanced at the couple walking in the opposite direction on the beach and there he was. I recognized him right away. Not a doubt in my mind. It was Dover Snelling. Just walking along with his beautiful wife. Rich. Happy." She spit out the words. "He had the things Nigel wanted and should have had. But never will."

"What did you do when you saw him? Did you speak to him?"

Mrs. Clark shook her head. Her lower lip quivered as she fought to go on with her story. "I knew there could never be any doubt that Nigel was dead. Never again. That was his body they fished out of the river." She dabbed at her eyes. "I got agitated but fought to control myself. And I succeeded. No one understood what was wrong. I tried to stay calm so I could watch and learn. And I did. I watched them return to that...that...palace...a right ugly palace, mind you, but huge—a size fit for a king."

Mrs. Clark stared into space. "As soon as I got to my nephew's house, I called London. Right away. To my family—I have three cousins who still live in the north of London—and then to mates of Nigel's. And you know what his old cohorts told me?"

She paused for dramatic effect. "They knew." Her voice faded. "They knew. All along they knew and they never told us." Her hand flailed within the confines of the high-backed wing chair. "My beautiful little brother, dead. They knew it before my mum died. They could have told her. But you know what they did?" Again, she spat out her words. "Nothing. They let that rat live."

Her face grew red. "When I called, they laughed. I heard them. And then Francis Whitton, he was Nigel's mate, says, 'Don't you go getting even with him or nothing. He's a big source of revenue for us, old Dover, he is.'" She mimicked the tough accent. "They was the ones who told me that he weren't Dover no more. They said he now used the name of Dallas Spenser. So I got my niece to alert the police in London. They didn't care no more. So I got her to call the newspapers. The tabloids, you know. But they didn't care neither."

"Did you call the local police in Loveladies?"

"We were talking about what to do next when the news came…he was dead. After that my nephew said we should stay out of it. It wouldn't look good. But then that reporter…I don't know how he found us but he did. He was here within two days. He wouldn't say how he found us or how he knew. But he knew, and he put the story in the paper. At least he didn't put our names in. How did you…?"

"How did I find your name?"

She nodded.

I told her that Jake Chandler had let her name slip. I felt protective of the reporter. "He didn't mean to tell me. I don't even think he knew. I was asking him some questions and he told me how…well, how not guilty…you were."

Pamela Clark chuckled as I changed the subject. "How did Dallas—sorry, Dover—get away with it? His family must have identified the body."

"No family. Just one of his old girlfriends. He had a slew of them. This one...I think he used this poor girl. She was built a bit odd. She didn't have many dates, I imagine. So my thought was that she made easy prey for Dover. I think she really loved him. She swore the body was Dover's."

"Do you remember her name?"

She shook her head as she pondered my question. "She had a pretty name. I remember thinking she was foreign but she wasn't. Just her name was. Isabella. Francesca. Fabiana. Something Spanish or Italian. The poor miss. A sad case by any name, to get tangled up with Dover Snelling. Not smart."

"Tell me about it." My shoulders slumped. Mrs. Clark observed me with horror. "Oh, no. Oh, God no. I never even met him. Please." My words faded.

"Honey, I don't know who killed Snelling, but if you find out, thank them for me. Better late than never." She picked up her tea and hoisted the cup as in a toast.

"No one in England did it, did they?" My voice betrayed my disappointment and resignation.

"It didn't seem that way to me. The scum he worked for knew he was alive. By the time they found him, he was doing okay. Married for money. They got a tidy sum from him each year. They told him to call it his tithe. They liked Dover...Dallas... whatever...alive." Her smile was comforting. "If you came to find out if I'm the culprit, I have to disappoint you." She raised her eyes toward the ceiling. "Maybe I let my dead mother down, but I didn't do it."

"Do you know a guy named Frankie in England?"

She thought hard and then said no. "Why?"

I explained about overhearing someone talking about Frankie at the funeral. She thought again. "No. I don't recall a Frankie."

I felt exhausted by disappointment as I said good-bye to Mrs. Clark and climbed into the Jeep. The petite round English woman stood waving on her tiny porch as I drove away through scattered raindrops.

Even as she shrank in my rear view mirror, I could sense her benevolence. I didn't think I'd found my murderer in Nigel Sims's sister. She'd given me home-baked cookies for the ride home.

Chapter 34

J ust because Mrs. Clark wasn't a murderer didn't mean her
brother or her nephew wasn't. I checked both names in
the phone book. No Henry Sims. No Harry Sims. One
Parker Sims. Listed with an address in Harvey Cedars. I
was fairly certain that Parker Sims had nothing to hide, but I
wanted to be the judge of that firsthand. I didn't want to follow him unnecessarily. Just size him up. Take a look. To judge
the book by its cover.

"The cover of the Talbot's catalog?" Andy asked when the
family came onto the porch of their faux Victorian in Harvey
Cedars.

Okay, the family did look a bit squeaky clean. A proud blond
dad, a proud blonde mom, and two adorable blond children
dressed in best preppie attire. Actually, it appeared the family
consisted of the statistically proper 2.5 children—but we would
have to wait several months to see if the new addition was
blond. I didn't see how the baby could avoid being a tow-head.

"I think the six-year old did it." Andy watched the little boy
as he charged across the porch to hug his mother. The family
headed out for a walk on the beach. Their Irish setter followed
them down the street.

"Hey, this little excursion could have turned out differently. This could have been a family of thugs with the motto 'the family that slays together stays together' tattooed on their arms."

Andy smirked. "Could have."

"They could have had automatic weapons and matching skull and cross bone insignias on the back of their leather jackets."

His smirk deepened. "Could have."

I wasn't going to win. I agreed the entire effort had been futile, but I wasn't concerned about the wasted time. What else did we have to do?

"Eat." Andy gets taciturn when hungry. Plus, I guessed that riding NJ Transit all day made him cranky—especially since he didn't locate the conductor who could be his alibi.

We drove to Kubel's—the mother restaurant at the other end of the island from Kubel's Too. It wasn't until our food was served that Andy and I had a real conversation. Or at least we were attempting a conversation when I spotted Hap Hathaway over Andy's shoulder.

"How are you two doing?" I smiled at Hap as he approached our table alone. The man-child didn't react. He looked at Andy expectantly, so I made the introductions. I didn't mention Dallas. I was surprised that Hap didn't either. He made small talk.

Hap had a buddy who lived in High Bar Harbor. He'd been over visiting him and thought they'd get something to eat. Hap related the details of this decision in painstaking detail. "So my friend, Skipper, he said he felt a little hungry. He works on a fishing boat and sometimes when they are busy, he doesn't eat all day. Not that he had the boat out today. But when he realizes he's ready to eat, he's ready to eat. So we got in his car...."

You get my drift. The conversation went on and on and on. Andy smiled politely and sneaked a steak fry into his mouth whenever Hap glanced my way.

Suddenly, Hap stopped talking. His big blue eyes stared past me. I glanced over my shoulder but I knew. Hap wasn't interested in the action at Kelly's boatyard. I could look all I wanted, but I wasn't going to glimpse whatever Hap saw. He would soon be speaking for Dallas. I knew it. "He's showing me a baby. Are you pregnant?"

My stomach did a backflip. I grew pale, but not as pale as Andy. More than two months in the sun undone by a single comment. Andy's tan disappeared.

I plastered a fake smile on my face. "You're way off this time, Hap." Silently I added, "I hope."

"No." He spoke in his most determined tone. "I see a baby. It's a boy. Twins. I think you are going to have twins."

I snickered. "I think *you* are going to have to come up with a different interpretation."

Apparently Dallas did, because Hap changed his story. He shook his head. "Not twins. One is older." He engaged in more purposeful staring. "All I know is that I am seeing two babies. Both in blue. Two boys."

Aloud, I promised to keep an eye out for the two. Silently, I promised to pick up a home pregnancy test. "Got names?"

Hap stared into space. "I see a J. You know two baby boys with J names?"

"Did they kill Dallas?" Andy asked with a lack of respect that came awfully close to the surface.

Hap delivered his "catching the culprit is not the point" lecture. Persistent little devil that he is, Andy wanted to know "the point."

"The truth," Hap stated seriously. "Your friend here is interested in the truth. I sense that you might have a fear of it."

"Is that Dallas talking?" Andy smirked.

"But I agree wholeheartedly." Hap shook his head and looked at Andy accusingly. "Dallas is slipping away." And so did Hap. Back to the bar. One thing about Hap, he wasn't into long good-byes.

"You barely disguised your disdain." I sneered at Andy, who had launched back into his meal with a vengeance.

"Well, you don't exactly treat him reverentially." He chewed a steak fry. "And besides, there is something odd about that guy."

"Something? Everything about Hap is odd." And it was true. In every aspect of Hap's being, there was just something a little off. His clothes, his haircut, his demeanor. All were close to normal. They just weren't.

"What's with the stare?" Andy asked.

"That's when you know he's going to call on Dallas for a visit—or rather when Dallas is about to pay a call. I think Dallas is the instigator."

"Listen to what you're saying. Do you actually believe him?"

"Of course not. I humor him." Even I noticed that I didn't meet Andy's gaze as I spoke. I took painstaking care in selecting just the right spot to bite into my burger.

"Are you sure that isn't the guy who hit you?"

I doubted it. I didn't think one of Hap's blows could hurt that much.

"Do you think he is completely nuts?"

"No. I don't think so." I considered my answer. "That's what worries me."

"Me, too." Andy excused himself and disappeared into Kubel's bar. He could have been going to the men's room. I had a feeling he wasn't. I leaned out of my chair and looked back into the bar. Andy and Hap seemed to be having a civil conversation. Andy was doing most of the talking. I went back to my burger. I finished the sandwich and Andy still hadn't returned. I peered into the bar again. This time Hap was doing most of the talking. He was staring over Andy's right shoulder.

Moments later Andy returned with a dazed expression on his face. "He says that he is telling the truth. His buddy, Skipper, vouched for him. He said Hap's been this way since high school. Ever since he nearly died in a head-on collision. They had a million stories." Andy took a bite of his sandwich and chewed it slowly before he spoke again. "He says no one put him up to it. He says he doesn't know Petino. He says he does not know Page." He cleared his throat. "He told me my grandmother wants me to remember the chocolate chip cookies she made for me."

"Did your grandmother bake chocolate chip cookies for you?"
"Every time I visited. But all grandmothers do." His eyes met
mine. "Don't they?"

Chapter 35

E-mail from Meg Daniels (DanielsMeg@hotmail.com):

Hi Everyone,

I guess you're wondering why you haven't heard from me lately. Figured I was in Antigua, eh? Wrong. Andy and I are still on Long Beach Island, but I don't have access to a computer regularly so this is the first e-mail I've sent in several weeks. Hope you don't mind my broadcasting one to all of you. I don't like to hog Oliver's computer when we are over here--even if he is currently embroiled in some basketball game.

Andy and I moved out of the Bruin's bedroom at Oliver's. Now Oliver, who will go anywhere there is ESPN2, spends most of his time on our couch--when he isn't dating. Oliver has finally found some mysterious woman--but he refuses to introduce her to us. I don't know whether he views the woman or us as the problem. I am very proud he is dating because I felt I had become his confidante and romantic advisor--no comments please. As his advisor, I recommended redecorating--a bit. So

that's kept me busy over the past month. We're
starting with his bedroom. I'm not asking him to
throw away any of his sports memorabilia--we are
just moving it out of the bedroom. I think he'll
get luckier if Dan Marino isn't watching every
move he makes.

The place where Andy and I are now staying
belongs to two lawyer friends of his--Leslie and
Bob. I haven't met them--they live in DC. The
house (modern and beautiful) sits at the southern tip of the island in Holgate. I don't even
remember these houses from the old days. The
house is spacious and faces south through humon-
gous windows. Except when a Nor'easter blows
through (and a couple have) we can see the top
of the buildings in Atlantic City above the
beach and ocean. The place is really great and
beautifully furnished in a kind of urban country chic look. (Luckily, Andy's friends are considerably wealthier than he is. I guess that's
not really lucky for me in the long run, is it?)

As nice as the house is, I am not getting too
comfortable. I am still visualizing Antigua. I
panic at the slightest sign of spring. If the
daffodils start blooming…or if the Peeps hit the
store shelves…I don't know if I will keep my
cheery disposition. (Again, no comments.) If we
are still here when they turn the traffic lights
on for the summer season, I definitely will not
retain my cheery disposition.

Hanging around Long Beach Island may not be what
I planned on doing this winter, but I am having
fun. I've always liked LBI. Seems more rustic to
me than a lot of shore spots. I guess because of
the trees (I think they are pine but in Harvey
Cedars they must be cedar, eh?) and because it
has no boardwalk. Andy and I sleep late (which
I love) and walk on the beach a lot (which I
love). So what's to complain about?

I will admit that it is a little colder in New
Jersey than in Antigua, but...okay, I have no
rationalization for that. I am a little disappointed but still having fun with Andy. And I
accept that my winter-in-the-Caribbean dream
might not come true--especially since we are
getting frighteningly close to the spring sol-
stice. Andy and Oliver did throw a small tropical party for me...sun lamps, fans, and frozen
drinks. I finally gave up on having only one
pair of jeans and one sweater I could wear outside. I now own a complete wardrobe of identical pullover sweaters (all cotton so they will
work in Antigua too) and jeans in a variety of
denim shades. That has to be it for wardrobe. I
don't want to use up my nest egg here.

Anyway, a lot of restaurants are open on weekends so we go out most weekend nights. Actually,
we go out most nights, period. Luckily Kubel's
Too and Buckalew at this end of the island seem
to stay open all the time. I drive to Stutz's
for fudge. Andy and I are trying all the breakfast places--there are a ton of them open on
winter weekends. I bought a cookbook at the
library (The Bitten Word) and have used it a few
times. All I have to do is pick it up and Andy
takes me out to dinner. He likes the cookbook.
He's just a little concerned about my execution
of the recipes.

The only social trip we made off island was to
Cape May to see George and Claude, who own the
Parsonage B&B there. We couldn't get a reserva-
tion for Valentine's Day, so we celebrated when
we went a few days later. Andy came through with
a romantic dinner (double date with George and
Claude), two rolls of quarters (for playing
skeeball), and so much fudge I got nauseous. I
gave Andy a basket full of socks. I know it
sounds dull but when Andy packed to come north,

he apparently thought it would be warm enough to go without socks. Therefore, my gift was quite thoughtful--if not the height of romanticism. But remember, he gets to keep the basket. He can use it again at Easter--in Antigua, I hope.

I know Andy and I should think about coming to New York or Philadelphia for visits--I'd love you all to meet him. But--we keep thinking we'll be leaving any day now. I do have a rental car now so maybe I will take a ride up someday.

The cops have still not made an arrest in the mur-der--and technically Andy is still a suspect--but they have to find the real killer soon. I want to leave town anyway but Andy, the more responsible party, feels we should wait. He doesn't want to force the police into arresting the wrong person (him). We don't hear much about the investiga-tion. The cops don't tell us anything--although I still run into that homicide detective. We hear so little that I actually like running into him--but all he ever says is that they are making progress. They don't tell the widow anything either. Oh yeah. I forgot to mention the other good thing about this house. It is even farther away from the widow's house than Oliver's. You can't move farther away and stay on this island. We do run into her occasionally. Accidentally? Sometimes I think she has an electronic device planted on Andy.

I hope you all get to meet Andy soon. I am still liking him--even after all these days just hang-ing out together with nothing much to do. I think that is a good sign. No skeletons have crawled out of his closet.

Andy is really keeping up a brave front. I know he is worried, but he tries to hide that from me. He's not doing much investigating at all now except looking for the NJ Transit conductor who

201

is his alibi--or would be if we could ever find him. He couldn't track the kid through the main office so now he rides. And rides. And rides.

I did ride up and down the Bay Head line with Andy fifty times looking for the conductor who took his ticket on the night of the murder. Okay, it was only three times but it felt like fifty. To him, too. He told me if I pointed out Dan and Lori's house in Brielle one more time, he would jump off the train. (Actually, he said push me off the train but since he is already a suspect in one murder I didn't want you to get the wrong idea.)

Our current plan is to leave town as soon as the murderer is arrested. With any luck we will be able to sail around the islands for a bit before we start up the inland waterway to come home. I don't have to start school until September, so that works for me.

Well, I guess you guys have real jobs and real lives, so I'll hit send. Hope you are all well. Write and let me know how you are doing--and if you don't hear back you'll know I am off to Antigua. I really believe we'll only be here a few more days.

Meg

P.S. You can't even see my bruises anymore!

Chapter 36

I checked my e-mail again before Andy and I left Oliver's.

From Suzie:
Meg,
If I don't hear back from you, I'll think you
got murdered.

Are you nuts? You don't know this guy. For all you
know he might really be the killer. And if the
widow is in on the scheme, I would worry about what
plans they have for you. I think you should listen to the police detective. I am only telling you
this because I care what happens to you. And why
did you two have to move somewhere to be alone?

From Tricia:
You are welcome to stay with us in Philadelphia
if you want to get away for awhile. I know Andy
doesn't want to leave the country, but can he
leave the state? We would love to meet him.

From Joy:
No skeletons! No skeletons have come out of his closet?

Come visit. We need to talk.

Joy

P.S. What bruises?

From Nanci:
You really should get some more clothes. If you want to go shopping give me a call. Maybe we could go over to Chestnut Hill. Call me and we can go next week.

From Amy:
Glad that you are still having fun with Andy. Happy to hear that you got to see George and Claude. They sound like a lot of fun. Are you sure you want to stay with Andy through this ordeal? I'm sure he'd understand if you wanted to leave. Maybe you could take classes in summer school--until he sorts out his legal problems.

From Dani:
I don't want to offend you, Meg, and I hope I am not out of line saying this, but has it ever occurred to you that you have really horrible taste in men? You can't really laugh off that Andy is suspected of MURDER. Not jaywalking. MURDER. Have I made my point? I know you can't get back into your apartment for several months, but my sofa bed in the living room is available. I really think you should consider getting away from that guy for awhile.

Dani

P.S. By the way have you ever met his parents? Any of his relatives? What is this friend of his like?

From Lindy:

Face it Meg. You have very bad taste in men. If I am not mistaken, your old boyfriend is currently awaiting trial on some sort of fraud charges. Now you are seeing someone whom the police have reason to believe is the prime suspect in a murder. Think it over kiddo. And come visit. New York is only two hours away.

Lindy

From Katie:

Do you think that someone is trying to frame Andy? If the police are finding evidence to support their charges someone must be feeding it to them. Hearing nothing must be so frustrating. I am sure it will work out just fine. I hope I don't hear from you again for a while because you are off to Antigua. On second thought, please keep in touch with us.

From Kevin:

You go, girl. You sure know how to pick 'em. But if you say he's innocent, I believe he's innocent. Just promise me you won't do any of the following:

*Wait outside for him in the driver's seat with the motor running

*Hide any small packages for him

*Carry something on a plane for him

I am sure he's perfectly innocent.

Kev

From Lisa:

You do remember that you promised to leave me that lovely Ebel watch that your parents gave you for high school graduation, right? If you're

not careful, I'll be wearing it to my wedding--
which, by the way, is September 15. Please stay
alive to get there. Chad and I discussed driving
down there to get you, but we are going to trust
your judgment--for now.

Lisa

From Mia:

Meg, someone is sending out e-mails over your
signature. I just got another one tonight. I
know you didn't send these because in them Meg
claims to have deferred graduate school, sublet
her apartment, and moved into a house on LBI
with her brand new boyfriend who claims to know
the owners whom she has never met. She also
claims that she is staying on Long Beach Island
because her boyfriend is suspected of murdering
his old girlfriend's husband. She also mentioned
that the only reason this murder suspect stopped
seeing the girlfriend regularly (under the guise
of investigating the murder) is that the cops
insisted. I know that no one with your SAT
scores would ever do something so dumb--so write
and tell me what you are really doing.
Worried about you,

Mia

From Eddie Bauer:

Are you ready for summer? Click here to get
ready for the beach.

From Amazon.com:

We've got mystery! Click here to add a little
mystery to your life.

From Air Jamaica:

Super Internet Specials. Click here to get away
from those winter blahs.

Chapter 37

"You know it isn't as bad as it sounds." I was in McNally's in Chestnut Hill with Nanci eating a roast beef sandwich. Actually, I was eating roast beef. Nanci was eating turkey. That was the way it was fifteen years ago, and that was the way it was now. When it comes to food, I can be very traditional—even risk-averse. That's why it was ridiculous for my friends to barrage me with e-mails reacting as if my stay with Andy on LBI constituted reckless endangerment. "You were about the only one who sent back an e-mail that did not attack Andy. They've never met him. How can they jump to the conclusion he is a killer?"

"That's the conclusion the police reached." Nanci stared at her turkey with more interest than was warranted. Her blonde hair flopped over her eyes so I couldn't really detect what she was thinking. "Meg, maybe they have a point. Andy does live a little on the edge. Does he even have health insurance?"

I was beginning to figure out why I never left Long Beach Island except for an occasional investigative foray. My situation did sound a bit unsavory. Unless you knew Andy. He exuded kindness and gentleness. Well, he *could* exude kindness and gentleness. And he always did toward me. I would just have to wait until this situation in Loveladies was cleared up. Then I would introduce him to my friends, and they would love him. Or learn to love him. I had enough battles to fight without fighting with my friends.

"You'll like Andy. You'll just have to trust me. In the meantime, maybe I should think about getting out of this cotton pullover uniform I've got going on. Maybe buy something a little sexier."

Nanci eyed my cotton sweater/jean combo. "You couldn't look less sexy."

With that supportive remark, we set out shopping. The day was cloudy, gray, and cold. The type of day that really lets you know you are not in the Caribbean.

Nanci and I ventured in and out of the same shops we had visited for years, plus a few new ones, in search of something more alluring than my jeans combo. None of the stores competed with Frederick's of Hollywood, but we did see a few items that might have spiced up my image. In the end, however, I just couldn't spend any of my dwindling funds on outfits for the northern climes. I still clung to the hope I'd be leaving for Antigua any day now.

"Oh no." I was comparing two items I absolutely did not need in a store full of items no one really needed when I saw them. All cheerful and yellow. Announcing spring's arrival.

"What's wrong?" Nanci responded with alarm to the panic in my voice.

"The daffodils are here."

Nanci glanced from me to the tin bucket filled with yellow flowers and then back to me. Clearly, she did not see the problem. "So?"

"So, I'm not supposed to be in the northeast U.S. to see the daffodils come out. I'm supposed to be in Antigua."

"They're imported, Meg. None of the bulbs in my yard are blooming. The daffodils aren't blooming yet. Really."

For the first time since the night I'd sat howling on the beach, I felt tears welling in my eyes. I was contemplating my colossal-loser theory when I heard the voice.

"Ms. Daniels? Meg?" The voice came from behind me. I turned and looked into a set of pale blue eyes in creamy skin surrounded by soft reddish brown curls. "You might not remember me. I'm Bonnie Spears. Emily Spears's daughter. You visited our house."

I remembered her; I just didn't recognize her. She was conservatively dressed, and I thought she appeared right at home on the upper end of Germantown Avenue. For that matter, she would have looked at home strolling in the English countryside.

"Bonnie, how nice of you to remember—and to say hello." I smiled warmly and participated in her idle chit-chat. Apparently she helped out in the store ten hours per week to get some experience. I was up from the shore for the day to get some clothes. School was going well for her. I was having a good time on Long Beach Island. Okay, I fibbed. I responded to all her comments, but my mind was racing. What an opportunity. There had to be something I needed to know that Bonnie could tell me. I read meaning into every coincidence in my life. Or at least I try to. I am still trying unsuccessfully to find meaning in coincidental happenings from years ago. Yet I cling to my belief. If some greater force put Bonnie and me together in this shop, there had to be a greater meaning. I just couldn't figure out what it was. Luckily Bonnie had the maturity of someone much older and kept the conversation going until I had organized my thoughts.

"Bonnie, I've thought of you from time to time. Wondered how you were coping."

Bonnie's expression gave the nonverbal response, "what do I have to cope with?" Her lips maintained that she was just fine—as if nothing unusual had happened to her in the recent past.

"Has your brother been home?" I casually returned the hand-painted mirror I'd been considering to the shelf. Too casually—it fell to the floor with a thud. Luckily it landed on an Oriental area rug—face down. As I scooped it up with a quick glance toward the service desk, I flipped the mirror over. No breakage. The woman at the register didn't catch my action. I was saved from buying the item as well as from enduring seven years of bad luck. The only bad luck was that I didn't see Bonnie's face as she responded.

"We haven't seen James since Christmas."

"Bonnie, I hate to pry," I lied. "But I'm curious. Are you and your brother close?"

She shrugged. "I guess we are. But he's in college now. He doesn't have too much time for me. For us. But my mother understands."

"Didn't he come home when the news broke about your father?"

Again, she shrugged. "No. He called a couple of times. But James didn't care. You know, Meg, we didn't know our father. Our mother took such good care of us...." She stared into space. "We missed having a father, but we didn't miss that father. Now that I know what he did...who could miss a man like that?"

I thought Bonnie better get to a therapist quickly before she showed up on a tower with a high-powered rifle. No one could handle betrayal this well.

"Have they found anything new about Dallas Spenser's murder?" Bonnie used the name with detachment as if the victim were not her father—well, her father using a new name.

Now it was my turn to shrug. "They aren't going to tell us anything." Beside me I sensed Nanci jockeying for eavesdropping position.

"You haven't heard anything at all?" For someone who claimed to have no interest in this man, Bonnie developed a surprisingly urgent tone in her voice.

"I guess the police are exploring lots of avenues." I didn't even believe the words as I said them. They were exploring one avenue. The wrong avenue.

I felt the stare on my back. Behind me a young man fidgeted nervously. The tall kid had a comical look largely because his long body perched on top of feet that were way too small. If she hadn't said that James was at school, I might have thought the two were brother and sister. But given the admiration in his gaze as he stared at Bonnie, I suspected that they had a different type of relationship.

"I think your friend is anxious to go."

She smiled graciously but made no effort to introduce him or include him in our group. "We're on our way to his house in the country, but I wanted to say hello." She said how nice it was to see me and excused herself—much to her friend's relief.

"Who's the girl?" Nanci tried to whisper.

"Long story. The victim's daughter."

"The boy is the son of the woman who owns this place."

"You know him?"

"No." She spoke through gritted teeth. "I heard him call her 'mummy.'" She held a string of tiny dolls in front of me. "Do you think I need these?"

"No one needs these," I replied through similarly clenched teeth.

Together we pretended to study the crafts as we watched Bonnie with the young man. As she neared, he pulled a hand full of daffodils from behind his back and extended them in her direction. Bonnie smiled and bent her head to smell the flowers. That was when I recognized her. Bonnie had been at her father's funeral, but with slicked back hair and wearing a leather jacket. She'd leaned so far into the casket that I'd included her in the group that came to verify Dallas's death. I hadn't recognized her at her home, but as she leaned forward it became so obvious. If she had no ill feelings, why had she checked out the body so closely? If she cared so little, why did she come to his funeral? When had she found out he was dead? When had she found out that Denver Spears was still alive and living as Dallas Spenser?

"That kid doesn't like you, Meg. He scowled at you the entire time you were talking to the girl."

"What?" I was watching Bonnie too intently to focus on Nanci's remark. Bonnie Spears called good-bye to a dark-haired woman behind the counter. Cessie, the woman with a light British accent, a nametag, and wide hips that seemed out of place on an otherwise wiry body, wanted to know if they were coming back later that afternoon. When the young man answered, he spoke slowly and deliberately in a childlike voice.

"He didn't like you." Nanci repeated.

"He doesn't know me. He probably doesn't like anyone who takes his girlfriend's time."

"I doubt if that's his girlfriend. She's way too cool for him." Nanci became distracted by hand-painted glassware from Central America and wandered away—as far away as one could wander in the small space. I continued to watch Bonnie and her friend through the window.

So did Cessie. She played with her short brown curls as she watched the twosome climb into a dark green van. Only after the van pulled away did the woman ask if she could help me. "Is there anything I can do for you?"

I pulled a bunch of daffodils from the tin bucket. "You must love daffodils too. I notice that's the only fresh flower you stock."

"Don't much care for flowers myself, but the customers seem to. Especially this time of year." The woman did not make eye contact.

Drawing Cessie into casual conversation wasn't going to be easy. "Is your son Bonnie Spears's boyfriend?"

"You know the Spears family?" The short woman eyed me suspiciously without actually catching my eye.

"I've met Emily and Bonnie. Never James. Bonnie is such a great kid. I just wondered if that was her boyfriend."

"That's my son." Despite her best efforts to appear irascible, she couldn't hide the love in her voice.

"Really?" I threw out the word because I had nothing else to say. I didn't expect a reaction. But I certainly got one.

Her pale brown eyes seemed to darken. "Takes after his father, that one. The way he looks, I mean. But he's mine. Took me thirty-six hours of hellish pain to push him out. Raised him myself. I ought to know."

Now I really had to search for a reaction. "Cute kid."

The woman didn't care whether I thought her son was cute or not. I got the impression she didn't care whether I bought anything or not. Apparently customer service was not a priority at Cessie's Collectibles.

Chapter 38

I decided to take the direct approach to turning Jake Chandler into my new best friend. I called and invited the reporter to lunch. Andy and I both felt sure that if anyone had a chance of cracking this case, it was the young reporter. I was given the assignment of hitching my wagon to Jake.

I wanted to know anything he was working on. Despite my best efforts to act casual, I guess I sounded a bit desperate. Jake probably knew I had no good information to offer him, but I did offer free food.

Jake said he would be driving to Edison for a job interview, but he could take the Parkway and "hop off" the highway on his way. I met him at The Stafford diner on Route 72.

Jake took full advantage of my hospitality. He ordered soup, salad, entrée, and milkshake and informed the waitress he would be ordering dessert. "Trying to bulk up," he explained.

Conversation was strained as I conveyed to Jake that I was just curious what he was working on. Jake was so busy eating that he barely noticed. "Your comment the last time we spoke was intriguing. I can't help wondering...did you find another life for Dallas?"

"Look, I know how you feel. I don't think Beck did it either, but I don't think being innocent is going to help him. The cops got no one else. And, I get the sense they are building a pretty good case."

A pretty good case? How could they create a good case out of nothing?

"And yes, I did find an earlier life for Dallas Spenser—I'm not going to print the story. It was too long ago so it has no real implications for the investigation. What would be gained?" Jake paused as a wave of honesty washed over him. "Actually, my editor thinks the story is dead. He won't print it."

My brow furrowed. "But what if these people were involved in Dallas's murder?"

Jake shook his head. "They aren't. They suffered enough. Do you want to know what Dallas did to them? He had an English girlfriend. She helped him with the Dover Snelling scam. Two whole years she waited to join him. To thank her, he gets her pregnant and then marries Emily. And know what the worst part is? His English girlfriend has a baby and at Dover's insistence she names him after his father, James, a no-good lout who left the family when Dover was a baby. Then Emily has a baby boy. Know his name?"

I mumbled my answer. "James."

"That jerk names his son with Emily after his father, James— as if he never had another son. Can you think of anything more negating? Anything more insulting to a child? To use his name again." Jake grew more pensive than I'd ever seen him. He shook his head as he gazed into space. Briefly. Then his entrée beckoned. He talked as he ate. "I think Denver saw the kid a couple of times, but he wouldn't call him James anymore. No, the kid had to have a nickname so his new baby boy would be the only James. No. I won't put that kid through what he would have to go through if I talked. He and his mother have suffered enough."

"Do the police know about them?"

Jake shrugged. "If they did their homework, they should."

"But you are the one who uncovered the other two lives. Do you really believe the cops are looking into his past?"

"Why set the police on them?"

"Because you don't know that they are innocent. And Andy is innocent. You know the cops are still looking at him."

"They won't find enough to charge Andy." Jake ripped off a piece of roll and covered it with enough butter to stop his heart on the spot.

"What? So Andy walks around forever under a cloud of suspicion. We need the cops to find and arrest the real culprit."

"I can't tell you who the 'real culprit' is. If I could, I'd have put that news in the paper." He stared at his hot turkey platter as he pronounced the words. I wasn't convinced he was telling me the truth, but I was convinced that he wasn't going to tell me whatever he did know. His eyes met mine. "I can tell you that Jimmy, the son Dover abandoned, did not kill his father. I know that."

"But how can you...?"

"Trust me." The reporter's eyes reflected a sincerity I had never seen before. "I know." I concluded that "feel" would have been a more accurate verb. Who knew that Jake Chandler had a soft side?

Getting more information about another past for Dallas was useless. Jake was not much more willing to talk about himself, but I did find out that he was orphaned at an early age and raised by his grandmother. "Not the warmest person on Earth. You know that New England reserve." Apparently not as well as Jake did. The kid reporter sounded bitter.

He should have been. Apparently she never provided lessons in etiquette. He explained that I was lucky that he could fit me into his schedule. His job interview was initially planned as a lunch interview, but the plans had changed. I thought he was the lucky one, as he was not the type of job candidate who would do well being interviewed over a meal. He slurped liquids and churned solids in his open mouth. I had wanted to see him in person to read his face as he answered my questions, and that was the only reason I could stand to watch him eat.

"How did you end up in New Jersey?" It was a casual question but apparently a tough one for Jake to answer. He shrugged. "I like the ocean. Had some friends here. I won't be here forever."

When I complimented him on his reporting, he smiled with bread-encrusted teeth. "Yeah, I did a good job, didn't I? That's how I got this interview."

"But you can't be done with the Dallas story." I issued a command. "Keep working on it. If you get more, your editor will see your point of view." I saw Jake as a beacon of hope.

"And you'll pay my rent?"

"Dallas doesn't have to be the only story you work on. Isn't there any other angle you can pursue?"

"Look, I can't say who killed Dallas Spenser, but I'm thinking that both of us might have been looking in the wrong direction."

"Meaning?"

"Dover Snelling fakes his death by drowning and resurfaces as Denver Spears. Denver Spears fakes his death by drowning and resurfaces as Dallas Spenser. Think about the night Dallas Spenser was killed. He had gone to the beach in the middle of the night with a kayak. Perhaps he was thinking of faking his own death yet again?"

I considered the scenario he had laid out and tried to ignore the sound of his chewing. It made perfect sense. The scenario. There was no explanation—or defense for—his table manners. "So you didn't stop. Is that what you're working on now?"

"I don't want you scooping me." Jake shoved turkey into his mouth.

My mood lifted as I searched for motives. I wasn't even appalled by the little stream of gravy working its way down Jake's chin. "Why would someone in his new life want to kill Dallas?"

"Why not? Was he telling them the truth? Did he ever in his entire sick existence tell anyone the truth?"

217

I shook my head. "But how did they find out he was lying to them? And why kill him? Why not settle for exposing him?"

"That is for me to find out. And, I must say, I'm doing a pretty good job of it."

"Please, give me a hint." I begged Jake, but he didn't respond.

"You'll just have to read it in the newspaper." He called the waitress over and ordered dessert. "Gotta bulk up, you know."

I smiled politely. The last thing I wanted to know was what Jake Chandler could do with a piece of banana cream pie.

Chapter 39

Oliver, suited up to play with the Jets if they happened to call, was reclining on the couch when I arrived at the house in Holgate where Andy and I were staying. He'd made himself right at home. He had his feet propped on the arm of the sofa, the remote in his right hand. "I brought my own," he explained, holding up a can of Bud in his left hand. "I figured I'd be stopping by a lot." He pointed to an empty carton.

Thirty cans of beer? I did the numbers. Oliver would be stopping by at least twice.

"Where's Andy?" Oliver asked, although I was the one who had just walked through the door.

"No idea. Did he leave a note?"

"There was a piece of paper on the floor inside the door when I came in. I think it had some writing on it."

I stared at Oliver. "In some circles, that could be called a note. Where is it?"

"Still there, I guess."

I retrieved the item. "He should be back...," I said as I glanced at the clock, "ten minutes ago. He took his baby to the garage for an oil change."

I grabbed a soda from the fridge that was now full of Oliver's beer supply. I plopped onto a chair across from Oliver. "So what's new with you? Love life still flourishing?"

Oliver's face tensed. "I'm not sure. Maybe I just don't understand women. She's hot. She's cold. She's hot. She's cold. I don't know what I'm doing to cause the change."

"It doesn't have to be you. Maybe she has a lot going on in her life." A rueful smile covered Oliver's face as I continued. "Stuff you don't know about. Ask her. Maybe she'll talk about it."

"I have asked. She isn't going to tell me."

I shrugged. "It takes time before people will trust you."

Oliver went back to watching ESPN. I stared out the windows at white clouds floating across a bright blue sky and pretended I was in Antigua. I didn't even try to pretend that Oliver was Andy. The two of us sat that way for two periods of a hockey game. Andy did not come home.

To call the pounding on the door "knocking" would be an understatement. The banging sounded urgent and angry. So angry that Oliver told me to lay back. "I'll take care of this." He checked through the peephole and then opened the door wide. Before he could speak, Page Spenser greeted him. "What the hell are you doing here?" Okay, maybe greeted isn't the right word. There was no time to search for a more appropriate term because Page brushed by Oliver and charged into the living room.

"Where's Andy? I've got to see Andy."

I was sputtering when I noticed that a woman had followed Page through the front door. It had to be Page's sister. Her younger, less conservative sister. The woman had Page's unusual coloring but a softer look. Her dark hair was longer and cut in a shaggy mop that completed a very hip image, which included a bare midriff and lots of silver jewelry.

"Guess who this is?" Page pointed to the young woman whose wide eyes suggested a kitten whose master has suddenly turned ugly.

I shook my head to indicate I hadn't a clue.

"This is Mrs. Delray Steelman."

Even as I spat out the words, "I don't know any Delray Steelman," the thought crossed my mind. "Isn't Delray a city in Florida?"

"You're damn right it is. Just like Dover is a city in England, Denver is a city in Colorado, and Dallas is a city in Texas."

What about a city name was so appealing to Dallas Spenser? And more significantly, what about Dallas Spenser was so appealing to women? To this woman?

Page, at least, no longer seemed to find the man so appealing. "That bastard was already remarried. He'd already started his new life. Before he had even faked his death—his next death—he was reborn in California. He was going to do it again. The bastard was going to do it again as Delray Steelman."

I thought back to my lunch with Jake and his description of the direction his investigation was taking. Then I looked at the fury in Page's eyes. The ambitious reporter had really stirred the pot this time.

"Do you know where the bastard got his new name?"

I shook my head although I suspected I knew. I remembered seeing the name on a memorial at the Barnegat Lighthouse. I didn't think DS had been wise in his latest "S" selection. As I recalled, Steelman was involved in a massacre on LBI, and not on the winning side.

By the time Andy came home, Page had told Oliver and me the whole story—at least as much as she knew. Earlier that day, Andrea Steelman, the wife—or really the bride, since she and Dallas (a.k.a. Delray) had only been married seven months—of Delray Steelman had shown up at Page's front door. Based on questions that a young reporter named Jake Chandler had asked her, Andrea had located the widow of Dallas Spenser to find out if she was now the widow of Delray Steelman—a man she'd reported missing from their home in Los Angeles several weeks earlier.

Andrea, stunned and speechless, sat on a hard wooden dining room chair and listened with wide eyes as Page summarized for us what she and Andrea had just learned. Page never met Oliver's eyes or mine as she recounted her story. She continued with her nervous habit of pulling at the third finger of her left hand, but there were no diamond rings to twirl. Apparently, Page had given Dallas Spenser an emotional divorce.

Dallas Spenser had made a few quick business trips to L.A. over the past few months. Or so he had told Page. He had really been paying visits to his young wife who was a film student in southern California. A very wealthy orphan/film student in southern California. He had visited her at the downtown loft he had purchased for her. Page had even known that he had bought several lofts as an investment. He never said where they were, although she knew he traveled to check on them period-ically. Now it seemed some were in his old name in Chicago, and some were in his new name in Los Angeles.

"He was checking the lofts all right." Page spoke through gritted teeth. She nodded at Andrea. "Tell them when you got married."

The woman was really more of a girl—almost waiflike. Older—but not by much—than Bonnie Spears. Tears welled in her eyes as she tried to speak. "Last July. On the fourth of July." A single tear spilled over and ran down her right cheek. "I didn't know he was already married. He said he was a wid-ower. I didn't know. I didn't mean to hurt anyone. I thought he loved me."

At that point, Oliver disappeared to retrieve a box of tissues that he placed on a table beside Andrea. As she reached for one, I spotted the gold watch on her wrist. She turned as if she felt my stare. "It's Del's watch. I gave it to him as a wedding gift. I put our initials on the back." She continued to sob.

"Oh that is just too…too…." Apparently Page couldn't find a word to describe Dallas's serial watch acquisition.

I had to give Dallas credit. He wanted to taste all aspects of life. Emily had been the prim, proper matron; Page, the strong busi-ness woman. Andrea was a hip young artist. Who knew what he had sampled before meeting Emily—after all, he had been over thirty when he met her. How many wives had he squeezed in by that time? I decided I would call Jake Chandler tomorrow. In the meantime Andy came home, and Page, much calmer but just as bitter, retold the story. Andrea, on the other hand, was far less calm. She was now openly sobbing—onto Oliver's shoulder. Oliver seemed to enjoy providing solace to the young widow—although technically she couldn't be a widow since she had never been married to Dallas/Delray legally.

Whereas I admired Oliver for his sensitivity, Page did not. She broadcast her resentment through a variety of hostile expressions that Oliver ignored.

Andy tried to comfort Page, but his efforts were half-hearted. I could tell his mind was spinning. What would this news mean to the murder investigation? The cops were certain the motive for Dallas's death could be found in his present life. Now it turned out we'd uncovered a new definition of current.

I listened to his side of the conversation as he called the police. "No. I am not calling to confess. There is someone here I think you should meet. Because she has something important to tell you. Page Spenser is here, too. Don't be snide, Petino. Yes she is here too. She lives here with me."

In the half-hour that it took Detective Petino to reach us, Andrea cried a bucket of tears—all onto Oliver's comforting shoulder. Page was in no mood for tears. She used a lot of words that rhymed with Smuckers. Andy and I gave up on trying to reason with her. She ranted and we nodded. Andy actually whistled a sigh of relief when the doorbell rang.

Detective Petino strode into the living room with long sure steps. He flashed a smile at me. "I've missed you, Ms. Daniels." He did his smirking thing. I ignored him.

He listened to the basics of the story and then turned to Andrea and Page. "I don't think we should talk here." Page was angry about being asked to move to the police station. Andrea didn't care. She would follow anyone anywhere as long as they provided tissues.

After the threesome disappeared out the door, Andy, Oliver, and I sat in the living room quietly trying to absorb what had just happened. Oliver spoke first. "You know, Dallas really had some hot women."

Andy and I stared at him. His statement was true, but given what had just happened, it seemed very inappropriate. On the other hand, it was very "Oliver." After making his pronouncement, Oliver returned to ESPN. Andy and I stepped out on the deck. It was cool enough that Andy and I had to snuggle to keep warm. There are some real advantages to cold weather.

We leaned on the railing and stared across the dunes to the water. Andy stood behind me with his arms wrapped around my waist. "So," he said, "how do you like my friends?" I turned my head so that he could see my smile. He lifted the hair that blew across my face to check my expression. "I'm not sure I've really taken all the right steps in my attempt to woo you."

"Just think of the kind of reaction you could have gotten with all the right moves."

We stood silently for awhile before we exchanged information from the day. Actually, I did most of the talking. I told him about my lunch with Jake and the news that Dallas not only had another identity at this end, but another family at the front end.

Together we worked on the chronology of Dallas's life. He was fifty-three when he died. That meant he was married to Page from thirty-eight to fifty-three. Before that he was married to Emily for six years. According to Jake, there was another son before that. That covered the three years after he left England.

"But Jake said the woman waited two years before she joined Dallas. Could that man have been alone for two years?" I doubted it. Was Jake working on it?

"Tomorrow, we'll figure out what to do next. Let's grab some dinner and get to bed early." He sealed the thought with a kiss.

"What's this?" He picked up a black item that resembled an oversized corkscrew.

"Your friends must drink some really cheap wine." I eyed the three inch hunk of black plastic.

Andy bounced the black plastic plug in his hand. "We'll just leave it on the coffee table. When Leslie and Bob come back, they won't be able to miss it."

Chapter 40

As soon as I opened my eyes, Andy started talking. "Just because we've uncovered yet another identity doesn't mean the murderer is part of that life. I mean, did Andrea look like a viable suspect to you?"

"What time is it?" The sky was growing light, but the sun had not risen above the horizon.

"Time to get up. We have a big day ahead." He jumped out of bed and disappeared into the bathroom. Over the sound of running water he demanded an answer to his question about Andrea. "Does she look like a killer?"

I had to admit she didn't—not that I actually knew what a killer looked like. I buried my head in the bedding.

Undeterred, the P.I. plopped on the edge of my side of the bed and lifted the corner of the pillow. Systematically, he reviewed our efforts. "The only missing link is Denver's son, James Spears. We should talk to him. Then we'll know we've covered all the bases. Come on. Get up." He sounded like a little boy.

While I showered, Andy managed to convince James Spears to spend his only free hour that day with us. We would meet the Princeton student at a restaurant both he and Andy knew. I was a bit surprised but, then again, Andy could be awfully convincing. I, of all people, knew that.

Andy wanted me to drive. He didn't say why, but I understood. Why give the cops any reason to pull us over? Even with me in the driver's seat he checked all the lights before we set out. "We'll get gas and a spare bulb for over the license plate on the way out of town." If I hadn't known Andy for several months, I wouldn't have realized he was nervous. But he was.

I may have been driving, but Andy was in control. Given the state of his life, I didn't protest. I took the wheel and followed the directions he gave to the gas station he chose and the pump he indicated.

"Can I help you?"

I looked out the window and groaned. "Hap, this isn't funny anymore."

The man's stare was as blank as usual. "What can I do for you?"

"Hap, this is getting ridiculous. I don't need your help."

"Yes you do."

"I do?"

"No self-serve in New Jersey."

Beside me Andy spoke with barely disguised disdain. "Meg, he works here. Hap works at this gas station."

"Oh." I didn't know that and couldn't pretend that I did. Only then did I notice Hap's name stitched on the flap of his pocket. "Sorry, Hap. I just assumed...well, anyway, could you fill it with regular?"

"Sure." Hap finished wiping grease from his hands and disappeared to the back of the Mustang. Andy's mood lifted. He smiled.

"Hey, it was an honest mistake."

"He came out of the bay. From under that Mazda."

"Sorry. I didn't notice." I sounded more than a bit defensive. His smile broadened. "I love you, Maggie."

Before I could respond he went in search of a bulb for the license plate. "I'd better get an extra tail light too."

When Hap reappeared at my window for payment, I waited for him to offer some words from Dallas. But he said nothing except "have a nice day."

"Maybe I'll see you around," I called after him cheerfully.

"Yeah, maybe." He shrugged and slinked back inside the station and under the Mazda.

"What, no call from Dallas?" Andy's smirk as he climbed back into the Mustang rivaled Detective Petino's.

"I guess he dumped me." I watched traffic for an opportunity to merge. "I'm all yours again."

Andy patted my hand on the gearshift. "I can deal with that."

The ride to Princeton went smoothly except for my hunger. I whined that I longed to stop at each diner along the way. Andy, however, had bribed James Spears with the promise of a meal. Lunch. A very early lunch that left no time for breakfast.

The restaurant was small and tucked away on one of the narrow picturesque streets in the center of Princeton. Andy directed me to drop him off and park in a municipal lot. When I got back he was sitting at a table—still alone.

"You are the most handsome man in this restaurant. Mind if I join you?"

At the next table, the women in pastel sweater sets, standard pearls, and blonde pageboys didn't bother to disguise their horrified expressions. "What audacity" was written across each carefully made-up face.

"Well, I am waiting for someone." Andy's eyes smiled at me.

"Your wait is over, you lucky boy." I pulled out a chair, snapped the napkin, and laid it in my lap. "You know you look lovely in that blazer."

Andy feigned modesty. "Well, I've been told I have a certain sense of fashion." Beside us the women exchanged disapproving glances. You can always count on the folks at the next table to pay attention—with the possible exception of any time you are choking on a fishbone.

"Anything else you're particularly good at?"

"I'd be happy to show you if you have some time later this afternoon." Andy poured me a glass of wine from the bottle he brought from the liquor store around the corner. I'm sure the women at the next table checked their watches to verify that it was not yet noon.

"For you, I'll make time."

Suddenly Andy's eyes narrowed. "He's here."

As I watched Dallas's son, James, follow the maitre d' to our table, I suspected he was the spitting image of his father. And, surprisingly, rather attractive. His hair was more blond than red. His freckles were subtle. His blue eyes were remarkable. In a blue blazer, khaki pants, and club tie he appeared to be something of a throw-back to a more genteel era—an era his sister assiduously avoided. "I bet he is the picture of his father, isn't he?" I whispered to Andy as James Spears approached.

For a college sophomore, James Spears displayed a surprising sophistication and a strong command of the social graces. His mother's influence was clearly visible. And when he spoke I understood why. Like Emily, he took control of the conversation.

"Look, I never saw my father after he left us. I was only four, but I saw how his death hurt my mother. When I was little, I used to make up stories. I understood that no body had been found, so I would fantasize about why he couldn't come home. What we could do so he could come home. I had a million of them—most of them involving superspies, aliens, and the Witness Protection Program. And then one day I was playing soccer. It was a game like any other. And I looked over at my mother. She was always there. And she was so good to my sister and me. And I stopped hoping. I missed having a father. I just stopped missing him. By then I couldn't remember what he looked like anyway."

Andy and I sat dazed as he finished. He'd barely taken a breath from start to finish. The only pause in his story came when he ordered. Andy cleared his throat. It had been a while since he'd spoken. "How did you find out that your father had been alive all those years?"

James Spears used his salad as a prop. I felt as if I were watching a performance. Make a point. Punctuate it with your fork. Make a point. Punctuate it with a sip of water. "Bonnie called me. A reporter had gotten in touch with them." Andy remained silent knowing James would continue. And he did. Explaining how numb he had felt. "I felt guilty because I didn't feel more. But I didn't. Bonnie wanted to go to his funeral when he died for real. I didn't care. I had no desire to meet the man—dead or alive. Not after I realized what he had done to us." James ate. "Maybe if he had lived, I would have softened. Grown curious. But as it was, I didn't care." He straightened in his chair. "Now, as for your problem, Mr. Beck. My mom told me that you are looking for information. I am really sorry that you ins...." We all knew he wanted to avoid the word "insisted." He switched tacks. "I regret that you went to the trouble of driving up here. I know nothing about my father or his death. My only contact with the entire situation was when Bonnie called. Of course, I've spoken with my family about it, but only briefly. I haven't been home since it happened."

James took a breath and Andy got another question in. At last. James had inherited his father's coloring and his mother's proclivity for rapid speech. "Did you learn that your father was alive before the day of his death?"

James appeared shocked. "No. No. How could I?" He seemed sincere, but I wasn't sure I believed him. "To me my father has been dead for years. If you are looking for a display of grief, you will, I assure you, be disappointed."

I guess in a way it was a wasted trip, but I felt better having seen James in person. It was like dotting an "i." Or crossing a "t." I wanted to see for myself that James Spears was a well-adjusted young man. That was exactly what he appeared to be. Well adjusted to death, anyway. Not particularly well adjusted to the passage of time. It was as if he had just wandered out of a

Noel Coward play. So, why did I have a nagging feeling he knew who Dallas Spenser was before Dallas washed ashore?

"There is one thing I should mention. It had nothing to do with my father's death. It happened last year. First semester. I got a phone call at school. It was from some kid who said he was looking for his father. He thought I could help him. He said he thought my father knew his father. I told him about my father's death. The first one—the one that wasn't real. He asked a lot about when and where and how my father had died. He was very polite. Thanked me. I told him I was sorry my father wasn't around to help him. That was it. He never called back."

"Did he give you a name?"

"He did—you know, right when I picked up—but I didn't retain it. I asked for his name and number so I could ask my mother, but he said he would call her."

"Did he?"

"I asked her once. She said she hadn't heard from him."

Then the main course came and we discovered that James Spears could eat with the same intensity that he spoke. He never completed another sentence until he thanked us for the meal and said good-bye.

Chapter 41

Page was pacing on our deck when we got home. Her pale blue eyes were icier than the wind that blew off the ocean. When Andy opened the door, she charged past him. She was the first one into the house, but she wasn't interested in staying for a visit.

Fueled by a newly discovered hatred of her late husband, Page had been wracking her brain to figure out how Dallas had taken all those pictures. She realized that he couldn't have. She had known all along that he was watching the action. That was part of the game. But after looking at the pictures she concluded that Dallas had not been watching from any of the camera angles. She thought she knew what was responsible for the poor quality of the photos on the Web. She was convinced that Dallas had videocameras planted in the room. She could estimate where they were, but she couldn't find them. She figured Andy was the guy to find them. "You're a P.I."

Andy didn't seem unwilling to help. He simply wondered if he was qualified. "I haven't worked with a lot of sophisticated equipment."

"I doubt if Dallas was capable of anything too sophisticated. The pictures weren't that good. You'll do." She rose. "You'd better bring a ladder." She headed for the door as if confident Andy would follow. He did. I followed him.

We put the seat down in the rental car, shoved the ladder into the back, and followed Page into her house. Yes, into. She had moved a sports car out of the garage so that we could drive right in. I noticed three kayaks on the wall. The rack had room for four. I understood why one was missing.

Page led us up four half-flights of stairs that climbed at odd angles to a cube near the top of the house. Like the house in Harvey Cedars, the décor did not suggest the scene of wild orgies. The decorating was stark and beautiful. Stripped down country with solid white linens. The main feature of the room was the expanse of ocean outside the window.

With the exception of a stack of papers in the center of the bed, Page had taped each picture on the wall of the bedroom. She'd printed out every page before having the Web site pulled down. From the way she had arranged the photos, it appeared they had been taken from five angles. From three walls, and one cornice above the wide window. The pile on the bed had been taken from a camera mounted on the ceiling.

While Page watched with visible anxiety and impatience, Andy set up the ladder and climbed the steps. In less than an hour he had located and disconnected all five of the tiny cameras. One in the air duct. One in the headboard. One in the bureau. One over the window. And, one in the overhead light. Five VCRs were stacked in a dropped ceiling. Apparently, the house had been built to accommodate Dallas's prurient interests.

Page opened the door to a bathroom that could have housed a family of four and threw the cameras into the black marble sink. She didn't say a word as she filled the shell-shaped bowl with water. She didn't have to. Her face said it all. If Dallas was not in hell, it wasn't because Page hadn't wished hard enough.

With trepidation, Andy asked if she wanted to watch the tapes. He held the cassettes out to her. "Please just destroy them." She didn't even look in his direction.

Now there was an example of trust. If she'd entrusted them to me, I would have destroyed the tapes—but only after sneaking a peek at them.

Andy reached into the bathroom and squeezed Page's shoulder. "I will." He disappeared down the stairs with the tapes under his arms.

Page's wide eyes met mine in the bathroom mirror. "He's a good guy." Her tone was warm, sincere.

"I know."

"I wish I had known." Her attempt to smile was not successful.

I slipped out of the room to leave Page to her task of destroying the electronic equipment. When Andy came back for the ladder he simply called good-bye to Page. She didn't answer.

Chapter 42

"Do you mind if I drop you off? I thought I'd take a train ride this afternoon. I think there's about fifty yards of New Jersey Transit track I might have missed."

"Do you want me to come along?" I demonstrated no enthusiasm for the task.

He answered pensively. "It's boring. You don't have to."

I didn't. Andy dropped me off at the house in Holgate with the keys to the Mustang. He kept the rental out of laziness. He didn't feel like changing cars or taking the ladder out of the back.

There had to be something productive I could do with the few remaining hours of sunlight to guarantee that I would see the clear green waters of the Caribbean within the foreseeable future. I had that sick-nervous feeling, knowing if I wanted something to happen, I had to figure out how to make it happen.

If I couldn't check out Dover Snelling's life in England, maybe I could check out Denver Spears's life in Pennsylvania. We'd talked to all members of the Spears family, but it couldn't hurt to check in and see what they were up to.

I didn't really have any questions, and I couldn't simply ring the doorbell and ask if I could hang out for a while. Maybe I could just watch. Why? Why not? What did I have to lose except a few hours? Only as I got close to the Spears's Main Line house did I recall telling Andy that a red convertible wasn't good for surveillance. Even I had spotted him. So it was vaguely ironic that I found myself circling the Spears' neighborhood in a classic car that people stared at the first time it went by—let alone the second, third, and fourth.

Luckily the roads that led to the Spears' house were relatively free of traffic. After circling the block a few times, I found a place to park about fifty yards from the end of the Spears driveway. Well, not actually a spot. A small opening on private property. I hoped the owners were away and not simply negligent about picking up their newspapers from the end of the driveway.

It only took fifteen minutes before I began to feel ridiculous. Nothing was happening at the Spears house—or rather outside the Spears house. Already the daylight was waning. It'd been a long day since Andy dragged me out of bed at dawn. Yawning, I almost missed Bonnie turn out of the driveway in a Saab. With little rationalization other than that I had nothing better to do, I followed. Bonnie started down Route 320 toward Conshohocken—probably on her way to work at the shop in Chestnut Hill, I thought. But she didn't go all the way into Chestnut Hill. She turned off Bells Mill Road into a small parking area for Valley Green Park. I slowed to watch as she pulled in next to a dark panel truck. According to the lettering on the side, the vehicle belonged to Cessie's Collectibles. If Cessie was paying her son by the hour, she was not getting her money's worth. The kid was lounging against the front bumper smoking a cigarette. Bonnie greeted her friend with a long hug that I deemed to be affectionate but not romantic.

Given the size of the lot, there was no discreet way for me to park there. I crossed Wissahickon Creek and found a hiding place for Andy's Mustang. Well, the car was not exactly hidden.

If a green minivan moved, the convertible would be easily visible from the street.

I spotted the two easily. Although they had moved to the trail through the park, Bonnie and her friend hadn't ventured more than ten yards down the path. Feeling both guilty and ridiculous, I doubled back and watched Bonnie across the water and through the trees.

The young man cried. Once Bonnie's arms went around him, his body shook with the force of his tears. Bonnie wept too. Okay, I wasn't close enough to be sure, but I think she cried. In the fading light, I saw her wipe what I assumed to be tears from her cheeks. Most joggers and walkers ignored the couple, but an occasional passer-by stared at the emotional display.

The occasional passer-by looked at me oddly, as well. Hiding in the trees would have been easier in a month or so. Not a bud had shown its face on any of the trees I was behind. I couldn't think of a good reason a person would lurk where I stood. In the spring, one could study the burgeoning plant life. In the fall, one could admire nature's beautiful display of color. In summer, one could enjoy the lush vegetation that gave the path its name—or simply hide in the underbrush. But in mud season? At this time of year, there was no excuse for what I was doing.

At least I didn't have to lurk in the trees for long. Bonnie headed back up Bells Mill Road toward Ridge Pike—and her car. My interest stayed with Cessie's son. He didn't return to the van, but continued to lean against the wooden fence. Even from my angle I could see that he was staring into space.

I decided to take a closer look. Since the kid had seen me in his mother's shop, I felt I should keep a fairly low profile. I pulled up my collar and walked by him quickly. He seemed lost in his own thoughts. I couldn't stare, but I did glance to catch his expression. I don't even think he saw me as I walked by. I could tell he was upset, but what did that prove? So, a guy who probably never met Dallas feels bad....

The sky was growing dark and the number of people enjoying the park was dwindling. I didn't want to be the last one off the trail, and it didn't look like I would be. The kid was still in the same position, wearing the same expression. I assiduously avoided looking in his direction as I passed him on my way out of the park.

I'd kept busy but learned nothing and concluded I'd wasted another day. To avoid a complete washout, I called Cass, my friend since first grade. Before I met her at McNally's, I called Andy to tell him I'd be home after dinner. He wasn't home, so I left a message on the machine.

Chapter 43

I had made the turn off Route 70 onto Route 72 when I first noticed the headlights following too closely. I didn't like to push the Mustang, so I moved to the right to let the truck pass. A broken yellow line stretched far ahead on the left. I saw no oncoming traffic. The vehicle was in the clear. The driver had plenty of time to pass but apparently was more interested in tailing me.

We tooled along past restaurants, bars, and housing developments, looking more like a two-car train than two individual vehicles. As we passed the last farm stand, closed for the winter, the realization hit me that maybe I had something more to worry about than the driver's bad driving habits. Especially since Andy had my cell phone in the rental car.

I slowed to force the driver's hand, but he wouldn't pass me. I sped up. He stayed on my bumper. Only then did I realize the guy was purposefully terrorizing me. It was a little late to catch on. The next stretch of the road was the darkest. It was several miles to the next roadside stand. Not that it mattered, since they would be closed for the season.

There was a time I'd known all sorts of shortcuts through South Jersey. But not the dirt roads that cut off the highway. If

I knew one led to safety, I would have taken it. I didn't know if any of the roads were passable or where they led, but I had a feeling it was not to safety. I stayed on the main road, stepped on the gas, and hoped for a speed trap.

There was no traffic to speak of—not surprising at this time of night and this time of year. Maybe that's why no cop caught me doing eighty.

I kept one eye on the road and one eye on the truck. I couldn't see how many people were inside, let alone who they were.

Suddenly, the vehicle pulled beside me. I saw one person, male, was behind the steering wheel. Actually, what I could see was the silhouette of a head in a baseball cap. I assumed the head sat on top of a male body. The vehicle was a windowless van, painted a dark color.

The driver moved to the right—into my lane. I had nowhere to go except the soft shoulder and then what looked like an old railroad bed. I refused to swerve. The driver of the van bumped me. Well, he made his truck bump my car. He swung the truck into the old Mustang and then pulled away quickly. Andy's beloved convertible swerved, but I quickly regained control. The van rammed me a second time. Harder. I swerved again, caught the side of the truck again, and headed off the road. I'd lost the battle. The car careened across the shoulder. I heard the sound of branches scratching the paint off the doors of the classic car. Andy was not going to like this. Above me, low-hanging branches ripped at the canvas roof. Andy was definitely going to be unhappy. Something cracked the glass in the side window. Andy was really going to be in a bad mood. At the moment, however, I had other things to worry about. I steered into the soft sand of the rail bed that lined the road. I slammed on the brakes, but to no effect. I hit a bump. The car took flight. I had my hands on the wheel, but there was no point in steering. The car was airborne.

I waited for something to stop my flight. Something in that case would be a tree, or perhaps a telephone pole. Amazingly, the car landed without extreme impact and hit another ramp. The brakes did nothing to slow the vehicle and the car took off again. I knew that lightning didn't strike twice. The next time the car hit the ground the chances that it would not hit an obstruction were nil.

I tried to remember where the telephone poles crossed the road. At one point they no longer lined the right side of the road but moved to the left. I didn't know exactly where that happened. Everything was happening so fast that I couldn't see any poles. I was afraid I wouldn't see them until they came through the windshield.

The car landed in the sand again and I continued to press the brake pedal. If my actions did anything at all, they caused the car to skid. The right side of the car started to rise. I felt certain the convertible was about to flip. I had just enough time to think "old car, no rollbar" when the Mustang righted itself and jerked to a stop.

I looked around for the van but was relieved to see no sign of it. Just to be sure I didn't encounter the driver, I crawled across the gearshift to the passenger door and threw it open. I hopped out of the car and ran into the pines.

If the Jersey Devil was in the neighborhood, I didn't want to see him coming since I couldn't outrun him. Unfortunately, the moon was full. I found a tree and hid behind it.

Even though I don't really believe in the Jersey Devil, I couldn't get my mind off the creature while I huddled there. I didn't believe that an eighteenth-century New Jersey woman had actually given birth to a devil in the pinelands. I certainly didn't believe that a two-hundred-year-old devil with hooves, wings, and a long forked tail roamed the present-day pine barrens. But I certainly did believe that some unexplained events had occurred in the huge pine forests of South Jersey.

While I watched and worried, no one approached the car. The night was still—the silence broken only by the occasional roar of a passing car, an occasional breeze through the trees and an occasional rustling in the brush that I sincerely hoped wasn't the Jersey Devil. Every urban legend I had ever heard had at some point in time been attributed to the Jersey Devil— although now that I thought of it, where would the Jersey Devil have gotten a hook for a hand?

I was pondering that thought when I sensed the presence. I was crouched behind some pine bushes watching the car. Slowly I turned to the right and there it was. I didn't quite know what *it* was. A big dog? A small horse? A misplaced coyote? The creature remained perfectly still, but I felt its power. The animal exuded strength. I sensed it. The force frightened me.

Whatever the animal was—and I was confident the creature was an animal and not a mythical supernatural beast—it seemed calm. It stuck its long snout through the bushes as if checking to see what I was watching. Slowly, the animal turned its head in my direction and our eyes met. I recalled someone telling me eye contact with wild animals was a no-no. I turned my eyes back to watching the car. Out of the corner of my eye I saw the animal do the same thing.

I knew this was only a temporary solution. The animal wouldn't do surveillance with me forever. I realized there was a possibility that the creature might wander away. But that was only one possibility. The other possibilities included making nice with me, cornering me, and ripping my throat out. I could visualize the last.

I glanced at the animal, which seemed to regard me with disinterest. "Hi," I said in a soft voice to establish a mood. The animal didn't react. It simply continued to watch me. Slowly, I stood up and started walking even more slowly toward the Mustang. I fought the impulse to break into a run the entire way.

After ten seconds by my watch, ten hours by my heart, I reached the open passenger door. The right side of the car didn't look too bad. A few bumps and scratches. But this wasn't the time to play insurance adjuster. I climbed into the front seat and pulled the door closed behind me.

Less than a minute later, the animal sauntered into the light of the Mustang's highbeams. Now that I could see the creature more clearly, I reached a few conclusions. Number 1, the animal wasn't 100 percent of any species. Number 2, the beast was 100 percent ugly. Number 3, the creature was vicious looking. I mean, his physical features made him look vicious. He actually appeared a bit bored. He stood in the light for a minute staring into the darkness. Then, with a glance in my direction, the animal sauntered off into the night. I breathed a sigh of relief. This was not the Jersey Devil. This was not a predatory beast. This was an animal with absolutely no interest in me. My guess? A lonely coyote that had somehow gotten ahead of his species' migration down the east coast.

Cars sped by—apparently without questioning why a car would be sitting off the side of the road with its lights on. I knew that if I wanted to summon help I was going to have to leave the safety of the car. I worried about the beast, but he seemed friendly enough. Unless something had put him in a bad mood since I'd last seen him, I didn't believe he constituted a major threat.

I suspected Andy was going to pose the bigger threat to my happiness. As I checked out the driver's side of the Mustang, I tried to envision his reaction. Andy wasn't going to like this at all. He loved his classic convertible. It had been a gift from his uncle. The sentimental value far outweighed the financial value —which from the look of things was currently hovering around zero. And I couldn't even see the full extent of the damage in the darkness.

The driver's door was smashed and would not be opening again. Not that it mattered. The buckled frame probably rendered the car undrivable. Andy was never going to take me with him to Antigua. Not now. I reached through the shattered window and snapped off the lights. Silly, really. Why worry about the battery? It was unlikely the car would ever run again.

I slowly walked to the edge of the road, slipping and sliding in the sand. Everything I possessed ached. I didn't recall hitting anything. I suspected the pain was from tensing during my unscheduled flight. I stood on the side of the road bent over with my hands on my knees. Standing straight was not a possibility. A full minute passed before I saw headlights approaching from the east. Was it the van? As far as I knew the truck had disappeared in that direction. Had the driver made a U-turn? I ducked back into the bushes. I could wait for an eastbound vehicle.

The car passed. It wasn't the van. It was a minivan. As the vehicle disappeared down the road, I saw that it was filled with tiny little tow-heads. A minivan full of kids. And I'd let it go. I decided to flag down the next car.

I stood on the shoulder waiting for the next vehicle. The wait wasn't long. I could see headlights in the distance—heading east. That was when I heard the roar behind me. A huge white light was cutting through the woods traveling along the old rail bed just as I had. Becoming airborne just as I had. Suddenly I realized the light belonged to an all-terrain vehicle. An ATV that might not see and certainly would not expect to find a classic Mustang in its path. I ran to the car, reached through the broken window, and turned on the headlights. Just in time. The light caught me in the eye as the ATV cut to the right and jerked to a halt at the edge of the highway.

"Wow." A kid with the height and build of a fourteen-year-old hopped off the bike and strode toward me. "Thanks for the heads up." He pointed at the headlights. In the dark, it took me a minute to figure out that he was older than fourteen. About fourteen years older than fourteen. My guess was that he had spent at least that many years behind bars. I found him as frightening as the animal that had recently vanished into the woods. Nonetheless, I found the man's composure astonishing.

"They say these things work on all terrains, but they don't expect you to run into a hunk of steel on a trail like this." He surveyed the damage. "What happened?"

I told my story with an emphasis on the animal that kept me company in the woods. "Sounds like a coyote. We don't got none of those around here."

I wanted to talk about the animal. Ted—that was the man's name, Ted—wanted to talk about Andy's car. While he did another car passed.

"I've really got to get help...."

Ted didn't seem to care. He interrupted. "That was one nice vehicle you ruined there, lady. My ol' lady do something like that and she'll find herself head first down the well."

"Well, that's a nice sentiment, but I'm just going to stand up here on the road and flag down help." I edged away from the man. By then, I had a feeling I needed help for more reasons than one.

"You don't need no help. I can give you a ride...." He also indicated that there were several other things he could give me—including the "big one," as he so romantically phrased it.

I declined all offers. I didn't know where I would sit on the ATV and didn't want to find out. "Oh look. Here comes a car." Luckily, it was a Jaguar with a cell phone. Actually, the next car wasn't a Jaguar with a cell phone. The next car that *stopped* was a Jaguar with a cell phone. I'd already been rejected by a Ford Escort, two Toyotas, a Mercedes convertible, and two more minivans while I fended off the stranger's offers—which by then included a lot more than a vanilla version of the big one. I sighed audibly as the Jaguar came to a halt.

An incredibly handsome man with an incredibly broad smile slid down the window of an incredibly expensive car. "You two got a problem?"

"I have several, actually." I nodded at Ted. "He doesn't have any problems. He brings his ATV down here from Trenton to ride late at night." My tone added, "if you believe that one." I kept my hand on the man's door as I said good-bye to Ted. "Well, you can climb back on that ATV now. Thanks for all your help."

Ted eyed me and then the man and then the Jaguar and then me. He sneered. "I guess I know where I'm not wanted."

I clung to the Jaguar's door. If the driver decided to take off he wasn't going without me—even if he dragged me to my death.

Ted mumbled as he made his way to his ATV. Once there he made a great show of climbing onto the seat. I was relieved when he finally tore away.

"Who was that guy?"

"Ever heard of the Jersey Devil?"

The guy chuckled. "There hasn't been a sighting of the Jersey Devil in years."

"Don't bet on it."

"What are you doing out here all by yourself?"

I pointed to my car. "I had a little problem."

He didn't ask any other questions. He called the police and had me sit in his vehicle until they came. He let me speculate on why someone had forced me off the road. "Well, I am kind of investigating this murder. They think my boyfriend did it, but he didn't. I'm sure."

The guy seemed relieved when the cop car pulled up. I asked for his card to send him a thank you, but he declined. He said helping was reward enough and then he hit the gas. His tires screeched as he pulled away.

Chapter 44

The uniformed cop who dropped me off behind the Holgate house wanted to see me inside. All I wanted to do was go inside, confess my malfeasance to Andy, get dumped, and cry myself to sleep. I'd long since stopped worrying about the possibility that someone was out to kill me. I had bigger problems.

The policeman seemed satisfied to watch me until I got to the back door. I assured him that I would be okay. "I can see the lights are on. Andy must be home."

I'd been relieved that Andy hadn't been home to take my call from the police car. The state of his beloved classic Mustang was the kind of news I preferred to break in person. But when I ran up the steps into the large living room, Andy was nowhere in sight. I found Oliver. Alone. Without Andy.

Oliver had spent so much time in the spot on the couch now occupied that his presence didn't seem at all unusual. He was reclining. He had a beer in his hand. He was dressed like Joe Namath. I guess I should have noticed he wasn't watching ESPN. He was listening to classical music. Vivaldi. I should have realized something was wrong, but I didn't. I charged into the room talking. "Oliver, someone tried to kill me." I plopped onto the other end of the sectional.

"Who?" He seemed interested—just not concerned.

"Well, Oliver, if I knew I probably would have mentioned that in my last sentence."

"You have a snide side, Meg."

"Only gets bad when I feel threatened—like when someone tries to run me off the road. Someone from Pennsylvania I think. They had no front license plate."

Oliver seemed oddly unimpressed. This had to be the biggest thing to happen today. Didn't it? "Aren't you going to ask me why I'm sitting in your living room?"

I shrugged. "Since we moved down here, you spend more time on our couch than you do on your own. Though you should have turned the heat up. It's cold in here." I made the suggestion, but I didn't get up to adjust the thermostat. I was too exhausted.

"You know what makes you and Andy such a good couple?"

"Our mutual love of skeeball and vanilla fudge?"

"Yeah, that too. But as of tonight you two have something else in common." His voice softened. "Someone tried to kill Andy tonight. Don't worry; he's going to be fine."

"Tried to kill him?"

"Tried. A bad shot, luckily. Got his shoulder. Really just nicked his upper arm." With his finger, Oliver circled the spot on his own shoulder.

"Someone shot Andy?" I sank back into the cushions. My gaze followed Oliver's pointed finger to a neat hole in the window that resembled a dark spider in the center of a glass Web. "Is he asleep?"

"Don't know."

"Don't know? Haven't you been in to check on him?" I tried to pull myself out of the hole I had dug in the cushions.

"The nurses do that."

"The nurses?"

"He's in the hospital. Didn't I mention that?"

"Why are we sitting here?" I managed to push myself off the sofa and onto my feet. "If he's in the hospital, we should be there."

"I was just waiting for you to arrive home, sweetheart."

Oliver drove his Jeep the same way he drove the Porsche. The ride was fast. The ride was erratic. The ride was scary. Even though Oliver spoke as quickly as he drove, he barely had time to tell me the story before we reached the hospital.

From what Oliver could figure out, Andy had been sitting in the living room watching tapes of *All My Children.*

"*All My Children?*" Now I was really worried.

"Apparently, someone shot him through the window."

"What else did he tell you?"

Andy hadn't told Oliver anything. Oliver had reached his own conclusions. "The videos were running when I got there. The hole was in the glass."

"What did Andy say?"

"Nothing. He was unconscious."

"Where did you find him?"

"On the floor. Right in front of the couch. Beside the coffee table."

I wasn't an M.D., but even I knew a bullet that grazed the skin wouldn't knock out a grown man. I put together a scenario from Oliver's story. Andy was watching videos. He got shot. He thought it was nothing. He got up to chase the guy but found he couldn't. He must have collapsed on the floor where Oliver found him unconscious. Andy's wound had to be a lot more serious than Oliver believed.

"I called 911 and the rest is history. The paramedics took Andy to the hospital."

Oliver waited because he heard my message that I was on the way. Given the circumstances, I guess it wasn't odd that Oliver checked our messages. It never occurred to me to ask why he had dropped by in the first place.

Chapter 45

I would not be able to identify the hospital in a line-up. Oliver pulled up to one of those big, square, modern buildings under one of those high, wide, brightly lit porticos. I jumped out of his Jeep and ran. An electric eye opened the door for me and I rushed inside—right past the white jackets and green scrubs gathered behind the high desk familiar to hospital visitors. I figured that if I acted as if I knew where I was going, a preoccupied staff wouldn't notice. They didn't. I had no idea where I was headed, but I knew that if I hesitated someone would stop me. Then, I'd never get back to the patients' area. I wasn't about to spend the rest of the night in the waiting room without seeing Andy.

I walked purposefully down the hallway glancing quickly into each treatment room without slowing. Why didn't this hospital have glass windows like the ones in the television hospitals? I felt like a voyeur peering in the doorways. Luckily, I didn't see anything too frightening—or any hospital staff. Must have been a slow night in the ER.

When I saw Andy, I put on the brakes. As I slid past the room on the slick floor, I grabbed onto the doorframe. I pulled myself back and peeked around the corner of the door. Andy looked great—even in a pastel, patterned hospital gown accessorized with a bright blue sling. He was resting on a narrow treatment table covered only by a thin white sheet. His eyes were closed, but the corners of his mouth turned up in a small smile. I tiptoed across the room and peered down at my sleeping friend. I was afraid that my touch would disturb him, so I just watched him breathe. To tell the truth, that was all I wanted to see—Andy breathing. I leaned close and let his familiar odor block the sterile hospital smell. Or most of it. After hours of treatment, Andy, himself, smelled a bit like a hospital. But I couldn't complain. He was not in surgery. He was not in intensive care. He was not in heaven. The bullet hadn't hit its mark.

Andy looked so content. At least until Oliver found the room.

"Heh, Andy, how the hell are you?" I'd never really noticed before how loud Oliver's voice could be.

As I warned Oliver that Andy was asleep, I realized that he no longer was. He groaned as he came awake. "They left me on this gurney all night. I didn't get any sleep." I didn't argue that he had, in fact, been asleep.

"Hi." As his pale green eyes peered into mine, I detected real joy.

"Hi." Ever the clever conversationalist, I responded in kind.

Andy reached out his right hand. I took it and moved around the cot to his right. "Are you okay?"

"They tell me I'll be a little sore, but I'm fine."

"You could have been killed." I fought back tears. What was this sudden display of emotion? I'd been so calm until this moment. Supported by adrenaline, I guessed.

"Maggie, I'm fine, really." Andy stroked my face. "Really. I am." He grimaced as he squeezed my hand.

Aside from the sling on his right shoulder, Andy appeared healthy but tired. I held his hand and stroked his hair while he told his story. Well, he didn't actually have a story to tell. He couldn't remember what happened. "I know that I heard the window break. I walked over to see what had happened and then...nothing. They told me I'd been shot. And actually, I'm starting to believe them." He struggled to adjust his shoulder. "This is beginning to hurt." He nodded at an envelope on the bedside table. "They gave me some drugs. I'll feel fine."

I gave Andy a single pill and held the glass of water to his lips. He took a moment to let the pill settle before he spoke. "Petino was here. Of course, he thought I shot myself. He just can't figure out how I shot myself through the glass. I gave him permission to search the house. Told him to check it out for himself. I assumed someone would be there. Didn't you see him?"

Oliver explained that the homicide detective hadn't yet arrived when we left. "The paramedics called some local cops, but they didn't hang around long. Do you suppose he'll think we did it together? That I shot you? We could have done that, you know."

Sometimes I wondered whose side Oliver was on. Andy cautioned him. "Oliver, the police can come up with enough ridiculous fantasies about my involvement in this crime. They don't need your help." The muscles in Andy's face were tight. Were they tight because of physical pain or because of frustration with Oliver? Or both?

I sent Oliver off in search of beverages. That Andy claimed to feel fine presented me with a dilemma. He was clearly well enough to hear about his car. His classic car. His beloved, classic car. His beloved, classic car that his uncle had given him. He was healthy enough to take the news. I knew that. But what if he had a relapse? My mind decided I'd better wait. But that decision did not stop my mouth from blurting out the truth.

"I ruined your car tonight." Tears flowed down my cheeks.

"Are you okay?" He reached for my hand.

"Yes." My sobbing stretched the single word into at least five syllables. "But your car...."

"Maggie. It's only a car. What happened? Are you hurt?"

Oliver chose that moment to reappear from the vending area. "Somebody tried to kill her, too. You two are quite the couple.

Soulmates maybe. Don't you think?" He popped the tabs on sodas for Andy and for me.

If Oliver didn't take the threat on my life seriously, Andy did. He wanted to hear every detail. He was worried about me, not the car. And hell-bent on finding out who had tried to wipe us out. But before we could leave the hospital to find out, Detective Petino appeared in the doorway, generating a force that drew all our eyes in his direction. His power went beyond his obvious physical prowess. His well-developed body appeared to block the wide hospital doorway. Not physically but psychically. No way I would dream of trying to escape past the cop. Especially given the expression on his face—an expression that Andy either couldn't read or could read but ignored.

"Petino, wait until you hear this. Someone ran Meg off the road on Route 72 tonight." Considering his condition, Andy's voice was surprisingly strong. I think his energy was fueled by the idea that at long last we would see a break in the case.

Little did we know that Petino thought the same thing. Well, not exactly the same thing. He too thought there would be a break in the case. He displayed no interest in either of our mishaps. He pulled a plastic bag from inside his jacket. "Ever seen this before?"

Andy took the plastic bag in his right hand. He appeared confused, but I recognized the item immediately. "It's that thing we found on the porch." Andy didn't seem to recall. "Remember, I said it looked like a giant corkscrew for a really cheap bottle of wine." I glanced at Petino. He didn't find my little joke amusing.

Andy peered inside the bag more carefully. "Oh yeah, for a really big bottle of wine." He looked at Petino optimistically— an expression I found a bit disingenuous given the cop's demeanor. "Do you know what it is?"

"Don't be coy, Beck. You know exactly what it is."

I don't really remember how the conversation progressed except that Petino got nastier and Andy got angrier. Neither Andy nor I had recognized the black plastic item because neither of us owned kayaks. The item was, in fact, a plug for a kayak. And not just any kayak, but for the precise model that Dallas Spenser owned. The model that washed ashore after his death. The model that turned up on the beach missing a plug. A plug identical to the one that Petino claimed to have found in the house where Andy and I were staying.

"I didn't know what it was or where it came from. For all I know my friends own a kayak."

"Didn't find one." Apparently, Petino had searched the entire house. After all, Andy had given him permission. I had already thought ahead to the trial. Could we claim that Andy was under the influence of drugs—albeit legal drugs—when he gave the cop the go-ahead? Would it matter?

"Why would I give you the keys to my house if I had anything to hide?" Andy made no attempt to disguise his disdain.

"You didn't hide anything. Plug was sitting right there on the coffee table." The detective's tone grew solemn. "I've told you this before, Beck. This time, listen to me. Get a lawyer. A good one. You're going to need one."

In the midst of the argument, Detective Petino asked me to step into the hallway. I didn't consider saying no to the cop. Once outside, I leaned on the wall. The detective loomed above me in a way I knew was threatening—although my claim wouldn't have stood up in court. He asked me to review with him what I recalled about finding the plastic plug. There wasn't much to tell, but I told what I knew.

The strength drained from his body. The position that had seemed so threatening felt suddenly intimate. "Look, Ms. Daniels, I may be...no, I know I'm out of line, but the handwriting is on the wall here. I admire loyalty, but when it's misplaced...for your own good, you should get out of this relationship—before he takes you down." He paused for a moment, then fixed me with a steely gaze. "And another thing, if I find you've misled me, I'll bring you up on obstruction charges. Believe me, I will. I will not hesitate."

I met his gaze. "Detective Petino," my voice was as firm as my stare, "Andy Beck did not kill Dallas Spenser. He did not care enough about Dallas Spenser to kill him. He did not care enough about Page Spenser to kill her husband. Tonight someone tried to kill him, and someone also came after me. I suggest you look into those crimes as they relate to the murder. I also suggest that if someone could get close enough to take a shot at Andy, they could get close enough to toss a plug onto the deck. I told you that's where I found it. If Andy had taken the plug from the kayak while committing a murder, do you honestly believe he would be so careless as to keep it? To drop it on the deck? To let me find it? Do you believe that anyone could be that stupid? Get real, Detective Petino."

According to the cop's eyes, he found my speech amusing, but it didn't put him in a good mood. He asked me to remain in the hallway while he talked to Andy. Oliver joined me. The cop had thrown him out of the room, too. I heard voices raised in anger. After a few moments the cop charged out of Andy's room and down the hallway. But he didn't take Andy with him.

I felt relieved. How low had I sunk? I'd had a good day. My boyfriend didn't get arrested.

Chapter 46

By the time we signed him out of the hospital, Andy was ready to go back to work. "To tell you the truth, I was shocked Petino didn't arrest me at the hospital. He must have had some doubt. Or a missing link that he needs. My time is running out. We have got to get to the bottom of this." For the first time I detected no trace of the calm reassurance. Andy was scared. "We'll start with Page."

"Andy, why don't we get some sleep first?" I knew that was what the injured P.I. should be doing. I was willing to bet that was what Page was doing. But Andy tolerated no talk of rest—or even a stop at home. "I don't want to tell my cellmates that I could have beaten the rap, but I needed a nap." While Andy struggled into a Dophins jersey from the back of Oliver's Jeep, he convinced Oliver to drive us directly to Page's. What drug had the hospital given Andy? Not a sedative, obviously.

Oliver didn't drive his Jeep any more responsibly even though a wounded man was belted into the front seat. We arrived at Page's home in Loveladies much earlier than legally possible or socially acceptable. Most of the windows faced the beach, so as we drove down the rutted private drive we could not tell if anyone was awake in the Spenser house. I wouldn't have been. The first traces of light were turning the black sky to charcoal gray. Once again I expressed amazement that the building was, in fact, a private home. The house looked more like a public building. A library. A school. A prison with heavy landscaping in place of razorwire.

Andy was out of his seatbelt before Oliver brought the car to a halt. The P.I. led the charge up the wide wooden stairs to the double doors in the glass wall. The inside of the house was dark, but not for long. Andy pressed the bell. Once. Twice. Relentlessly. He stopped only to bang on the door and call out to the occupant. "Let us in, Page. We have to talk to you. Now."

I'd pegged Page as the type to arrive at the door in a black silk negligee and satin mules. She looked even sexier in the oversized man's shirt she had thrown over—well, I don't exactly know what she had thrown the shirt over. The shirt was all I could see. That and the long shapely legs that stretched below the shirttails. The pale oxford cloth complimented the blue of her eyes. Her hair was charmingly tousled. Apparently, her face didn't require make-up. And, she had just had a good night's sleep. The jealousy I had fought so hard to overcome popped to the surface. Until that familiar scowl covered Page's face.

She appeared annoyed to see the three of us. Of course, I can't blame her for being annoyed. If we had been from the Publishers' Clearinghouse Prize Patrol she probably would have been annoyed. It was not yet 6 A.M. She flung the right door open and extended her arms toward the left panel to make sure we didn't think we were getting inside. "What?" She didn't sound at all concerned. She was angry.

"We need to talk to you." Andy brushed by the scowling woman. I mumbled apologies as I followed. Oliver seemed embarrassed and confused as he followed us—possibly because he brushed against a marble sculpture that threatened to topple off its pedestal. Oliver managed to steady the statue before he joined the rest of us in a sitting room that opened into the kitchen.

"This better be good, Andy." Page opened a door and disappeared behind it. When she emerged she was wearing a pair of jeans that she had probably pulled from the dryer. For the first time she noticed that Andy's arm was in a sling. "What happened to you?"

"You don't know?" Andy's tone was even.

"Know what?" Page pointed to a white leather sofa and, with some difficulty, Andy lowered himself onto the cushions.

"I'll make mimosas." Oliver ran into the kitchen and dug through drawers, cabinets, and the refrigerator to come up with ingredients. Oliver had several basic approaches to dealing with life's problems. Most involved crushed ice and all involved alcohol.

While Oliver played bartender, Andy told Page about the attempts on his life and mine. She smoothed her hair and kept her eyes on the floor as she listened. Page's face registered surprise. I was sure of that. But her expression showed more. Behind the mask she plastered into place, her mind was spinning. She might not have done the deeds, but I was willing to bet she knew who did.

The only emotion Page was willing to express was anger. "Andy, what on Earth would make you think I had anything to do with an attempt on your life?" Absentmindedly, she took a mimosa from Oliver's hand and immediately slipped the goblet on the table beside her. Andy did the same. I took a drink and drained it. Oliver finished up his shortly after I did and refilled both our glasses. While we drank, Page and Andy continued to argue.

"I didn't say you did it. This," he pointed to his shoulder, "has to have something to do with Dallas's death. I think you know who shot me. If not, I think you know something that would help me find out who did it. I don't think it's a coincidence that someone tried to kill Meg and me on the same night."

"What makes you think it's the same person? One person couldn't be in two places at once. Why shoot you and not shoot Meg?" Page used her wide eyes to sell her opinion to Andy.

He wasn't buying. "I believe the same gun that killed Dallas was used to shoot me. Ballistics will verify my hunch. I can't believe the two incidents were unrelated. Maybe the killer did not have the gun yet when they ran Meg off the road—maybe they were on their way to pick up the gun."

"At your house, Andy?" Page flashed a look that was both flirtatious and challenging. It probably worked better under different circumstances.

"Look, Page, I'm sick of this. You know I didn't have that gun. Who tried to shoot me?" Andy dug into his pocket and pulled out the envelope filled with painkillers. I took it from his hand, shook one out, and returned it to him with my mimosa.

"There's alcohol in here." Andy swallowed the pill before protesting. "I thought it was orange juice." He pushed the glass towards me. "Are you trying to kill me, too?"

Page didn't seem at all concerned about Andy's health. She was more concerned with defending herself. "I have no idea who shot you. Maybe it was one of those people you talked to about Dallas's murder."

Andy groaned. "Page, every lead you gave me was a false one. You kept me running around to distract the police. I know that. Now tell me the truth."

"I don't know the truth, Andy." Page's words were measured.

I didn't think she was lying. Exactly. I think she had us on a technicality. Maybe she didn't know beyond a shadow of a doubt, but on some level she knew.

Chapter 47

The sun had risen above the horizon by the time Oliver dropped Andy and me in Holgate. Later, Andy told me he'd never understood the derivation of the phrase "falling asleep as soon as your head hits the pillow" until he saw me drop onto the couch that morning. There was no pillow, but I didn't care. I didn't even notice. I fell asleep in my raincoat.

It seemed like only moments later that I felt Andy shaking my shoulders. "We shouldn't have left her alone."

"It's okay." I mumbled. In my half-conscious state—make that 10 percent, not 50 percent—I had no idea who *she* was. And less interest in finding out.

"Wake up. We have to keep an eye on her."

"You go ahead. I'll wait here." I yawned, rolled over, and buried my face in the cushions.

"She was upset. I could tell. I still think she knows who shot me. Who tried to kill you. If she knows, she may try to get in touch with that person, but she can't afford to have a call show up on the phone records. I think she'll go see the perp."

"Andy, I am so tired. I was up all night." And I didn't mention that I topped off a night without sleep with two large mimosas. A fact Andy did not throw in my face.

I felt him sink onto the edge of the sofa. He didn't touch me or speak to me. He didn't mention that he was up and he'd been shot only hours before. He just sat there—projecting sadness and disappointment. I could feel the emotion through my trenchcoat.

"Are you going to sit there all day?"

"Dunno," Andy mumbled. He began to bounce his legs.

"Are you going to bounce your legs all day?"

"Dunno." He continued the action.

I rolled onto my back and stared up at him. "How long have I been asleep? Or rather, how long did you let me sleep?"

As he stared at me, I thought I saw traces of a grin on Andy's lips.

"How long, Andy?"

"I fixed the window."

I squinted and saw tape holding a piece of shirt cardboard in place. I didn't think fixed was the correct verb. "How long did that take? Thirty seconds?"

Before he could answer, I fell asleep again. I know we had some conversation after that, but I can't quite recall what we discussed. According to Andy, he discussed following Page and I discussed my senior prom, the future of Russia, and the recipe for Barnegat Bay Clam Fritters in the Ocean County Library cookbook.

Andy had to shake me again to bring me to consciousness. "Are you listening to me now?"

"Unfortunately." I tried to pull away, but Andy was stronger at his weakest than I was at my peak—and I was nowhere near my peak.

"Can't you go alone?"

"And leave you alone and unprotected?"

Andy really knew how to play me. I opened one eye, spotted the remote control, and handed it Andy. "Okay. I'll go. But please, let me sleep just fifteen minutes. Please. That's all. Fifteen minutes." I knew my getting up was important, but I didn't believe that I was physically capable of standing without at least a few moments' sleep.

"Watch your *All My Children* tapes." He protested, but I interrupted. "I won't tell anyone that's what you were doing when you got shot. Hey, if you want to watch *All My Children*, it's okay."

"I wasn't watching *All My Children*."

"Oliver said an *All My Children* tape was running when he got here. He said the tape ended as he walked in."

"No, I was going to watch the tapes I brought back from Page's. I had just started the first one when I got shot." He thought for a moment. "I guess Dallas taped over *All My Children*. The tape must have been running out when Oliver got here. I felt his body stiffen. "Oh, oh." He jumped up—if one can say a recently shot man can jump—and ran—if one can believe a recently shot man can run—to the entertainment center. "Thank God."

"You kept the tapes from Page's?" Andy nodded, not nearly as sheepishly as I felt was warranted. "You promised to get rid of them."

"I will."

"When?"

"After I review them. I need to see if there is anything in them that relates to the murder. I didn't want to upset Page, but these videos might constitute evidence."

"And you forgot that you had the tapes? You gave Petino permission to search the house when you had those tapes here."

"That doesn't mean he looked at them. It doesn't look like he did. He really didn't have permission to." I suspected that argument would be a hard one to win in court. Andy grew pensive. "I hope he didn't. My having pornographic movies starring Page Spenser wouldn't really look too good."

I couldn't argue that point. "You should watch the tapes now so you can destroy them as quickly as possible—unless of course Dallas managed to tape his own murder. But stay away from the window." My eyes headed toward half-mast.

"Maybe Page told someone I had the tapes. Maybe that's why they shot me. Maybe there is something in these videos."

"But Page trusted you to destroy the tapes. She didn't know you took the tapes for any reason other than to destroy them. Did she?"

He mumbled that he didn't think she knew but let the conversation lapse. As I dozed off, I heard the tape rewind and then start. Just as I was losing consciousness, I heard a familiar clipped voice. "Oh my God." That exclamation was followed by Andy's repeating the same words. "Oh my God."

I lifted my head and after ten seconds or so my eyes were able to focus. There on the television screen in living color was Oliver Wilder—cavorting naked with Page Spenser.

"Well, at least that woke me up." I stared at the screen. "Did you know?"

Andy shook his head. "No idea."

I stared at the screen. "What does it mean?"

I could feel Andy's anger, but I sensed it was directed at my question and not at Oliver's actions. "It means Oliver is having an affair with Page. That's all."

"Yeah, but Andy...."

"He told us he had a girlfriend. I can understand why he did not tell us who she was." He hit the stop button and then rewind. "He has a right to his own life. I just hope Page isn't using him."

I just hoped Oliver wasn't using us, but I realized there was no point in trying to discuss that point with Andy. He was struggling to force his one good arm into his jacket. I pulled myself off the couch and tried to help. Finally, in exasperation, he yanked the sling over his head. The sound of Velcro ripping free made the action sound violent. "I'm fine. I don't need this thing. Let's go."

With that he was gone. I ran as best I could to catch up and climbed into the seat beside him. The car was in gear and his right foot was on the gas. He lifted his left foot off the brake before I pulled the door closed. It slammed shut as, to the accompaniment of squealing wheels, the car flew out of the driveway.

Chapter 48

I was asleep with my head on the car window and drool on my chin when Andy poked me. "Here we go." I opened my eyes and, as I squinted through a yawn, saw Page's black Mercedes pull out of the driveway. The driver neither sped nor dawdled. She might have been headed to the grocery store. My guess was that she was not.

We trailed Page down Long Beach Boulevard by ten car lengths, but distance hardly mattered. At that early hour ours was the only other car headed south on the road. This was one time Page's self-absorption worked in our favor. Page was unlikely to notice us in our innocuous white sedan. Page was unlikely to notice anyone in an innocuous white sedan.

She traveled slightly under the speed limit as she followed the signs to the bridge and Route 72. Despite his injury, Andy drove. He claimed the spot where the bullet grazed him barely hurt, but I saw him grimace at each of the turns. I hoped that no heavy-duty defensive driving lay in our future. I didn't believe Andy was up to it. Of course, after the previous night's activities, I knew I wasn't up to it.

After all the time I'd waited for a real investigative opportunity, we'd finally gotten some action. And I couldn't stay awake.

Once we were on Route 72, I told Andy I was just going to close my eyes for a few moments. Route 72 cuts straight across the Pine Barrens, so we would encounter no twists and turns to disturb my sleep.

Andy sounded surprised. "Don't you want to show me where you ran off the road?" What impressed me is that he referred to my being run off the road, not his Mustang's. "I thought you'd want to provide me with every gruesome little detail."

I wanted to—I just didn't think I could. I was still tired and more than a little bit sore from my unexpected flight into the woods. "I'll show you on the way back. It will be easier for me to recognize the spot." My head fell back against the window and I assume my mouth fell open again. I was asleep in a minute and for a minute. "Where are we going?" I sat upright as the car made a right.

"I have no idea." Apparently, Andy had never followed this route before. He pulled to the side of the road to let Page increase her lead over us before he started down the long stretch of macadam that cut a swath through the pine forest. Where the road through the pines led was anyone's guess.

"At least it's paved." My optimism about the road was misplaced. The pavement ended about a mile off the highway. Page's Mercedes continued on, throwing a cloud of dust into the air. That could only be good news. No way she could see us through the dust trail her Mercedes created. I was surprised when Andy pulled the rental car onto the shoulder and stopped.

"Aren't we going to follow her?"

"In time."

I didn't ask for clarification. He was the professional. After a minute of watching dust settle on the road, I was asleep. Suddenly, Andy threw the car in gear and the sedan jerked back onto the road. The action startled me into consciousness. When my eyes were fully open, I could tell that Page must have turned. "Slump down and pretend you're a child." I did as I was told and started asking if we were there yet. Andy clarified that looking like a child was sufficient; behaving like one was overkill. After about a thousand yards, moving very slowly, we passed the third driveway on the road. I spotted Page's car about thirty yards down a gravel drive that led to an old farmhouse. On the porch a small woman in workclothes waved to Page. The woman interrupted her greeting to glance in our direction as we passed. "I think I know her." It took me a few seconds to figure out why. The small build with an unusually large posterior, the short dark hair in stark contrast to the white skin. "She runs a store in Chestnut Hill. She's Cessie something. I'm sure she is. Her son is friends with Bonnie Spears."

As the thick woods hid us from the women's sight, Andy and I each speculated as to why Page Spenser would be acquainted with the friend of her dead husband's daughter from a previous life. I couldn't think of a logical explanation. Neither could Andy—and he was the professional.

After about fifty yards, we came upon a road that cut back into the woods at a thirty degree angle. Andy turned in and drove slowly, peering into the woods on the right. "We should be able to get access to the house from the back."

We?

Spotting another turn some thirty yards ahead he turned again. "This should take us behind the house."

Andy handed me his cell phone. "Call Jake Chandler and see if he knows what happened to us last night. Ask if he's heard anything. And, see if he talked to Cessie and her family in the course of his investigation." Andy parked the sedan across the road and told me to stay put. "I'm going to check this out."

I wasn't surprised Jake had not yet arrived at work. I was more surprised that he had already left his home. I reached his machine. "Hey, Jake. Meg Daniels. I was wondering if you knew anything about a guy that Bonnie Spears hangs out with sometimes. His mother runs a store on Germantown Avenue in Chestnut Hill. Her first name is Cessie. Bonnie introduced me to the kid once, kind of." Then I took a shot in the dark. The kid did have red hair that he clearly didn't inherit from his mother. "I was thinking...is this the son you mentioned that Dallas...

Denver…I guess it was Dover who abandoned him? Remember you said that Denver named him James—Jimmy, I think you said. I was wondering if he lived out here in the pines. Anyway, if you get this message give me a call." I started to hang up when I remembered the principle intent of the call. "Also, did you hear anything interesting about Andy and me lately? Give me a call." I gave him the cell phone number.

Then I sat and watched the woods. Watching dust settle with Andy began to seem exciting.

Chapter 49

I was sitting where Andy left me, minding my own business, when Cessie's son ran across the road about thirty yards in front of me. I pondered my situation. Andy had told me to stay put, but the kid was clearly fleeing. Watching him disappear into the woods, it seemed so obvious. This had to be the Jimmy that Jake had referred to. This had to be the kid that Andy spotted in the dunes outside the Spenser house.

I wasn't thrilled with the prospect of venturing into the pines alone. The last time I ventured—unwillingly—beyond the fringes of the thick woods, I'd almost died. Things had gotten so bad, I'd made one of those pledges that if I ever got out I would devote my life to doing good. Going back to graduate school was the first step in keeping that promise. Now, as I considered following Jimmy, I wondered if deferring school for a sailing trip could be construed as breaking that promise. Breaking? No. Postponing. That was the word. Certainly, applying and registering for school was proof enough of my sincerity. Divine forces would have no reason to think I had reneged; thus, I concluded, they had no cause to punish me. I walked into the woods.

Prickly needles scratched at what little skin showed as I followed the narrow path beaten through the pine trees. After about fifty yards I came upon a small building. Well, it was a building in the same sense that Jake Chandler's compact was a car. I had hoped to find Cessie's son, but I saw no sign of life near the shed. What I did see was an array of targets hanging from trees. Targets with bullet holes strategically placed in their centers. A long wooden plank stretched under the targets. On the ground underneath, tattered tin cans were scattered across the dust. From the looks of the cans, the kid had managed to hit them. Could he hit a moving target? I bet he could. I made my approach hiding behind tree after tree.

Despite my best efforts at stealth, I made a pretty noisy approach through the leaves and twigs. I stopped periodically to listen for evidence of anyone else in the area—especially anyone shooting a twenty-two.

I was surrounded on three sides by woods that could hide anything or anyone. The shack's door was straight ahead of me. Did I want to announce myself, or did I want to take the kid by surprise? Scare him? Startle him into pulling the trigger?

I stopped in front of the rickety wooden door. "Jimmy? Are you in there?" I knocked lightly. "Hello, anyone here?" If they were, they weren't admitting it. "Jimmy?" Nobody answered. Maybe no one was inside. Maybe there was someone inside, but his name wasn't Jimmy. Or maybe the kid, whatever his name was, was in there and didn't want me to know. I stood still and listened. I was willing to bet the shack was empty.

The old wooden slab yielded readily to my left hand. I didn't want a bullet to greet me. I stepped to the side and, without putting myself in the doorway, pushed the door open. A swath of dull light cut across a room crammed with what appeared to be gardening tools. No sign of the kid. No sign of life. If the shed had any windows, they were covered. Not that the day—which hadn't brightened much since 6 A.M.—held much light to sneak in. I whispered Jimmy's name, doubting he was in the dark building but not really doubting that was his name. I pushed the door wide open to admit additional light. I saw a great place to hide a murder weapon, but no kid. I moved into the doorway.

I'd become so absorbed with the inside of the building that I forgot a key point. If Cessie's son wasn't inside, he was outside. Suddenly, the force of two hands slamming into my shoulder blades plunged me into darkness and onto the floor. My head crashed into a table leg. I raised my arms to deflect falling flower pots. When the torrent of clay containers stopped, I rolled onto my back to confront my assailant. What I saw was the door slamming shut. What I heard was the sound of a creaky metal lock sealing me in the shed.

I called out. "Hello. Is that you, Jimmy? I'm Meg Daniels. I'm a friend of Bonnie's. I just wanted to ask you a question."

I stumbled to my feet and rushed to the door. There was no lock on the inside. The door responded to my tugging but would not open. I leaned on the door and talked through the old wooden slats. "Jimmy. It's Meg. You saw me at your mother's shop. I'm a friend of Bonnie Spears. You can let me out. I only want to ask you a question." Actually, I had two questions. I didn't mention that the questions were "Was Dallas Spenser your father?" and "Did you kill your father?"

I pressed my ear to the door but heard nothing. Not even the sound of crunching leaves. I reassured myself aloud, "This place is not structurally sound. You can break out."

As long as I was sealed in the shed, I figured I might as well check around for the murder weapon. I ran my hands along the front walls for a light switch and found none. I wasn't surprised.

The shed was only about five feet wide. I had determined that when I approached the dilapidated structure. Now I positioned myself at the entrance and started to pace off the length. I've seen cartoon characters step on rakes that flew up and hit them in the face. For laughs. I'd always wondered how they did that—now I knew.

I laid the rake against the front wall and rubbed my left cheek. Without ice, the bump promised to discolor and blow up. I'd barely gotten rid of my last shiner. All this violence could not be good for my complexion.

Hoping to find the murder weapon—or at least a flashlight—I moved through the shed, touching each item. Gently. No use identifying the gun by discharging a bullet into my face. I turned my attention to the right side of the shed. Moving toward the back of the building, I slid my hands over assorted pots, plastic bags, and garden tools assembled on a tabletop. No gun. No flashlight.

To my left I felt handles of assorted pieces of gardening equipment. With the memory of the rake fresh in my mind and on my face, I kept my feet to the right. Seven footsteps into the shed, I bumped headlong into a third table. Reaching forward, I found shelves. Running my hand along them I discovered familiar shapes: hammers, screwdrivers, nails of different sizes.

Slowly I touched every item on the workbench. No flashlight. No gun. It was a tedious job, but since there weren't any other demands on my time, I pressed on methodically. After ten minutes of careful searching, I was growing bored and frustrated. Then I heard footsteps in the fallen leaves. The steps circled the shed. I heard a splashing sound. Even before the smell reached me, I knew. I was alone. I was vulnerable. I was about to be toast. Literally. With adrenaline pumping at rates unknown to an endomorph, I slammed my hands against the walls of the shed. "Let me out. Please. Whoever you are, please let me out. Jimmy. You are Jimmy, right? I'm a friend of Bonnie's. Let me out of here!"

The only response was the glow and crackling of flames. The stench of gasoline was giving way to the acrid smell of smoke. The glow of the fire outlined a small six-pane window on the back wall. I climbed up and over the table, knocking the bench to the ground. I ripped a cloth from the front of the window and pushed on the window frame. The bottom pushed out. Even if I'd dieted religiously and exercised as I'd promised on New Year's Eve, I wouldn't have fit through the space. I tried forcing the window with my hands. It didn't move. I grasped for the hammer. Delighted to feel the cold metal, I beat frantically on the hinge that kept the left side of the window from flying free. The smoke was attacking my lungs, but I didn't feel my strength diminishing.

Finally, the hinge broke. I turned my attention to the right. After many frantic blows, the rusted hinge wouldn't budge. I abandoned the hammer and pushed with both hands on the right side of the window. The glass was growing hot to the touch. Smoke curled through the shed. I pushed again. The right side of the window broke free. I hoisted myself onto the sill and spun around. My legs now slipped easily through the opening. Holding the window up, I pushed myself off the side of the shed so I'd fall clear of the flames. When I hit the cushion of pine needles and leaves, I didn't look back. I crawled to the edge of the woods and pulled myself to a sitting position against a narrow tree trunk.

As in an explosion, the shed was suddenly engulfed in flames. I didn't have time to dwell on my near miss. Someone had just tried to kill me. Someone who was probably still nearby.

I surveyed the area around the shed but didn't see my killer. That proved nothing. The woods could easily hide my attacker. Whether or not the killer was nearby didn't matter. I couldn't move. I coughed and gasped for breath. My lungs burned, and my eyes watered. I was helpless to do anything but watch the shed burn. Then, I saw the silhouette against the flames. The figure was running toward me. I tried to rise, but I got no farther than my hands and knees. "Meg. Stop. Meg. It's okay. It's me."

The speaker's legs came into view in lovely black boots of soft leather—probably Italian. Confusion registered on my face as Page knelt before me.

"Meg. It's me. You're okay. Let's get you out of here." She pulled me to my feet and draped my arm around her shoulder. Hunched down, with me hanging around her neck, she dragged me about five feet into the woods and then headed toward the road.

"What happened? Who did this? Do you know who did this to you?"

"Not you?"

Page sneered. "Not me. I'm no murderer. But whoever did this might still be here. Keep moving. Come on. You can do it."

Her right arm held me up. Gradually, my running motions became running. That helped our movement through the trees. I tripped repeatedly but wasn't doing badly for an out-of-shape, attempted-murder victim who had recently fought her way out of a burning building.

Page propelled me onto the road, opened the door of her Mercedes, and pushed me into the front seat. "Are you okay?" With that, the good-hearted Page disappeared and the more familiar Page reappeared. "What the hell were you doing in there anyway?"

Chapter 50

I started my explanation in the middle, without mentioning that we had followed her here. If Page had figured that out, she didn't let on.

"Andy went to see Cessie…and her son. Is his name Jimmy? What is his last name? He ran across the road while I was waiting in the car. I saw him come here but…aren't you going to call the fire department?"

Page peered through the woods at the burning shack and shrugged. "I think it's too late for that place."

"Maybe. But what about the rest of the state?"

"We'll go back to Cessie's house and call." I checked the car for signs of a mobile phone and found it hard to believe there wasn't one. "I saw the smoke from there. I was afraid it was coming from Jimmy's office. That's what he calls this place. Called." A gentle smile crossed her lips. "Jimmy is a sweet boy. People make the mistake of thinking Jimmy is retarded. But he's not. In many ways, Jimmy is normal. Even exceptional." The smile on her face was replaced by a frown. "What happened at the shack?"

"I called Jimmy's name, but he wasn't inside."

"Are you sure?"

I felt a moment of panic followed by a moment of anger. "No. No way. I'm sure."

I jumped at a small explosion in the burning building. I really thought a phone call was in order, but I'd left the cell phone in the rental car and Page claimed not to have one.

"Did Jimmy lock you in there?"

"I didn't see him, but he must have."

In the distance, a shrill whistle summoned the volunteer firemen. Police sirens moved in our direction. Apparently someone had made the call.

"But did you see him lock you in or set the fire?"

"No."

With squealing tires, Page backed the car around so it straddled the road. Then she pressed the gas pedal to the floor. The force carried the sedan's front wheels over the high shoulder. With great effort the back wheels followed. With marked driving skills and alarming speed, Page steered the car down a narrow road—actually more of a dirt path.

Leaves and branches brushed the car as we sped down the path. As we emerged from the makeshift road I saw a dilapidated farmhouse. She drove across a small patch of lawn and slipped the car onto the driveway. She pulled up behind an old van with Pennsylvania plates. I assumed I knew what that meant. But there must be a lot of vans with Pennsylvania plates. I probably needed more information before I accused Jimmy of trying to kill me twice. Probably.

We were stopped in front of the house and Page was out of the car before the door opened a crack. Cessie peered out.

"Cessie, I'm afraid your shack is burning. It sounds like police and firemen are on their way."

"Yes, I hear." She was inappropriately calm.

"Is Andy Beck still here?"

"Andy Beck?" Cessie's eyes had a faraway look in them. "I'm sorry. I've never heard of any Andy Beck."

Yeah, and I'd never heard of Pepperidge Farm.

"Is Jimmy here?"

Cessie didn't know how to reply to that question, although I was fairly certain she had the right answer.

I threw my door open. Page and I both saw the shock on Cessie's face as she caught sight of me. Why? She couldn't possibly remember me from my one visit to her store.

"Why...." She seemed flustered. "I didn't expect...." She corrected herself. "I didn't know you were here. Please come in."

Suddenly Page and I were on the same side. I whispered my concerns in her ear as we headed for the porch. "Andy didn't leave. Our car is still sitting on the road. Did you see her face? I don't think we ought to go in." I changed my mind before she could respond. "But we have to. Andy could be in there."

Page chewed her lip nervously. "This has turned out to be a real mess." Page had a penchant for understatement. And for going wherever she wanted. She charged up the stairs, pulled the front door out of Cessie's grasp, and pushed past the surprised woman. I followed her into a narrow hallway—like a puppy.

"Cessie, where is Andy?" Page's tone was firm. "We know he was here."

Cessie shrugged. "Oh, is he that P.I.?" She tried to affect innocence. Hers was a pathetic effort. "He left. He said he parked on the back road."

Well, that was true. He had. But how had he gotten lost between here and there? He was not in the car when Page led me to her Mercedes. I didn't see him with Jimmy. Maybe he was following Jimmy. I hoped that he had decided to do some reconnaissance in the woods, but a churning in my stomach told me he hadn't.

"Wait in there." Cessie pointed into a dark living room. I obeyed. I had no other plan and not much energy. My throat ached from the smoke and my body from everything else that had happened.

Page went to Cessie and bent down to speak confidentially. Her movements were sharp and urgent. The two stood in the hallway arguing. Actually, it was Page who was doing all the arguing. The two moved through a swinging door into an adjoining room. Before the door swung into a smaller arc, I glimpsed a kitchen that needed renovation sometime in the nineteen fifties. I heard their urgent whispers continue. Not that I could make out what they were saying. I couldn't even figure out how Page knew Cessie. Or why Page had come here today. She obviously thought that Cessie or her family had something to do with the attempt on Andy's life as well as my accident on Route 72. I had to admit I agreed.

I went to each of the living room windows and peeked out, expecting to come face-to-face with Andy peeking in. It didn't work out that way. No sign of Andy. The room was uncomfortably dark. The roof of the porch that surrounded the house wouldn't have admitted much light even if the windows hadn't been covered by half-drawn shades, sheer curtains, and heavy drapes. Nonetheless, I could see around the room well enough to know that Andy was not hidden behind any of the dark couches or overstuffed chairs.

I was beyond nervous. I was scared for Andy. Where was he? Was he with Jimmy? Had he left of his own accord? It was possible that we had just missed each other—but unlikely. "Andy." I called him in a stadium whisper. "Andy, where are you?" I circled the room calling his name. I don't know what I expected. There were no hiding places in the crowded space.

The house had been built a hundred years earlier in an era when heavy dark woodwork was the epitome of good taste— and apparently the people who built this house had a lot of good taste. And, a lot of money. It was obvious, however, that the people who maintained the residence now did not have a lot—of taste or money. The furniture that crowded the room appeared way beyond well worn. Yet, the style suggested a former elegance—as if an English duke had furnished the country house and then sold it to the farmhands. Farmhands who clearly couldn't afford to heat the place. Even in the darkness, I could see my own breath in the air.

A mirror with prominent age spots hung over a brick fireplace. I stood on my toes to check on what I expected would be a bruise on my face, but all I found was a red streak down my cheek. I poked it to make sure it still hurt. It did. After I poked it.

While the women continued their argument, I checked out a row of photos in cheap gold frames that lined the mantel. The pictures included the usual baby and school photos. Jimmy as an infant in his mother's arms. As a toddler in a carriage pushed by his mother. As a young boy with a baseball bat with the man I assumed was his father. Then I looked at his parents' wedding picture. The portrait revealed a dark, little man no more than an inch taller than his five foot, two inch bride. In front of the couple, a beaming Jimmy held his mother's bouquet.

I thought of the strapping six foot, four inch strawberry blond Jimmy had become. I considered recessive genes—briefly. Then I thought about adoption. In the few short moments I'd conversed with Cessie in her store, she'd managed to squeeze in some moaning about childbirth. I ruled out adoption. Then I thought of tall, red-haired Dallas Spenser. My guess had been right. It had to be. No, this was too obvious—and too easy.

I was still pondering the thought when the front door opened and Jimmy flew in. "Jimmy." The sight of me stopped him in his tracks. "Jimmy. Where have you been? Where is Andy Beck?"

A look of shock crossed his face. "He's gone?" Excitedly he took a few steps down the hallway and slid back the closet door. I saw Andy slumped on the floor, bound, gagged, and apparently unconscious.

Chapter 51

"What did you do to him?" I ran to Andy. "Call an ambulance now!" I yelled at Jimmy. "Better yet, go get the firemen—they're right down the road." I reached into the closet and gathered Andy into my arms. I was relieved to hear his breathing. "Get me a knife. I need to free him."

"I'll call the firemen." Jimmy started for the door again, but a stern voice stopped him cold in his tracks. The voice belonged to Page.

"Jimmy, what the hell have you done now?" Page held open the swinging door to the kitchen and posed like a gunslinger come to town to set things right—and possibly to do a little shopping. In her casual attire and gold accessories, the woman made the scene look like a *Vogue* fashion shoot. She took three long strides to the closet door where I cradled Andy in my arms. I was whispering his name, but he wasn't responding.

"I didn't...I didn't...I swear," Jimmy stammered.

"I know, Jimmy." She spat the words with disgust. "You never hurt anyone." She shook her head. "Do you understand, Jimmy, that you just can't kill everyone who gets in your way?"

Jimmy headed for the door. I figured he wasn't going for help; he was trying to get away from Page.

"Don't you move, young man." Now it was his mother's turn. "You stay here until we figure out what we are going to do about this situation."

"Is anyone going to help Andy?" I screeched as loudly as I could given my raw throat—a throat that felt considerably worse after I screamed. Everyone stared at me—including Andy. Apparently my hysterics had brought him back to consciousness. "Oh, Andy, thank God you're okay." I kissed his forehead gently. "What happened?" Only then did I think to peel the duct tape from his mouth. Probably would have been less painful if I had removed the tape while he was unconscious. He protested. "God, Maggie, what are you doing to me?"

"Me?" I was tempted to drop the P.I. onto the floor, but I was afraid he would lapse into unconsciousness when his head hit the uncarpeted hardwood. "I'm your only friend in this room, buddy, so if I were you I wouldn't mess with me. Now, would someone please untie this man?"

Jimmy looked to Page who looked to Cessie. "Cessie, I see absolutely no point in keeping him bound. We need to figure out what we are going to do—and what we are not going to do. And, I would like to emphasize, what we are not going to do is kill Andy. Or Meg." My name was an afterthought. "Let's get Andy back on his feet and then we will all sit down and talk this out. Which is probably what we should have done in the first place." Page helped me move Andy out of the closet and into a sitting position in the hall. "What did you hit him with, anyway?"

"Frying pan," Cessie replied matter-of-factly.

"So you're the one." Page smiled ruefully. "Dallas told me he had an old girlfriend who bopped him with a frying pan."

"He'll be fine." Cessie informed me, but her tone wasn't reassuring. "I'll cut him loose. Page, you get some ice for his head. Jimmy, you are not to move."

The kid backed into a corner and did not move.

While the two women were in the kitchen, Andy and I held a brief, whispered conference. Jimmy did not appear at all interested in eavesdropping. I told Andy my hunch about Jimmy's identity. He told me that he'd gone back to the car and called Petino on the cell phone before he'd confronted Jimmy. "Don't worry. Petino will get here. By the way, where were you?" He sounded indignant.

"Long story." There was no time to tell it. The women were back. Cessie knelt down and used the knife as she had promised—to free Andy. Page passed the icebag to me.

"How did you know that I shot at him?" Jimmy asked Page with a trembling voice.

"Jimmy." Page feigned patience but demonstrated exasperation. "You used the same gun. Didn't you?"

Jimmy nodded sheepishly.

"I told you to ditch the gun, didn't I?"

Again Jimmy nodded.

"I told you to throw it in the ocean, didn't I?"

I could tell that Jimmy was almost too scared to nod.

"You told me you did. Why didn't you?"

Jimmy shrugged. "I thought I might need it. And I did." His face lit up. "I did need it."

Page was nothing short of imperious when she answered. I understood why none of Andy's friends had liked Page—although I couldn't quite figure out why Andy had. "Jimmy, think about it. Who is the only person on Long Beach Island who knows Dallas and Andy?"

Jimmy thought the question over but didn't come up with an answer.

"I am, you ninny. I am. Now what do you think the police will think? Let's see. Someone shoots Dallas. Someone shoots at Andy. Ballistics will show the bullets are from the same gun. What else could you have done to call attention to me? Go on national television and explain how I helped you flee after you murdered my husband? I tried to help you, Jimmy, but it's over.

I don't know what we do now, but I do know I am not going to jail for you."

"I didn't kill Dallas." Jimmy mumbled. As if he was tired of telling Page the same thing over and over.

"Where is the gun now?" Andy took a pragmatic approach.

"I'll get it." Jimmy headed for the door—eagerly.

"No!" Andy and I shouted in unison.

"Stay right here." Andy issued the command and Jimmy obeyed it. "We can worry about the gun later."

Page's anger faded. She knelt before Andy and took his face in both her hands. "Andy, I am so sorry. I lied to you. I never meant to hurt you or put you in danger. I just wanted to help Jimmy. I owe you an explanation. Let's get you up. I'll explain. I'll start at the beginning."

Page and I helped Andy to his feet and to a seat at an old kitchen table. Cessie provided a glass of water, which he drank eagerly. She refilled the old jelly glass and filled a glass for me. A glass of water wasn't going to cure my problems, but it definitely soothed my throat. I asked for another, but Cessie didn't notice. Her attention was focused on her son.

Jimmy kept his distance, which, considering the havoc he'd wreaked on Andy, suited me just fine. He kept trying to move toward the door, but Page caught him every time. Finally, she pointed to a straight back chair and told him to sit down. He complied obediently.

Page was ready to confess. To abetting Jimmy. To framing Andy. To hiding Jimmy Hoffa. Getting her to talk was not a problem. Shutting her up was going to be the difficult part.

She started at the beginning—a time she defined as several weeks before the murder. Some of what she said was news to me. Some was news to Andy. Some was news to Cessie. I could not tell with Jimmy. He was sulking, punctuating Page's comments with the same sentence, over and over: "I didn't kill my father."

A few weeks before his death, Dallas had asked Andy to investigate a prowler. He apparently felt that he was being watched at night at his beach house, though he didn't notice anything odd in New York. When Andy reported that he'd spotted a young kid hiding in the dunes, Dallas had a good idea who it was, thanked Andy for his efforts, and told him no further investigation was needed.

Shortly thereafter, Jimmy presented himself at the door of Dallas and Page Spenser's Loveladies house. He knew Dallas was his father, Dover Snelling. Dallas denied everything. Page, however, believed the kid. She followed him home to the farm we were visiting now. There she met Cessie Wax and confirmed that Dallas had fathered her son, Jimmy.

Here, Cessie took over the story, but only after instructing Jimmy to wait on the glider on the porch. He did so obediently. Was I the only one worried that Jimmy had stashed the gun on the porch? I kept one eye on the back of his head through the window while Cessie told her story.

"Brain injury is a really tricky thing. In some ways Jimmy is fine. In other ways, he's still like a child."

"Dallas didn't want him because of his brain damage?" Andy asked.

Cessie snorted. "Dallas, as you knew him, didn't want him for a variety of reasons. Dallas didn't want *us* for a variety of reasons. He had met Emily by then and was living as Denver Spears. He wanted to forget his past. I was the only vestige of his past life. I waited two years in England for that man. I was faithful to him every moment while he lived in Boston. Over that time I sent the money he...appropriated...the part that he couldn't carry. I even smuggled the rest of the money for him into the U.S. When I came to this country, he had taken the bulk of the money and started a new life. By the time I got to Boston, looking for Dover Snelling using the alias Danvers Sullivan, Dover had assumed the identity of Denver Spears. I followed him to Philadelphia. I couldn't believe...I didn't want to believe that Dover no longer wanted me. I thought we'd marry. I was so happy when I found out I was pregnant. I was so stupid. I thought Dover would be, too—or at least that he would come to like the idea. I actually thought that when I told him he would insist on marrying right away. And in a way that is what happened. He did insist on marrying, but not me. That's when he told me he was going to marry Emily. I asked him what she had that I didn't. He smirked and said, 'Frankie, you are so bloody dumb it hurts.'"

"Frankie?" I asked, thinking of the man at the funeral.

"He called me Frankie. My name is Francesca. Francesca Wexford. Dover changed his name to Denver Spears. I just started going by Cessie. Just in case. It was his idea. I figured we'd get married and I'd be Cessie Spears. Frankie Wexford would be gone forever. When I married, my name changed— although not much. But even with the change from Wexford to Wax, I felt relieved. I was always afraid someone from England might track me down. Funny, I didn't worry when I was with Dover—by then he was Denver Spears—anyway, I didn't worry. Not because getting caught wasn't a possibility, but because I didn't care. I was mesmerized by the man. I don't know what he had."

That made two of us.

"When he left, I felt so vulnerable. That scam…it was Dover's scam, not mine…but I had helped him. If anyone suspected, there were financial transactions they could trace. But I guess Dover had more to fear than I did. From his compatriots in England…the cops…and me. Anyway, Dover…Denver…that man bought me this place to keep me out of Philadelphia. He said he was protecting me, but he really bought me the farm to get rid of me."

"And he never saw Jimmy?" Andy asked.

"If only. I wanted him to be involved in Jimmy's life, but he was married…eventually he had another son. I couldn't let it rest. What a fool…."

Page took over. "I never knew about Cessie or Jimmy until Jimmy showed up at our door. When I found Cessie, she told me how Dallas had thrown Jimmy in anger and injured him."

"Into the brick wall in the garage." Cessie shook her head. "I should have had him arrested then, but I covered for him. Because he paid me off. After that he bought me my business. In Philadelphia. I insisted. And he paid me to keep me quiet. Until he died."

"The first time or the second time he died?" Andy asked the question, but I'd been wondering the same thing.

"Both times, actually." Cessie sighed. "I had to admit I was a bit suspicious when Denver Spears died—having seen Dover Snelling die before him. I never really believed he was dead, but I didn't have the money to track him down. The business produced just enough to let me hang on to this place. But I knew. I knew that someday I'd find him again. He liked cars, Dover did. When he was Denver, too. So whenever I saw an antique car show I'd drop by and look for him. And then, last fall, I was riding through Freehold...don't even remember where I was headed...and I thought I'd stop and take a look around a classic car rally...." She shook her head. "There he was. It was so easy. He was standing right there. The fear in his eyes when he saw me. I loved that, I did. I didn't say nothing to him then. I waited. I heard someone call him 'Mr. Spenser.' And I followed him home. He was staying in Loveladies. From then on, getting back on the payroll was easy." She chuckled. "Sort of a short-term benefit."

"But I will take care of you." Page reached across the table and squeezed Cessie's weathered hand. "That's why we have to figure out what we are going to do about Dallas's murder."

I had the funny feeling something illegal was about to happen at the old kitchen table—at least if Page and Cessie had their way.

"Did you tell Jimmy immediately? After you found out?" Andy was all business.

"Tell him? I never told him. At that point I didn't want that man in Jimmy's life. I never told him."

"So, how did he find him?"

"I figured he found an envelope—I got a money order every month—and got curious."

Figured? Her son kills his father and she doesn't worry about how he found out where his father was living?

"I didn't care how he found out. He'd always been curious about his father. He was always snooping around. I always tried to discourage him. But he was good. He was smart. He found the Spears family last year. Don't ask me how he did that, but he did." Cessie shrugged. The action appeared to require a great effort. "I wasn't worried about how Jimmy did it. I was worried about how he might get hurt by that man. Hurt again."

Page explained how after Dallas rejected him, Jimmy had returned with his photo albums. He felt his father might want to see what his son was like growing up. "He was so sweet. Not at all threatening. He believed Dallas would want to know him." Page's voice quavered. I began to believe that she had a heart.

"Dallas had a gun he claimed was for protection. He never registered it. I don't know where he got it. He pulled it out and held it on Jimmy. He told him he should go away and never bother him again. He said horrible things." Page shook her head. "I knew that Dallas could be sharp, but I never...." She cleared her throat and continued. "Dallas told Jimmy that he disgusted him. He called him names. Told him a kid like Jimmy could not be his son. He wasn't good enough. He said that if Jimmy wouldn't leave, he would. He handed me the gun and strode out the sliding doors to the beach without even a backward look at his son. I put the weapon back in the desk and spent a little time with Jimmy. Maybe half an hour. I thought he had calmed down when he left. It was only about ten minutes later that he ran back into the house through the doors Dallas left through. He was waving the gun...Dallas's gun...and crying. He didn't want to kill Dallas. He kept saying he never meant for his father to die. And he didn't. I swear. I saw his face. He didn't mean to kill Dallas."

"I didn't kill Dallas," Jimmy yelled through the window. He leapt off the swing with such force that the wooden seat hit the wall three times before the arc of its swing grew weaker. Cessie ran to the door to stop her son from fleeing, but her concern was unnecessary. "I did not kill him." Jimmy almost knocked his mother down as he charged into the room with heavy steps. His fists were clenched and his face was red. "He was my father. I loved him."

Page ignored Jimmy's protests. True, she had never seen Jimmy take the gun and, true, she had never heard the shot that killed her husband. "But who else could have taken the gun from the drawer?"

Did the name Page have a familiar ring? I kept the thought to myself.

When Jimmy appeared at her door, Page said, she felt sure she understood what had happened. "Jimmy kept moaning that he didn't want his father to die. He was sorry. He didn't want his father to die. Over and over again."

"I didn't want my father to die." Jimmy's grief was visible on his unlined face.

"Finally, I got him to lead me to the beach. Dallas was float-ing face down in the water. I couldn't believe that Jimmy had done it. But after what Dallas had done to him...I couldn't let him go to jail. I couldn't."

Page admitted that the plan was hers. Her tone was calm, but her thumb pulled at the skin on the third finger of her left hand where she'd worn her wedding ring. "I wanted to make it look like an accident. If the body never showed up, it would be assumed that Dallas had accidentally drowned."

"Dying was something he had a lot of experience in." I never learn. There are certain moments when irony doesn't play, and this was one of them.

"So...." Page eyed me harshly. She was so good at conveying annoyance. "I got Jimmy a wet suit. Then, we put Dallas into the kayak. Jimmy paddled him out beyond the breakers, pulled the plug, and swam back to shore. The tide was going out and I fig-ured it would carry the body out to sea. At worst, if the body showed up it would appear to be a random shooting."

Good plan. Random shootings are everyday events on LBI. One could hardly step onto the Loveladies beach without dodging bullets. My thoughts must have registered on my face because Page answered the question I never asked.

"I know it was an unlikely scenario. But what else could we do? Dallas was already dead. He'd hurt Jimmy so badly. I could not let him ruin his life."

I knew there was a philosophical debate inherent in that statement, but I wasn't going to argue the point.

Page turned toward Andy and leaned forward to emphasize her alleged sincerity. "I was sorry that they suspected you, Andy. I never meant...I just wanted to confuse the cops. To slow them down until the evidence got cold." Her tone asked for understanding. I myself didn't believe that anyone should be that understanding. But it wasn't up to me. She was talking to Andy. "That's why I let the cops know about our past. I hinted that you and I were still involved. I told them I wasn't sure if you were there the night Dallas died. I never said you were. I just never said you weren't." She turned to me. "And it was really silly of me to hit you that night on the beach." She made the statement matter of factly as if I'd know all along that she was my assailant. "I was waiting at Oliver's for Andy. I don't even recall why now. I was probably going to send him on another wild goose chase. When you came by in the cab, I recognized you. I followed your cab to the beach. I guess I figured you would lead me to Andy. It was silly. Stupid. You see, the cops had asked if Andy had a temper. I'd said yes just to confuse the issue. Seeing you alone, I knew what the police would think if you had a...." She didn't finish the thought. "Please forgive me. I just wanted to make some marks. Dark enough to attract the cop's attention."

I could probably forgive her for hitting me, but not for keeping me away from Antigua. I hoped they gave her the chair or whatever it was they gave criminals these days.

Page was running this meeting. Cessie Wax stared into space. Every muscle on her face betrayed her pain. She clutched her son's arm. For support? To restrain him? I wasn't sure.

"So the point is, we have to protect Jimmy." Page issued an order. "Given what Dallas did to him, he was justified."

"Why won't anyone believe me? I didn't kill him. He was my father." Jimmy's eyes beseeched Andy and then me to believe him. He turned to Page. "Why don't you believe me?"

"Jimmy, it's okay that you hated Dallas. I understand why you'd want to punish him."

Jimmy screamed. The next thing I knew he was lifting the end of the table. The beverages, the centerpiece, and the salt and pepper shakers slid down the green formica and landed in a heap on the cracked linoleum. I looked from the broken pile to Jimmy. He was ranting and crying. His mother tried to catch his flailing arms. One caught her in the chin and she fell to the floor. Jimmy didn't notice. Page bent to help the sobbing woman while Andy climbed over the two to grab Jimmy. The furious youngster turned and grabbed the kettle and threw it against the wall. It hit a ceramic owl and bounced off a chair and into the hallway. Andy grabbed Jimmy from behind and held the kid's arms tight against his body. The pain reflected on Andy's face made it clear to me he couldn't hold on for too long.

"Why won't you believe me? Why won't anyone believe me?" Jimmy was sobbing from rage.

He worked his way free of Andy with a headbutt to the P.I.'s nose. Andy fell to the ground. Jimmy kicked him while he was down. We all started to rush the kid when he reached into his thick white cotton sock. Of course. A sock would be a good place to hide a gun.

I froze. I wasn't the only one in the room who did. While Andy writhed in pain on the floor, Cessie, Page, and I played statues. Arms extended as if we could stop a bullet with our hands, we all cautioned Jimmy to simmer down. None of us noticed that Andy's cries of pain had stopped until he reappeared from behind the overturned table, bloody and bellowing. He grabbed the startled young man's arm and wrestled him for the gun. "Get down!" he screamed at us. "Get down!"

I had no problem following his orders. I ducked behind the refrigerator. Across the room, Page found cover behind a metal pantry cabinet. Cessie, however, moved slowly toward the fighting men. "Please, Jimmy. Please. Give me the gun. Give me the gun. Please." The distress in her voice was painful to hear. Cessie Wax's sad life was getting a lot sadder.

I jumped at the sound of the gunshot. If that was the sound of a small caliber pistol, I sure didn't want to hear a larger gun at close range. But my interest in the acoustics of gunfire was short lived. I jumped up in search of Andy. He and Jimmy were spinning out the door. The gun was pointed towards the sky. I didn't see any blood on either of the men. I checked Cessie and Page. They were both still standing. I didn't spot any blood on either of the women. I ran to the door and pushed it open. I saw Andy sprawled on his stomach at the bottom of the stairs. His hands gripped Jimmy's ankles. The gun lay about six feet ahead of the young man who was trying to break free from Andy's grasp. Then I heard the command.

"Freeze." The single word was followed by the sound of many guns being cocked—just like in the movies.

"He did it." I spoke to no one in particular as I pointed to Jimmy.

Men with weapons pointed in our direction moved toward the house. I stood motionless, as did Page and Cessie behind her in the kitchen.

Andy called Detective Petino to his side. "I do not have a gun, okay?" Only after the detective agreed and announced the news to his cohorts did Andy pull a tape recorder from under his shirt. "I hope you don't mind, but I took the liberty...." He handed the tape to the cop. "I think it speaks for itself."

"Can we move?" I asked impatiently from the spot where I had frozen upon command.

Petino nodded at me. "You can. Everyone else wait until we get to you."

I rushed to Andy. He rolled onto his side and into my arms. His face was white and streaked with blood from his nose. As I stroked his cheek, I noticed the blood on his shoulder. "You're bleeding. Have you been shot?"

He made a weak attempt at a shrug. "Not lately. But you know, I don't feel so good."

With that, Andy passed out in my arms.

Chapter 52

The police were still there when they arrived. *They* were the new odd couple.

"You two know each other?" I asked the question. Andy and I were sitting on the side of the porch with our legs dangling over the side. If the porch had ever had a railing, it had long since disappeared. A paramedic knelt beside Andy and ministered to his reopened gunshot wound. I wrapped myself in the blanket the EMS officer had provided for Andy.

"We met in the driveway." Jake pushed his way up the stairs past the medical equipment. "Is Jimmy okay?"

"He's in the kitchen with his mother and Page." At the time, I didn't notice that Jake knew exactly where the kitchen was. I was fixated on the other arrival.

"Hap, what are you doing here?"

He stared. What else would Hap do? "I don't know yet."

This was getting weird. Hap showing up in the middle of nowhere—dressed like a fireman no less.

"How did you get here?"

"I'm a volunteer fireman. I work in a lot of towns. When I got to this fire, something drew me here. I walked through the woods. I ran into that Jake guy in the driveway. He told me who lived here, but it made no sense to me. I don't know these people. Who are they?"

Very cautiously, I explained who lived in the ramshackle farmhouse. I didn't mention murder or blood relationship to Dallas.

"Can I sit down?" I'd never seen Hap rattled before. He was beyond rattled. What had I said to upset him? He leaned against the porch beside me. Turns out it wasn't what I had said. "It's too much. Too much." Hap protested—not to me—to an invisible presence.

"What is he telling you?" I knew without asking that Hap would claim to be talking to Dallas.

"He's showing me those baby boys. He's telling me one of them sent him to the other side. He didn't want to go but his son pushed him."

Poor Jimmy. He could protest all he wanted. No one on the side of the living believed him. Now votes against him were coming in from the other side.

Jake was going to put the story in the newspaper tomorrow. I couldn't see any harm in filling Hap in now. I told him that the police were going to be talking to Dallas's son about his murder.

"Was this guy Dallas relentless?" Hap lay back with his head on the floor of the porch. "I am going to have to send him away." He closed his eyes and massaged his temples. "He is really coming on a bit too strong." After that, Hap had nothing to say. As far as I could tell, he had passed out.

"Hap?" I leaned back and slapped his cheek lightly. He groaned but didn't open his eyes. "Hey." I called the paramedic who was putting the finishing touches on a new bandage for Andy. "I think we have a problem over here. He's out cold."

I don't know what Mitchell the paramedic did but, within three minutes Hap was conscious and protesting that he was fine. "Is he gone?" He sounded hopeful.

"Jimmy?"

"No." He stared into space and then let out a deep sigh. "Dallas." He jumped to his feet. "I gotta get outta here or he'll try to come back." He looked around the area frantically.

"Where's your car?"

"I came on the fire truck. It's gone." He sounded panicked.

At that moment, two paramedics rushed out the front door with Jimmy strapped on a stretcher. Cessie Wax trailed behind, trying desperately to keep a hand on her son's shoulder. Hap, Andy, and I watched the activities—Andy and I with interest, Hap with fear. He put both hands to his temples and massaged them roughly. I heard a low moan coming from his lips.

"Jake, are you leaving?" I asked as the reporter stepped onto the porch.

"He is." The next person out the door, a young cop in uniform, answered for him.

I laid my hand on Hap's arm. "Would you mind driving Hap back to his car?" I asked Jake for the favor.

Jake didn't even ask where that was. He agreed. The cop recorded Hap's name and address and told him that the police might be in touch. Hap was polite. He didn't know if he could be of help but would be happy to make the effort. I am sure the cops had no idea what that effort might entail.

Hap turned to thank me. "Does this make sense to you? I have a woman who wants to contact you. She's showing me keys. I see a red and white cookbook. It has a pocket in the front. I think she wants you to see that the keys are there."

"Ready, fella?" Jake called to Hap.

"Thanks for getting me a ride." Hap smiled at me. Of course, he hadn't gotten a good look at Jake's car yet. "Gotta go." Hap waved over his shoulder as he followed Jake to the driveway. "Who are you?" He asked Jake as the two headed along the side of the house.

Andy wrapped his good arm around my waist. "If I thought Jake moved fast before, think how well he'll do with Hap as a source."

The two young men were chatting amiably as they got into Jake's old car. Jake was animated. And Hap? Hap was looking around nervously as if Dallas might somehow catch up with him. He was in the car with his seat belt fastened by the time Jake got the key in the ignition.

"What was that Hap said about the keys?" Andy pulled me close.

"He said that a woman wanted me to know that the keys were in the cookbook."

Andy snorted. "Well that doesn't make any sense."

"Actually, it does." I shook my head in what I considered an intelligently thoughtful manner. "I can remember my mother waving the keys to the old convertible I had when I was in college. She was walking into the kitchen and she said she was going to put them in a safe place. But I never remembered what she said. And I never found them."

"He said they were in a cookbook?"

I nodded.

"Well, were they?"

I smiled. "I don't know. I kept that cookbook when my parents died, but it's in storage. We'll have to wait to find out."

"All those years you never once opened that cookbook?" Andy didn't sound particularly shocked.

"You're surprised?"

"No. I'm impressed. With your mother. She really knew a safe hiding place when she saw one."

Chapter 53

"I can understand why you might be reluctant to help Jimmy." Cessie Wax apparently had a flare for understatement. "I know that over the past few days he has tried to warn both of you off."

Warn us off? I thought the phrase she needed was *knock us off.* Over the past week, Jimmy had tried to murder both Andy and me. Now, his mother was sitting in our living room asking us to postpone our departure to help clear her son.

Cessie and Bonnie Spears showed up in Holgate as Andy and I were packing our bags. We were ready to say good-bye to LBI. The house was clean. The window was fixed. The sun had set. One more night on Long Beach Island and we were off to Kennedy for our flight south. Then they arrived.

I wasn't sure how the two had found us. They'd come in from the front, the beach side—the vantage point from which Jimmy had shot Andy. I assumed Jimmy gave them directions to the house—since he had visited at least twice before when trying to frame and kill Andy.

I was the one who heard the knock. I stuck my head around the corner of the living room wall and saw two forlorn faces peering through the glass. I was surprised enough to see that one of the faces belonged to Bonnie Spears, but I found it especially hard to believe that Cessie was on our porch. But there she was. Dwarfed by her foul-weather gear. Buckles fastened; hood up. Knocking on the sliding glass doors. Looking tiny and cold and pathetic. Asking for help.

"I know that Jimmy did not kill his father. I know he didn't. He claims that everything Page says is true, but he still says he didn't kill his father. He says he didn't and he doesn't lie to me. Ever." Cessie Wax was now seated on the white couch with a cup of hot chocolate that she barely sipped—although she seemed to find the warm cup a good antidote to the cold night.

"Never. He doesn't lie to me either. Ever." Bonnie was emphatic. Her look that night was innocent. No make-up. No hair gel. No nose ring. The latest transformation made me worry. I didn't like to be manipulated—mainly because it was so easy. I found myself responding to those big blue eyes that appeared so much larger and so much more innocent without heavy make-up weighing them down. "I know I've only known Jimmy for a year, but I trust him."

"Go on," Andy said.

"When Jimmy told me what happened I told him to go to the police—or at least talk to you." Bonnie flashed her eyelashes at Andy to emphasize her alleged innocence. "But he wouldn't. Page told him that he would go to jail if anyone found out that he was at the Spenser house that night. I know she wanted to protect Jimmy. She went all out to help him, but Page doesn't know Jimmy. She doesn't understand what a kind boy he is. She believes he's guilty."

Heaven knows I don't like to side with Page but I had to go with her on this one. If a guy shows up in the middle of the night with gun in hand crying that he never meant for his father to die and then led me to that same father's body floating in the ocean with a bullet in the back, I'd be a bit suspicious. Especially when that same boy tried to kill two more people within the month. Okay, I'll admit my opinion was colored by the fact that Andy and I were the two people he had tried to kill. But attempted murder is attempted murder—and I didn't believe for a moment we were talking about attempted scaring.

Cessie and Bonnie found a sympathetic ear in Andy. He had only pity for the boy who'd been hurt so badly by his father. We all knew that Jimmy did not dispute Page's version of what she witnessed. He did, however, dispute her assumption about what happened when she was not present.

According to Jimmy, he had run out to follow Dallas but had stopped on the deck. He needed to figure out what he could say to win his father's affection. By the time he reached the beach, he found Dallas lying in the shallow water. He knew Dallas was dead. He saw the bullet hole and the circle of blood on Dallas's back. When he saw the gun a few feet away on the beach, he was afraid the tide would wash it away. According to Jimmy that was why he picked the weapon up and ran to find Page.

Jimmy liked Page. He trusted Page. He had witnessed her attempt to persuade Dallas to take responsibility for his son. So Jimmy turned to Page when he found Dallas's body. And she had helped him. She told him he would go to jail if they didn't get rid of the body and the gun. He believed her, but she did not believe him. Andy believed both of them.

"I don't doubt at all that Page wants to protect Jimmy." Bonnie sounded sincere. "She knows Jimmy had a motive. He did. I admit that. But so did I. And so did Mrs. Wax. And so did my mother...and my brother...and Page...." Bonnie let her voice trail off. There was no use in going through the entire list of people who had a reason to want Dallas dead. Might as well read the Manhattan phone book aloud.

"I don't know where else to turn," Cessie said in a trembling voice. Her wild eyes and shaking hands betrayed the emotions she was trying to hide.

I leaned forward and took the cup of chocolate from her hand. The place was already clean. I wasn't about to deal with a big brown spot on the light Dhurri rug. At the same time, I speculated that Cessie must really be in trouble if she chose us to help her. Didn't she have any friends?

"You're private investigators." She awarded both Andy and me the same professional status. "The police are finished with their investigation. They aren't going to try to clear Jimmy. You know how that feels." She gazed at Andy beseechingly.

Andy looked sympathetic. Perhaps he had forgotten the only reason he was capable of empathy. The only reason he knew what it was like to be falsely accused. The only reason the cops had targeted him. Page and Jimmy had tried to frame him. And, I just want to mention one more time, Jimmy had tried to kill him.

Watching Andy, I saw him demonstrate one of the qualities that made me admire him. I was in awe of the kindness he showed the mother of the boy who had tried to destroy his life. At that moment, there were two things I was sure of. One, I really loved him for helping the woman. Two, if we didn't clear this up I was never getting to Antigua.

I was flush with happiness and annoyance.

Chapter 54

"We'll give her two days. That's it. I swear we will be on a plane within seventy-two hours. I promise." Andy raised his hand to confirm his pledge.

"You look like a boy scout."

"The one on Dallas's Web site?"

"Ugh. I was beginning to forget about that." I pulled the big comforter around me and gazed out over the ocean. I had thought this morning would be our last in the king-size bed overlooking the Atlantic Ocean. I had hoped it would be the last.

Andy slid the glass door back to admit fresh air that smelled suspiciously like spring. Suddenly, getting to Antigua didn't seem so urgent. Not compared to what we could do to help a kid whose tough life was about to get tougher. "What can we do in forty-eight hours?" I'd asked this before, but with a very different intonation.

Andy would start by talking to Page. She was out on bail and back at her house in Loveladies. "I'll go over the details of the night Dallas died. This will be the first time I've questioned her since she stopped protecting Jimmy." I wanted to add "and

framing you," but I figured I'd beaten that horse enough. I should be happy that Andy was so forgiving. Someday that characteristic might work in my favor.

Andy felt, and I agreed, that Jake Chandler was the other person who knew the most about the case. "See if he forgot to tell us anything. Every other time you and he gossiped, he was trying to protect Jimmy. He might have been holding back. He must have been. Just talk to him, see what he knows." Andy offered no more specific instructions for me, but he did outline his plans for the day.

"I'm going to call Cessie Wax. Remember James Spears said he got a call a year ago from a kid looking for his father? I'm assuming that caller was Jimmy and that was how and when Jimmy met Bonnie. Cessie may know. If she doesn't, she can ask Jimmy. I need to see if I'm right."

"And if you're not?"

Andy shook his head. "Maybe it was an old buddy of DS from any of his many lives."

"Or a son from the missing years?"

Andy sighed. "Sometimes my head hurts keeping this man's lives straight."

After Andy left, I reached Jake at home. He was cordial, but I did not get the impression he would be thrilled to see me. He had probably moved on to other stories, I figured—at least until the trials related to Dallas Spenser's death got started. He told me I could meet him at a bar in Pleasantville if I really wanted to see him. He would be going there anyway for a late lunch. His tone said, "if you insist on joining me, you can." My tone said, "I insist."

As I got into my jeans, shirt, and red sweater, I pledged that as soon as I hit Antigua I would burn these clothes, along with the boat shoes in which my feet had spent the last six weeks. I dropped Andy off at Oliver's, where he borrowed a car. The good thing about Oliver was he always said yes and never asked why. I think that was true of all aspects of his life. I took the rental car and I headed for the Garden State Parkway. As I

passed the gas station where Hap Hathaway worked, two things occurred to me. Number one, did Hap know how the scene at the Wax house had played out? Number two, did I need gas? I checked the gauge. The needle was on E. I never expected to put gas in a car I didn't own—no matter how long I drove a rental—no matter how many rentals I drove.

As I pulled up to the gas pump I wished that everyone could know the joy of gassing up in New Jersey. No self-service. No getting out in the cold. No standing staring at numbers flipping—quickly on the price, slowly on the gallons. No waiting in line while fifty walk-in customers buy lottery tickets.

A lanky man attired mostly in grease strode across the cement to the pump to my left. Over my shoulder, I asked him to fill it up. He put the pump in and disappeared. I looked around for Hap Hathaway, but the man-child was nowhere to be seen. When the attendant returned to collect, I asked for Hap. "I thought I might see him today."

The guy grew serious. "You a friend of Hap's?"

"Kind of. I know him. I haven't seen him in a couple of days. I wanted to fill him in on a few things."

"Well, ma'am, I hate to tell you this, but Hap was in an accident. He's in the hospital down in Somers Point. He's not doing that good."

"What happened?" My concern at Hap's condition overrode my concern that a man in his twenties had called me ma'am.

"I don't know the details. From what I hear he can't recall, but he was beaten up bad."

"Beaten up? By a person?"

The guy nodded. "Looks that way, ma'am."

"Who would beat Hap up?" Even as I said the words, it occurred to me that not all people appreciate uninvited guests from the other world. I reworded my question. "Who do you think might have done it?"

The guy wiped his hands with a rag blacker than the oil stains on his hands. "I couldn't say, and like I said he apparently does not remember."

"When did this happen?"

"Don't know exactly. His girlfriend called me this morning."
Hap had a girlfriend? A living one? Now I was really shocked.

"I have to call and check on him. Do you have his room
number?"

"No. They won't ring his room anyway. Well, they wouldn't
earlier. You can try." I nodded that I would and started to pull
out. "Hey!" The man yelled and I jammed on the brakes. "Be
sure to ask for him by his real name."

"Right." I hit the gas and then the brakes again. I had no idea
what Hap's real name was. I looked back at the man.

"Jim. Jim Hathaway."

I thanked him and resumed my trip. Hap was on my mind for
the entire ride. I'd last seen him walking into the sunset with
Jake, and I started thinking maybe Jake could shed some light
on the situation.

Jake was in the bar when I arrived. I am sure the establish-
ment had a name, but the management apparently felt no need
to put the moniker on the outside of the building. The regulars
knew where to find it. No one else would want to. The bar was
not the kind of place many women frequented—especially
alone. Given Jake's pose as an ace reporter, I expected his hang-
out to be full of jaded reporters at the bar trading stories about
gangsters, politicians, and movie stars. What I found was a place
half full of men who appeared to have given up on life. And
Jake. The glasses in front of the reporter told me that he had
been following many beers with many shots for many hours
before I slipped onto the barstool next to him. Jake said he was
going for a late lunch. He just neglected to mention that first he
was going for an early binge.

"Jake, I just got the worst news."

"Hello to you, too." Jake lifted a glass to toast my arrival.

"You won't believe what happened to Hap. Did you hear?"

"Hear what?"

"What happened to Hap."

"What happened to Hap?"

I held up my hands to silence him. "Let me do the talking, okay?" I told him what the gas station attendant had told me.

"He's alive? Could he tell the cops what happened? Where did it happen? Where did they find him? Is he going to be okay?" Jake took a long drink of beer. When he finished he had more questions, starting with, "Was it an accident?" I guess it's a reporter's job to ask questions. Jake had a million of them. I did not have any answers.

With uncertain steps, Jake led me to a booth. He fell onto the bench, spilling most of his beer in the process. He gestured frantically for another drink. Much to his disgust, I ordered a Coke. He sneered, but then he remembered Hap. "Poor Hap. Didn't really know him, of course, but he seemed like a really good guy. Little odd with that talking-to-the-dead thing going on."

"Maybe you could investigate."

"Yeah. Maybe I will." He grabbed his next drink out of the waitress's hand before she could get it to the table.

"I'm the designated driver," I reassured her as I took my Coke.

"Look, Jake," I said when we were alone again. "Andy and I were wondering if there is anything you didn't tell us, back when you were protecting Jimmy. We want to help him. He says he didn't kill Dallas, and we believe him."

Jake didn't answer. He drained his beer and followed it with a shot.

"Jake, what's wrong? I can't sit here and pretend I don't know that you have a bit of a drinking problem."

"No problem. Trust me. I'm just letting off a little steam. I had a rough week." I stared at him until he made eye contact. "Really."

I hadn't driven fifty miles to handle Jake's problems. "Is there anything you can think of that might help Jimmy out of this mess?"

"I...I don't know how I can help him. I would if I could. I told you he was innocent, didn't I?"

"You always said that. Always."

Jake looked disgusted as he waved down the waitress. He asked for another round.

"New shift. I have to see some I.D." The woman wasn't happy about either development.

"Hey, I can vouch for him. Plus, he's been drinking here for an hour or more."

"Lady, it's obvious you're old enough to drink. I need to see the kid's I.D."

With effort, Jake produced a New Jersey driver's license. The woman scowled at the license, scowled at Jake, and went off to get him a beer and a shot.

"How old are you, anyway?" I plucked the I.D. from Jake's hand to check the date of birth. I didn't get that far. My eyes remained riveted on the name on the license: James S. Chandler. James. Jake was a nickname. Jake's given name was James. In that instant, I knew. Even before I had time to recall Jake's indignation at Dallas's giving the same name to his second son after disowning the first. Even before I thought of Boston. Cessie had said that DS had moved from Boston to Philadelphia. Jake had been raised by his grandmother in Boston. I checked the date of birth field and did a quick calculation. Jake was born smack dab in the middle of Dallas's missing years. My mind was racing as I passed the license back. All the evidence was circumstantial, but it was all pointing in one direction.

I knew my face looked strained. Unnatural. I couldn't figure out what my natural expression should look like. I tried a smile. "Well, you really are legit." I tried to keep my breathing even. Even if Jake did turn out to be DS's son, there was no reason to assume he killed his father.

Who was I kidding? I was sitting across the table from a killer. And Jake knew I knew. His eyes told me. First. Then his mouth told me. "You're smarter than I thought."

"Is that a compliment? I'm not actually smart enough to figure it out."

Jake chuckled and waved at the waitress to hurry up. On the one hand, I didn't think he needed another drink. On the other hand, I thought it was in my best interest that he have as many beers as he could hold. He wasn't very big. A couple more drinks should knock him out. Then I could slip away.

He ordered two more rounds when the waitress delivered his next. Then he drained the beer, downed the shot, and slid the empty glasses back onto the waitress's tray before she had a chance to leave the table.

Sandy with the well-worn nametag and the persistent scowl sneered at me. "I'm the designated driver," I assured the late-shift waitress. "Bring me another Coke."

Jake started working on his next drink. "So now you know."

"Know what?"

"Everything. I can see it on your face. You know that old 'DS' as you like to call him was my father. At that point, he was called Danvers Sullivan. That was the first name he used when he came to the U.S. When he arrived in Boston, when he charmed my mother. When he abandoned my mother. To become Denver Spears. To marry Emily. To father James." Jake spit the name. "Danvers Sullivan. But he was the same guy. The same rotten-to-the-core slimeball who called himself Dover Snelling and Denver Spears and Dallas Spenser. He left my mother like he left all the others. Didn't fake a drowning or anything that dramatic. Didn't have to. He broke my mother's heart and it killed her. All I ever had of him was one lousy pic-ture—one picture and this ridiculous head of hair. I couldn't even be tall like him. I'm tiny like my mother. She was so tiny. He hurt that tiny little woman. She was so sweet. So kind. I barely remember her. Just from pictures. I don't even have a picture of us together. The three of us. All I have is one, just one, photo that she must have taken. He was holding me. I was only about six months old. We were at an antique car rally. I think that's why I love old cars so much. Isn't that pathetic? Aren't I pathetic?" Now that he was talking, his interest in drink-ing seemed to be fading. I encouraged him to drink up. I needed him to get drunk, pass out, and forget we ever had this conversation.

"Do you think I was wrong to kill him?"

I shook my head. "He was a bad man. A cruel man."

Jake slammed his fist into the table. "But he was my father." I saw tears welling in the young man's eyes. "And l loved him. And I hated him. And I killed him." With that Jake's eyes closed and his head fell forward onto his chest. What did one do with an unconscious killer? Before I could figure that out, his head popped up and his eyes flew open. "Now, where were we?"

Chapter 55

If alcohol really destroys short-term memory, there was no way Jake would remember confessing to Dallas's murder. By the time I pulled up in front of his house, he didn't even know who I was—although he apparently found me darn attractive.

"Why don't you come inside and we'll have a little fun?" Jake woke up, asked the question, and fell back to sleep. The reporter was dead weight in the front seat of the rental car.

"Come on now, Jake. Let's get you inside." Jake was small, but still too much for me to lift. I opened the passenger door and yanked on his arm.

"What?" Actually, he said, "Whaaaaa?" He opened his eyes and looked around but found it impossible to focus on anything. "Where am I?"

"You're home. It's time for you to go to sleep. You'll feel better in the morning. We'll talk then."

Jake struggled to his feet. He leaned on the passenger door and surveyed his home as if he had never seen it before. "I live here?"

"Yes, you do." Jake was far too drunk to wonder how I knew. "And you're going to go inside and go to sleep."

"Okay," he said cheerfully. After I pulled him to his feet, he lurched forward toward his cottage. He was unsteady, but moving forward. I didn't wait to see if he made it all the way or not. I locked myself in the car and burned rubber pulling away. Driven by my greatest fear—that Jake would sober up, realize what he'd told me, and kill me—I headed out of town, pausing only to make a call from a bank of phone booths on 9th Street.

Andy didn't answer. "Andy, if you're there, pick up. Pick up!" I started screaming into the machine before the message ended. "Andy, please. Listen to me. Get out of the house. No. Wait at the house for me and we'll leave. Don't go to sleep. Whatever you do, don't go to sleep. Cessie Wax was right. Jimmy didn't kill Dallas—Jake Chandler did. He's Dallas's son. It's a long story. We have to get to Petino. Tonight. If we do it in the morning...if he wakes up...he'll kill us...I mean, why not? He's done it before. I'm on my way to get you. Do not fall asleep. I think he's out for the night but...I gotta go. I'm on my way home."

Andy got my message only minutes after I left it and called the police immediately. Somehow or other he got in touch with Petino and persuaded the detective to meet us. Petino, in turn, had persuaded some poor county employee in High Bar Harbor to host the meeting. He agreed with Andy and me that if we stayed in the Holgate house we would be sitting ducks for Jake Chandler—should he sober up and come in search of me. Petino drove down from his house in Toms River and, on his advice, I picked Andy up and drove north from the southern tip of LBI. "Half the people who visit this island don't even know that High Bar Harbor exists. Even if Chandler starts combing the island, he isn't going to find you there."

Petino was right about High Bar Harbor. I never knew the neighborhood existed where virtually every property had a great view of the Barnegat Light—although in hindsight I could remember Hap Hathaway's mentioning it one time. Poor Hap. It seemed obvious now that he was another of Jake's victims. We wouldn't know for sure until we could talk to Hap—if he could remember, that is—but I was convinced my fears were correct.

I took no solace in the fact that Andy and I were the ones who had put Hap in Jake's car. Okay, I was the one. Hap had probably started channeling Dallas, and once Jake realized that he knew the truth he had tried to silence him. Suddenly I caught myself. What was I thinking? I didn't for a moment believe that Dallas had been talking to me through Hap. Did I?

When we found the address Petino had given Andy, a young county investigator opened the door to yet another waterfront house. I was wondering how the guy could afford a spread like this one when he mentioned that he was housesitting for his parents. "So please, no gunfights or bloodstains. Okay, Petino?"

Petino didn't make any promises, but he was optimistic as he led us to the back of the house. He figured that if Jake was going to make a move, he would go to Holgate and then to Oliver's house. Andy and I both looked at the detective with concern. "Wilder?" We nodded. The cop made a call on his cell phone. "A car will pick Wilder up and bring him here. I doubt Chandler would think to go after him—but who knows how clearly he's thinking. He could go looking for you and...." The detective changed tack. "Let's play it safe."

Every move the detective made told me he believed my story. That was a first. But there was something he didn't understand. "Why would Jake Chandler tell you?"

"I have one of those faces."

Petino smirked. He glanced at Andy, who nodded. "She has one of those faces."

"Really. I'm always the one they ask for directions. Anywhere. England. France. Hong Kong. Once in Mexico City a woman came up to me and asked me for directions in Spanish."

"So you speak Spanish?"

"No, I don't—which I told her."

"In Spanish?" The cop wanted to know.

"I can say, 'I don't understand' in Spanish. And I understood enough to know that she was saying, 'How can you not understand? All I want to know is....'"

"So you do speak Spanish?"

The cop was giving me a headache. "Let's get back to Jake. He confessed to me. He knew I had the whole story figured out. I think he liked bragging that he'd gotten away with killing Dallas. When he was drunk. When he sobers up I don't think he'll be too happy. But I believed him. I'm sure he did it."

"If you say so." The detective shrugged. "And I do believe you."

"Well, that's a first." Now it was my turn to smirk at the detective.

"I'm not going to apologize to either of you. We were acting on sound evidence in investigating Beck." He nodded at Andy but spoke to me. "I am sorry that people you knew were callous enough to try framing Beck, but we were only acting on what appeared to be very persuasive proof of his guilt." The detective looked tired. The tight skin on his face appeared to sag—just a little. His dark eyes were surrounded by red. "In my own defense, I must say that I never got a bad feeling about you, Beck." He shrugged. "I usually trust my instincts, but never at the expense of the evidence." Andy nodded as if he understood. And I was sure he did. Even I did. And I certainly could not fault the cop's responsiveness now.

Petino had arranged for surveillance on Jake Chandler until we straightened everything out. It appeared he was still inside his house—or actually almost inside his house. The young reporter had passed out in the doorway with his head inside and his feet outside. He hadn't yet moved. Petino wasn't willing to make a move on the guy simply on my say-so. Not because he didn't believe me, but because the drunken confession would not stand up in court. When the cop spoke, he spoke to me. "Will you wear a wire?"

"Hey." Andy interrupted. "That could be dangerous."

"I'm not saying it won't be, but we will do everything we can to protect her."

Okay, it was one thing to risk my life to save Andy. But he was in the clear. I would be risking my life to clear Jimmy Wax. A kid who had tried to frame my boyfriend for murder. A kid who had tried to kill me. A kid who had never gotten a break in his life.

"How do I get Jake to talk to me again?"

"We'll work with you. Coach you. You'll do fine."

I turned to Andy. He shrugged to let me know that the decision was mine.

The first thing in the morning I was on the phone to Jake. "Jake, it's Meg. Are you awake?" He mumbled that he was now. I cut him off. "Don't talk on this phone. But we do need to talk. Meet me at Barnegat Light. Can you be there by noon?"

He groaned.

"Jake, we need to work something out for both our sakes. I want to be your friend. Understand? When can you get there?" I had to remind him that he had to pick up his car. I also had to remind him where his car was.

He agreed to meet at noon. "It won't be easy, but if you insist...."

Once again, I insisted.

Chapter 56

I was wired and standing on the walkway by 11:45. I'd been trained on techniques to elicit a confession and not much else. Once I got Jake to talk into my baseball cap (where the microphone was hidden), my part would be over. When the cops in the blue van in the parking lot gave the word that they'd heard all they needed, an undercover officer in a red jacket would walk by, signaling me. Then I would make my excuses and get out of the way so the cops could take Jake.

I knew I was surrounded by police—all hidden or disguised. Nonetheless, I felt nervous as I stood on the long walkway that topped the jetty. Occasionally, an officer walked by and mumbled news about Jake's progress. Two cops from Cape May County had followed him to the county line, where the Atlantic County cops took over. At last the mumbled news was that the Ocean County police were tracking Jake's moves.

Noon passed, but no sign of Jake. It was close to 12:30 when he appeared in front of the lighthouse.

I remembered telling Andy I could take Jake. If appearance were any indication, it would be especially easy that day. From what I could deduce as he came down the walkway, he was teetering on unsteady feet. He didn't even appear to reach his usual diminutive height. He wore oversized sunglasses that made his undersized head look even smaller.

As soon as he reached me, he fell against the railing. "Why did you drag me up here?"

I pointed the brim of my hat at the reporter. "Jake, we need to talk. And not on the phone."

"About what?" Jake was irked and wanted me to know it.

"Do you remember our conversation last night?"

He reached a finger under his sunglasses and rubbed his right eye. "Some of it came back to me on the drive up here." His voice was devoid of emotion. I wished he would drop a hint about his attitude. "Why did you pick such a cold spot?"

"Jake, given what you told me last night, I didn't want to take the chance that we might be overheard."

"So we couldn't go to your place?"

"Jake," I did my best to sound earnest, "I didn't tell Andy anything about our conversation." The ease with which I lied alarmed me. But lying to a killer was not like lying. Right? "Do you remember what you told me?"

Jake studied me. I turned my head so the wind blew my hair onto my face and hid as much of my expression as possible. My guess was that Jake remembered the entire conversation but was deciding whether to admit he remembered or not. Apparently, he reached no firm conclusion. "Maybe."

"Jake, I believe you. I believe you killed Dallas Spenser, but I'm not going to the cops. Look, I'm leaving town. I'm leaving the country. Your secret is safe with me. All I ever cared about was clearing Andy. Before I go, I wanted you to know that. I'll never tell. But I would like to help you figure out a way to get Jimmy out of jail."

"Don't you think I would if I could?" He sounded truly anguished. As he leaned forward with both elbows on the rail I bent my hat forward to catch his words. "I never meant for him to go to jail. He's a good kid." Jake stood straight and pulled his old tan raincoat around him. "Tell me again why you dragged me out here."

I pointed the brim of my hat at his face. "I wanted to be where no one could hear us when we talk about how you are going to make sure that Jimmy does not go down for a crime you committed."

"It's going to rain." The effort to turn his face to the sky caused Jake visible pain.

I checked out the cloud cover. "Not for a while. We're not going to be here all day. We have to figure out a way to get Jimmy off without your confessing to Dallas's murder."

Jake put a hand on the railing to steady himself. "I can't stand up much longer. Can we sit in my car?"

Could we? Petino told me not to leave with Jake. But Jake wasn't suggesting a ride. He just wanted to sit down. That sounded okay. We'd be closer to the police van in the parking lot. Maybe the signal would be better. I believed Jake was telling the truth about why he wanted to sit in the car. I'd watched him tie a load on the night before. I understood his pain.

I was all solicitude as we walked slowly to the parking lot. "Jake, you should be careful when you drink. Did you tell anyone else you killed Dallas?" I turned my hat brim to catch his response.

"Do you think I'm an idiot? Why would I tell anyone I killed Dallas?"

"That's my point. You should keep it to yourself. It's lucky you told me, and not someone who cared. I mean, there was a time I would have. But now...like I would care who offed Dallas Spenser! From what I know now, he deserved what he got."

Jake didn't agree or disagree. I didn't think his silence was the result of strategy. He was just too hung over to talk.

Jake's old Toyota was easy to find. There were five cars and a van in the lot. Two of the cars and the van belonged to the cops. One car was my rented sedan. One car was a Land Rover. And then there was Jake's deteriorating compact.

As he unlocked the passenger door, I wondered whatever possessed him to lock his car doors. But he did. Both of them.

I got in, then reached over and unlocked the driver's door for him. He fell into the front seat with a groan. "Man, how much did I drink last night?"

"Too much. You should be more careful."

"Aren't you going to close the door?" He nodded at the passenger door that I'd left standing wide open. I argued that we weren't going to move the car. He argued that we'd gotten into the car to stay warm. Even I had to admit that his argument was stronger than mine.

The door had barely slammed shut when he turned the key. "Hey," I said quickly, "I thought we were going to talk here."

"I'll run the heater." That was only half of Jake's plan.

Turned out that Jake had a favorite spot for confidential conversations. He wouldn't tell me where it was, but he assured me that I'd love it. "We're talking about some high stakes issues. You may be smart about a lot of things, but not necessarily about finding a spot for a confidential conversation. That's part of my job. Trust me on this one." He turned the heater on full force. I grabbed my hat to make sure it didn't blow into the back seat. Of all the things that didn't work in the car, the fan wasn't one of them.

"Warm." I wiped my brow with the back of my hand.

"Take off that hat if you're hot."

"This?" Boy, I was really quick with the retorts. I touched the brim nervously. "Can't. Bad hair day. Now it'll be worse. Hat head." Luckily, Jake seemed to accept my explanation, because he did not continue to express interest in my headgear.

He made a left out of the parking lot and headed south down the island. I would have checked in the side mirror to see that the cops were following, but the car didn't have a side mirror. A metal stump indicated that it had once but, judging by the rust, those days were long gone. I assumed...make that hoped... make that prayed...that the police were behind us as we drove across the bridge and out Route 72 to the exit ramp to Route 9 South. "Oh, we're taking 9 South. Why?"

"Because that's where the place is."

If Jake found it odd that I commented on almost every sight we passed, he didn't let on. He just nodded as I expressed surprise at stores, gas stations, and street names. "Oh, downtown Tuckerton. Oh, here's the Tuckerton seaport. Hey, I've never been. Why don't we stop there? Oh, we're turning left. Already? We just passed the seaport."

Jake didn't appear to be concerned. I noticed that he wasn't in the habit of checking his rear view mirror. Under normal circumstances that would have worried me, but these weren't normal circumstances.

Jake was not in a talkative mood. He turned the radio up loud and searched for a song he liked. I couldn't decide what kind of music he liked because for the entire ride he didn't find a single cut he could live with for more than thirty-two bars. Periodically, he would turn the radio off, say something about how bad his hangover was, and then start the search again.

"Next time you should get a tape player. Or a CD. I guess that would be better." I tried making small talk.

"Think so?" I thought Jake was being sarcastic, but he continued. "I wonder if you can even get a new car without a tape player."

"I wouldn't know. I live in New York. We take cabs."

"You like that? Living in New York?"

"Yeah." I was really having trouble making conversation. If Jake knew me better, he would have known something was up. Luckily, Jake didn't know me at all.

"New York City. I think that's where I'm gonna go. I'm gonna get a new job and move."

I'd never been down the road Jake had chosen. Of course, I verbalized that thought. At first it looked like any number of roads I had been down. Nice enough. An intersection or two. A few housing developments. Signs to a local golf course. Then the neighborhood changed, although "neighborhood" was not actually the correct word—unless you were a seagull.

"Great Bay Boulevard. Never been here." I smiled at Jake. Luckily he didn't turn to catch my expression. The smile wasn't convincing. Jake didn't care if I had been here or not. As he had told me before—and would tell me again—this was his favorite spot for important conferences. "Jimmy Hoffa like it here?" I joked, although I knew even if Jake Chandler had a sense of humor this was not the time to call upon it.

On a beautiful summer day, I am sure Great Bay Boulevard is gorgeous. Even on this increasingly overcast day, the road possessed a stark beauty. If I hadn't been riding with a killer, it wouldn't have appeared so ominous.

Wherever Great Bay Boulevard went, no one was coming back from there. Ours was the only car on the road. By the time we stopped for the first light—controlling traffic on a one-lane bridge—my heart was racing. The sight of a boatyard might have calmed my nerves if anyone were there. But I saw no cars, no people—no signs of life at all. The light turned green and we crossed the one lane bridge.

"Wow, a one-lane bridge." I spoke for the benefit of the eavesdropping cops. I glanced back over my shoulder as if admiring the bridge, but hoping to find a cop car behind us. Nothing. I turned my eyes to the front. The road stretched ahead into the wetlands. Far in the distance on either side I saw wires stretched from pole to pole through the tall grass. I could only hope they ran along roads but, even if they did, I doubted the roads would meet the one on which we traveled.

I saw buildings off to the right but they appeared to sit in the vast spread of wetlands. "What is that building?" I elaborated for the sake of the police. "It looks like some sort of abandoned factory. A big thing. Like a steel mill."

Jake flipped the radio on and began his search for the perfect song. What he found was static.

I talked over the noise. "Is that a Coast Guard station over there? Ahead of us to the right."

Jake looked puzzled at the extent of my description. I pointed.

"I can see it."

"Is that a Coast Guard station ahead of us to the right?" I asked again.

"What do you think?" Jake sneered and snapped off the radio. Although it was the last thing we needed, he turned up the heat.

"Well, it's white and has a red roof." I spoke loudly for the cops' benefit. I hoped they could hear me over the fan. "Oh, a second light. Another one lane bridge. Is this the road they call Seven Bridges Road?" I wished I had counted bridges. We'd gone over some small bridges as well as the ones marked with lights. How much longer could this route continue? It seemed to stretch forever into the future. That thought marked the first time I considered the possibility that this road might constitute my entire future.

Jake turned and studied me. "Do you ever have an unexpressed thought?"

I studied him surreptitiously. I saw no bulges on his person that could conceal a gun, but I knew they made some pretty small models. I eyed the trash on the floor of the backseat. Anything could be hidden back there. A small gun. A large gun. A small accomplice. Jake's mood appeared to be dictated by his hangover. Was his usual exuberance dulled by too much drink—or by the realization he would have to kill again?

The end of the road came into view and I found myself thinking it might be a dead end in more ways than one. A metal barrier marked the boundary of the paved area. The Coast Guard building stood to our right. The only access was by a high wooden trestle that stretched above the wetlands. There was a single car parked at the foot of the trestle. I could see other vehicles parked around the elevated building. There were people out here—not that any of them saw us, but I hoped Jake was considering that possibility. I mentioned the cars just to make sure he did. He did not appear to hear me.

"Now this is where you go to have a confidential conversation." Jake parked, and opened his door. "Come on." He strode away on his surprisingly long legs. I noticed that he was moving with more confidence than he had at the lighthouse. Good news for him. Bad news for me?

He waited at the metal barrier to play the gentleman. He wanted to help me over. I was still thinking attempted murder as we climbed over the low fence onto the thick log beyond. We hopped down and trudged through sand over rocks and into mud. The tide was low but Jake made sure we moved right to the water's edge.

"Open your coat." He patted me down. I anticipated his next statement and made sure I did not look up or reach for my hat when he said, "I was afraid you were wearing a wire. Let me check under your hat." I lifted the sports cap gingerly. "I can see you're clean, not that it really matters. A bug wouldn't work here even if you were wired. But I wanted to know."

"Why wouldn't a wire work here?" I asked with an undeserved level of interest.

"Where do you see a receiver? No car followed us down the road. I made sure of that. You know, Meg, you could have been in Antigua right now. Sitting on your boyfriend's boat sipping tropical cocktails, but no...you have to do the right thing. Try to help Jimmy. I like that about you. I did the same thing. That was one of the reasons I killed Dallas."

That quickly, my job was done. Jake had confessed. I could go home now. If the police came and got him. Unfortunately, I saw no evidence of law enforcement in the area.

"I killed Dallas Spenser because he deserved it—partially because of what he did to Jimmy. Jimmy just happened to be there that night. I didn't mean for that to happen."

He gazed off into space. I took the opportunity to check the area for arriving police. I spotted no action.

Meanwhile, Jake was spilling his guts. "Jimmy wouldn't have ever been there if I hadn't tipped him off about his father's whereabouts. I'd been looking for my father for years. I found Jimmy last year and told him who and where Dallas was. I had not planned on telling him. I was just gathering information about my father." His tone made "father" sound like a dirty word. "And then when I found out how much he loved his father...even after what he'd done to him." Jake shook his head.

"I didn't tell Jimmy because he loved his father. I told him to cause trouble for Dallas. And then I led Jimmy to the Spears family hoping that together they would all create some big disruption in Dallas Spenser's nice little life." Jake's eyes sought mine. I fought my urge to search for approaching police and met his gaze. "I didn't have any altruistic motives. I could say I told Jimmy the truth because he had a right to know. If that were true, how come I never told him that I was his brother? He'd been looking for his father for years, but his mother managed to keep him in the dark. I was too dumb to see any danger to him in letting him see the light. It's all my fault. All of it."

I moved closer to point my hat in his direction just in case he was wrong about the capabilities of the police receiver. "I was watching Jimmy and Dallas arguing. That's how I knew about the gun. The window was open a crack. I grabbed the gun when the room was empty, followed Dallas, and shot him. Just once. He fell face down in the water. I figured if he weren't dead, he would be soon enough. I didn't even know Jimmy had happened upon the body until that day at his house when the police picked him up. I heard that call on a scanner. I didn't know what was going on, but I figured I better check it out."

Behind Jake I saw a flat-bottomed boat with three men in dark clothes. I hoped they were cops.

"I felt protective of Jimmy, but I was only protecting him from the embarrassment of having his personal life exposed. I didn't know he would become a suspect."

I kept my eyes pointed toward the ground so I could catch the boat's action without looking at it—and tipping Jake off.

"I know you were worried about Beck, but I figured they couldn't convict him. If that had happened, I would have come forward. Really." My eyes met his briefly. "I would have. I didn't know that the merry widow was planting evidence. How could I?"

My only response was to step into the tiny—and surprisingly mild—waves. I absentmindedly kicked shells and rocks that lay in the shallow water. Jake moved in response to me. Step by step I moved him closer to the grass—and the three men in the boat. They appeared to have wedged their flat-bottomed craft in the seagrass.

He kept talking like the villain in a James Bond movie who explains his entire diabolical plot, giving 007 time to escape certain death. At least I hoped that's how this was going to play out. I saw Jake as the villain. I, of course, was the dashing, if in this case distaff, secret agent.

Jake sighed. "Things didn't go the way I wanted. I didn't plan it, you know. Killing Dallas." Well, there went first-degree murder. I convinced myself I was actually helping Jake. "It was serendipity."

"Well, serendipitous for you." The words were out before I knew it. I didn't mean to interrupt his confessional stream.

Jake sniggered. "You're right. It wasn't serendipitous for Dallas, was it? Or Hap. I feel really bad about that kid. He seemed nice, but man was he creepy. He kept telling me that Dallas was in the car." He shivered.

"What did Dallas say?" I wanted to know. Jake frowned at me. "I mean, what did Hap claim Dallas said?"

"Well, given that Hap ended up beaten to a pulp in the Pinelands, what do you think Dallas said?"

I could easily guess. I nodded and sneaked a glance at the boat. The vehicle was well hidden in the tall grass, but I could see it was empty. I didn't see the men anywhere.

Jake's voice grew soft. "Hap said Dallas—my father—had forgiven me. You know, I didn't even know how Dallas could have known who I was. Or that I was the one who shot him. He never saw me. I shot him in the back."

"Why didn't you try to talk to him?" My question was sincere. For the moment, I didn't care about the cops.

"You forget. I was outside listening to him talking to Jimmy. Talking. You couldn't call what he did talking. He berated. He belittled. He humiliated. Why would he have treated me any differently? I was just another rejected baby James."

Out of the corner of my eye I caught sight of two men moving cautiously through the tall grass.

"You know what I thought when I heard about his new life? His new wife? I thought, no more. No more disposable children. No more sons growing up without a father." Jake gazed across the Manahawkin Bay at Long Beach Island. "Yes, one of the reasons I killed Dallas was because of what he did to Jimmy. But I really killed him for what he did to me. I am so sorry it worked out the way it did."

Now I was feeling guilty. Dallas was a rotten bastard. I wanted to help Jake as much as I wanted to help Jimmy. At least I thought I did until Jake reached inside his jacket and pulled out something dark. At least he tried to. "Gun, gun!" I screamed. The two men rushed the reporter from behind and knocked him face down into the water. Uniformed policemen materialized from other hiding spaces in the grass to provide backup. Jake was shouting and flailing around in the shallows. When the commotion died down, I realized he was yelling, "Cell phone! Cell phone!"

At least the cops didn't shoot.

They pulled Jake to his feet. When he looked at me, I saw no anger in his eyes. "I was going to call the cops anyway," he said. "I couldn't do it to Jimmy. I couldn't do it. Maybe I'm not that bastard's son. Not really."

I felt sad seeing Jake in police custody. One of the cops pulled his arms behind his back and snapped the handcuffs into place. "Okay, Opie. Let's go." The officer read Jake his rights as he pushed the reporter toward the road.

I hadn't even noticed Andy move into position beside me. "You okay?" He wrapped an arm around me and gave me a little shake.

"Now I feel terrible for Jake. I feel like we should help him." I watched the reporter tripping up the path. "I don't like this business, Andy."

"There's nothing nice about murder." He took my right hand in his left and squeezed.

"I shouted 'gun.' I could have gotten him killed."

Andy offered a rationalization and another reassuring squeeze of my hand. "Under the circumstances, anyone would have thought it was a gun."

Petino emerged from the path and, with his head down and his hand planted in his pockets, strode across the sand to the spot where I stood next to Andy. "You done good, Ms. Daniels. Thank you." He smiled with pursed lips and reached for my hand awkwardly. By the time I extracted mine from Andy's, Petino had withdrawn his hand. We settled for a nod. "I'm going to ride with Chandler, but Investigator Mira will take you two home. I'll be in touch."

From my viewpoint keeping in touch wasn't necessary, but I thanked the detective and smiled politely. He patted my arm clumsily and expressed his gratitude again. Apparently, the gesture was supposed to make me forget that he had tried to send my boyfriend to the slammer. Maybe someday he would discover that I never forget.

"Beck." Petino nodded at Andy who reciprocated with a knowing nod of the head. I knew that he had gotten past his differences with Petino. He's nicer than I am.

Andy wrapped his arm around me. "So, how are you feeling? Being a hero and all?"

I leaned into his wool jacket. "I don't feel like a hero. You know, I really thought he might kill me."

"It seemed like a real possibility there for a while," Andy said with alarming calmness. "When we were bringing the boat in."

Without pulling myself out of his grip, I turned and stared up at him. "And still you guys took your time. Couldn't you have waited another few minutes? I was enjoying watching my entire life pass before my eyes."

Andy ignored my sarcasm and gave me a big hug. I needed the embrace to keep me composed and make me warm. "You okay?"

"Sure. Now I am. But Andy, I had seen the light by the time you guys made your move. A minute later and I would have been so far gone that I couldn't have come back. I think I actually saw my parents calling me into that bright white...."

Andy interrupted as he leaned me back in his arms. He was smiling. "Did anyone ever tell you that you have a tendency to exaggerate?"

"You're not taking me seriously, Andy. I was really scared."

He chuckled as he made several unsuccessful attempts to brush the hair from my face. "If you were a normal woman you would have been scared long ago."

I felt no need to question the normal woman allegation at the moment but made a note that the time would come.

Andy grabbed my hand. "Let's get you out of those wet shoes and into something warmer—like Antigua."

Gently, he led me towards the police car that would take us back to LBI. As he lifted me across the big log at the end of the path, I gazed back across Manahawkin Bay towards Long Beach Island. "Andy, can we come back here someday? Under different circumstances? It's really beautiful. I'm really glad I found out about this place." I sighed. "You know, I am always lucky in my bad luck."

Andy raised an eyebrow as he placed me on the road.

"Okay, what happened to me—getting driven here by a murderer I thought wanted to kill me—*that* could be construed as bad luck." I pointed to the wide expanse of beauty surrounding us. "But look at the great end result. We found this gorgeous place. That's good luck."

"Maggie," Andy said as he patted me on the head, "I think we have to work on raising your expectations."

Chapter 57

We were stretched out on the deck of Andy's boat—at last. The sun was warm. The water was warm. Only the margaritas were cold. All was right with the world. Well, with the immediate thirty-five-foot world of Andy's sailboat. But for the next few months that would be my world.

"I didn't think I would live this long." I leaned back. In my white shorts and T-shirt, I was actually overdressed—maybe even a little warm. "You know, every time I come back to this part of the world I'm shocked by the color and clarity of the water. Every time." I had been waiting to make that claim for more than a month.

Andy was at the helm, guiding the *Page One* across open waters. On his face I saw complete joy. I'm sure he saw the same in mine. We sailed for awhile without speaking.

"You know, Andy, you were one of the few people on this planet who did not have a reason to kill Dallas. Between his various families and the people he put on the Web, there had to be hundreds of suspects."

"Let's not think about Dover/Danvers/Denver/Dallas/Delray again until we sail into Barnegat Bay this summer. By the time we return to Jersey we should get some answers."

We had gotten some answers before we'd left. Notably, we had heard the news that Hap Hathaway was going to make a full recovery. Andy and I had stopped at the hospital to see him. Holding his hand was the sweet blonde girl who had followed him out of the Bayside Diner only weeks before. "No wonder they call him Happy," Andy mumbled as we watched the angelic young woman care for her injured beau. I'd asked Hap if Dallas was happy with the way things turned out, but Hap said he had not heard from him since his accident. He hadn't heard from anyone on the other side. He seemed a bit relieved. Andy seemed relieved that now Hap wasn't conferring with the deceased, he would have time to work on the Mustang.

"Yep, I can wait until summer for the answers. Let's leave that behind us." I agreed. "But, you know, I can't see how they can nail Page on obstruction when she was obstructing a crime that never happened. Now, hindering prosecution. Interfering with an investigation. That's different—don't you think?" Page was out on bail, but still facing charges related to protecting Jimmy.

"I don't know, Maggie. And I don't want to think about that entire episode of my life. Not while we are enjoying this incredible day." He paused. "Although I can't believe we...okay, I...I'm the professional...I can't believe I wasn't more suspicious of Jake Chandler in the first place. I mean, I should have figured out that he had gathered all that information before Dallas died. No one is that good at research. And I should have guessed that someone put Bonnie and Jimmy together." He shook his head before changing his tone abruptly. "Anyway, I'd like to put all that behind us and enjoy the day—although I do worry a little about Jimmy." Andy sounded sad.

All charges against Jimmy relating to the murder of Dallas Spenser had been dropped, which was ironic considering that charges against Page were still pending. Jimmy was at home with his mother. He still faced the possibility that he would be charged for his attempt on Andy's life and mine. Andy and I just wanted whatever was best for Jimmy. We could afford to be magnanimous. After all, his efforts to hurt us failed. Under normal circumstances the kid wouldn't have been a criminal. Under any circumstances, he wasn't going to be a successful criminal.

"I have a feeling things will work out for him," I said.

Andy nodded. "I'll be interested in seeing what happens to Page."

"Yeah, me too." I no longer yearned to see Page in jail. I was not anxious to see her, but I had a feeling she wasn't going to be a part of our social circle. No matter how noble her motivations, she had sent the police after Andy—and had an affair with his best friend to keep tabs on how well her efforts were working. "But you know my biggest question? Why did Dallas insist on getting a new Rolex from each wife? Didn't anyone ever mention that he could remove the engraving and keep the watch?" This was a secret I felt Dallas had taken to his grave— that, and the reason he was so reluctant to call a divorce lawyer.

"Probably a symbolic thing," Andy said. "I doubt we'll ever really know the answer. It certainly won't come out at Jake's trial. Though he may cop a plea, of course."

I only hoped we wouldn't be summoned to testify any time soon. I'd finally gotten to Antigua and Andy's boat, and I was not going to let anything interfere with my romantic fantasy. Well, almost anything.

Oliver stuck his head up the hatch. "What a gorgeous day. I'm so glad you guys asked me along. I'll admit I was reluctant at first. But Page did such a job on me...now, a little time like this on the open sea...I already feel like a new person." Oliver interrupted himself. "Thanks, guys."

Oliver handed each of us a cold drink and then stretched out across from me. It was just like old times—only with warmer air and without ESPN. I closed my eyes and let the breeze wash over me. All I could hear was the wind in the sails and the soft sound of the boat cutting through the water. Nothing could wipe the smile off my face.

More Great Books
from Plexus Publishing

KILLING TIME IN OCEAN CITY

By Jane Kelly

"*Killing Time in Ocean City* is a unique, riveting, engaging mystery that all fans of the genre will find immensely satisfying."—*The Midwest Book Review*

After being jolted from a sound sleep by police early in her vacation, Meg Daniels discovers that her former boss has turned up dead near her rented beach house in Ocean City, New Jersey. Along the way the action shifts from Ocean City to Atlantic City to the Pine Barrens, with Meg frantically hunting for answers while she herself becomes a target of the killer.

The familiarity of the author to the shore areas of South Jersey brings a fun, real-life dimension for the local reader to this suspense-filled "whodunit."

Hardbound/ISBN 0-937548-38-3/$22.95

CAPE MAYHEM

By Jane Kelly

"Lots of local color, a memorable cast of characters, a fast paced plot, and an irresistible heroine."—*Herald Newspaper*

Temporarily unattached, Meg Daniels arrives in Cape May for what should have been a romantic off-season holiday, but instead finds herself in the middle of a mystery. Overnight, a certain female guest at the Parsonage Bed & Breakfast has undergone an impossible transformation. Suspecting foul play, Meg enlists a hunky investigator in the local DA's office, as well as the B&B's spunky co-owner, to help her figure out a killer of a question: "Who was that lady who checked in with Wallace Gimbel?" The weather is frosty, but the trail is hot as Meg and friends unravel the truth behind a scheme marked by imposters, infidelities, and—if she's right—even murder.

Hardbound/ISBN 0-937548-41-3/$22.95

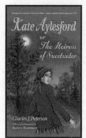

KATE AYLESFORD
OR, THE HEIRESS OF SWEETWATER

By Charles J. Peterson
With a new Foreword by Robert Bateman

"Plot twists, colorful characters, timely observations, lyrical descriptions of the Pine Barrens, and ... an unusually strong and well-educated female protagonist."—*Robert Bateman, from the Foreword to the new edition*

The legendary historical romance, *Kate Aylesford: A Story of Refugees*, by Charles J. Peterson, first appeared in 1855, was reissued in 1873 as *The Heiress of Sweetwater*, and spent the entire 20th century out of print. As readable today as when Peterson first penned it, *Kate Aylesford* features a memorable cast of characters, an imaginative plot, and a compelling mix of romance, adventure, and history. Plexus Publishing is pleased to return this remarkable novel to print.

Hardbound/ISBN: 0-937548-46-4/$22.95

PATRIOTS, PIRATES, AND PINEYS: SIXTY WHO SHAPED NEW JERSEY
By Robert A. Peterson

"*Patriots, Pirates, and Pineys* is excellent ... the type of book that is hard to put down once you open it."—*Daybreak Newsletter*

Southern New Jersey is a region full of rich heritage, and yet it is one of the best kept historical secrets of our nation. Many famous people have lived in Southern New Jersey, and numerous world-renowned businesses were started in this area as well.

This collection of biographies provides a history of the area through the stories of such famous figures as John Wanamaker, Henry Rowan, Sara Spenser Washington, Elizabeth Haddon, Dr. James Still, and Joseph Campbell. Some were patriots, some pirates, and some Pineys, but all helped make America what it is today.

Hardbound/ISBN 0-937548-37-5/$29.95
Softbound/ISBN 0-937548-39-1/$19.95

DOWN BARNEGAT BAY: A NOR'EASTER MIDNIGHT READER
By Robert Jahn

"*Down Barnegat Bay* evokes the area's romance and mystery." —*The New York Times*

Down Barnegat Bay is an illustrated maritime history of the Jersey shore's Age of Sail. Originally published in 1980, this fully revised Ocean County Sesquicentennial Edition features more than 177 sepia illustrations, including 75 new images and nine maps. Jahn's engaging tribute to the region brims with first-person accounts of the people, events, and places that have come together to shape Barnegat Bay's unique place in American history.

Hardbound/ISBN 0-937548-42-1/$39.95

OVER THE GARDEN STATE & OTHER STORIES
By Robert Bateman

Novelist Bateman (*Pinelands, Whitman's Tomb*) offers six new stories set in his native Southern New Jersey. While providing plenty of authentic local color in his portrayal of small-town and farm life, the bustle of the Jersey shore with its boardwalks, and the solitude and otherworldliness of the famous Pine Barrens, Bateman's sensitively portrayed protagonists are the stars here. The title story tells of an Italian prisoner of war laboring on a South Jersey farm circa 1944. There, he finds danger and dreams, friendship and romance—and, ultimately, more fireworks than he could have wished for.

Hardbound/ISBN: 0-937548-40-5/$22.95

To order or for a catalog: 609-654-6500, Fax Order Service: 609-654-4309

Plexus Publishing, Inc.

143 Old Marlton Pike • Medford • NJ 08055
E-mail: info@plexuspublishing.com
www.plexuspublishing.com